Klabund: Short Stories, Part One

I0563136

KLABUND

SHORT STORIES,

PART

ONE

Translated by Jim Doss

LOCH RAVEN PRESS   SYKESVILLE, MD   2025

Printed in the United States of America

Cover Art: Front cover, Klabund in 1925.
          Back cover, Klabund with Frank Bruno, Walchensee, 1915.

Cover and book design: Jim Doss

ISBN 979-8-9905505-4-4

Loch Raven Press
140 Milrey Drive, Suite L
Sykesville, MD 21784
www.lochravenpress.com

Table of Contents

Introduction
  Biographical Sketch   2

PART ONE: Celestina   (1912)
    Forward   14
    The Grünberg Campaign   16
    The Apparition of Saint Hedwig   19
    The Astronomer   22
    Celestina   23
    The Emergency Baptism   25
    The Sad Prince   27
    The Oder Nixie   29
    The Parable   31
    The Burglar   33
    Crossen   35
    The Dancer   38
    The Valet   40
    Violinist Heinrich   44
    The Flyer   49

PART TWO: The Man in the Top Hat   (1911)
    The Man in the Top Hat   52

PART THREE: Klabund's Carousel   (1914)
    Tapioca   56
    The Roof Tile   57
    The Homecoming   58
    The Garden of Saint Veronica   60
    The Jockey   62

The Lass	64
Blonde Hair	65
The Duchess of Este	67
The Weakling	68
Abysses	72
The Winner	73
Phryne	74
Marching to War	75
Waldemar	76
Test of Style	78
The Smile of Margarete Andoux	79
The Suicide	81
The Brown Devil of Adrianople – A Bulgarian War Story	82
But Love	85
Little Lorbeer	86
Balaschew	90
The Lover	91
Stassi	94
The Third	96
The Poem	98
The Invention	98
The Child	99
Adventure	101
The Birthmark	102
Revolution	103
Novella	105
Professor Runkel	106
The New Poet	110

PART FOUR: The Commissary Wagon (1914)

Revolution in Montevideo	114
Il Santo Bubi	116
The Golden Death	118
Farewell	120
The Bear	121
The Wealthy Young Man	124
My Brother Said	125
The Corporal	127
In the Russian Camp	128
Flower Day in Northern France	130
The Black Flag	131
The Stamp on the Field Postcard	132
The Young Polish Shooter	133

The Revolutionary   135
The Widow Pulko   136
Bed No. 13   138
The Regular's Table   140
Bartholomew and the Young Man   141
Does Your Watch Glow at Night?   144
Short Hike   146
Mittenwald   148
Autumn   149
All Soul's Day   150
Nights   151
The Dying Soldier   152
The Flyer   153
Hölderlin   154
The Battle Line   156
The Commander   156
The War Correspondent   158
The Ballad of Forgetting   160

PART FIVE: **Short Hike**   (1915)

Short Hike   176

PART SIX: **Legends of the Saints**   (1921)

Foreword   180
The Saint of Sorrow   181
Saint Loy   181
Saint Eustachius   182
About the Holy Child Saint Quiriacus   182
Saint Florian   183
Saint Francis   183
Saint Irene   186
Saint Jerome   186
Saint Cyprian   187
Saint Someone and Saint No One   188
Saint Notburga   188
Saint Thais   189
All Souls' Day   190
Saint Petronella   190
Saint Macarius   191
Saint Nicholas   192
Saint Gregory   192

The Image of the Virgin Mary............................194
Saint Genevieve............................194
The Seven Holy Sleepers............................195
Saint Goar............................196
Saint Augustine............................197
Saint Elisabeth............................198
Saint Catherine............................199
Saint Dorothea............................200
Saint Luke............................200
The Nine Muses............................201
Saint Cecilia............................202
Saint Alexius............................203
From Our Dear Lady............................203

PART SEVEN: Little Klabund Book   (1921)

Short Autobiography............................206
Katharina............................207
Ferdinand Cortez............................208
The Transformation of Harun al-Rashid............................210
The Two Realms............................210
Child in the Cradle............................213
Little Songs for Irene............................214

PART EIGHT: The Chaotic Decline of the West
(1922)

Prologue............................226
It was the Morning of a Rainy Autumn Sunday............................226
Reporting for Duty............................227
In the Ninth Month............................228
The Slow Combustion Stove............................229
World History from the Psychoanalytic Perspective............................230
A Proposal for Decency, That is, for Wickedness............................231
The People's Commissar............................232
The Age of Absolutism is Dawning...............................233
Biography............................234
Elegantly Furnished Rooms............................234
Mucius Mauke............................235
Cubism............................236
The Yellow Man............................237
The Journalist............................238
The Two............................239

The Chain   239
The Bedstead   240
The Literary Society   241
The Goldfinch   242
The Cricket   243
Fable   244
The Proverb   245
The Uncle   245
Just a Quarter of an Hour   245
Paula   246
Boschel   247
The Man with the Mask   247
Brigitte   250
The Tooth of Time   257
The Gambler – A Scene   258
Letter to Asta Nielsen on the Occasion of Her Hamlet Film   260
The Hot Water Bottle   260
The Demonic Otto   261
The Mass Grave   262
The Boxer   262
The 99th Return of Buddha   264
Fidelity to Women   266
The Typewriter Bureau   267

PART NINE: **The Last Emperor** (1923)

The Last Emperor   270

PART TEN: **The Poet and the Emperor** (1923)

The Poet and the Emperor   284

PART ELEVEN: **Thu-fu Recalls the Great Chinese Poet Li-tai-pe From Exile**

Thu-fu Recalls the Great Chinese Poet Li-tai-pe From Exile   288

PART TWELVE: **He - A Story** (1923)

He – A Story   292

PART THIRTEEN: Letters to Walter Heinrich   (1924)

Letters to Walter Heinrich   298

Klabund: Short Stories, Part One

Biographical Sketch

1. Introduction: Klabund's Place in German Literature

Alfred "Fredi" Georg Hermann Henschke (1890-1928), known by his pen name Klabund, occupies a unique position in the annals of early 20th-century German literature. His works, characterized by lyrical expression, stylistic innovation, and an ever-present exploration of existential themes, reflect the complex socio-political environment of the time. While other literary figures such as Thomas Mann and Bertolt Brecht gained greater international fame, Klabund's contributions as a poet, playwright, and translator have left an indelible mark on German cultural history.

Klabund's distinctive voice is particularly significant in the context of German Expressionism, a literary and artistic movement that emerged in response to the rapid modernization, political upheaval, and existential anxieties of pre- and post-World War I Europe. His works, while rooted in the Expressionist tradition, often ventured beyond the confines of the movement, incorporating influences from Eastern literature, historical narratives, and personal reflections on mortality.

This brief biography aims to outline the life of Klabund, touching upon his evolution as a writer and intellectual, his engagement with contemporary literary movements, and the personal struggles and health issues that helped shape his worldview.

2. Early Life and Formative Years (1890-1910)

Klabund was born on November 4, 1890, in Crossen an der Oder at 1:00 a.m., a small town located in what was then part of the German Empire (now Krosno Odrzańskie, Poland). Crossen was a small Prussian garrison town with around 7000 inhabitants, loyal to the emperor, provincial and conservative. His family belonged to the middle class. His father, Dr. Alfred Henschke (1858-1936), was a pharmacist at the Adler-Apotheke which was located at Dammstrasse 344/45, and was appointed to be of the magistrate in 1893, a position he remained in until 1930. He was also elected to the unpaid position of first deputy mayor in 1907, which he held for seven years. His mother, Emilie Antonie (1867-1945), a housewife, ensured the household ran smoothly. His upbringing was comfortable yet provincial, and from a young age, Klabund displayed both intellectual precocity and physical frailty.

Despite the relatively ordinary circumstances of his early life, Klabund's childhood was marked by a deep emotional sensitivity, an acute awareness of life's fleeting nature, and a fascination with literature. By the age of twelve, he was a young gifted pianist with larger than average hands and already engaged in writing poems, although at the time, he had no idea that this early passion would shape his entire life. Klabund's delicate health also became a key part of his formative years. He suffered from recurring bouts of illness, particularly high fevers and bilateral pneumonia, which caused him to be hospitalized in Crossen for six weeks in 1907, and would later be diagnosed as "closed tuberculosis" and dominate his adult life. A 1912 letter is the earliest written confirmation we have that Klabund knew he had tuberculosis. Up until the middle of the twentieth century, a diagnosis of tuberculosis was roughly the equivalent of receiving a death sentence that would be carried out at some unknown, unpredictable time in the future. In the early 1900's, there were primarily two ways to fight this disease, and both were rarely successful. The first technique was to attempt to mobilize the patient's immune system through long climatic cures in wooded highlands, through a "healthy diet" and by avoiding strenuous activity. With the second technique, following the research of Berlin doctor Ferdinand Sauerbruch, doctors tried to defeat tuberculosis surgically: through a resection of the ribs. By means of a "pneumothorax," whose noisy effects Thomas Mann so mockingly described in his "Magic Mountain," part of the lung was shut down. This second option was not viable for Klabund since both of his lungs were affected and he could potentially experience a dramatic deterioration in his condition at any time.

His father, a stern but loving figure, expected Alfred to follow in his professional footsteps. Pharmacy, like many middle-class trades of the time, was viewed as a stable and respectable career. However, Klabund's early schooling revealed a different trajectory. His teachers recognized his literary talent, and he excelled in subjects like literature, history, and philosophy, even as his physical health continued to decline.

In 1909, upon completing his early education, Klabund moved to Munich to study medicine, largely due to the expectations of his family. Munich at the time was one of the intellectual and artistic hubs of Europe, home to a vibrant community of writers, artists, and thinkers. The shift to Munich exposed the young student to a broader world of artistic and literary experimentation. Here, he first encountered the currents of modernism that were sweeping across Europe.

Despite his initial dedication to medicine, his attention quickly shifted toward literature and philosophy. He began attending lectures on philosophy, philology, and history, further cementing his interest in these intellectual pursuits. His time in Munich also allowed him to engage with Expressionist artists and writers, whose works reflected the growing sense of existential crisis that pervaded European intellectual life at the dawn of the 20th century.

By 1912, Alfred Henschke had officially abandoned his medical studies in favor of a full-time literary career. This period also marked the adoption of his now-famous pen name: Klabund. As Klabund explains it: "I created the name Klabund one day in a mood of serious self-parody, but I gave it so much of my blood that it began to live alongside and above me, becoming a reflection of my art and worldview... Klabund emerged from Klabautermann – the mischievous sea ghost that appears to sailors on foggy nights as a harbinger of doom – and from Vagabund. The name points to the vagabond-like days of my early student years..." The symbolic weight of this name is significant – it reflects Klabund's itinerant spirit, his status as a wanderer through both physical landscapes and the realms of human thought as evidenced by the many themes and settings within his literature.

> The It of things to which I've pledged my being
> Softens into the You of reverie.
> I will love my soul unceasingly,
> In its peace, in its frenzy.
> Beloved, eternal upon my lips:
> I am and was and will always be Klabund.

As "Klabund," the young writer fully embraced the bohemian lifestyle of the avant-garde literary circles in Munich and Berlin. He became a part of the burgeoning intellectual community that included figures such as Frank Wedekind (1864-1918), Heinrich Mann (1871-1950), and the young Bertolt Brecht (1898-1956). Klabund's work from this time was heavily influenced by Expressionist themes of alienation, urban chaos, and the search for spiritual meaning in an increasingly industrialized and dehumanized world, with the expectations of war and social conflict between the classes always looming large.

3. Expressionism and Early Literary Output (1910-1914)

Klabund's early works – primarily poetry – were deeply rooted in the Expressionist movement, which sought to reject the materialism and realism of the late 19th century in favor of more subjective, emotional, and often apocalyptic visions of modern life. His first major poetry collection, *Morgenrot! Klabund! Die Tage dämmern!* (Dawn! Klabund! The Days are Breaking!) (1913), embodies the key elements of Expressionist aesthetics: intense emotions, vivid imagery, and an exploration of existential anxiety.

In 1912 Klabund wrote to Walter Heinrich, an occasional writer and bank clerk in Crossen who went by the pen name Unus: "To impress you a little, here are a series of numbers and titles. I have written 597 poems, 29 novellas, 13 one-act plays, 1 novel, a collection of aphorisms, as well as fragments and collections of material for dramas and novels of the highest style (Don Juan, Nausicaa, Adam and Eve, etc.), essays, etc." While only Klabund knows if this was a bit of an exaggeration or not, it demonstrates the type of productivity Klabund would maintain throughout his literary career.

In the winter of 1912, inspired by the writer Villon, Klabund sent some verses to the theater critic Alfred Kerr (1867-1948), who published them in the magazine *Pan*. These poems, written in a coarse and cheeky style, caused a bit of a public stir. The Imperial Censorship Committee found grounds to charge Klabund with "the dissemination of obscene literature." They heard the opinions of Frank Wedekin, Max Halbe (1865-1944), Erich Mühsam (1878-1934), and Richard Dehmel (1863-1920), who objected to these charges which also implicated Kerr by arguing the poems had artistic merit. The trial lasted from September 1913 to January 1915. The judiciary ultimately fined Klabund 50 Reichmarks, only to have the verdict overturned a year later.

This period also marked Klabund's growing fascination with death and the ephemeral nature of life, themes that would persist throughout his career. His lifelong battle with tuberculosis, coupled with his intellectual engagement with Expressionist thought, made him particularly attuned to the fragility of human existence. His poems often meditate on impermanence, mortality, and the disillusionment of the modern age.

In collections such as *Morgenrot!*, Klabund's poetic voice expresses a mixture of despair and wonderment. The natural world, in his work, is often a place of both beauty and terror, filled with fleeting moments of grace that contrast sharply with the bleakness of urban life. For Klabund, the modern city represents a place of alienation, where individuals are disconnected from one another and from the natural world. Yet, even in this disenchanted landscape, he seeks moments of transcendence, whether through love, art, or spiritual reflection.

Klabund reflects on the book *Morgenrot!* that: "I have absolutely nothing: no paper, no money, no profession, not even a proper apartment. As a bait for credibility, rhymes are accompanied not by 'hot' but cheerful 'sexual distress,' ensuring that something primal and vivid is not missing from this lyrical portrait of Samuel Klabund – by himself."

Klabund was also heavily influenced by German Romanticism, particularly the works of Friedrich Hölderlin (1770-1843) and Heinrich Heine (1797-1856). Like these earlier poets, Klabund imbued his work with a sense of longing for a lost ideal – whether a spiritual utopia or a pre-modern world untouched by the corruption of modernity. His use of lyrical, often musical language, as well as his interest in myth and folklore, connects him to this Romantic tradition, even as he critiques the very notion of romantic ideals in a modern context. In 1913 Klabund came into contact with Alfred Kerr's Magazine *PAN*, though he continued to publish in the magazines *Jugend* and *Simplicissimus*. Beginning in 1914 he contributed to *Die Schaubühne* (Show Place), which later changed its name to *Die Weltbühne* (The World Stage).

Klabund completed the manuscript of his first novel – *The Ruby – Novel of a Young Man* in May of 1914 and sent it to his mentor Walter Heinrich in Berlin. The novel was intended to be published by the Erich Reiß Verlag, but disputes between the author and the publisher and the outbreak of World War I prevented its release. *The Ruby* was eventually published posthumously in 1929 by Phaidon in Vienna.

By this point in time, Klabund was destined to live up to the "vagabond" part of his pen name as he frequently changed his place of residence from Crossen to Munich to Berlin to Locarno and other cities, and when his tuberculosis began to severely impact his health he sought healing in the Swiss spa town of Davos.

4. World War I and Changing Attitudes (1914-1918)

The outbreak of World War I in 1914 marked a turning point in Klabund's life, both personally and professionally. Like many intellectuals and artists of his generation, Klabund initially greeted the war with a mixture of excitement and patriotic fervor. He saw the conflict as a way for Europe to purge itself of its decadence and moral decay, viewing it through a lens of romantic heroism. However, this initial optimism would quickly give way to a more complex and critical perspective as the war dragged on, exposing the futility and horror of modern warfare.

Due to his poor health, Klabund was unable to serve on the front lines, in spite of his repeated efforts to enlist, but he followed the war closely and responded to its events in his writing. His early war poetry, while still somewhat idealistic, began to take on a darker, more cynical tone as the scale of the destruction became clear. In works like *Kriegsfibel* (War Primer), a collection of war poems written between 1914 and 1918, Klabund grapples with the senseless violence and the moral degradation that accompanied the conflict.

Kriegsfibel (War Primer) stands as one of Klabund's most important wartime works, capturing his evolving disillusionment with the war. The poems in this collection are characterized by their stark realism, eschewing the romanticized depictions of battle that had characterized his earlier works. Instead, Klabund presents the war as a grotesque and meaningless spectacle, in which human life is reduced to little more than fodder for machines and bureaucracies. Klabund's shift from early enthusiasm to deep cynicism about war culminates in his 1918 novel *Bracke*. The novel is a scathing critique of the social and political structures that led to the war, as well as a meditation on the personal toll of violence and destruction. *Bracke* is one of Klabund's most explicitly political works, and it represents his growing disenchantment with both the war and the nationalist ideologies that had initially fueled it. The novel's central character becomes a kind of anti-hero, whose moral confusion and emotional detachment reflect the broader sense of disillusionment felt by many in post-war Germany.

It would take almost three year before Klabund recognized the senselessness of the war and on June 3, 1917 published on open letter to Kaiser Wilhelm II (1859-1941) in the Neue Zürcher Zeitung (New Zurich Newspaper) urging the Kaiser to abdicate with passages like: "Be the first prince to voluntarily renounce his fictitious rights and bow to the Areopagus of human rights. Your name will then be mentioned among the truly great in the new books of history, where the history of humanity will no longer be written in terms of coalitions but in terms of the history of the human spirit. Then you will establish the people's kingdom of the Hohenzollerns on rock; whereas it is now only a cloud formation that, if you do not recognize the time, will soon be vanished in the rising storm." Many believed his future wife influenced his transformation toward pacifism. Needless to say, this letter did not go over well with all citizens, and cause much resentment and hard feelings toward Klabund. In September 1917, Klabund addressed the controversy of his earlier war poetry to Munich journalists: "These poems were written three years ago at the beginning of a horrific war – when no one knew where it was heading, and when everyone was deceived about its goals. I have greatly changed my opinion about the war; my 1915 Chinese war poetry, more like the pack wagon, and later Moreau, show the path that leads to absolute pacifism, on which ground I now stand."

On a personal note, in 1918 Klabund married Brunhilde Irene Herberle (1896-1918) on June 8th, whom he had met in a sanatorium for lung patients. She was a passionate pianist who loved to play the music of Schumann and the tubercular Frederick Chopin. Larngeal tuberculosis also occasionally rendered her voice nearly inaudible. He calls her Irene in his poems because to him that word meant peace. Klabund described her in a letter: "I am married: to a woman who is entirely animal, entirely child, entirely butterfly, like those beings around us." Rumor was that she was pregnant at the time of their marriage. On October 17th she gave birth to daughter Irene Fiete Anny after a seven-month pregnancy, and was operated on due to complications. Klabund's wife survived until October 30th. On February 17, 1919 the daughter also passed away. Klabund sent a telegram to his friend Walter Heinrich: "Irene has called her child to her today." Klabund wrote several books of poetry dedicated to his first wife, such as *Small Verses for Irene*, and *Sonnets to Irene*. Klabund blamed himself for Irene's death.

> I was your death. I murdered you.
> I am guilty that chaos, like a crater,
> Bursts open and spews its fire. I am the father
> Of anarchy, red and overflowing upon us.

> I was your death. I murdered you.
> In vain the pious father warned me;
> I desecrated you, dolorous mother...
> I killed you with my own child.

> The rule you wielded with the lily,
> I overthrew in the fever of my caste.
> You smiled. You blessed. You loved.

> I glared darkly. Threatened. Cursed. Hated.
> And while you sifted gold from dust,
> I ran to debauchery, bellowed, drank, and reveled.

5. Postwar Work: Cultural Exploration and the Search for New Forms (1919-1928)

In the aftermath of World War I, Klabund entered a period of intense creative output. The political, social, and economic chaos that followed the war deeply influenced his work during the 1920s. Yet, even as he engaged with the traumas of the war and its aftermath, he also began to explore new forms of artistic expression, venturing into drama, historical fiction, and cultural translation.

In early April 1919, Klabund received a telegram that a friend from his Munich student days, Erich Mühsam (who would later be incarcerated at Fortress Niederschönenfeld with Ernst Toller), had been arrested, and Klabund was asked if he could help him. However this raised suspicions about Klabund and the possibility that he might be part of the Munich insurgents so he was taken into "protective custoday" from April 17th to April 26th in the Straubing prison. The "anarchist" Erich Mühsam was one of the leading figures of the Bavarian Soviet Republic. He was arrested by the counter-revolutionary troops of the Reichswehr and sentenced to fifteen years of fortress imprisonment. Klabund became a victim of his own efforts to help his friend, and was himself accused of participating in Spartacist activities. The political ideologies of socialism, democracy and revolution in reality meant little to him. He was merely committed to trying to help a friend. In the end his "help" achieved nothing, and his ten days of incarceration were documented in his book *Tagebuch im Gefängnis* (*Diary in Prison*). Upon release, Klabung writes: "Free! Outside again! Alive again! I am still too agitated and nervous to contain the waves of emotions coursing through me... Today, I plan to visit Nuremberg, the Hirschvogel Hall, and Hans Sachs. At the Hans Sachs House, I will tip my hat for the first time in nine days and pay reverence to the Germany I love."

During this time, Klabund also became active in the cabaret scene in Zurich and Munich at the Cabaret Voltaire, the Bavarian Cabaret, The Beautiful Bird, and other venues. There he met fellow writers such as Bertolt Brecht, Hugo Ball (1886-1927), the founder of Dadaism, his wife Emmy Hemmings (1885-1948), and other German writers and performers. Klabund was an occasional performer and his ballads of love, murder, alcohol and other frivolities made him a popular performer as he shot a few mocking arrows at both himself and the audience, but he didn't come under the Dadaist influence and remained true to his own poetic instincts. During his time in the cabarets, Klabund also met Maria Kirndörfer (1893-1981), aka Marietta di Monaco, about whom he wrote the novella *Marietta – A Love Story from Schwabing*. Marietta became known as the poet's muse and famous through her close friendships with poets like Joachim Ringelnatz (1883-1934), Frank Wedekind, Fred Endrikat, and Klabund. She recited their works on stage.

Like his health, Klabund's finances were on a constant rollercoaster ride with dizzying highs and depressing lows. As a bestselling author of the time, money would come into his pockets based on the popularity of his books, but then it quickly evaporated again as the poet helped those in need and usually picked up the tab at parties and celebrations. He also would occasionally support penniless students until he himself was in need of help again and had to call on his friends.

One of the most distinctive aspects of Klabund's postwar work is his deep engagement with Eastern literature, particularly Chinese and Persian poetry. This fascination with non-Western cultures set Klabund apart from many of his contemporaries, who remained focused on European literary traditions. Klabund's translations and adaptations of classical Chinese poetry, particularly his translations of the Tang Dynasty poets, introduced German readers to a new literary form that emphasized simplicity, natural beauty, and philosophical reflection.

In addition to Chinese literature, Klabund was also deeply influenced by Persian poetry, particularly the works of the Sufi mystic Rumi. His fascination with Eastern spirituality reflected his broader search for new forms of meaning in a post-war world. For Klabund, Eastern literature provided an alternative to the disillusionment of modern Europe, offering a vision of inner peace, harmony with nature, and a transcendence of the material world.

In the 1920s, Klabund began to focus more intensively on drama, producing several important plays that would secure his reputation as a major figure in the German theater. His most famous play, *Der Kreidekreis* (The Chalk Circle), was first performed in 1924 and became an immediate success. Based on an ancient Chinese folk tale, *Der Kreidekreis* tells the story of a legal dispute over a child and the wisdom of a judge who determines the child's true parentage.

Der Kreidekreis was notable not only for its narrative structure but also for its fusion of Eastern and Western dramatic traditions. Klabund's play would later serve as the inspiration for Bertolt Brecht's *The Caucasian Chalk Circle* (1944), one of the most important works of 20th-century theater. Klabund's use of the chalk circle as a metaphor for justice, loyalty, and truth resonated deeply with audiences, and the play was praised for its universal themes and innovative staging.

In addition to *Der Kreidekreis*, Klabund wrote several other plays during this period, including *Karfunkel* (1923) and *Xantippe* (1920), both of which reflect his continued interest in history and myth. His plays, much like his poetry and prose, were marked by a lyrical style, a fascination with moral ambiguity, and a desire to explore human relationships in the face of societal collapse.

6. Personal Struggles: Illness and Relationships

While Klabund's literary career flourished during the 1920s, his personal life was increasingly dominated by his struggle with tuberculosis. The disease, which he had contracted in his youth, worsened as he grew older, forcing him to spend long periods in sanatoriums, primarily in Davos. His experiences with illness and isolation are reflected in many of his works, particularly his later poems, which often meditate on the themes of suffering, death, and the passage of time.

In 1924, Klabund met celebrated actress in Berlin's theater scene Carola Neher (1900-1942), who would later become one of Brecht's most famous collaborators, on a streetcar in Munich near the Café Stefanie. Klabund keep staring at her until she whispered to him: "If you want to stare at me without any shame, you have to go to the theater. I'm playing Hugenberg in Frank Wedekind's play *Pandora's Box* at the Kammerspiele tonight." After the play, he waited for her by the stage exit, hands her his business card and insists on another meeting. In the spring of 1925, severe blood poisoning forces Carola Neher to spend several weeks in the Breslau Friederici Sanatorium, where she must be operated on immediately after admission. On May 7, 1925, she and Klabund were married in the sanatorium. Their relationship was passionate, but troubled, largely due to Klabund's deteriorating health in combination with the demands of their two artistic professions which requires Carola and sometimes Klabund to move to the various cities where the theaters are located for her parts. Klabund writes to Herman Hesse (1877-

1962): "I live, blown here by fate, still in Breslau, the (bulwark of the East), a damp, unfriendly place in Prussian Siberia. How often I long for the warm, tender Ticino." Neher is cast in Klabund's play *The Chalk Circle*, and he creates parts in subsequent plays for her such as *The Burning Earth* and *XYZ*. On May 30, 1928, Carola Neher and Klabund depart from Gottfried Benn's (1886-1956) apartment for their trip to Brioni. For Carola Neher, it is a holiday of one and a half months before starting rehearsal work as "Polly" in the premiere of Brecht's play *The Threepenny Opera*, and for both, it is their last holiday together. During this trip, Klabund completed work on *Borgia*, his last novel. In July, Klabund contracted a fever again, and needed to return to Davos immediately, where the patient, critically ill, arrived exhausted in the middle of the month. The doctor diagnosed pneumonia once again. On the evening of August 13th, Klabund's life began to fade away. His doctor had not expected the end so soon. Carola, the doctor and a night nurse stood by Klabund's bedside, hardly recognizing him, as he gently passed away on August 14th at 4:30 a.m. Klabund described his wish to be cremated: "I would like my ashes to be scattered over the sea. Then I will end up like Jonah in a whale's belly, or a flounder will swallow me, and one day, a fat gentleman from Königsberg will invite me to dinner. But perhaps I will reach the bottom of the sea safely, yes: perhaps I will reach the bottom of all being." The burial took place in Crossen at the Bergfried Cemetary on September 9, 1928 with the poet Dr. Gottfried Benn delivering the eulogy for his deceased friend.

In his eulogy, Benn said: "I knew him in the times when he was nothing, and in the times of the brilliance of his name. The best years were probably those when, shortly after the war, he lived in a small street in southwest Berlin, in a small room with only one window and no bed; he slept on a sofa, and when you visited him in the morning, he was lying on that sofa, completely covered with manuscripts, newspapers, letters, and journals, working tirelessly and feverishly, as he did his whole life. These were the years of the second period of his poems, his novels, and the years when the thought of the 'Chalk Circle' came to him. They were also years of illness, and I often went to him as a doctor. Sometimes I called him in friendship 'Jens Peter,' which were the first names of the great Danish novelist Jens Peter Jacobsen, to whom he resembled physically, and who suffered from the same illness and died. I often saw violets in his room, Chopin's favorite flowers, his other companion in illness. Once we read together the last words of Chopin, which he wrote on his day of death: 'My attempts are completed according to what was possible for me to achieve' – the farewell words of a true artist who had experienced the fragmentary nature of the individual, words of silence and restraint, as Klabund could have written them too, whose fundamental characteristic throughout all the years was one of deep, brotherly modesty."

Years after Klabund's death Carola Neher married Anatol Becker in 1932 and left Germany following Hitler's ascension to power in 1933. She first emigrated to Prague, where she worked at the New German Theater, but went on to the Soviet Union in 1934, where she met Gustav von Wangenheim and worked with him at his cabaret Kolonne Links. In 1936, during the great purge both she and her husband were denounced as Trotskyites, resulting in their being arrested on July

25, 1936. Becker was executed in 1937, while Neher was sentenced to ten years in prison. She eventually died of typhus at Penal Colony No. 6 of the Federal Penitentiary Service of Russia in Orenburg Oblast.

7. Conclusion: Reassessing Klabund's Legacy

Klabund's early death cut short a brilliant literary career, leaving many to wonder what further contributions he might have made to German literature had he lived longer. Despite his relatively short life, Klabund left behind a significant body of work that continues to be studied and appreciated today – 25 plays, 14 novels, numerous short stories and books of poetry. His poetry, plays, and translations are admired for their emotional depth, stylistic innovation, and cross-cultural reach. Klabund's ability to bridge the literary traditions of East and West, his exploration of human fragility, and his engagement with the existential crises of his time make him a vital figure in both German literature and the broader tradition of European modernism.

In recent years, there has been a renewed interest in Klabund's work, as scholars and critics have sought to recontextualize his contributions within the broader framework of modernist literature. His unique blend of Eastern and Western influences, his engagement with existential themes, and his lyrical mastery make him a key figure in the literary history of the early 20th century.

While his works may not have achieved the same widespread popularity as those of Brecht or Thomas Mann (1875-1955), Klabund's legacy remains significant. His ability to capture the emotional and intellectual turbulence of his time, coupled with his desire to seek new forms of artistic expression, continues to resonate with contemporary audiences.

Ultimately, Klabund's life and works offer a powerful testament to the enduring human struggle for meaning in a world marked by uncertainty, impermanence, and suffering. His voice, though often melancholic, is one of hope, suggesting that even in the darkest moments, there is beauty to be found in the fleeting and the fragile.

Part One:

Celestina

Celestina is considered to be the first published work
by Fredi Henschke. It was published in 1912.

Celestina

Forward

A book that brings what I present in the Old-Crossen stories is uncertain, subjective – and, in the strict historical sense, unfortunately – rather dubious riffraff!
   – Klabund

To the Memory of Johann Joachim Möller (1659–1733)

Dedication
Highly esteemed Archdeacon, dear Colleague, revered Friend!

Permit me, as someone approximately two centuries your junior, to humbly dedicate this little book to you. I may be two centuries younger than you — but, alas! — not two centuries wiser. As a renowned expert in Hellenic antiquity, you will surely agree with me when I say: since Plato, the world has not changed. And the noble spirits of all subsequent centuries can still "shake hands" with him.

For a small eternity now, you have enjoyed the well-deserved heavenly peace after a life full of toil and labor, richly blessed. You converse with Aristotle, Erasmus, and Doctor Martin Luther — whom you nearly idolized, despite your childlike fear of idolatry — on philosophical and theological principles worthy of contemplation. You have also deepened your fleeting acquaintance with the small, unassuming, wrinkled Prince Eugene of Savoy, whom you glimpsed from afar here in Crossen in March 1710, recognizing the mighty soul within him. Surely, in your discussions with the illustrious gentleman, you did not miss the chance to address strategic themes — for a true fighter for the Word of God, as you were, is well-versed in war and its stratagems.

Allow me once more to call you "friend." For if we had been fortunate enough to live in the same time, we would surely have become friends. Already, we are united by the seemingly incomprehensible joy in a wholly unprofitable and materially unrewarding pursuit, which we nevertheless labor at, just as bakers, tailors, and district court clerks labor at theirs. We do not hesitate to regard this endeavor — chronicling and composing — as work equal in worth to baking cakes, rolling pills, or quarrying stones, even if it does not leave us with rough hands or compel us to appear outwardly bedraggled.

Such contemplative activity, as chronicling and composing, always bears a certain stigma in the eyes of the diligent, bourgeois world — a blemish that, my esteemed friend, we will hardly ever erase. Not even with a whetstone, not even through the most inconspicuous existence. Because our efforts rarely, if ever, lead to gold and glory, we belong to the so-called penniless artists, a category that, besides chroniclers like us, also includes painters, musicians, and contortionists. But let us console ourselves, dear friend, for we find our solace within ourselves.

In our "works" (which people only deign to call "works" after our death), they see only the polished final product, never the earnest and often desperate effort behind it. Who knows, for instance, that you dedicated your entire life to your grand *Croatian Chronicle*? That, to provide an accurate account, you searched through 200 libraries for a letter you deemed significant for the history of the town? An extraordinarily arduous undertaking for your time.

Now, my most esteemed colleague, I undertake here a task diametrically opposed to your objective endeavors: what I present in the Old Crossen Stories is uncertain, subjective — and, in the strict historical sense, alas, quite dubious rabble. Yet, I hope the lack of external historical truth in my accounts is compensated for by the inner truth of the stories I reveal. If these tales do not always conform to the iron rules of ecclesiastical morality, as you, esteemed Archdeacon, might prefer: do not hold it against me. People — especially the people of Crossen — are simply like that. Nature is colorful, with red, blue, yellow, and violet flowers. Likewise, there are red, blue, yellow, and violet characters.

And any city that produces people who are gray, stiff, and dull, like burnt prairie grass, one indistinguishable from the next — such a city would deserve to vanish from the face of the earth. For variety, as you might have put it, is what makes the world the world and life worth living.

Thus, if you, in the hereafter (which you once called the "better place," though you might now revise that opinion based on the facts of your experience), read and dream over these little stories during your nectar-sipping twilight hours, cloaked in the smoke of your immense tobacco pipe adorned with the turbaned Turk's head: smile. Smile with the smile of those who have transcended, who play only as spectators in the theater of life.

But perhaps, if you truly reflect, that smile (as with every smile) is a form of longing. For one does not always realize, while living, how beautiful it truly is to be human.

Smile, and around your kind, aged lips, the Graces will dance.

Yours in profound esteem,
Alfred Henschke

Preface, or Prologue, by Peter Puchner to His "Remarkable Events" (Crossen, 1738)

To the Honored Reader, Befitting His Station!

Although many books are available to everyone, bearing titles that boast much about their contents but in truth consist only of sentimental farces or crude anecdotes — books for which many squander their money only to discover, upon reading, that the author has merely borrowed material, reworking passages from a thousand old and new sources — you, esteemed reader, have no such worry with this little book. Here, you will find only genuine and truthful events that once transpired in and around the beautiful town of Crossen, situated in the Marches near Silesia on the Oder River. These accounts have never before been published and are presented for your enjoyment.

This work, previously well-known under the title "Remarkable Events and Historical Accounts Concerning the Town of Crossen," has long been unavailable in bookshops. It has now been expanded with various useful and highly curious pieces, bringing the total number of chapters to thirteen, with the expectation that it will be all the more enjoyable and beneficial.

Since it has become fashionable to publish books in formats and sizes so large they rival baskets and can only be transported by handcart, and since reading such books to completion could take several years (provided the reader is not rescued from this ordeal by the solace of sleep), we have modestly slipped this small volume out from under the bench. We hope that every reader, particularly the residents of Crossen, will carry it with them, study it often, and find heartfelt pleasure in the curiosities recorded here from bygone times. We trust that posterity will not withhold its due gratitude for this effort.

If some parts of the book do not meet the taste of one or another reader, let them not hastily lay all the blame on the author. Instead, let them first examine themselves in a mirror and judge accordingly.

Thus, we conclude our prologue with the following blessing:
"Omnipotent Great One, preserve the walls of Crossen from fire, war, plague, and infamy, for many years!"

Your most humble servant,
Peter Puchner

Crossen, in the month of October (Wine Month), 1738.

The Grünberg Campaign

In the year 1477, on July 27th, the Crosseners invaded the Grünbergers' territory, capturing 150 of them and bringing them to Crossen. The Memorabilia Crossensia reports this event in its gray objectivity with nothing more than this bare fact. Why this terrifying raid of the Crosseners into Grünberg territory occurred (indeed, no less horrifying than the Tartar invasion of Silesia in 1241) remains unaddressed by the Memorabilia, nor does it wish to address it. For the mischievous charm inherent in the prelude to this bloody campaign must have seemed to its strict historical conscience like superfluous frippery that ought not to burden posterity.

But I, who know the entire prehistory of this war (likely the only living person today who does), hold a decidedly different view. To me, what the memorabilia omits is precisely what is most worth knowing, complete with a delightful moral, making it both instructive and enjoyable reading for all, especially for dear young ladies.

At that time, there lived in Crossen a cloth-maker named Joachim Dürr. He had two daughters, Margareta and Barbara, born on the same day, who in their blonde beauty were so alike that not even their father — let alone a stranger — could tell them apart at first glance and say, "You are Barbara, and you are Margareta." Since they seemed of one mind and inseparable, always strolling arm in arm on the streets, tenderly leaning against each other, people were relieved of the difficulty of addressing them individually. In the town, where no similar pair existed, they were simply called "the twins."

This went on for some time, and everyone was content in their way: the parents, the two girls, and the townsfolk, for the twins were a true golden delight to the eye. Back then, there were mostly Slavic black, curly-haired heads around the area. When the twins reached a marriageable age, many young men would have gladly sought their hands — if only they had known which one they were actually in love with: Barbara or Margareta.

In the year 1476, it so happened that a young cloth-maker from Grünberg, a business associate of Joachim Dürr, visited Crossen and enjoyed his hospitality for several days. Just as he was about to return to Grünberg, the city gates were slammed shut before his eyes. It was said that Duke Hans of Sagan was marching to besiege Crossen, which soon proved true. Duke Hans believed he had rightful claims to Crossen, which had recently come under the control of Margrave Albrecht of Brandenburg, and sought to seize the beautiful town by force. However, his plan was thoroughly thwarted by the brave citizens of Crossen, and the young Grünberg cloth-maker, finding himself within the city walls, lent his own effort to the defense.

During the skirmish, he received a minor grazing wound on his right cheek, which gave him a convenient excuse to be tenderly cared for by the twins in the house of his host. This led to the peculiar outcome of him falling in love — not, as one might expect, with both sisters, but rather (and he insisted firmly on this) with Margareta alone. He claimed he could distinguish between them by their eyes, wherein love resided, and he asked for Margareta's hand in marriage. He spoke to her father, who quickly called for the mother. Both were deeply moved and happily gave their consent — for once one of the "imps" was out of the house, the other, just as pretty and cheerful, would soon find a husband as well, as the difficulty of choice would be resolved.

The Grünberger was then sent to fetch Margareta. He went out, and by chance, encountered one of the twins alone in the hallway. In his excitement, he mistakenly brought Barbara into the room instead. Barbara, smiling, gave no indication of the error. She received her parents' blessing in the arms of the handsome Grünberger and was happy and content. For she loved the Grünberger, while Margareta cared nothing for him — a true rascal she was — but let events take their course, eager to burst out laughing with Barbara in their chamber that evening.

The Grünberger left the next day, as a capable young man (regular postal carriages did not exist then), of course on foot, escorted by the parents and the twins as far as the Glogau Gate. He returned to Grünberg with the promise to come back soon and not deprive his bride too long of his cheerful presence. This he indeed did, visiting Crossen repeatedly in 1476 and later in the spring of 1477.

For the summer of 1477, on July 26th, the wedding was arranged. The ceremony took place in the church by the market, where Margareta Dürr and Heinrich Wenzel from Grünberg entered into the marital bond for life. But beneath the guise of Margareta, it was Barbara who stood before the altar. Thus far, the girls had carried out their prank — for the Grünberger still insisted wildly and vainly, as on the day of their engagement, that he loved Margareta and her alone, and that he felt only a brotherly affection for Barbara. Yet, in truth, he was passionately enamored with Barbara, kissing her fervently and behaving as if madly in love with her.

After the wedding, a modest meal was held in Joachim Dürr's garden under the open sky. The next morning, after the consummation of the marriage, the young couple departed for Grünberg, accompanied by the heartfelt blessings of the parents and the mischievous waving of Margareta, who now began to harbor all sorts of anxious thoughts. That evening, Mother Dürr entered Margareta's room just as she was about to climb into bed. And since people at that time still went to bed completely naked as the Lord had made them, Mother Dürr froze in the doorway. For the figure standing there in her fair nakedness bore a small, coin-sized brown birthmark on her left upper arm — the distinguishing mark of Margareta by which the mother had always been able to tell her daughters apart.

Margareta fell weeping onto her pillows, and the horrified mother immediately understood — or at least thought she understood. She ran downstairs to her husband, and the two quickly agreed that the Grünberger had brought an indelible disgrace not only upon their family but also upon the entire city and the Holy Roman Church. They summoned some neighbors, held counsel, and ultimately decided to not only seek retribution against the Grünberger but also against the Grünbergers as a whole, who had always carried their heads high and fancied themselves superior to the honest folk of Crossen.

The next morning, the entire citizenry was roused, and armed with spears, axes, and swords, a force of about 400 men marched toward Grünberg. There, unsuspecting festivities were underway in a forest clearing about half a mile outside the city walls — a celebration in honor of some saint or Grünberger, who knows. Among the revelers, the newlywed couple Heinrich Wenzel and Margareta (alias Barbara) Dürr danced merrily on the meadow. Suddenly, with wild cries and shouts, the Crosseners burst forth from the bushes. Before the Grünbergers realized what was happening, and unable to resist since they had no weapons, they were surrounded. The women and children were let go, except for one: the unlawfully abducted Helena alias Barbara alias Margareta, for whom the Crosseners had launched their assault. Among the men, 150 were captured, along with the pipers and musicians, who, after playing for the Grünbergers' dancing, were now forced to march at the head of the procession back to Crossen, playing wild victory marches.

To Heinrich Wenzel, all this seemed like a wild drunken dream, and the idea that he was the cause of the Crosseners' raid, as he gleaned from the hints and conversations overheard while trudging toward Crossen, simply made no sense to him.

In Crossen, the 149 Grünbergers were imprisoned, while Heinrich Wenzel, his wife, her sister, and their parents were summoned before the council. There, Heinrich learned of his crime: that he had unlawfully abducted Barbara Dürr, to whom he was not married, instead of his rightful spouse, Margareta. Heinrich pleaded his innocence, insisting that this woman (pointing to Barbara) was the wife granted to him before God and the world, and that he had come to know and love her under the name Margareta.

Against this stood the testimony of the twins' mother. The father and the judges scratched their heads, for now that they saw the twins side by side again, they were once more confusing them. Then Margareta stepped forward and resolved the matter in a way that, while dubious, was fortunate enough that no one could, or wished to, object. With a mischievous spirit upon her, she solemnly declared: it was indeed correct that Heinrich Wenzel was married to this woman (pointing to Barbara). She must know, for she herself could not recall standing before the altar. That woman, although always called Barbara, had been baptized Margareta, while she herself had been baptized Barbara. She remembered this clearly from her baptism, although she had never bothered to correct the misunderstanding since they were rarely addressed individually, and it had not been worth speaking up.

Thus, it turned out that the woman called Barbara was, in fact, Margareta, and her marriage to the Grünberger cloth-maker Heinrich Wenzel as Margareta Dürr was therefore valid. The judges (keen to avoid a scandal involving the church) embraced Margareta alias Barbara's Solomon-like wisdom. Everyone breathed a sigh of relief at the happy resolution of the affair: the couple, the sister, the parents, the townsfolk, and not least the 149 Grünbergers, who were immediately released and sent home with elaborate apologies.

This is the true and remarkable story of the Crosseners' raid into Grünberg territory, which took place on July 27th, 1477, in the 629th year after the founding of the city.

The Apparition of Saint Hedwig

In the local council library, there is an old folio volume bound in pigskin. Its contents arouse little curiosity, but its cover immediately catches the eye. The bookbinder (who ruined and destroyed many old, valuable manuscripts by exploiting them, unaware of their worth, for his bookbinding artistry) used several pages of an old handwritten Vulgate to save on pigskin.

This manuscript, written in a monk's hand, is still clearly visible and legible: it contains passages from the letters of Peter and Paul, and the portraits of the two apostles are finely and meticulously crafted as initials in blue, red, and gold. At first glance, the portraits of the saints impress only with their physical beauty (a quality perhaps too generously bestowed upon them as apostles). Upon closer inspection, however, a peculiar discovery emerges. The faces of these pious men bear a strange, girlish sweetness and delicacy, such that one might reasonably conclude: perched upon the slender, austere, and stylized bodies of the saints are two playful, lily-like blossoms, pretty young women's heads.

And upon further examination, the apostle portraits turn out to be depictions of the same beautiful young woman. Around the mid-15th century, there lived in the Franciscan monastery here (which stood where today's New Market is located) a devout and learned Brother Theodorus. Though only 29 years old, his scholarship was so considerable that it was proverbial in the region and even as far as Frankfurt. Thus, the prior entrusted him with the task of transcribing a Vulgate Bible, as the local monastery lacked one. Brother Theodorus eagerly took up the task. With a fine-tipped brush and black ink, he meticulously wrote out the Gospel of Matthew, then Mark, Luke, and John, and so on, even completing the Acts of the Apostles. But when, months later, he reached the Epistles (by which time spring had arrived), his focus faltered. His work slowed to a crawl, like a sluggish brook. Through the barred window of his cell, his gaze often wandered with the birds into the clear silver-blue sky, and though his lips murmured prayers, they seemed ready to burst into secular and unholy springtime songs. One day, as he was delicately painting the "P" of the Apostle Paul, his eyes strayed from the parchment to gaze longingly out the barred window. He started abruptly, for he had seen Marja, the most beautiful girl in town, the daughter of a boatman, walking through the morning sunlight across the meadow — Marja, for whose sake the boatmen and mercenaries stabbed curses into their fists with their knives — yet none of them could boast of even the slightest favor from her. The young cleric rose from his stool and began pacing restlessly in his narrow, dim cell. He had encountered Marja once before on the street, and now it seemed to him that her lively brown eyes had climbed the monastery wall like lizards, searching for something, or someone. The blood rushed crimson into his pale, ascetic face. Could it be he for whom Marja's eyes had leapt over the monastery wall? He banished the unholy thought indignantly, but no matter how fiercely he dismissed it, it stubbornly returned. Falling to his knees, he prayed fervently to the Virgin Mary, summoning her image to his mind. She appeared to him, yet her face shone with Marja's features, smiling down at him with a sorrowful allure.

With a sigh, he rose and resumed his work. But as he completed the Apostle Paul's initial in red, blue, and gold, behold — Marja's gentle face gazed back at him from the saint's blue robe.

Brother Theodorus prayed through the night, but the night was sensually mild, as spring nights sometimes are when summer already trembles within them. The memory of Marja pressed upon him with force: her gait, her slender hands. Never, never before had a woman seemed even remotely worth looking at. Now the devil's temptation sent him Marja, the little fisher girl — could she embody his destiny? He did not want to succumb. He fought... for a week... for fourteen days... and every day during those fourteen days, Marja passed by the monastery, her lively brown eyes climbing the monastery walls like lizards, searching for something... someone...

To escape her, he requested that the prior send him on a preaching journey to the villages. Exhausted, broken in body and soul, he returned to Crossen one evening.

Two weeks had passed again, but still Marja's image burned within him. Walking between willow bushes, through the Oder meadows, nearing the town, he suddenly stopped in his tracks. The moon hung behind clouds. Suddenly... he shuddered... from the damp meadow mist arose the vision of a woman. He wanted to flee... but she seized him. He tried to make the sign of the cross... but she prevented him. And then, he let himself sink, helpless, into her arms.

"So it is with monks," says a chronicle from that time. "Once they have tasted blood (though before, they may have been the tamest creatures of house and monastery), they become like wild men."

Brother Theodorus even dared, one night, to enter the garden near Marja's home. They stood in a tender embrace beneath a linden tree when suddenly the moon broke through the clouds, and with it, from the house, a crowd of shouting, gesticulating people. Marja's parents had long since grown suspicious. Armed with poles and cudgels, they advanced upon the trembling monk, whose tongue froze in terror in his mouth. But Marja stepped forward and cried out (for when women are quick-witted, they are often exceedingly so): "Fall to your knees and pray, for behold, Saint Hedwig has appeared to me!"

At this, they all (for stupidity requires only a forceful command to act upon) fell to their knees, believing the gray outline of the Franciscan's habit in the dim light to be a woman's garment. (They did not suspect that Marja's lover was, in fact, a monk.) He, however, raised his arms and blessed them. And so, more frequently and undisturbed, Saint Hedwig continued to appear to the beautiful fisher girl, Marja.

Note: Professor Lüddecke of Crossen (to name at least one reliable witness) and the author have both had this book in their hands. It was last housed in the large cabinet that once stood in the city council chamber and was later moved to the ground floor of the treasury building. The book has recently vanished under mysterious circumstances, at least temporarily, despite the author's frequent and diligent efforts to locate it. It would be a shame if nothing remained of the book except the charming (if somewhat frivolous) tale of the "Apparition of Saint Hedwig," which the author has endeavored to record here.

The Astronomer

I found the following charming tale in a small Latin book that I purchased several years ago at the flea market of the Auer Dult in Munich. It was titled: Origines urbiutn oppidorumque Germaniae, Nuremberg 1609, published by Johann Pfeiffer. I translated the piece very freely from Latin and, for the sake of better artistic effect, modernized it somewhat here and there. The text speaks only of a city called Crossen, as the letters indicate. Whether this refers to Crossen on the Elster or perhaps Crossen on the Oder, I leave it for historians and philosophers to determine (and I do not consider an investigation of this matter unworthy of being a doctoral thesis in philosophy. For those interested, I am happy to provide any information on sources, etc.). I recount the tale simply and plainly as it presents itself and ask you always to bear in mind the fact that it is, after all — just a fairy tale.

In those ancient times, when everyone still addressed each other informally and dreams grew on trees like golden apples, six dwarfs lived.

They were small, like three-year-old children, but each had a huge mouth as big as an ox's. They claimed that, unlike other people, their soul was not a mouse, but a rat, and that it needed such a large opening for its strolls. However, others believed that their mouths had stretched so wide because of their foolish chatter.

Since they were too small to pick the dreams from the trees and couldn't find a better occupation, these six dwarfs founded a skat club. Their names were letters; back then, people had no desire to spend hours laboring over long words.

The first, adorned with red hair and always found to be thoughtful, was named n. The second, who was amazed by everything and bald, was named o. The third, β, was named so because he chased lizards along the sunny wall.

The fourth, r, was named for his rolling r when he spoke. The fifth, e, laughed bleatingly like a goat, so they named him e. The last one, finally, was called c because he eternally suffered from a bad toe.

For a year, they played skat from sunrise to sunset. Then c grew bored, and o agreed with him. They decided to court six women of similar stature and with equally large mouths. After marrying the dwarfs, these six women formed a ladies' circle, and the six families founded a city. The city had to be by a river because c wanted water nearby to cool his bad toe.

One day, a man arrived in this city with a black-haired, blue-eyed boy. This startled and annoyed the dwarfs: all of them had blonde hair and blue eyes, and they considered the strange man to be a revolutionary.

The stranger had an enormous physique and massive, slap-ready hands, so they feared him and insulted him only in secret.

As long as the boy was small and played happily and innocently with their children, things were tolerable. But the boy grew older and decided he wanted to study astronomy.

For a year, they played skat from sunrise to sunset. Then c grew bored, and o agreed with him. They decided to court six women of similar stature and equally large mouths. After marrying the dwarfs, these six women formed a ladies' circle, and the six families founded a city. The city had to be by a river because *c* wanted water nearby to cool his bad toe.

One day, a man arrived in this city with a black-haired, blue-eyed boy. This baffled and annoyed the dwarfs: all of them had blonde hair and blue eyes, and they considered the strange man to be a revolutionary.

The stranger had an enormous physique and massive hands made for slapping, so they feared him and insulted him only in secret.

As long as the boy was small and played happily and innocently with their children, things were tolerable. But the boy grew older and wanted to study astronomy.

Since he always held his head high to observe the stars, they soon called him arrogant. From all the stargazing, the boy's eyes became farsighted, so he had difficulty seeing things up close and failed to greet the dwarfs. They felt deeply insulted in their honor and would cry out among themselves: "He is conceited; we're too insignificant, too dwarfish for him. Yes, yes, young people these days — once they go to university, they become pretentious and no longer acknowledge people like us."

And so, they plotted how to make him feel their hatred.

...One night, the young man retrieved a star from the sky — a testament to his profound skill. He sent out his soul in the form of a swallow, and it had plucked the star from the celestial meadow.

He displayed the star in the town hall and charged an admission fee to view it.

The dwarfs — c, o, β, and r — came and were astonished to find that they only saw a grain of sand. They denounced him as a fraud.

Their dirty words pained the young man, and he realized that their souls and eyes were formed differently and that they could not understand him.

"We can catch stars better than that," they said, trying to shame him and elevate themselves. "We'll shoot them down!"

One of them had an idea: "Look at our eyes — don't they shine just as brightly as the stars?" So, they shot at one another's eyes and perished in their own foolishness.

The astronomer moved to another city where he was better appreciated.

Celestina

It was not very long ago, after Crossen was completely burned down to its foundations, leaving not a single house standing except the sacristy, which was saved by the blood of a calf that ran there and extinguished the flames. At that time, Johannes Sultano arrived from the distant land of Venice. After constructing buildings in a beautiful and foreign style in other cities, he was commissioned by the council of Crossen in the year 1538 to build a market hall. Sultano brought with him a maiden named Celestina, whom he referred to as the child of his late sister. Her beauty rose above us like a rare star, and her name, Celestina — meaning "the Heavenly One" in our language — seemed to suit her perfectly. She had black hair and black eyes, as dark as the night reflected in a pond, yet a glow seemed to emanate from her. When she walked through the streets, proud and graceful as a young deer, windows and doors rattled, hearts trembled, and young and old alike leaned out to delight in her presence. But among the women of the town, pale envy and red hatred arose. They whispered behind her back that she turned men's gazes and thoughts away from them. I, who write these lines for posterity while the white strands of old age fall sparsely over my brow, recall my golden youth and hear again the Venetian's Italian laughter, twittering around me like swallows. Oh, my youth! Requiescat. We young lads — above all, my friend Christianus Licht, the son of a legal assessor in Frankfurt, a law candidate, and myself — boldly courted the Venetian maiden. But she only laughed and mocked us: "Dare not, you fair-haired rabble!" Her scorn for the love of us blond men cut our souls as if with knives, driving us to spend many nights drowning our fiery blood in taverns and brandy houses, to the detriment of our studies and morals. The women, however, found no peace until they slandered her with vile and outrageous accusations. The first among them was the wife of Councilor Gottwald, who, when Celestina affectionately caressed her child one day in the street (for though she scorned us older men, she dearly loved children), violently snatched the child from her arms, wailing and crying that Celestina was an immoral person, bound for the executioner's block. She claimed that anyone touched by her would become unclean and was obliged to purify themselves in church. Celestina laughed, suspecting not what crime she was accused of, and replied, "Is the executioner's servant not also a man — and a handsome one at that?" From that day forth, the women — and reluctantly the men — avoided her, though many a secretive, enamored glance still fell her way, like a mouse peeking from its hole. For it became known that she often strolled alone to the Glogau Gate, where the executioner and knacker lived with his young assistant, Martin. Executioners and knackers were considered dishonorable and despised, and anyone who touched them or dined with them unexpectedly had to perform public penance. A cup from which an executioner drank was his alone, for no one else would dare to drink from it. But Celestina loved the executioner's assistant, Martin, who was dark-haired and wild-eyed like her and a fierce companion. That year brought a curious phenomenon: a new species of bird was caught in the area, the size of a thrush, with a thick beak like a waxwing, but its body was entirely bright scarlet. The obstinate women (for female cunning knows no end) managed to file an accusation with the council, demanding that Celestina be tried as a witch. They claimed she had summoned these unknown birds with her hellish arts to frighten the town. Many rational men protested against this accusation, as women, it is universally acknowledged, lack reason entirely. I was among the protesters, for though my love for her had not died despite my wild indulgences in Bacchus to ease my melancholy, it was all in vain. The trial was held, and the judgment passed: she was to be burned publicly on the market square. The day of her execution dawned, bright with sunshine and Italian blue skies. From early morning, the market swarmed with people like locusts in bad years. At 10 o'clock, the executioner's cart arrived, drawn by a donkey, with the executioner and his assistant Martin walking alongside. Celestina stood within, her delicate ankles bound, clad only in a white chemise. Never had I seen such a woman — and with my seventy years, I doubt I ever will again — whose face and slender form, despite the madness of her love, bore such pure beauty, almost sacred in its grace. The cart stopped in the market. A heavy silence fell over the crowd. A theologian approached her from the circle, but she shook her head and smiled. And as this smile shimmered on her pale cheeks, the executioner's assistant Martin, who in his simplicity had believed the judgment and shunned her as a witch, fleeing her once cherished love, stepped forward, seized her bound hands, and cried, "She is my wife, my wife!" Lifting her in his strong arms as if she were a child, he held her close. The crowd gasped as if struck by a whip. Everyone looked at their neighbors in embarrassment, not least the judges. For they were now compelled to honor the ancient law of the land: a witch could be freed and absolved of her bonds if a man claimed her as his wife. The chief judge ordered her release. Martin, the executioner's assistant, knelt before her as though before a saint, tears glittering like daggers in his eyes: "I too am a man! A man! Not a beast!" Then he lifted Celestina, who had fainted, into his arms again and carried her, oblivious to her weight, through the Glogau Gate to the knacker's dwelling. To this day, the saying persists among the people: "When executioner and witch meet, the devil himself blesses the marriage."

The Emergency Baptism

Around the year 1500-something, the chamberlain Jacob Häberle lived in this town. His ancestors came, as the name suggests, from Swabia. And he had retained a good deal of Swabian coziness. But there was one thing he couldn't stand for: anything related to religion. When the pure and unadulterated Protestant doctrine, as preached by Luther, began to take hold in Crossen, he was immediately on board with fiery and holy zeal, quickly transforming from a submissive Catholic to a wild and vehement Protestant. But his wife remained quietly loyal to the old doctrine that her enthusiastic heart trusted, and no matter how hard he tried to bring her to his side, he fought in vain against her devout stubbornness. After seven years of marriage, they had a child, a boy. The parents were beside themselves with joy, and he was to receive the name Martin in holy Protestant baptism, as the father rejoiced. His wife, not wanting to provoke him, didn't object to the name. While he thought of Luther, she could derive the name Martin from St. Martin of Tours. But the Protestant baptism! She was lying in bed after childbirth and was too weak to seriously resist his forceful will. However, since she remained inwardly and faithfully a follower of the papacy and wanted to pass on its blessing to their child, she decided to secretly oppose her husband. One day, when he was out of the house, she secretly baptized the boy, before he had been baptized Protestant, with the Catholic emergency baptism, as every adult Catholic is authorized to perform in an emergency. She then calmly allowed the regular Protestant baptism to take place for herself and the boy, believing it to be ineffective in her simple heart.

The boy grew up healthy and lively and became a clever and sharp-witted fellow. "The boy must become a pastor," Jacob Häberle said one day when he was quizzing him on his Ovid vocabulary. "Yes," she dreamily confirmed, thinking only of his church.

When the boy was 14, his mother thought it was time to explain his true faith to him. The boy became very embarrassed, fiddled with the buttons on his jacket, and didn't know how to respond. Of course, Jacob Häberle soon learned of his wife's trick, cursed in true Lutheran fashion (like Martin Luther, who never minced words). However, nothing could be done about the emergency baptism – but of course, it didn't count, Jacob Häberle thought. With this belief, he sent his son to the University of Frankfurt on the Oder at the age of 17, where he was to pursue "the study of theology." But the faculty raised concerns about enrolling him. For Frau Fama had informed them of the emergency baptism. When they made a fuss and demanded various signatures from him, threatening him with eternal hellfire, which he was unwilling to give, he quickly put an end to the nonsense, shaking the dust of Frankfurt from his feet and shaking off the Swabian Protestant theological curses from his mind. For he had inherited energy from his father but the enthusiastic rapture from his mother. As he considered this in the bare guest room, he suddenly discovered his Catholic heart, and since he couldn't become a Protestant clergyman, he decided at least to try his luck in the Catholic Church. He knocked on the door of the bishop in Ansbach, and they welcomed him gladly. Of course, the emergency baptism performed by his mother was fully recognized. Thus, Martin Häberle gradually became a Catholic vicar and eventually a priest in Augsburg, Bavaria, while his father protested in vain from afar and his mother prayed for the Madonna's blessing upon him.

Years passed. When Martin Häberle reached the age of thirty-five, the widowed Countess of Brühl, who had her widow's residence in Augsburg, took him on as her confessor. She was a wealthy, stately, and still beautiful lady, although, in terms of age, she could well have been his mother.

He had not thought about his semi-Protestant origins for years, only in heavy dreams did they sometimes weigh on him like a nightmare — now, however, as he sat comfortably in his armchair after dinner, opposite the countess by the fire, watching the logs lick the grate with red and yellow tongues, thoughts came to him in their cozy togetherness that would certainly be allowed to a Protestant clergyman, but not to a Catholic confessor. Gently stroking his black cassock, like the fur of a dark animal, he told her, half-seriously, half-jokingly, like a *bon mot*, about his Catholic emergency baptism and his main Protestant baptism.

The countess listened attentively and said (and looked at him innocently with her large blue eyes), "But then you are — Protestant! So you can marry!" He looked up, surprised. Then he smiled (having, as a confessor, probably gotten to know women well). "Are you serious, Your Grace?" She played with a ring on her finger: "Absolutely." He stood up. "The discussion today, Your Grace, has made me thoughtful. I ask permission to reflect on it further, according to the strict rules of logic." He kissed her hand and left. When the door slammed behind him, the countess rang for her maid.

"I'm afraid, Madeleine, we'll have to have the old two-bed cot brought up from the floor again. Do you understand me?"

Martin Häberle did not sleep for three days. Finally, he completed the treatise that he sent to a Most Reverend Archbishop, in which, with Jesuitical subtlety and razor-sharp logic, he proved that he — was actually a Protestant. And (so to speak) that he didn't need to convert to Protestantism if he intended to enter the holy state of marriage.

This is the wonderful and edifying story of Martin Häberle, who, after already having suffered the emergency baptism in his youth, performed it once again on himself in his prime, under the holy sign of almighty Venus.

The Sad Prince

Once upon a time, in the days when Crossen was still a duchy, there lived a prince named Conrad in the castle at Krakow. Like all princes, he suffered dangerously from life itself. But while the other princes distracted themselves from their illness — dancing, loving, laughing — an endless sadness bloomed within him, the toxic sweetness of which could not be contained. From his eyes radiated a painfully alluring, insurmountable sorrow. And the girls who saw them, wherever they were: in the hall, on the street, or when his gaze, like two dark falcons, descended from a window of the castle upon the adoring crowd — these girls immediately began to cry bitterly and would have gladly kissed the sorrow from his eyes and lips, if only he could have become happier. But the prince did not know the cause of his pain. He had a room built for himself, round like a pavilion, which was entirely lined with mirror glass. There he sat for hours, entire afternoons, painfully lost in his own gaze, until tears began to pour down his cheeks and chin, tears that brought him no relief.

"What am I supposed to do in the world, I, a prince?" he philosophized. "There are so many princes, three dozen at every royal house. And if they are cheerful and full of life, it is because they do not feel how unnecessary they are. The work I do could be performed by my chamberlain, apart from his chamberlain duties, as a side task. And if only I, as an ordinary person, still represented or created some kind of value! But my impulses and my talents are shared equally by 10,000 others. If I think — then the minds of those ten thousand think precisely the same thoughts, bound in the same straitjacket of logic. If I kiss — I kiss with borrowed lips. The only thing that distinguishes me from them is my immense sadness. Does it mourn for aimless purposes, for directionless goals? Oh, I don't even know what purpose and goals mean: these words sound to me like out-of-tune brass bells, which I will never bring into harmony. I only have my sorrow." And he went and sat in his room, staring into the mirror glass, which seductively absorbed his image.

"He must be given a mistress," stammered the old, lean court physician. "A mistress," echoed the foolish circle of courtiers. "A mistress..." — the cry rang out among the people, and was sung by the dear girls, each of whom secretly longed to see herself at the left hand of the handsome, melancholy prince, walking through the high, cool halls of the palace. But the council of state rejected them all, those who thronged by the thousands at the door of the prince's bedroom, infatuated with his dark, sorrowful eyes — none thought, deep down, to make him cheerful and happy. Each one only wished to let the spell of his sorrow work its magic on her and learn to weep and gaze as he did.

The State Council selected a girl from the royal theater ballet, one of exceptional beauty and radiant youth. Never had a more perfect body been seen, one that united the beauty of flowers, sky, sea, rock, tree, and animal within itself.

But within this wondrous body there was no soul. It had fled because it feared its ambivalent power, and it wandered without substance over heath and forest, in cities and clouds. Therefore, this beautiful girl was also the only one who had never thought of the prince. Her feeling was like an empty vessel that only rang when struck with a mallet.

The prince accepted the mistress without surprise and hardly regarded her with more curiosity than one might give to a gifted ring before placing it on one's finger. Then he laughed, a pliable, trembling laugh that fluttered like a bird to the dome of the room, only to fall suddenly and dead back to the ground. All who heard it shuddered — only the little ballerina smiled, helpless and foolish.

One day, when the prince sat in his mirror pavilion, tormenting himself with his own gaze, he suddenly noticed that a strange transformation was taking place with his face in the glass: it began to shimmer with grayish-white and greenish hues, and his eyes sank into their sockets, resembling infinitely long and thin funnels. His usually stubborn brown hair was being pulled out like useless weeds by an invisible hand. For the first time in his life, the prince rejoiced. This must be death. He pondered the miracle — and the more he pondered, the more splendidly he painted his future; he would no longer see his eyes: they, the origin of his burning sorrow. And he commanded the construction of a mausoleum. It was built a hundred fathoms deep beneath the earth, with ten thousand black-marble steps leading into a hall illuminated and made of black marble, in which stood a black-marble coffin, its walls several meters thick. In the coffin lay a tiny black-marble chest. Into this, when he would eventually die, his two eyeballs were to be placed. Thus, the prince intended to silence the pain of his dark eyes forever. For he feared that these eyes, unless they sank completely into the earth, might still cause misery beyond the grave and devastate the people. The court physician chuckled: "Yes, yes — a mistress, that always helps, a tried and tested remedy. His Highness is now in an enchanting humor." And the foolish circle of courtiers echoed: "...enchanting humor." "Enchanting humor," it rang through the people, and bonfires were lit on the mountains as on Midsummer's Eve, rockets soared, yellow, red, and violet, artificial suns and stars exploded and spun like wild wheels, and the beer vendors and innkeepers made good business. One time, the prince took his mistress into the mirror pavilion. Brilliant and light-glittering, the mirror reflected the bright beauty of her body. He gazed into her face — and was startled. Through her physical form, he saw his mirrored self grinning at him like a flat, ugly skull.

And he kissed her, pondering whether the path to death lay through woman. He called her more often to the pavilion. There — into the mirrored glass — the soul of the beautiful woman strayed on its wanderings, almost by chance, yet guided by his unconscious impulses. She had grown heartily weary of the vagabond life and the hospitality of tree and river and cloud and beast. She longed to feel herself again: not scattered across the world, but with the world gathered within her. The prince and the mistress entered the pavilion in the evening. When the soul recognized her body, she submerged herself blissfully within it, disregarding worry and fear. At the very moment when the highest beauty of body and soul united and became apparent in the silvery-blue eyes of the girl, the prince fell dead to the ground. He died with a laugh of redemption. When they attempted to bury him in pomp and ceremony, and the court physician and the undertakers washed and embalmed the corpse, they found that he had no eyes. They were greatly puzzled: could eyes be lost? No, at worst, stolen! They speculated about the thief until the priests one day dragged the girl, his mistress, before the tribunal. And indeed — through her eyes, the prince looked out: but the sorrow had vanished, and where it subtly lingered, it was transfigured by goodness and pure grace. The priests wanted to gouge out her eyes, to fulfill the prince's command and place them in the little marble chest. However, the judges and jurors opposed the clerical demand. They sensed that this woman carried the soul of the people in her eyes.

The Oder Nixie

In the year 1659, towards the autumn, the construction of the water tower in the market was completed. The master stonemason Hanns Erdmann also participated in the construction, having carved the hideous heads that spout water beautifully and with artistic care. To celebrate the completion, he, along with some apprentices and good friends, went out to Hundsbelle and made himself comfortable at a local wine tavern with a 1658 vintage, a year which had produced excellent wines — against the wishes of his grumpy wife, who had let him go only after much nagging and arguing and was, in general, quite a devil (as will be revealed in the course of this story). There in Hundsbelle, he sat, far from business, and — sighing happily— far from his quarrelsome wife, in the cool shade of a lime tree at a wooden table, and thoroughly enjoyed the golden 1658 wine. His gaze was tenderly fixed on the vineyard hills, where the 1659 vintage glimmered in heavy grapes in the evening sun. Hanns Erdmann, in his spare time and private life (and when his wife wasn't looking), was a kind of artist, and artists always have a passionate fondness for nature and its charms, which undoubtedly includes wine, ranking among the highest. He expressed his enthusiastic reverence for nature well into the night, and the bell from Crossen signaled the 11th hour when they finally thought about heading home. Arm in arm, a swaying chain, they marched out of Hundsbelle, waking half the village with their loud singing of the beautiful song: "We have it, we have it, yes, we have it!"

How this came to pass, none of the party-goers could recount — but, in short: when they arrived in Crossen, Hanns Erdmann had vanished; the middle link of their chain was missing, the chain which, after he must have fallen out, had closed itself again. How that night had unfolded for him, he confessed to his wife the next morning, when he arrived home pale, hollow-cheeked, and very quiet, but nonetheless comforted by her. And we can do nothing but recount this confession here, although there are well-founded indications that the story actually played out quite differently. This, too, will become clear to the discerning reader as the story unfolds.

This is what Hanns Erdmann told his sullen-looking wife:

As you must know, (the wife shakes her head suspiciously) he had a tendency toward solitude, which sometimes overtook him with sudden and stormy force. Therefore, last evening, he had gently detached himself from his companions to be alone on the way home, so he could peacefully indulge in his thoughts and philosophy. And then, something strange and incomprehensible to the rational mind happened to him.

He was walking along the footpath down by the Oder, and while he was think-ing affectionately of his dear wife at home (the wife smiles grimly in disbelief) — suddenly, the waters surged before him, and a wonderful woman was carried aloft by them, a beauty such as he had never seen before (the wife frowns), looking just like a real woman down to her breasts, but from there on she was scaled and tailed like a fish. She had deigned to address him—he, who stood quite dazed before the apparition—in a kindly manner (the wife: "Just you wait!"), and her speech went as follows: "Do not be afraid, oh man, who is honored to cross my path. I am the Oder Nixie, whom few have seen without being carried off dead in my arms. But I do not desire you — only your art! Look upon me properly, and then go, make a statue of me in stone, and have it erected in my beloved city of Crossen, so that the citizens will always have my face before their eyes and give me the reverence that is my due." At that moment, the moon went behind the clouds, and when it reappeared, lighting up the willows, the Nixie had vanished, and although he called (the wife: "Just wait, you scoundrel, did you want her back!"), she did not reappear. However, he was determined to carry out her request, feeling as though some otherworldly force was compelling him. Indeed, Hanns Erdmann, pale and hollow-cheeked as he was but with fiery eyes, immediately went to his workshop and did not rest until the lines and features of a woman had emerged from an awkward sandstone block, looking human down to the breasts, but scaled and tailed like a fish from there. He worked nonstop for 14 days, and then the fountain was finished, and he offered it to the magistrate, who recognized the high art embodied in it, bought it for the city, and had it placed before the Stone Gate.

But Hanns Erdmann's wife was jealous of the beautiful Nixie, who had so completely captivated her husband's mind that he spent every evening out of the house, no longer paying any attention to her scornful remarks. She schemed to find a way to catch him (and the Nixie) in the act.

Then chance offered her a helpful hand. One day, while she was at the fishery, she saw a pretty girl pass by with a net full of fish in her hands. By chance, she looked into the girl's face and stopped, surprised.

Where had she seen this face before, not exactly the same, but — similar? She wracked her brain. After a few minutes, jealousy gave her the answer.

She went to the fountain in front of the Stone Gate. Indeed, it was the Nixie, the Oder Nixie, the one she had encountered at the fishery! She kept the discovery to herself, but at the next fish market, she went back to the fishery, and indeed, there was the Oder Nixie again, having just caught a batch of fish and turning to leave. She followed her discreetly — until Sichdichfür, where she disappeared into a small eatery. It finally dawned on her: the Oder Nixie was the proprietress of a (and moreover notorious) eatery in Sichdichfür! She completely shattered her husband's argument with the reasoning she used against his fairy tale about the Oder Nixie. At the very least, he walked around for days with his head bandaged.

But in order to rid herself of the public shame forever, she plotted against the magistrate, insisting that it was an embarrassment to the city for an indecent cook to leave a legacy to posterity. Eventually, the magistrate agreed and sold the Oder Nixie to a private individual, who was eager to acquire her, if only for the amusing story attached to it, and also enjoyed the honorary title of art connoisseur. She stood in his garden for a long time, until less art-loving descendants, forced by a prudish neighbor, disavowed the Oder Nixie and buried her in the garden. Today, she rests in the garden of Mr. Koch, and anyone who digs deep enough might still bring her to light — an amusing *document humain* of Crossen's past.

The Parable

Below, I will record the parable that the mayor of Crossen, Augustin Heinrich Krause, gave on March 7, 1675, as a response to Swedish cavalry captain Ernst Garzken, who, under the assurance of Swedish protection and friendship, demanded the opening of the city gates.

Well, Captain, this is how things would fare for us if we yielded to you, and entrusted our fate to the Swede: a fox, a carp, and an eagle happened to meet one evening at a bay of the river. The carp wanted to get a little fresh air before going to sleep. He stuck his oval snout out of the water and breathed through his gills. The fox came to the water to drink and took his usual evening sip.

But the eagle perched on a gnarled willow stump and rested from a long journey.

After the three had courteously complimented each other, the talkative carp soon began a conversation: "I would love to see the world," it puffed, flipping its gills back and forth, causing air bubbles to rise to the surface of the water like delicate silver spheres. "You, Mr. Fox, and you, Mr. Eagle, have it much easier than we poor carp. We are forever bound to our element and tied to the company of frogs and ducks if we want to hear about the world. My God, ducks and frogs are an unrefined and loud crowd. And in the end, one does want to do something for one's education!"

"Help is available," said the fox thoughtfully. "What do you think, friend eagle, if the three of us undertook a world trip together? Alone, we struggle through the world; you cannot swim, I cannot fly, and our friend the carp cannot walk. But together, we are a perfect being: The carp will carry us both safely across rivers and seas on his broad back, you, friend eagle, can rest from your long flights on my brown private divan, and travel with the carp comfortably and luxuriously, as if in a state carriage across the land, and during mountain trips, you can carry the carp and me in your strong talons and bring us over valleys and crags." The eagle, who loved solitude and would have preferred to continue the journey alone, looked astonished and indignant. In the end, however, he agreed to the plan, and they decided to set out at the first light of dawn.

The carp could not sleep from excitement, and when he finally fell asleep, he snored so loudly that all the frogs in the neighborhood began croaking irritably. At the crack of dawn, they gathered to discuss the first route. Since the fox and the carp were both very curious, the eagle, as the most worldly and well-traveled of the three, who knew at least superficially the river and plain, the domains of his two companions, was to head first into the high mountains. So, the eagle took the fox in his claws, the fox took the carp in his mouth, and all three took to the air.

The eagle, with powerful wings, flew towards the distant Alps.

After only a quarter of an hour, the carp began gasping and confessed to the fox that it was feeling very unwell and, if the congestion continued, it would likely have a poor experience of the journey. The fox, who had forgotten his breakfast in the excitement of planning that morning, became hungry and, without hesitation, ate the carp.

The eagle heard nothing of the conversation between the two, as his full attention was focused on the goal that he was drawing nearer and nearer to. After the meal, the fox was very satisfied with himself and the world, and he looked at the landscape with interest from the bird-fox perspective.

In the evening, the eagle landed on a bare, rocky peak.

"Where is the carp, friend fox?" said the eagle, astonished.

"He was on his way when he saw a river and jumped in; he couldn't stand the thirst anymore, as he groaned to me, so I let him go. In general — with people of his type, there is always the danger that they will fail at the first unfamiliar effort. They can't control themselves."

"You're right," said the eagle. "Now we still have to cross a small gorge to reach our night quarters. If you don't mind..." and he grabbed the fox and carried him with his strong talons to his young brood in the nest — for the evening meal.

"The carp, that is the Silesian people, the fox — that's you. The Brandenburg eagle eats both of us — even if you should devour us first." "Good heavens," laughed the Swedish captain, "I have little desire to be served to the Brandenburg eagle as an hors d'oeuvre..." ...but it was all to no avail. The same captain fell in November of the same year during the Brandenburgers' capture of the town of Wollgast.

The Burglar

Old Hieronymus Sporn, who, according to Hundsbelle, had a small estate on the Oder, feared neither God, the Devil, nor the Swedes. The sufferings in life, the wickedness of people, the hardships of the times had early on forged him into a hardened fatalist, to whom war, plundering, mistreatment, robbery, theft, and "Swedish liquor" could do no harm, only driving him more surely back into himself and to his books, from where he calmly tolerated all the baseness and foolishness that unfolded around him. His ironic calmness had often protected him from the worst — the looting of his library. Once, a French corporal, with several soldiers who cursed while rummaging for gold and silver, broke into his home! The corporal pointed the tip of his sword at his chest: "Votre richesse...?" Calmly, Hieronymus Sporn grasped the tip of the sword with two fingers of his right hand and brought it to his forehead: "Voilà, monsieur!" The Frenchman, like all of his kind, was receptive to a witty remark, lowered his sword, saluted, and courteously took his leave with his comrades.

On March 16, 1675, Hieronymus Sporn, as usual, fearlessly went on his evening walk — even though the Swedes, who had set an ultimatum to Crossen on March 7th (either the city paid subsidies or it would be raided), had made themselves at home on the mountain before Crossen and all sorts of vagabonds: robbers and murderers, hoping for loot, were following in their wake.

Old Hieronymus Sporn, who was now nearing seventy, hobbled along, armed only with his oak staff, without anything happening to him, and completed his usual walk. Lost in melancholic thoughts, which took him back to the bad times of his youth, to that dreadful year of 1631, when the Imperial troops nailed his mother, who had resisted their vile wishes, by her breasts to a tree and drowned her like a cat in a rain barrel, he entered his house and opened the low door to his study. A sharp, unpleasant odor struck him. He lit a candle. Then he saw that the window was open. He stuck his nose out of the window. A cool, fresh breeze greeted him. The smell remained in the room. Suddenly, a faint, sawing sound came from somewhere in the room.

He gripped the oak staff tightly and looked around attentively.

Then he hobbled straight toward the curtain that separated his study from the bedroom and pulled it back.

He involuntarily wrinkled his nose but controlled himself, leaned forward, and smiled at a schnapps-scenting, snoring vagabond who was leaning against the doorpost.

The vagabond wore a tattered soldier's uniform, had a wooden leg, and appeared to be at least 50 years old, judging by his dirty gray beard. In his right hand, he brandished a short, dagger-like knife.

Hieronymus Sporn regarded him for a few seconds and shook his head disapprovingly as the dagger blade gleamed in his eyes. Then he pushed him forcefully and stepped back a step, waiting for the effect. The vagabond was startled, blinked nervously into the light with his eyes swollen from drink — and awoke. The astonishment at seeing the small old man before him was so great that he stood motionless, almost fearfully, maintaining his previous position. "What does he want here in my house?" Hieronymus Sporn began the interrogation.

The vagabond, intimidated not only by his own drunkenness but also by the old man's piercing eyes, didn't dare to lie. He stammered: "S... s... s... steal."

"What did he want to steal, eh?" Hieronymus Sporn, feeling so much pity for the human foolishness that at that moment was embodied in the drunken rascal, softened his initially stern tone to a comfortably indifferent one. "G... gold."

"But he can't even run away!!" Hieronymus Sporn pointed to the wooden leg with his oak staff.

"N... No," said the vagabond, staggering to the other side, where the other doorpost kindly supported him.

"I don't have any gold, do you understand?"

Hieronymus Sporn tapped him on the head with the oak staff.

"I have... a knife," said the vagabond. "Do you think I'm afraid of his – knife?" The vagabond grunted: "No." "Then give me your knife!" The vagabond made an effort, but he couldn't do it. He leaned his whole body on his right armed arm, pressing it against the doorpost. "Let the knife fall," ordered Hieronymus Sporn. "I'll pick it up." With a clink, the knife fell to the floor. Hieronymus Sporn picked it up.

The drunken scoundrel followed his movements with a blank stare.

"Ah!" The connoisseur within Hieronymus Sporn awoke. "Look at that. The handle is exquisite ivory work." He hobbled over to his study desk, smiling. "You'll allow me to examine it by the light?"

"You may, sir." The scoundrel nodded graciously, almost losing his balance.

"I don't want to inconvenience you any longer." Hieronymus Sporn turned back to him. "You know what? So you don't cause any mischief with that thing, leave it with me. You can go to the devil for all I care. You understand me?"

The drunkard barely heard the word "devil" before he started trembling and nearly became sober. "Or, if you don't leave soon and voluntarily, I'll dissect you with your own knife and prepare you like that one over there!" He pulled back a second curtain. A yellowish skeleton grinned lecherously at the vagabond. He barely caught sight of it before, completely sobered up, he bolted screaming from the doorpost, leaped across the room in three bounds so that his wooden leg clanked three times on the floorboard, and swung himself out the open window into the darkness. Hieronymus Sporn closed the window with a smile. He then he returned to the table, once more admired the dagger hilt, and took a small leather-bound notebook from the cupboard in which he recorded his various collections and curiosities. He wrote: "March 10, 1675, acquired a beautifully crafted Venetian knife..." He smiled again as the grotesque silhouette of the vagabond came to mind. Then he went to the bookshelf, lifted a huge book with both hands, and carried it to his work table. He opened it and began to read. The title of the work was: *The Revelation of Nature and Natural Things* (as well as many strange and subtle effects) by the highly learned and widely renowned Mr. Hieronymus Cardanus, Doctor of Medicine in Milan, described in Latin, translated into understandable German by Hulderich Frölich of Plawen, printed in Basel in 1562 by Sebastian Henricepetri.

Note: The "Swedish drink," an invention of Swedish soldiers, was prepared as follows: they would throw the person to whom the drink was to be given onto the ground, insert a funnel into his mouth, and pour as much water through as possible until the body swelled. Then they would stomp on the person's body to expel the water – and repeat the process.

The "Swedish drink" should not be confused with the modern "Swedish punch," which, when consumed in moderation, is quite palatable. The former nearly always resulted in death or long illness.

Crossen

(From the "Curious Months" of Mr. von Schelmuffsky, a fabricated travelogue from the 17th century. Previously unpublished.)

Then I arrived in Güntersberg, a village, I might add, very nicely situated on the Oder River, which is famous far and wide for its sturgeon farming, where the sturgeon are kept as domestic animals, just like cattle elsewhere, and have been so tamed that they follow you, I might add, like a little dog, wagging their tails and begging for a piece of bread. Güntersberg boasts an admirably beautiful church, entirely built of wood, and curiously adorned with two perfectly identical tall towers at both ends. After changing my shirt, which, to say the least, didn't look too clean since I hadn't taken it off for two weeks during my very arduous journey, and after the Carthusians had provided me with a regiment of boarders, I loaded my pack onto my back and hiked straight across the Raven Hills and past the gallows, where a thief was fluttering like a wisp of straw in the wind, towards Crossen. I must say that the town of Crossen presented a rather impressive appearance from a distance. It lay like a dumpling in broth, as the entire surrounding area was covered with water, since the Oder River flows into a large lake there, which is called the Aue. This German word, Aue, however, should be seen as a distortion of the Latin word "Ave," and the name of the lake should be understood as a reference to the ancient custom of people praying *Ave Maria* when the waters began to rise and creep into their homes. As I descended the hill and stood on the quaint wooden bridge, oh my goodness, how my heart sank. For beneath the bridge, the Oder River rushed and swelled like a cataract, causing the bridge to sway, and I feared it might float away at any moment. In the lanes and streets of the town, on the dike, in the land alley, in the butcher's alley, the scene was curious enough to defy description. Barrels, tubs, and rafts, made from broken planks, floated by, filled with jolly men and women who sang, shouted, and drank as they passed through the streets. In one such barrel, which he expertly directed with his walking stick, the mayor passed by gallantly, while I waded through the raging waters with my pack on my back.

I then very politely tipped my hat, and he responded with the same courtesy, even bringing his boat alongside and inquiring if I might be the distinguished person traveling under the name of Schelmuffsky, who had already been reported to him from Frankfurt by a messenger on horseback. I politely replied that I was indeed that person, and asked if he knew of a suitable lodging for me in the city, as I was not particularly inclined to continue waddling like a duck in the cold water any longer. The mayor then cupped his hands to his mouth like a funnel and shouted through them, and it sounded, to my ears, as though an ox were being slaughtered. Soon, however, a fine little boat, fully lined with pink velvet, came around the corner, steered through the current by a boatman using an iron pole about 12 ells long. He stopped beside me and raised his wide-brimmed hat, offering a gracious speech in which he mentioned that the distinguished person, who concealed their high birth behind the name Schelmuffsky, might deign to board the magnificent boat that had been made available to me by the Senate of the town of Crossen for the duration of my stay. Good heavens, how quickly I jumped into the luxurious boat, taking my pack with me, and soon sat comfortably back on the pink velvet cushions. However, water from the Oder River was running into the boat from my pants, as I had already been wading in the water for over eight hours.

The boat now swiftly brought me to the grand town hall, where the entire Senate, in full regalia, greeted me at the front stairs. They were dressed in a very peculiar manner. All of them wore violet pointed beards, their faces were whitened as if with plaster, and on the tip of their noses, as well as on both cheeks, glowed round, fire-red spots. Their garments consisted of black sacks, dotted with yellow spots. Good heavens, how astonished I was as I saw these people strutting about so oddly. Even when I spent a full 14 days at the court of the Great Mogul in India, I had never seen anything like it. The eldest member of the Senate, whose head was adorned with a pointed blue cap, gave a well-composed speech, which, due to his age, he stammered out. Meanwhile, his head wobbled like a perpetual motion machine, and I, the devil take me, feared that it might roll off and fall onto the cobblestones. I replied very politely, as if I were one of the bravest fellows in the world, and I didn't fail to recount the story of my strange birth and the tale of the great rat. Oh, how the men opened their mouths wide and could surely tell that something truly bright was sparkling in my eyes. The eldest then began again, removed his cap, and invited me to follow him. He wished to show me the magnificent chambers that the esteemed Senate had made available to me for the duration of my stay. They had taken up the entire first floor of the town hall, and within it were a bedroom, a living room, a drinking room, a dining room, a bathing room, a workroom, and a waiting room. For my visit, 33 young maidens, dressed in the fashion of the land, had been appointed. Their hats were so large and heavy, like mail coach wheels, that to look into one's blue eyes, one had to unscrew the hat first. Their dresses were wide at the top and narrow at the feet, like men's trousers, so that they could only move in a hopping manner, like toads. The girls now danced before me, very elegantly. I cannot express how gracefully they could place their steps. These same maidens, however, became so enamored of me, sighing time and again, "Graceful young man!" that the Senate had to remove them from my service for their own safety and lock them away in the town prison for the duration of my stay, lest they drown in the Aue from love-sickness.

After I had spent a full 8 days in Crossen, and the Senate had gifted me with a huge piece of purple cloth, which had been manufactured there and was worth 100 gold gulden, I loaded my pack onto my back and set off toward the Glogschen Gate, heading for Grünberg...

Notes: 1) "Schelmuffky's Truely Curious and Very Dangerous Travelogue by Sea and Land" (published 1696/97) is one of the most brilliant works in the field of German comic literature. It is only a pity that it is so little known to today's readers. A new edition was recently published by Inselverlag Leipzig and Martin Mörike's Verlag Munich. An adaptation by Karl Pannier is available in Reclams Universal Library (No. 4343) for 20 Pfennig.

2) This site in Güntersberg was unfortunately destroyed during the last reconstruction of the church (1909).

3) A rather unfortunate interpretation of the German word "Aue."

The Dancer

God knows, I've never bothered about fools, my fellow human beings. Yet, even in my early youth, they fawned around me, the women licking my mouth, and the men bleating about the great duties that life imposes — how I must one day become an upstanding fellow — and how, with my considerable talents, I would surely make it to town clerk or even deacon.

At that time I was a ten-year-old boy, but I saw behind their flattering, twinkling, greasy and dripping eyes, and what filth they were, and how they carried their dirty mockery within themselves, not realizing when they, their joints trembling from drinking, pointed to their bellies and croaked: Ha, see what a man I am, and how I've made something of myself in the world! They were always content with themselves and did not know that unrest of the mind from which all youth and all life flows. So I soon separated myself from them and hated them, and ran out into divine nature, which is more powerful than all reason, and in its mirror I saw myself and my goals. For hours I lay on the meadow, covered by a willow bush, in the grass, and saw and heard the blue sky bell ringing above me. Or I stood on the Kienberge and traced with blessed fingers the gentle lines of the Rusdorf hills into the violet evening sky. There I knew what in me cried so strongly: I, I must recreate the world from the dark chaos that surrounded me — if I were even to remain alive. Life had meaning for me only as I ordered and interpreted it. I wanted to be an artist, a painter like Holbein and our Albrecht Dürer had been. When I made this realization (I was 17 years old and ready for the study of university letters), it struck me with pride and terror at the same time. I was different from the others. And exposed to their rage and the revenge of their majority, when I preached my doctrine of the sanctity of art. For I thought of the dreadful fate of that Polish nobleman Casimir Lynzynchski Podsedek Brzeski, who was sentenced to death, and whom they called an atheist. He was imprisoned on October 21, 1689, in Warsaw by the Bishop of Vilnius, because among other terrible blasphemies they found in his damned writings this sentence taken from the hellish sulfur pit: *Deus non est Creator hominis, sed homo est Creator Dei*: God is not the creator of man, but man is the creator of God. – But what, I thought at that time, does art preach if not this? And am I an atheist if I seek God in myself? In my blood, I had an aversion to any structured and roofed worship of God, as it is presented by churches. If I wanted to pray, I went to the pines in the forest, to the butterflies on the meadow. And my aversion to church buildings was only softened when I encountered the Gothic, magnificent structures like the St. Sebaldus Church and the Church of Our Lady in Nuremberg and Munich. For I fought hard with my parents, who could not understand my unusual and unconventional disposition, that they should let me move to Nuremberg and Cologne, where I intended to learn the art of drawing and engraving. I succeeded in this against their will. For I knew the Bible well, and it says there: We must obey God more than men. And I trusted in my God.

Thus, I bravely looked around in Nuremberg, Munich, Augsburg, then in Cologne and Lübeck, and after I had learned something proper, I returned to Crossen in the autumn of 1711.

Homesickness lies upon us Northerners like a disease in our blood.

Here is the translation of the provided text: There, I was immediately greeted with the latest news: that the shooting range on the moat had been demolished and rebuilt in front of the Stone Gate; that in June, a mason's apprentice, Samuel Klopsch, had fallen three stories while cleaning the eaves at the house of Eustace Möller, the town musician, in the market square, but had survived and could still work; that a farmer's wife in Rußdorf had given birth to three live children who were perfectly healthy and identical in every way — and such other curiosities. Also, King Augustus of Poland had passed through Crossen on July 27th with three wagons, and the greatest event and honor was yet to come, as Tsar Peter of Moscow, who had passed through here on September 18th with five wagons on his way to Dresden, would be returning in the first days of November. To receive him, the Prince of Brandenburg, Friedrich Wilhelm, would arrive tomorrow. On the day of my return, however, it was the 28th of October.

The town was in a state of great excitement, as though they were preparing for a royal hunt. Flags in Brandenburg and Russian colors hung from the houses, and the doors of the inns were adorned with wreaths of fir branches. For the announcement that the Muscovite Tsar would stay in Crossen for a full three or four days had drawn many visitors and curious onlookers. I strolled leisurely and contemplatively through the streets, greeted a few acquaintances, and enjoyed the lively tumult, as is naturally in us artists. In the evening, I went to Salt Square, where it was like a fair. Beer and brandy vendors had set up their tents, and on a bumpy dance floor, young couples spun joyfully under the starry sky. There were also various show booths, where one could see a family of bloodsuckers or vampires, the wheel of the world, a bear, rats as big as dogs, a Chinese man, an Indian fire-eater, and more. After peeking into a few of them, I stopped in front of a booth where the sign read in crimson letters: "Nadja, the Most Beautiful Dancer in the World — Dance Poetry." The words "Dance Poetry," which I had never heard before, struck me as particularly captivating, and although the barker, a thick woman shimmering in a silver armor, inspired little confidence, I handed over my coins and stepped behind the dirty curtain separating the world outside from the stage. A mediocre musician played an introductory foreign war march. Besides me, about two dozen other spectators waited, among them several fine young men, sons of respectable citizens, for the performance. They amused themselves by drinking water from a flask and spitting it at each other.

The music picked up pace, soon turning into a frantic gallop, a discordant bell rang, and suddenly, without us knowing where it came from, a black costume adorned with light green ribbons whirled in the center of the stage, from which a pale yellow head sprang up and vanished again, two pale arms flashing like lightning across the room. The music slowed, the dancer's movements became gentler, more graceful, and sensually overwhelming. Only then could one make out her delicate, soft facial features, her mahogany-brown hair, the childlike slenderness of her figure, the deadly fragility of her hands — and as she, in the manner of the war dance she performed, raised her right arm stiffly like a sword and a dagger flashed between her fingers, there was not a single person in the audience who would not have willingly died at her hands. Her eyes seemed to fly out of her head like two fireflies. They shot straight at me and buzzed through my brain in an instant.

The dance overwhelmed me so much that, drained of all strength, I staggered out of the booth into the cool night, but only returned home to Steinstraße after a long detour.

I did not sleep a wink that night.

The eyes of the dancer gazed at me wherever I looked, from the night.

I had no interest in the following day, whether the Crown Prince or Tsar Peter came; it left me indifferent. An unyielding force pulled me toward the dancer in the salt square.

I found her in the morning, leaning against the wagons of the wanderers. Her gaze swept over the Oder. When she heard my hesitant steps, she carefully turned around and smiled.

I approached her as if it were the most natural thing, didn't ask if she remembered me or could even remember, and took her hand. She wouldn't have understood me anyway. Neither spoke the other's language. She was Russian. She took my hand, held it for a moment, and then suddenly turned it so that the palm was facing up. Then, she bent her pale, delicate face over it and tried, intently, to read it with her blue-black gaze. She was reading my fate. When she raised her face, it seemed to me as though years had passed, and she looked into my eyes once more, smiled sadly, and shook her head... Since then, I have not been able to love any other girl. The eyes of the foreign dancer, whom I had seen for only a few minutes, never left me for the rest of my life.

I threw myself passionately into my art. But it, too, became dedicated to her. Again and again, I had to paint the dancer as a Madonna.

This is my story, the story of my life. For both, fate is cast: one receives a sword, another a book, and another a dancer.

We must all bleed for our deepest self. The most important thing is that we bleed.

The Valet

(A story from the turn of the 18th century)

In the entourage of Count R. — who owned a knight's estate near Crossen and whose extraordinary wealth allowed him the most extravagant whims and eccentricities, was a young man who, at first, attracted little attention. However, through a series of peculiar events, events that only later, in retrospect, revealed themselves as truly strange, he became, if only for a day, the talk not just of the

Count's inner circle but of the entire world. The Count had engaged him as a valet on the strength of excellent references, one of which was from Baron F., his brother-in-law and friend. Albert quickly won the Count's trust with his refined and quiet manners. He read the Count's wishes from his glance and gestures and performed his duties with a fanatical zeal that greatly astonished the Count, until he gradually became accustomed to it and could not do without the care and discretion of Albert's presence. Albert was about 22 years old. He wore his dark hair, which had a faint bluish sheen, parted in the middle, and his light eyes were protected by very long eyelashes, so that his sharp, piercing gaze sometimes seemed to break out of the foliage like a lance. His nose had a slight bump, but his face did not appear disfigured; his otherwise soft features were instead more marked by it. A faint bluish sheen lay on his upper lip. The most beautiful thing about him were his narrow, delicate hands. The Count sometimes could not resist stroking them. "You are an aristocrat, Albert," he said with a smile. "It is as if they are so sick and pale with the memories of their ancestors." "From their hope," Albert replied. The Count looked at him in astonishment.

The Count also confided in Albert about his many love affairs. He gave him all his instructions verbally, needing only to say a few suggestive words, and Albert would understand him completely. This relieved the Count not only from prolonged discussions, but also from long moments of reflection, which Albert anticipated for him. The Count's mistresses did not look unfavorably upon the young man, so confident in himself, who spoke little yet accomplished much. More than one became enamored with his slender gait, which, in its measured poise, betrayed something calculated, even coquettish, and gave him furtive nods. He noticed them but merely smiled, quietly dismissive and melancholic. One morning, when Albert entered the Count's bedroom to assist him in dressing, the Count called him closer. Lying on the bedspread was a small, red velvet box. The Count pressed a hidden button to open it and took out a golden ring adorned with an enormous, wondrous turquoise. Without saying a word, he reached for Albert's hand and slipped the ring onto his finger. Albert trembled, his eyes widened in shock, and his breath came in gasps. Then he fell to his knees before the Count, tears streaming down his face as he kissed his hands. But suddenly, he sprang up, cast a look of horror at the Count, and stormed out the door.

For several days, the Count could not shake the memory of this incident. He had never been accustomed to such overflowing emotional displays from his servants, whose gratitude for favors had always been cold and superficial. Was it gratitude, confusion about the precious gift, that had thrown Albert out of the regularity of his controlled and circumscribed movements and feelings? The Count thought of asking Albert. He thought it would be psychologically very interesting... but in the end, he refrained, fearing he might unintentionally open wounds in Albert's soul. For he was the first servant who seemed to have something resembling a soul. After a week, he had forgotten the seemingly minor pains of his servant in the midst of new adventures and pleasures.

Albert wore the ring with a holy reverence, never taking it off, even at night. He now completely distanced himself from the other servants, with whom he had already kept his distance as far as possible, since they, jealous of his favored position with the Count, made crude and vulgar insinuations about an immoral relationship between him and the Count. It pained him on the Count's behalf, seeing him so vilified, and he blushed fiercely every time such a poisoned word shot at him from ambush, but he remained silent to spare the Count from anger and pain.

In the meantime, the Count embarked on a love affair that drove him to an unusual extravagance of both his money and his energy. He, now nearing forty years of age, increased his passion to such a frenzy that he seemed no longer in control of his senses and, to win her favor, was willing to sacrifice hundreds of thousands. It was in vain that his friends urged him to be reasonable; it was in vain that his brother-in-law, and best friend, Baron F., traveled to try to calm him down and used all logical means to hold him back from his folly. He would not listen to any argument, and like an immature, childishly infatuated young man, he, who had been led through all the tricks and pleasures of love, had no other weapon against her than a monotonous: "I love her, I will love her forever, and I will perish without her." Albert also mediated the correspondence and the almost daily meetings between the Count and his lady. He also made great efforts to protect his master's financial interests, though he did not succeed as he had hoped. The lady, a widow of a mid-level official and of lowly origin (her father had run a small brewery), was as beautiful as she was reckless. She found herself suddenly in a position, thanks to the Count's generosity and his willing devotion, to satisfy all, even the most nonsensical and unnecessary desires, and although she had been a thrifty housewife to her late husband in their very brief marriage, she now lost all sense and oversight and allowed gold coins to roll through her small hands by the thousands. An apparently inexhaustible fortune can drain away like a river in the desert.

Albert saw that, unless the lady's actions were brought under control, the Count's ruin was imminent and he set about trying to save him. His influence over the Count in this case was very limited. Logic had no effect. He said, "If I perish, I will perish with her." So he had to find a way to influence the lady in some way. Fortune gave him the help he needed here. The lady, tired of the Count's extravagant caresses — for her love for him had always been rather superficial and heavily influenced by his wealth — yearned for distractions and adventures that all the theaters and variety shows the Count provided for her could not fulfill. As she had daily opportunities to admire Albert's quiet, modest, yet unyielding demeanor, which was heightened by the disciplined self-restraint he practiced, she suspected in him, in terms of worldly knowledge, a kindred spirit. The Count sometimes seemed to her to possess a terrifying fineness of taste in matters of art, such as music, and so she soon found herself genuinely drawn to Albert. He held the threads of her fate taut in his hands.

As soon as Albert recognized the lady's mood, he set about nurturing and subtly encouraging it. He would look her straight in the eye when speaking to her, and she would draw a dark desire from his gaze, so much so that she often faltered in her speech and did not know how to continue. He made sure to accidentally touch her hand, causing her lips to tremble, and thus he drove her into a passion no less intense and boundless than the Count's own. Her eyes rimmed, and frequent bouts of illness befell her, so the Count became very concerned and sent for the doctor several times a day. When Albert felt the lady was pliable enough, one afternoon he entered her boudoir and, without further preamble, said to her with his firmness, which softened the gentle sadness in his eyes, that he wished to fulfill her longing for love, provided she swore to him an oath — he said the word "oath" twice, while looking at his hands, which the lady gazed at with anxious delight — an oath to protect the Count's fortune and not exceed a certain sum each month, while he presented the dire consequences of further waste in dark images before her eyes. The lady, although she vaguely sensed the degrading nature of her situation, was so weakened by desire that she immediately agreed and repeated the oath he had spoken to her, sinking into an armchair in tears. Albert approached her, kissed her hair softly, and promised to give her his love on one of the coming nights. "Give me a token," she said through her tears, as she felt that he might yet slip away from her. He left her the ring the Count had given him as a token and took his leave. The Count did not recall ever having seen his servant in such a cheerful and lively mood as that evening when undressing. Albert told him the funniest stories about the surroundings, about the Count's friends, and portrayed some of them in their human weaknesses and follies so well that the Count could not stop laughing. But in the end, Albert became serious, and as he wished him goodnight, he was filled with intense unease. He hesitated, then grabbed the Count's hand wildly and covered it with many kisses. The Count, disturbed by the heat and intensity of the kisses, quickly withdrew his hand. The next morning, Albert, who had presumed the Count was still in the bedroom, entered his study without knocking. Like Lot's wife, he stood frozen at the doorframe. He had caught the Count and the lady in an intimate embrace. The lady, scarlet with shame at being so exposed by her true lover, hid her face sobbing in the cushions of the divan. The Count, enraged, leapt up, and in his embarrassment and fury, unable to find words, he waved Albert out with a hasty, angry gesture, in which disgust trembled. But Albert stood stiff and frozen, his eyes glassy and empty like two dead balls, fixed on the Count. Then his body began to tremble and convulse, his nostrils quivered, he tore at the curtain with both hands and with a horrible scream, bit into it, falling to the floor along with the curtain, which had detached itself from its rod. The Count carried the unconscious lady into the next room and instructed the people who had been summoned by the noise to take Albert to his room and immediately call the doctor.

Albert lay as though dead on the mattress. A faint bluish-white foam shimmered at his lips, and the color of his hands and face had turned a yellowish-gray. The doctor arrived. During the examination, only the Count remained present. When the doctor tore open Albert's shirt, he suddenly turned to the Count with a look of astonishment and inquiry.

"It's a girl," he said softly. Then Albert opened his eyes, and when he saw the Count, he smiled a wistful smile, as if asking for forgiveness: "The ring..."

It was her last word. That evening, she died. She could not survive the sight of her lover lying in the arms of another woman. For a week, the fate of this girl, fantastically embellished by the newspapers, was the talk of the whole world. The Count, however, was shaken to his core and fell into a melancholy from which no woman could save him. He placed the ring in her grave, and with the ring, his own life.

Violinist Heinrich

Outside the city, down the Oder, near the vineyards, he owned a small estate. Every day he came into the city, old Heinrich, with his wrinkled farmer's face, his protruding scruffy chin, and his brown, merry little eyes always grinning. On his formerly straw-blond, now dirty gray hair, he wore a faded cap whose brown color had taken on a greenish and blackish hue. His rough suit showed numerous patches and stains. In his right hand, he leaned on a willow cudgel, while his left hand dragged a canvas bag that contained the products of his small farm: cabbage, fruits, which he sold in the city — and a violin. This violin was his everything. He always carried it with him, and he could offer no greater honor to anyone than to show it to them or even play a little tune on it. It was because of his tender love for the not-so-great violin—he had inherited it from his father, who had bought it from a traveling musician for a few thalers, that he had earned his nickname "Violinist Heinrich," by which he was widely known. When he appeared on the street, boys and girls would run to him shouting, "Violinist Heinrich, Violinist Heinrich, play us something! Ah, you can't play, ah, ah!" Violinist Heinrich paid them no mind and limped quietly on; he didn't hold it against the children, and his face had the same grinning expression as always. It was known that he was a bit dim-witted, just as it was known that his relatives, whose property adjoined his own, had taken advantage of him. Much of what was rightfully his had already been claimed by a clever lawyer during the inheritance settlement. But they didn't stop there; time and again they brought lawsuits over various strips of land against him, and they mostly won. The relatives would have gladly taken all his land, which was fertile and, with proper management — Violinist Heinrich didn't understand that, he let everything grow as it would, as God let it grow — it would surely have produced very good yields. They would have gladly taken the whole estate from him, which they would inherit if they could manage to have him declared mentally incompetent or wasteful. He didn't understand how to handle money at all. He spent a considerable portion of his inherited wealth on the railway. He had already been to Berlin, Frankfurt, Leipzig, and Dresden, though no one really knew why. Now and then, he would board the train and leave with his beloved violin. When he returned, he would tell everyone who would listen how many thousands of marks he was offered for his beautiful violin in Berlin or Leipzig, and how people had admired its rich tone and praised his playing. There was no further information to be gotten from him. Once, after returning from the nearest larger city, where he had happened to win a lawsuit at the regional court, he told a particularly touching story. He told it to the cook and the maid of the Adler Pharmacy, to whom he had brought beets for the midday meal, for the goose roast, as the apothecary loved beets with his goose. "Yes, my dear, these are beautiful. these are fine beets, just as the apothecary likes them," he said to the cook. Then he turned to the maid, who had just started on April 1st — today it was the fifth or sixth, and whom he didn't yet know. "Ah, a new young lady, a beautiful young lady, yes, yes, well, good day too," and with that, he offered her his calloused hand. The girl laughed and shook it. She was a pretty, cheerful girl of 17, who had already heard about the strange old fellow from the cook. "Yes, Mr. Heinrich. I've heard of you; you play the violin beautifully," she said. "Yes, yes, yes," said Heinrich, grinning. "And what happened to me recently, yes." "What's going on, Mr. Heinrich? What have you experienced? Tell us," the cook chimed in, eager for a new violin story. "Yes, yes, so, I was in Cottbus, in the waiting room at the station, you know, where I had a lawsuit, and I still had time before my train left, so I sat down calmly, third class of course, with my violin, of course, yes, yes. And there at the next table, there were some young people talking, and they kept looking at me, and suddenly one of them gets up and comes over and bows and says, 'Excuse me if I disturb you, but aren't you the famous Violinist Heinrich?' The famous Violinist Heinrich, he said, yes, yes. 'And wouldn't you like to play something for us? I am,' I forget his name, but he was very young and yet already a professor at the musical conservatory. I wondered how he knew me, but I said, 'At your service, Mr. Professor, if it pleases you and the others,' and I took my violin and played, yes, yes. In a quiet place and in the Grunewald, there's a wood auction and 'Hail to Thee, Victor's Crown,' and many others, yes, yes. And when I was done — by now, more people had gathered around and were listening — then the professor came up to me and thanked me on behalf of the others and asked me to accept a thaler as a keepsake. I didn't want to at first, but he insisted, and he said I was an artist and my violin was very valuable, yes, yes, yes, my violin," Heinrich finished, gazing lovingly at the canvas sack, in which the contours of the hidden violin were sharply outlined.

The girls had a hard time holding back their laughter, and the young one had tears in her eyes. Finally, she said, nearly bursting out laughing, "Yes, Mr. Heinrich, you are an artist, but please, won't you play something for us? You see, I haven't heard you yet," and with that, she looked at him with feigned sincerity in her pretty brown eyes. The old man met her gaze, looked awkwardly down, but had to look back up at her pretty face. "Yes, yes," he said awkwardly, and rummaged for the violin in the sack. He stroked it tenderly as one might stroke a child's hair, plucked at its strings as one might pinch a child's cheeks, lovingly and tenderly.

Finally, he positioned it, tuned the strings, and drew the bow across them, causing them to screech loudly. The girls laughed to each other, trying to hide it. Violinist Heinrich didn't notice; his eyes were gleaming. And now he played. Folk songs, waltzes, as he had heard them; everything mixed up, mostly correct, not always pleasant, as his bow scratched too much. When he finished, he said, grimacing even more: "Yes, yes, my violin." Then he carefully packed it back up, wrapping it first in a large, colorful silk scarf. The maid said, "That was beautiful, Heinrich. You are really an artist, but hopefully, the lady didn't hear it," she added, with twitching lips. She had to hold back her laughter with difficulty. Violinist Heinrich grinned more happily. "Yes, yes, my violin, well, goodbye, young lady, goodbye." "Goodbye, Mr. Heinrich, and come back soon."

He had already descended a few steps when he turned back and called up, "What's your name, beautiful young lady?"

"Anna, Mr. Heinrich, well, goodbye." The girls slammed the door shut, and inside the kitchen, they collapsed onto the bench, laughing so hard that they had to dry their tears with their aprons. "Oh God, I can't take it anymore, what a silly old fool," the young maid sighed happily. But Violinist Heinrich went home with a look of bliss on his face and paid even less attention to the street boys than usual. "Anna, yes, yes, Anna," murmured his dry lips, "my violin, yes, yes."

Almost every day, even when he had nothing to bring for the household, Violinist Heinrich now came to the pharmacy, and if only for a few minutes, to say good day to Anna and play a short tune on his violin. With the same tenderness he gave to his violin, he now regarded the young, pretty girl — he, the sixty-year-old man who had never really paid attention to women and had lived his whole life for his violin. Anna soon sensed why Violinist Heinrich came so often and secretly made fun of him. After all, she had her sergeant, but she didn't show him her mockery, and for the sheer joy of playing along, she pretended to like him and threw him affectionate looks. Violinist Heinrich was filled with pleasure whenever she shook his hand or looked at him, and his eyes gleamed with delight. He brought her small gifts — silk handkerchiefs, delicate tins, especially fine fruits from his garden. She accepted them gratefully but secretly laughed at his foolishness. Then he stayed away for a few days, and the girls thought perhaps he had felt their ridicule and was offended. But he had made a big decision. "Anna, yes, yes, Anna," he murmured to himself as he hobbled through his overgrown garden. Finally, he had made up his mind. He put on his best coat, tucked his red silk handkerchief, featuring the Battle of Sadowa, into his pocket, took the violin and the linen bag, and went into the city. He found Anna alone, the cook had gone to fetch something; he asked if he could go into the kitchen with her. "Well, Mr. Heinrich, you look so formal today?" "Yes, yes, beautiful lady," Heinrich stammered out his speech with difficulty. "You see, I'm a man, I've never looked after women in my life, and I... you see, I haven't lost my bloom; I'm decent, as my mother made me, that's how I am. And you see, even though I'm almost sixty, I'm still strong and could take on some young man. And I've got my livelihood, and it's enough for two, and so I wanted to ask if you would take me as your husband. I'm not a bad catch, yes, yes, beautiful lady, and I like you very much, very much, yes, yes," and with that, he looked at her tenderly.

Anna didn't know what to say. She suspected that he meant it seriously, but since mischief was always in the back of her mind, she answered: "Yes, Mr.

Heinrich, your proposal honors me very much, and I do like you a lot, and I wouldn't be opposed if you waited a little while." "Many thanks, Miss Anna, many thanks, I'm not a bad catch, yes, yes, in the summer, we could have the wedding," he said, with a satisfied grin. "Well, Mr. Heinrich, in the summer. But now I don't have time. You must excuse me. Well, goodbye, Mr. Heinrich, see you soon." "Goodbye, Miss Anna, goodbye, yes, Anna." Happy and with a content grin, he hobbled away. When Anna later told the cook about the proposal, she nearly burst out laughing.

Anyone passing by Violinist Heinrich's property these days could see through the dilapidated fence as he proudly strutted through the garden, fiddling and singing in his croaky voice: "Wedding, yes, yes, wedding with a beautiful lady." By now, it was May, and Violinist Heinrich brought Anna lilies-of-the-valley every day. One day, he invited her to visit him, saying she should see what kind of household she would come to. "Yes, Mr. Heinrich, I'll come next Sunday afternoon when I'm free." She was looking forward to this new fun. Heinrich tidied up the two rooms and the kitchen and put on his holiday coat. Anna really came. Her sergeant accompanied her to the corner, where the footpath led across meadows and past hedges to Heinrich's property. Heinrich stood at the garden gate, watching. When he saw her turn the corner, with her graceful walk, slender figure, pale face, and the white blouse that suited her so well, his previously anxious features brightened, and he hobbled a few steps toward her, violin in hand. "Good day, Miss Anna." With a clumsy bow, he handed her a bouquet of lilies-of-the-valley. "Good day, Mr. Heinrich, thank you very much." "Yes, yes, Miss Anna, the weather is very nice today." He looked up at the clear blue sky, which was already sending down considerable warmth. "Well, then let's have a look at our garden." He opened the gate and let her go ahead. The paths were overgrown with weeds, and the flowerbeds, among the lily-of-the-valley, peacefully grew dandelions, bird's foot, and fat hen. He led her up a small hill, part of which already belonged to the neighbors, his relatives. There, on the hill, Violinist Heinrich had built a bench around a walnut tree. He sat down and invited Anna to join him. She sat next to him. From here, there was a lovely view over the meadows and willows to the Oder, where a tugboat with a dozen coal barges was chugging and puffing against the current. "Yes, yes, it's lovely here, Miss Anna, you don't have such a view from your kitchen." "It's very nice," Anna said, but her desire for further teasing had faded, and she began to feel bored.

Heinrich the violinist raised his violin and played "In a Cool, Shady Vale." He played more softly and tenderly than usual. The notes trembled through the silence, blending with the distant sounds of the river and the city. Anna felt a softness in her heart, pity for the old man. He stopped. "You played very, very well, Herr Heinrich," she said. "Yes, my violin," he grinned contentedly. From the Oder, the steamer's horn sounded, deep and hollow. He stood up and took out his pocket knife. "What do you want to do with that?" Anna pointed to the neck slicer. "Yes, yes, Fraulein Anna," he smiled awkwardly. She looked up at him in surprise. He leaned over the bench and carefully carved a heart into the bark of the walnut tree, with "A. R." inside and "K. H." beneath it. Her name was Anna

Rutschke, and his first name was Karl. She couldn't help but laugh out loud when she saw the heart. "Yes, Fraulein Anna, as a keepsake." She stood up and adjusted her dress. "I must go now, Herr Heinrich." "Yes, yes," he said. He was very sad. He had set the coffee table at home for both of them, the two cups with gold rims that came from his parents. One showed the Cologne Cathedral, the other read "out of love." He had taken both from the closet, where they had collected dust, and cleaned them properly. In the absence of a tablecloth, the table had been covered with the violin case. He had bought cake as well. Now she was leaving. He escorted her with his violin to the garden gate. "Well, goodbye, Fraulein Anna, and I hope all goes well for you, yes, yes." "Goodbye, Herr Heinrich, and see you again," she gave him her small white hand. He stood by the door, watching her hand disappear around the corner, until the white blouse was out of sight. Then he turned and locked the door. "Yes, yes, Anna, Anna," he murmured to himself.

The summer holidays arrived. Anna traveled with her family and the children to the spa. Heinrich the violinist said goodbye to her the day before her departure. He remembered that she had promised they would marry in the summer. But he dared not remind her. "When she comes back," he consoled himself. Now he sat on warm summer evenings under the walnut tree with his violin in his arms, smiling at the inscription in the heart and occasionally playing a dance. Then he stood up, stomped his feet to the rhythm, and sang: "Wedding with a beautiful lady, yes, yes."

The holidays were nearing their end. Meanwhile, the relatives had succeeded in pushing through the guardianship procedure against Heinrich the violinist. This time with greater success: the guardianship was pronounced. The trial had taken place at the regional court in Cottbus. Heinrich the violinist had his lawyer file an appeal with the Supreme Court of the Reich. It was unsuccessful. "Yes, dear Heinrich, I'm sorry, but there is nothing that can be done, you must accept it," said the lawyer with a shrug. Heinrich the violinist replied, "Yes, yes," and went to Berlin. They would hardly find any cash with him. In his poor, tortured mind, the most nonsensical thoughts crossed his mind.

He had himself shown the way to the royal castle, wanting to speak with the Emperor. When Anna returned, what would she say? She wouldn't marry him. "Anna," he murmured to himself as he wandered around the castle, looking for an appropriate entrance. Finally, he asked a soldier: "Excuse me, soldier, but could I not speak with the Emperor?" The soldier looked him up and down. "Move along," he said. Heinrich removed his hat and limped away. He then asked some passersby where he could speak with the Emperor. They looked at him with pitying smiles and walked on. He didn't know what to do. Until late in the evening, he stood in front of the castle, waiting for a miracle, waiting for the Emperor to appear. Then he went back to the station, his wrinkled face hardening. Deepest despair lay in his eyes. He sat down in the waiting room with his violin on his lap. The train wouldn't leave until early morning. He hadn't eaten in the last two days, and he ate nothing now.

In the afternoon, he reached the station of the small town. From there, it was a half-hour walk to his cottage. When he entered his apartment, he saw that his relatives had already been there. They had broken down the door, likely looking for his money rather than for him. He sat down on the bench and stared at the floor. He felt weak and miserable. The hunger was becoming unbearable, but he ate nothing. In the evening, he dragged himself up to the hill and sat down under the walnut tree. A humid, dark summer night hung over the land. The frogs in the Oder marshes croaked incessantly. A few stars flickered through the dark clouds. A late bird fluttered through the air. The branches of the trees rustled. It was as if the branches were breathing in their sleep. Heinrich the violinist sat motionless, his violin pressed tightly against his waist. His lips murmured: "Ah, yes, Anna, Anna, now I won't marry a beautiful lady, no. Now I only have my violin, yes, yes, my violin." He pressed it tighter against himself and laid his feverish cheek against the cool wood. He sat like that for hours.

As morning dawned through the branches, he tried to pull himself together. He was too weak. With great effort, he turned around and looked once more at the heart and its inscription. "Yes, yes, Anna." Then he lifted the violin. With great difficulty, he managed to hold it and drew the bow across the strings. The trembling, hoarse sound echoed through the morning silence: "In a Cool, Shady Vale..." Barely had the last faint notes faded when the violin clattered to the ground. Violinist Heinrich wanted to bend down to it. He collapsed beside his violin onto the dew-soaked grass, his hands desperately clutching the violin in a death struggle, while the first rays of sunlight gleamed on his white hair. — They could not release his clutching hands from the violin. They had to bury him with his violin.

The Flyer

Georg Henneske was the first flying non-commissioned officer in the German army. When he, the son of a Markish farmer, came home on leave, his home-town, located not far from Crossen, had already been in an uproar for several days. Upon his arrival, everyone who could walk rushed to meet him halfway, and some brave souls even walked half an hour to the Baudach train station to greet him. Children and half-grown girls sat in the cherry trees lining the street, waiting for him to come. Now he was here. The whole village crowded around him so closely that he could hardly catch his breath. His mother wept, saying, "Georgi, my Georgi," and the pastor exclaimed, "What a divine providence!" "Children," Georg Henneske laughed, "children, I'm starving!" Then the crowd dispersed only to quickly regroup for a procession that would lead him to the table in a dignified manner. It had been set up outdoors. The village took it upon itself to honor him with a meal. There were about seven courses, and each one included veal in some form. Along with the meal, they drank sweet, new cider. After the meal, when the wine began to take effect, people grew bold. They dared to speak to Georg Henneske, to ask, to make requests. "Georgi," his mother marveled tenderly, "you can fly now!" "Won't you show us a little flying?" timidly asked little Marie. "Oh, no," laughed Georg Henneske, "that's not something you can do just like that. It requires a special apparatus!" "He surely has one in his pocket," grinned the shepherd mischievously. "He just wants to keep us in suspense." "An apparatus, that's something you wind up, right?" asked his youngest sister, Anna. She was thinking of the tin elephant he had once brought her from Berlin. A rod ran mercilessly through his belly, and if you turned it a few times, the elephant began to wobble, tap his trunk on the floor, and suddenly run around the room in confused circles like a weasel. "No," said Georg Henneske, "I don't have the apparatus with me, because it belongs to the state." "I see," said the shepherd, nodding his white-haired head, "the state. That's another new invention." "Exactly," laughed Georg Henneske. "So tell us about flying and how one learns it, Georgi," his mother asked. She was so proud of him. Then Georg Henneske stood up, and everyone rose with him. "Alright, I'll do it. Listen!" He jumped onto a chair. They gathered around him, excited and devoted to his will, like a herd around the leader. They lifted their heads, eagerly, and the blue sky lay in their eyes. Georg Henneske, however, stretched out his arms, shook them against the light, the joy of a triumphant figure flashing in his eyes, and when he spoke, it blazed from within him. He himself felt so light, so joyfully light, the ground sank beneath his feet, his arms spread out like wings, swaying, and like an eagle, he soared high and steep into the blue. The whole village stood as one, bending a hundred heads to the sky. And they watched Georg Henneske float in the ether, calm and clear, farther and farther, until he vanished from their sight.

Part Two:

The Man in the Top Hat

The Man in the Top Hat is a crime novella
that was published in 1911.

The Man in the Top Hat *A Crime Novel*

The clock struck: four quick, bright chimes, followed by six slow, heavy strokes. As if on cue, an ear-splitting clamor arose: through the gray November mist came shrieks and whistles, as though all the wicked spirits of winter twilight had been unleashed. The shrill whistle of Kulmann's sugar factory began, and like a siren in a stormy night, the whistle of J.C. Robn's cloth factory joined in a howling chorus. Within five or ten seconds, the suburb echoed with the ghastliest concert of factory whistles.

From the A. Kerner Metalworks Corporation, the black stream of laborers was already pouring out. A dark, indistinct throng surged through the gates, only to dissolve a hundred meters beyond into ten, twenty, thirty smaller groups. Like conspirators and rioters, they crept hunched and stooped through the fog. In the first alleys, these groups split into smaller clusters again. In threes and fours, they trudged through the dirty streets, sullen and silent, until a crude jest from a companion forced a harsh laugh from them.

Karl Schleifer walked his way alone. He hurried to get ahead and have no one in front of him.

With his left hand in his pocket, he swung his blue tin coffee can with his right. When it struck his kneecap, it hummed: hmmm... hmmm..., always the same monotonous tune.

He turned into a busier street. A chain of shop girls crossed the roadway, laughing and giggling. He stopped to watch them. A sergeant rushing by accidentally bumped him with his bayonet. "Pardon," the sergeant said, politely saluting. Karl Schleifer glared after him, resentful. He hated the military, and even a chance touch from a soldier kindled a treacherous rage in him.

He shuffled on. Electric lamps flickered in the shop windows. Unconsciously, he paused before a jewelry display, his greedy, glistening eyes darting over the glittering items and necklaces.

It's no use, he thought. It's no use. I can't steal them. They'll catch me.

Slowly, he moved along. A memory from his school days surfaced abruptly.

> Erdem fere tempore P. Crassus, cum in Aquitania pervenisset, quae pars, ut ante dictum est, et regionum latitudine et multitudine hominum est tertia Galliae existimanda, cum intellegeret...

It was a complicated sentence. He had failed to translate it once in his third year and been punished by having to learn it by heart. It had stuck in his memory ever since. Now he puzzled over it: Publius Crassus — who was he again? Why am I even thinking of him? Damn it, what good has it done me to attend higher school until the third year? Nothing, absolutely nothing! Did it make me something better? No, I'm a scoundrel, a workhorse, a germ spreader like all the others. Turning screws and valves — what a wonderfully intellectual and health-promoting occupation, day after day, year after year. They never move you to a different department. You're a specialist! You only know how to turn screws, day after day, year after year.

What if I bought a secondhand Caesar on Saturday instead of schnapps? Maybe that would help. I'd really like to know what happened with Publius Crassus when he reached Aquitania.

Karl Schleifer crossed the Elisen Bridge. He had to firmly hold onto his sports cap as the west wind whipped around his pale, beardless face. He shivered, despite wearing a dirty black jacket over his blue work smock.

The country road began. Houses stood sparsely along the way, one-story, rarely two, surrounded by small front gardens.

The road was empty, except for footsteps approaching in the distance. He looked up. In the light mist, he discerned an elegant man in a top hat. Perhaps an assistant doctor from the St. George Hospital outside the city, heading to a festivity. Or the director himself.

The darkness was considerable. The gas lamps in front of the hospital loomed like pale yellow globes in the misty haze.

The man in the top hat and Karl Schleifer passed each other. Karl deliberately bumped into him, consumed by senseless rage. The man in the top hat said nothing and calmly walked on.

That's what is vile about it, thought Karl Schleifer. He knows why I bumped into him. Now he's thinking to himself: "What a plebeian. He hates me just because I'm dressed more decently than he is, like a bull hates the red cloth. He can't control himself! What a base character!"

And the vile thing is: he's right. That's exactly how it is. Why is he dressed better than I am? Why is he finer? Why am I so wretched that I have to hate him — have to hate him?

Karl Schleifer abruptly turned and ran after the man in the top hat. The man turned around. In the dim light, his pince-nez gleamed.

The gleam stabbed Karl Schleifer in the eyes, intensifying his fury. He knocked the pince-nez from the man's face.

The man in the top hat made a gesture of disgust. "Are you drunk? What's the matter with you?"

Like an animal, Karl lunged at his throat and strangled him.

The man in the top hat was slender and could only weakly resist.

Karl Schleifer voluntarily turned himself in to the police. The trial was a bizarre spectacle. The accused refused to testify and admitted only to the act of manslaughter. The motive for the crime remained entirely unclear. The victim's watch, wallet, and briefcase were found intact. There was no indication of any connection between Karl Schleifer and the murdered young doctor, nor was one conceivable.

Karl Schleifer was sentenced to 15 years in prison, with mitigating circumstances taken into account.

Published in 1911.

Part Three:

Klabund's Carousel

(Erich Reiß Verlag, Berlin, 1914)

Klabund's Carousel

Farces by Klabund

Oh, a gloomy rain is falling,
And tear-stained winds are blowing.
No, – I want to lie down in bed
And look after my dolls.

Playfully, from the pillows I form
White, burning figures,
Which must obey me:
Children, young gentlemen, and whores.

Tapioca

Tapioca went through life with his hands in his pockets, sometimes stopping to look at this and that, but in the end, nothing came of it. He felt neither boredom nor desire, neither love nor pain. One day, it might have been around Pentecost, as he turned a corner, he bumped into a hat box, which was being carried by one of those pale girls who, in early spring, could make even old men feel delighted. He lifted his hat, and suddenly they were talking, and Tapioca thought for the first time about trying marriage. Because to make her his lover — that would have been too much work for Tapioca. He would have had to conquer her. Tapioca married the pale creature. He was surprised how little the new state of affairs affected him and returned, with his hands in his pockets, to his usual path. This went on for seven months. In the seventh month after the wedding, a small creature, weighing two and a half pounds, appeared, which was immediately wrapped entirely in cotton, as it couldn't even generate its own body heat. When Tapioca asked what this meant, the doctor replied, "It's your son." For the first time in his life, Tapioca understood what life, and especially his own life, was all about. Could that delicate little thing become a Tapioca like himself? After the doctor left, he pressed in the child's fragile skull, turned on the gas, and lay down in bed beside his sick wife. The newspapers turned the story into a "Shocking Marital Tragedy" for their readers — though, in truth, there was nothing, absolutely nothing, behind it.

The Roof Tile

"My God," said Abraham Mesecheck, and he wasn't entirely wrong, for a roof tile had fallen on his head. He soon lay dead. The incident was gently communicated to his wife. She collapsed into fits of sobbing and uttered dark words, which she hissed out, jerking like a clogged garden sprayer: "The Müllers... of course... the Müllers... and it's a scandal... that such a thing is even tolerated... a masseuse!" – As long as the city existed (it existed for 937 years), no one had ever had a roof tile fall on their head. At most (in the Middle Ages) a meteor or (in modern times) an airplane. But a roof tile? No. – The whole city quivered and buzzed in agitation like an anthill. The site of the accident was cordoned off by the police, and Sergeant Roball drew a magical circle around the roof tile with a piece of chalk. For the tile alone lay safely and comfortably, a little stained with brain matter, still in the school alley. For Abraham Mesecheck's earthly remains had already been removed by the sanitary unit. – Where had the roof tile come from? That was the big question. Was a roof defective? And which one? God help the homeowner! – All the roofs near the scene of the incident were thoroughly examined to see if any tile was missing. Nothing was found. No clue. "It was Providence!" said the city councilor and headmaster Krausebeck. For he belonged to the liberal electoral association and taught natural history. Providence could not be acknowledged by the magistrate as the official authority, which only believed in the dear Lord. But who had done it? A roof tile. Well. A roof tile must have come from somewhere. It doesn't just fall from nothing. The opinion of Mrs. Emilie Mesecheck, the late Abraham Mesecheck's wife, could not be taken seriously, as Miss Müller, firstly, did not live in the school alley, and secondly, had been in a commission in Berlin at the relevant time.

They were in great embarrassment. For they had to report the incident to Berlin: Ministry of Culture, Department C III 734, a.

Then a small street urchin appeared, dirty, intelligent, with a piece of buttered bread between his hand and mouth. He was the only eyewitness to the incident, having witnessed it from five steps away, and could pass on the last words of the deceased to the mayor, who was interrogating him, and to posterity.

"My God," Abraham Mesecheck had still called out.

"My God?"

"My God!"

"Nothing else?"

"Nothing else!!"

Now everything was clear: that the dear God Himself had thrown the roof tile. Abraham Mesecheck had seen Him (in a vision) and, terrified, had called out His name. The dear Lord had wanted to punish Mesecheck — probably because of Fräulein Müller. The Consistory, represented by Archdeacon Kohn, accepted this hypothesis and refused to provide a religious burial service for Abraham Mesecheck.

Abraham Mesecheck had to be laid to rest outside the cemetery wall, among the suicides and criminals.

The Homecoming

When Moritz Jeckel was released from prison and came to his wife, he thought he was having a good day and said: "Marie, put on your good blouse."

She was standing at the wash tub scrubbing. When she heard him, she lifted her rough, red hands out of the water, dried them on her rolled-up skirt, and turned her faded face toward him, which was still a little pretty.

"You're starting again. You must be crazy. Instead of working, you think I'm going to do it again for you, after I've done everything for you, and now..."

He turned crimson with rage and struck the wash tub with his walking stick so hard it made a loud noise. "Woman, I'm telling you, put on your blouse, don't make me angry."

She didn't dare object to him anymore and crept into the room. You slut, she thought, you slut.

"Machta," she said to a thirteen-year-old child who was crouching in a corner over a well-thumbed, dirty book and sucking on a slice of bread with plum jam, "Machta, watch the little one, I'm going out, father is home."

The child didn't move and licked his left thumb.

She changed in front of a small broken mirror.

"Didn't you hear, father is home. Don't you want to say good morning?"

"Alright," said the child. He was indifferent to everything. Now there would be beatings every day again.

Moritz Jeckel washed his hands in the tub, set aside his bundle with the small savings from his prison labor, and whistled cheerfully between his teeth: "Where there's singing, there you may rest easy — Evil people have no songs."

The woman stepped out of the room, wearing a dark blue striped blouse and a black bonnet.

"What?" he said, throwing his thick muscular arm around her waist. "I'm not a bad man, am I, Marie?" And he started singing again, loudly, "Where there's singing..."

She looked at him fearfully. "You've probably already had a drink, haven't you?"

"Of course," he grinned, "of course ... Come."

He pulled her along. "We're going to pick up Pölemanns Karl."

Pölemanns Karl was just resoling a rather ungraceful ladies' boot. He stroked his straw-blonde, mighty mustache, which was oddly out of place on his frail figure, put on his black Sunday jacket, and went along.

"There you are again," he said, eyeing Moritz Jeckel from the side. "Here I am," said Moritz Jeckel, "here I am."

They went into Petersen Gustav's distillery. A so-called gypsy band, two fantastically dressed violinists, and a skinny woman beating a tambourine performed a dreadful piece of music. The smoke-filled air stood thick and impenetrable like a gray wall.

"Greetings, you multitudes," Petersen Gustav always made excellent jokes, and today he made a particularly fine one, as he was happy to have found his best customer again.

"Yes, back from wandering!" Moritz Jeckel shouted, as the band was playing fortissimo.

Pölemanns Karl let out a booming laugh that one would hardly expect from his small body.

"So, three bottles," Petersen was already bringing them. Moritz Jeckel stomped up to the platform, grabbed the ugly woman by the chin, and gave her ten pennies.

"What's going on?" Petersen Gustav asked briskly. He was never sober, for business reasons.

Marie's eyes stared and gleamed. She had already finished half the bottle. Moritz Jeckel was on his second. Pölemanns Karl cautiously pinched Marie's right thigh and noted a fairly decent amount of flesh.

Moritz Jeckel noticed this when he had the third bottle brought over. He laughed so loudly that the fortissimo of the music faded miserably into the background.

After the sixth bottle, he checked his money: there was only enough for one more.

"Ho ho," he thought, staring at Pölemanns Karl, whose broad hand was gently resting on Marie's rear.

Then he grabbed him and pushed him behind the wooden partition.

"You buying a round?"

"No," grumbled Pölemanns Karl, "I don't have much left either."

"But if I promise you something, will you buy me a round?"

"What are you promising me?"

Pölemann Karl belched.

"If you buy me five rounds, you can —"

"What can I do then?"

Pölemanns Karl became curious.

"You can have her tonight — you understand."

"Huh?"

That sounded highly unlikely to Pölemanns Karl.

"So, are you going to buy me another round?"

"As you wish," said Karl.

Moritz Jeckel drank four more bottles.

Bloated and reddish-blue, he lay under the bench and bellowed: "Wicked people — don't have a so-o-o-ng... so-o-o-ng... so-o-o-ng..."

Pölemanns Karl and Marie stumbled and swayed, arm in arm, on their way home. Marie waved her one hand enthusiastically in the air and kept shouting incessantly, "You're a good man, you — good man."

Pölemanns Karl played the harmonica, the tips of his otherwise proudly curled mustache hanging down, wet. His eyes were squinted, seeming to be framed above and below by two sharp red lines.

And he played a tricky melody on his harmonica, a tricky tune:

"Dideldum, Di–del–dumm, di–del–dumm..."

The Garden of Saint Veronica

(dedicated to Herr W(alter). H(einrich).)

It wasn't really a garden at all.

Just a moderately large piece of undeveloped land, overgrown at the edges with blackberry bushes, like the countless ones that grow in Brittany. It always lay there, gray-green and dull, only in the summer, when the heather awoke, did it shimmer, a single melancholic violet blossom.

In one corner of the "garden," there stretched a dirty white little house, proudly glowing in the midday sun as if it remembered a better youth, reaching into the blue sky that shone like a vast transparent beryl above the world.

This house was inhabited by Saint Veronica and her two sons.

Her name was Veronica: painters, who were searching for seascapes and character heads in the small village on the Breton coast, or bathers who, having strayed here from St. Malo, Cote Neuf, on sailing trips and beach walks, had named her and her meager, barren field the Garden of Saint Veronica.

She was a stout, rather unholy woman, whose breasts sagged under her blue blouse like two half-filled flour sacks. She could curse like an East Prussian street trader. Only more flowery, more Breton. "You stinking jellyfish, you brazen lobster!" she would call her Prosper. But she pulled herself together in front of Celestin. He would have beaten her.

Her two sons were named Celestin and Prosper. Prosper, the eighteen-year-old, was a lively, cheerful young man who loved jokes, girls, work, and, as far as a Breton is capable, cleanliness. Celestin was twenty-one, covered in filth, vermin, and idiocy, and was marked by an astonishing combination of physical strength and laziness. He never did anything. At most, he carved childish toys, swords, and spears out of wood. Even the strongest lads and men were reluctant to engage with him. His biceps delighted connoisseurs and athletic enthusiasts. The girls feared him, and despite his filth and dull wit, he had already slept with most of them.

Like the rest of the village, the family of Saint Veronica made their living from oyster fishing.

Every morning, Prosper and Saint Veronica waded out to the Rocher de Canale, equipped with oyster rakes and barrels.

They had been selling their catch for years to Herr Biberac, a materials dealer in Paris, rue de Verrerie, who sold them partly fresh, partly marinated.

For transporting the barrels to the nearest train station, which was a few kilometers from the village, they used a rickety, creaky cart pulled by a horse. This horse was the pride of the Holy family, and even Celestin showed a certain attachment to the lame creature. The rest of the village only kept mules, but this horse, named Pierre (though it was a mare), set the family of Saint Veronica apart, giving them an unusual prestige that they would not have traded for a respectable, real halo. Oh, if only this horse had merely been lame! But it was afflicted with every ailment a horse could have — chest bulges, sluggishness, cataracts, baldness — just enough for them to balance each other out. It would have been instructive for veterinarians to know what diet kept this miserable creature upright. It did its job with sluggish enthusiasm and, despite its age, had no intention of dying. Pierre's skin color had a greasy, gray-green sheen, streaked with red, bloodshot patches left by blood-spotted typhus. Its enormous ears flopped to the sides like elephant ears. Whether this made it hear better was doubtful. The painters claimed it couldn't hear at all. Furthermore, its entire body was alarmingly thin, with each rib protruding individually.

The presence of a tail was demonstrated by a tiny stump, to which a straw broom was tied in summer, when the fly infestation became too severe, so that Pierre could better fend off the flies.

This idea had come from Celestin. He occasionally had ideas that seemed to occupy him. All day long, he lay in the garden, on heather and soil. When it got too hot for him, he crawled under a blackberry bush. Toward evening, he engaged in mouse hunting. He lay on his stomach, waiting, and caught field mice with his bare hands. Then he bit off their heads and tossed them aside.

In the evenings, Prosper would go to Mehna, the shoemaker's daughter. But she did not listen to him, although she loved him. She said he had to marry her. He promised he would and spoke to his mother about it.

Celestin also had a desire for the girl and followed her with vulgar remarks. She ignored him.

One morning, Saint Veronica was very surprised that Celestin wanted to go out to the oyster bank. But she gave in and stayed home; three were not needed for fishing.

"The dredging net," said Celestin, "Let's take it, brother. We're going deep today, huh?"

Prosper was surprised and said, "If you say so."

Celestin grinned.

In the evening, Celestin returned without Prosper.

"Prosper fell into the water, couldn't swim, I couldn't either, dead," he said, placing the rakes and nets back in their place. Fishermen later brought his body.

Saint Veronica suspected what had happened, but she was afraid of Celestin, fearing he might strike her.

Celestin wrung the water from Prosper's thick hair, as one wrings a wet cloth.

Every night now, he crept to the shoemaker's house. Mehna once poured water over his head. However, he dared not harm her. She was the only one whose eyes he feared.

One evening after Vespers, when the farmers and fishermen sat smoking in front of their houses, women and girls mending nets, and the children playing cops and robbers — something whinnied helplessly and hoarsely down the village street. It was Pierre, and riding on him, saddleless and long-legged, so that his legs brushed the ground, was Celestin. His head was wrapped in a red cloth, turban-style. In his right hand, he held a pointed wooden lance, as if preparing for a tournament. In front of the shoemaker's house, he turned the horse and made him walk and parade up and down. The whole village stood silently in a row. Every eye and nose itched to laugh, but no one dared laugh out of fear of Celestin. Then Mehna appeared in the door, opened her wide eyes to fully take in the strange spectacle, and laughter rang out from her, so bright that it sounded like an Ave bell was swinging in her chest. And just as a thousand bells answer the first peal, so this laughter, once it flowed, rolled down the entire village street, mockingly driving the now-shy Pierre ahead of it. It was only in the garden of Saint Veronica that Pierre stopped and threw Celestin roughly and vengefully into the grass.

"Good," he thought. "Good. If I can't have her, then no one else will either."

Saint Veronica, seeing him lying there so pitifully on the ground, lost all respect for him and shouted, "You stinking jellyfish! You brazen lobster! You filthy cockroach, where do you come from?"

And day after day, he lay in the garden again, unless he had to go out to the Rocher de Canale — Saint Veronica struggled to manage on her own — and reached for the mice. He caught the field mice with his bare hands. And when he caught them, he bit off their heads and threw them away. "That's how it goes, little brother, that's how it goes," he grinned.

The Jockey

The race ended in a very interesting and completely unexpected way. After Imperator had been leading until a hundred meters from the finish line and victory seemed certain for him, Atalanta, who had been running in fourth place, suddenly surged forward, driven by a furious force, and crossed the finish line in a light, seemingly effortless gallop, a length ahead of Imperator.

There was tremendous excitement, the crowd pressed forward, the stablemen rushed to the scene, but before they could lift Jockey Harsley, who had ridden Atalanta, off the horse, Atalanta shied, reared up, and threw the jockey, who was too weak to hold on, onto the grass. He fell so awkwardly that a wooden stake pierced his chest, and he lost consciousness. They shouted for a doctor, for the medical team, who immediately arrived and carried him to the clinic. For weeks, the jockey fought with death under excruciating pain. His lungs had suffered severe injuries. He coughed up blood. Night after night, a nurse kept vigil at his bed. One nurse could not handle him, as fever-induced rage attacks, like wild dogs, gripped him, pulling him out of the pillows.

And through all his fevered dreams, one word echoed, first faintly, softly, affectionately, then more pleading, more demanding: "Tilly." And finally, even by day, only this one word appeared on his lips: "Tilly." They tried cautiously to find out the meaning of this word, but he never regained full consciousness. "Perhaps his fiancé," said the professor. But no one knew of a fiancé. "A lover," said the young assistant doctor, making a clever, self-assured face. He had never been seen, like other jockeys, with girls from the demi-monde or society women. Finally, they speculated that it was a secret lover. But wouldn't she have inquired about him by now? Hadn't the accident, draped in sentimentality, been reported in all the newspapers? So, it must be a lady from high society, one who could not dare to emerge from the protective shadow of her anonymity?

The word "Tilly" sounded more and more stormy, plaintive, and hopeless from the sick man's lips. An essay appeared in a major newspaper, titled "Tilly..." with a few dots, but nothing came of it, Tilly did not make herself known.

One day, when the attendant was trying to feed him his second breakfast – milk – with a drinking tube, he jumped out of bed before anyone could stop him, knocked the glass tube aside so the milk spilled over his pillow, and leaned against the window. "Tilly," he whispered, staring out. A horse had neighed down in the street.

The nurse reported the incident to the professor. And now it became clear to everyone: he longed for a horse named Tilly. Soon, she was found in the stable of Herr v. W., Jockey Harsley's employer. It was Atalanta, whom the jockey had named Tilly. And he had only named her that for himself, no one else was allowed to call her that.

"We shall allow him this joy," said the professor, "he has at most a week left."

On a warm morning, the sick jockey, wrapped in blankets, was driven to the hospital courtyard. A crystal-clear blue sky arched over the buildings, sparkling behind the green leaves of the lime trees. Some convalescents from the third ward walked quietly and contemplatively along the radiant gravel paths in their grayish, dirty hospital clothes.

Suddenly, the gate at the porter's lodge was opened, and Atalanta was led in by a servant. She pranced with small, coquettish steps, swished her tail, and held her head straight and stiff toward the sun. Her brown smooth coat reflected gleaming highlights.

The jockey had his eyelids closed.

When he heard Atalanta's gait, he opened his eyes and joyfully raised his arms. She whinnied now — right near him. And stood still. He was able to grab her head. He trembled and wept. The nurse propped him up on the pillows, and then he grasped her head with both hands, pulled it down to him, and kissed her broad, hay-scented mouth, through which her breath puffed in barely visible white clouds.

"Tilly," he said, smiling, and sank back, sighing in bliss.

The professor signaled for the animal to be taken away again. Tilly looked at him with a long, smooth gaze, then turned and pawed the ground. Before anyone could react, she lashed out and struck the jockey in the forehead. He died instantly.

"A moving death," said the old professor.

"...to be sent to the beyond by his lover," said the young assistant doctor, writing the death certificate.

The Lass

"You're touchingly impudent," said the girl – but she didn't mean it seriously.

"The moon is behaving outrageously conspicuous tonight," he remarked with a melancholic look at the pale night sky. Fields and bushes lay dusted white with light.

The light was like that on sultry summer days just before sunrise.

The girl laughed: the way girls laugh in the excitement of love, cooing, sobbing. A voice called from inside the house: "Anna."

"I must go in," she offered him her lips for a kiss, "sleep well, Herr Adjunct." She had already disappeared around the corner.

He waited a minute, then entered the house from the main entrance, from the village street.

In the front parlor, a few carters and farmers' sons were cursing, sniffing, and drinking their corn liquor.

He kicked open the door to the dignitaries' room. It was empty. He sat down at a table. The innkeeper came and lit a kerosene lamp.

"Much honor, Herr Adjunct, what may I get you?"

"Half a glass of red wine."

He thought for a while, hesitated, then finally reached for his wallet and placed a twenty-mark coin on the roughly planed wooden table.

The innkeeper brought wine, a glass, and a napkin. He set a corner of the table.

"Herr Innkeeper!" The man had already been about to leave and turned around. "This is for you." He pointed to the gold coin.

"Should I change it?" the innkeeper said, obligingly.

The other man waved it off. "It's all yours."

He listened for noise in the front guest room. They were making so much noise and clamor that the glass in the connecting door rattled.

"If you let me into the girl's room tonight!" he added slowly. Then he took a sip and looked at the innkeeper expectantly. The innkeeper's eyes lustfully caressed the yellow gleam. "She's not my daughter," he whispered uncertainly.

"Should I light another lamp?" said the Adjunct, "maybe it's hard to see properly?"

"Fine," the innkeeper hastily blurted out, as if he couldn't get rid of the words quickly enough, "if the girl has no objections, what do I care?"

The innkeeper was called to the front room. He took the gold piece like one catches a fly, bowed, and said, "I hope you rest well, Herr Adjunct."

"Anna," said the innkeeper the next morning, "come, give me your hand." She stood at the barrel and washed glasses, wiped her hand on her dress and gave it to him. As she withdrew it, she saw a five-mark coin lying in the hollow of her palm.

"What's this?" She looked over to the innkeeper, puzzled.

He grinned. "Herr Adjunct has shown his gratitude to me, here, half is for you."

The coin fell with a clink to the floor. At the same moment, her face flushed bright red and then went snow white.

That evening, she was found hanged from the bedpost.

Blonde Hair

No woman in the village had such rich, blonde hair as she did. All the women envied her for it, and the ladies of the town, both old and young, who came out to the village on their walks from the town, an hour away, looked admiringly at the beauty of her blonde hair, which she wore high, mighty, and golden on her head.

In the town, she was generally known as Blonde Hair. Many didn't even know that she was real, for she led a wonderfully disguised existence as a kind, blonde fairy in fairy tales, which the imaginations of nurses and nannies told boys and girls about.

In the earlier days of her marriage, she would sometimes sit in the evenings on the stone bench by the house, loosen her hair, and let it roll over her fingers, watching with serious eyes the tender play of the evening sunbeams as they touched the yellow strands with tired hands. But then came the days, months, years of worry and secret grief that bleached her eyes, left her soft skin yellow and chapped — only the golden sheen of her strong hair remained untouched.

When the farmer married her, he knew why he was marrying her. Neither he nor anyone else in the village ever thought for a moment that she would do physical work. He acquired her from her father like a piece of jewelry to be placed in one's living room, to be paraded in on Sundays at church, but also to be enjoyed by candlelight at night.

She had gone to him because she liked him and because she wanted a child from him.

When he didn't give her a child after a year, she wept and wept into her hair, so that the tears leaped silvery like beads of mercury over the flood of blonde hair.

And again, after a year, she bit her lips and looked at her husband with angry eyes, eyes he didn't know in her, making him laugh awkwardly and unhappily.

Then she became silent and haughty, no longer had a friend, and kissed him only reluctantly with cold lips. Eventually, she turned away in disgust from him, as he began to smell of brandy, falling more and more into ruin, wasting strength and money with other women, maids, and prostitutes in the city. One day, she had her bed moved into an empty gable room and had it furnished for herself, for she had learned that the prostitutes had given him an ugly disease and a disgusting rash.

There she sat for days by the window, like a matron in the armchair, gazing out at the sunless northern sky — though she was barely thirty years old — and did not see her husband for weeks. Sometimes, there was a thumping up the stairs, followed by a cautious, urgent knock at her door. She listened to his laments and self-blame with disgust, remaining silent until he left again, grumbling and staggering.

Then came the bailiff. Her husband was absent. The bailiff treated her with a challenging politeness. She paid him no attention. "I cannot starve," she said quietly. Her father had died in the first year of her marriage. After the bailiff left, she took a small white powder that she had secretly obtained long ago. Her husband found her sitting as usual in the armchair, which bore the bailiff's seal. When she stared at him strangely, he approached her and raised his arms in a pleading gesture. Then he understood and trudged to the tavern, where they credited him a shot, and fetched the mortician. They laid her out in the former best room, on two chairs, as the carpenter refused to deliver a coffin.

When night came, he kept vigil over the body. Without any particular feeling, guided by an instinctive sense of duty. He sat on the stove bench, staring at the ground, smoking bad tobacco that he had somehow scrounged up, for no one would lend him anything after the village had learned of the bailiff's visit.

The full moon shone through the window, casting a glowing light over her yellow hair. As he looked at her, a fairy tale from his childhood came to mind. And he vaguely realized that he had once sensed this image dimly within himself.

He slept for a while, then woke with a burning sensation in his throat. The bad tobacco had dried him out; he coughed and felt a raging thirst. Water would not quench it, he thought, water would not quench it — where can I get schnapps? The innkeeper won't lend me any more.

He hobbled across the room a few times, looked at the village street, deep in snow in the pale moonlight, and sat back down on the stove bench. He shifted back and forth on it a few times and fell asleep again.

When he woke, it was bright outside; it must have been about four or five o'clock. Roosters crowed, dogs barked, and wagons creaked through the damp sand. The thirst had now become unbearable, and he clutched his throat, making gurgling sounds. The desire for alcohol overtook him. He looked at the dead woman. Then, in a flash, a thought struck him.

Her blonde hair gleamed through the bluish twilight.

He rushed to the window. There was no one to be seen outside. He looked around nervously, pulled out his pocketknife, a so-called "frog picker." Trembling with lust and fear, he cut the dead woman's blonde hair from her head. He picked up a dirty piece of newspaper from the floor and wrapped the hair in it. Then he quietly, quietly went out, through the back garden, climbed over the fence, and ran, panting, along the country road toward the city, but soon turned right into the woods to avoid being seen.

When he arrived in the city, the shops were just opening. He went into the first barbershop he came to and rummaged the hair out of the newspaper. "See, Mr. Barber, see, feel it — it's real, it's real," he called. The barber, addressing his assistant, said this and, although he admired it thoroughly, found a few things to complain about, such as that it, unfortunately, had a slight reddish tint, but still —

The barber paid him twelve marks, because he had a kind of pathological preference for blonde hair.

The farmer staggered into the nearest distillery and drank the very worst cheap liquor, the kind you can get for ten pfennigs a quarter liter, and got horribly drunk.

The next morning, he woke up in a bush in the city park and stumbled, unsteady on his feet, like a sleepwalker, back down the road to the village.

He found his house empty, and as if by instinct, he swayed toward the churchyard. He heard human voices and saw people standing by an open grave. The pastor was saying a few comforting words (no one knew she had taken her own life) — but the farmer shuffled right up to the grave, and with a trembling head and dead eyes, looked down.

Suddenly, he swallowed hard and spat the entire contents of his stomach down into the grave onto her coffin.

The Duchess of Este

One day, his father received the news that he had become engaged to the Duchess of Este. Although the father possessed a large fortune, he hesitated and had investigations carried out in the capital to find out about the inheritance dispute, the ministerial connections, and the state of the princely uncle. The claims of the beautiful duchess turned out to be entirely accurate. Every morning, she would drive in front of the princely palace, and the porter would already be standing, holding his blue gold-trimmed cap, ready to open the carriage door and escort her up the marble stairs covered with red carpets. But when it rained, he held a large black umbrella over her, and her small patent leather shoes would tap anxiously and quickly over the damp sidewalk, so quickly that he, formerly a non-commissioned officer in the Lüben Dragoon Regiment, could hardly keep up.

The duchess was invited to visit her future in-laws. A whole floor was made available to her, and the servants wore crimson livery, as she had once revealed to her fiancé her passionate preference for the color. In the stairwell, a silver bucket hung from thin silver cords from the ceiling, filled with red carnations. And Corner, the clever black poodle, carried a red carnation around for days, holding it in his snout, lacking a buttonhole.

The duchess's behavior and character were deemed charming, her manners flawless, and her tailor genius. But the most beautiful thing about her were her black eyes, which seemed to shimmer with a cheerful melancholy, as if they had once gazed into the horrors of life and could never quite recover from that terrible image. She left for the capital after four weeks without her fiancé. He had suddenly had to go to Baden-Baden on a matter of honor, as an assessor in the court of honor. His father saw her off. Several times, due to his excitement, his monocle, which was attached to a red silk cord, fell from his eye. His hand, encased in yellow kidskin, held hers in a long, friendly farewell. In the end, his lips bent toward her hand for a kiss. Corner, the clever black poodle, stood by, wagging his tail, held on a leash by a servant, and carried a red carnation in his mouth.

In Berlin, the Duchess of Este was greeted at the train station by three gentlemen. Two of the men handed her grand bouquets of red roses and carnations, smiling politely. The third man had only red lips and fiery red hair, and it was on him that her eyes most happily rested. The other two became jealous and telegraphed his father, and only one word: "barmaid."

His father locked himself in his study. After an hour, he understood, rang for his servant, and asked if the ordered shipment of oysters had arrived.

Meanwhile, the Duchess of Este and her fiancé were on their way to Vienna. She intended to introduce him to her parents. They stopped in Breslau and entered the waiting room. Unfortunately, the shoelace of her left shoe came undone. She went outside to seek the help of the restroom attendant. He anxiously checked his watch. She had already been gone for a quarter of an hour. He stood up and walked to the platform. A fast train in the direction of Sagan—Guben—Berlin slowly departed the hall. From a first-class compartment, a small pale hand waved. Then he heard a dear, familiar voice and saw two eyes that seemed to shimmer with cheerful melancholy:

"Goodbye, Egon, it was too nice — but you are a fool."

In the distance, from a first-class compartment window, a batiste handkerchief with the coat of arms of the Dukes of Este fluttered.

His father made no reproach.

"In the annals of Venus," he said, while his monocle fell from his eye, "she is recorded among the duchesses. As for me," and he cleared his throat, "I would not withhold the rank and honors of a queen from her."

Secretly, he commissioned the detective agency "Greif" to investigate the whereabouts of the barmaid Lotti Maier.

He had, after all, come up with a very fortunate idea.

The Weakling

The young lawyer strode through the streets of the city toward the open countryside, hands in his coat pockets, chin pressed into his collar, which seemed to be the only thing preventing his nodding, swaying head from rolling down onto his chest and into the filth of the streets.

"I cannot confide in anyone; I cannot talk to anyone — only to myself. I have friends — fine — but what am I to them? What are they to me? We talk to each other: dreary, endless rows of dead words — often I can't even manage that — and we call it understanding when they see me as they want me to be. And I present myself to them — exactly as each one wishes. My father, my mother, my acquaintances: they all form narrow, fixed ideas about me, each a different one. And to each, I seem different. The worst part is: I feel it, feel it as I play the witty conversationalist here, the anxiously refined aesthete there, the coarse and vulgar cynic in one place, the boastful man of honesty in another, the sly snooper elsewhere. And I must play these roles. Do I not sometimes feel a dangerous fear of losing my very self, since I have so little acquaintance with it to begin with?

"When I was fifteen, sixteen — I was not an unattractive boy — I fell in love with many girls, sisters or friends of my friends. They overlooked me. When they giggled and acted like silly young things, chasing each other breathlessly, squealing through the house or garden — I stood aside — with the demeanor of a funeral director. But it was my own loneliness I was imploring them to share. I tried to convince myself that they were silly geese, laughing and fluttering before me in their white flowing dresses, beating their arms like fledgling birds. Geese, whose absurd, chattering behavior was not even worth contempt. And I assumed a haughty, dismissive expression, one that said: I forgive you, but you are foolish and incomprehensible. You consort with oxen and donkeys — how I envied those oxen — such blatantly ungainly, brazen, childish boys to whom you grant your favor. A hundredth part of that bestowed upon me would have been heaven's grace.

"Now and then, one would come to me: but I could not speak to her, no matter how sweetly she sat beside me, coming as a comforter. Gladly would I have confessed to her the torturous agony I was enduring.

"Naturally, she found me dull — I have no talent for joking — smoothed out her dress, left, and told her companions that I was an odd and surely a little mad fellow.

"I have never known the feeling of unselfconsciousness — or only when, in an excellent role, I forgot myself.

"I rage with lust for woman and reality. Three women have loved me; they must have grasped some atom of solidity amidst all my groping, fumbling unrest — perhaps something they themselves breathed into me — and then clung to it in self-deception. I loved none of them and deceived both them and myself as long as I could. Since then, I have worn out my feet and soul, my eyes staring out of my head, searching for a woman who could understand me without my having to speak to her. I know nothing of myself except that I am weak and incapable of any will for myself, however much I rage and thirst with longing for strength and purpose. Yes, without even looking her in the eyes. Only my fingers want to trace the shape and outline of her head and body, and her spirit. For I am blind. And see only with my nerves.

"I remember: when my lover visited me at night for the first time, my nerves went into overdrive, and whatever heart I possess raged and screamed in anticipation whipped by desire. It cried out in a Don Juan drama that I feverishly sketched two hours before she arrived. Even as she perched on my lap, I was still scribbling away at that cursed poem, which churned and thudded inside me like a machine. We got into bed: properly, like silver-spooned newlyweds, modest and reserved. She had been driven back into herself... and was near tears. She left as she had come... I failed — not due to physical incapacity. I thought it for the first time on that most tormenting of nights, which awakened in me an unshakable disgust at my own wild impotence and drove me out to the train station, onto the first train that happened to be leaving. The spectacle repeated itself; I lacked the slightest confidence in myself the moment I believed I could rise above it. Only prostitutes temporarily gave me that confidence, as I proved myself with them to be the most potent of butcher's apprentices.

"And now I have been tasked with defending a young woman who stabbed her unfaithful lover in the chest at night. To defend the woman I admire — the woman in whom I worship the instincts with adoration — to defend, justify, excuse her — when I am instead tempted to hymnically praise her act. She is too worthy for justice, that whore of the weak — of which I am one. Was it perhaps for this reason that I became a jurist, an advocate of the law, because I felt a little safer under its protection? Justice: the straw grasped by the shipwrecked? Should she, this powerful woman, be destroyed by justice? Better that I should perish at the hands of my own disheveled fate. What does it matter to me? I want to save her. She will find a new lover and bear children who will seize life by the horns like a bull. I, on the other hand, am a Sunday hunter of hares — ones I purchase at the poultry shop..."

The lawyer turned back toward the city. From the plowed fields rose a fresh breeze that reached his nose: the earth breathed calmly and clearly, like a child in its first sleep. To the north, the line of hills traced its delicate contours against the light evening haze, like the silhouette of a naked, resting boy's body: unfinished, austere, and soft at the same time, its languidly graceful irregularities of form were enchanting.

To the young lawyer, the landscape's erotic shimmer struck his consciousness with unpleasant pain. He turned left at the bridge and walked toward the detention center. The custodian greeted him. "May I speak with my client?" A servant, who seemed to consist solely of a grotesquely bloated face and an oversized, jangling keyring, clattered ahead of him through the poorly ventilated corridors. "Number 7. I'll wait outside." He let the lawyer in.

Twilight, tinged with a faintly rosy breath of sunset, filled the medium-sized, damp gray room, presumably intended for two prisoners. The lawyer stopped at the door, his gaze darting uncertainly past her to the dark wall, which seemed to reflect back a distorted image of himself, like a mirror. He straightened slightly from his hunched posture. Then he fumbled with the black-rimmed pince-nez, which sat loosely and threatened to slip off.

With a ridiculous effort, he forced himself to speak: "I have... something to tell you."

She waited.

He sighed. He wiped the sweat from his forehead. "I can spout the dumbest phrases, turn legal jargon over a spit like a roast over the fire until it's smoked beyond recognition. But as soon as I touch — ever so cautiously — on matters of the soul, my tongue is tied, and my mouth sealed shut..."

There she sat before him on the cot, broad-hipped and strong like a creation of Rubens, her face red and full. The unruly waves of her blonde hair clung to her forehead. Her large, powerful blue eyes suddenly collided with his in an abrupt jolt: like two teams of horses charging at one another and suddenly rearing up. He held her gaze and began speaking in his thoughts. And each thought wrote itself onto his face as if onto a tablet. But the woman looked up at him and read:

I love you, wonder of my world, which knows no miracles except you. Mistress — in whose roaring eyes rivers rush, from whose sources my soul had not even known. I love you. How I love your sharp, platinum-white teeth. That they might rest on my lips or cheeks! That they might carve into my neck and chest sweet, painful furrows! From these, perhaps, new life could sprout within me.

The blood with which you stained yourself, I want to kiss from your hands. Oh, your strong hands! Oh, your good hands! How delicate and certain they were as they gripped the knife! Even now, I see a knife gleaming in your hands. Strike. I love you for all the torment your strength has prepared for me. How will you ease it? — I love you. — I want to save you. Only in that way can you also save me. Trust yourself to me. For the first time, I am earnest in my will.

She stood and interrupted his speech. Her gaze answered:

"Leave. You mean nothing to me. How weak! How wretched! You deceive yourself. Your will is never followed by ability. Should I give you so much of my essence that I am destroyed, while you would only barely manage to persist? I want no salvation. I am saved. Go."

He slunk away like a beaten dachshund with crooked legs, through the dimly lit hallway, where faint streaks of oil barely illuminated the way, and out the door of the building.

His path led again across the bridge.

Across the fields, under bare walnut and fruit trees, always along the river. The mountains pressed closer to the water, leaving only a narrow path. He walked it, leaping, singing, and psalmizing.

Ahead of him, a chalk-white, steep promontory jutted into the stream. It lay there like a giant crouching woman, leaning on her hands, pressing her arms into the full flesh of her massive breasts.

Toward this woman his longing turned, and in her, his mortal yearning believed it would find itself.

Abysses

She was at least twenty-seven years old. But one wouldn't have guessed it by looking at her. Every young man in the small town who cared even slightly about his reputation had been in love with her—or must have been. Law clerks, lieutenants, apprentice pharmacists.

When Erwin Frauenhofer met her, she had strawberry-blonde hair.

He declared, "I will kiss the dust of your shoes; I will write you sonnets, worthy enough to be dedicated to the Virgin Mary herself."

She laughed. "Many have said that to me before — how banal!"

He replied, "I will scourge myself like a flagellant before his deity; I will do anything you desire of me. I will love you — but only for half a year."

She asked, "Anything?"

He confirmed, "Anything!"

"For half a year?"

"Only for half a year!"

How amusing, she thought. But why shouldn't I accept?

It's never lasted longer than half a year anyway.

He suffered from unusually strong hair growth, like Samson.

"Grow a full beard," she demanded.

He did.

"Come to the Sunday market concert in red trousers, a yellow vest, and a light blue tailcoat."

He appeared as instructed. The street boys and apprentice locksmiths jeered. The high school students laughed. The officers dropped their monocles.

The townspeople shrugged. Magistrate Berndt called the state asylum.

At that point, she decided to end the foolish demands, and they were deeply in love.

Gradually, she learned to truly love him. And she loved him as she had never loved anyone before. Yet it gnawed at her that she knew nothing of his soul, and no matter how hard she tried, she could not descend into its deepest recesses. He remained as much a stranger to her as on the first day. And yet, she loved him.

It was the last day of the six months, a frosty winter's day. They went for a walk together. Dressed in a white golf jacket that revealed the delicate shape of her breasts and a form-fitting white wool dress, she looked like a naked nymph.

The frost-covered trees stood like mighty ostrich feathers. They walked over the pine hills. The river in the lowland carried blocks of ice, drifting and grinding alongside each other like children at their mother's breast.

They stopped at the "Steep Wall," which dropped vertically toward the river.

"Today is the last day." A foolish rage clenched her heart. She loved him and did not understand him.

"You promised to do anything for me in these six months. Do you remember?"

"I remember." He said it quietly, without joy.

As if gripped by a rigid trance, she stood there, her eyes half-closed, the muff pressed to her lips.

"Then jump down this cliff."

He stepped close to the edge, silent.

"Tomorrow, you won't love me anymore..."

He raised his arms. She trembled, wanting to scream, but she saw nothing.

"On the contrary," he said, tipping his hat with a smile and stepping back quickly.

"I already don't love you today. May I have the honor of escorting you back to town?"

Before he could stop her, she had vanished into the depths. A scrap of her white dress fluttered on a barren tree stump.

"How strange," muttered Erwin Frauenhofer into his beard this time.

The next morning, he had it shaved off.

The Winner

Never before had there been a more beautiful boy than Boris. His eyes were blue, his hair silver-black. White lace cuffs fell over his pale, infinitely slender, infinitely wistful hands. When he passed by the girls' schoolyard during a break, the girls trembled like helpless animals behind the fence that separated them from the street — and from Boris. Boris was so extraordinarily handsome, his creator had poured so much into his body that there was nothing left for his soul. Boris was stupid, and his beauty was a trap for virtue and an obstacle to true ethical existence. It reached the point where Boris became genuinely troubled by his beauty and thought: very stupid.

Nikita, on the other hand, was clever — very clever. But he was the ugliest person one could imagine. Even people who were fully aware of the aesthetic worthlessness of appearances, such as priests, hardware merchants, and district councilors, could not help but loathe him. His head was pointed like a banana, his eyes squinted — one upwards to the left, the other downwards to the right. Saliva constantly dripped from his distorted mouth. He limped and carried a hump on his back like a market woman with a basket of potatoes.

Boris and Nikita were the best of friends and always walked arm in arm through the streets.

Nikita sought Boris's friendship only out of calculation, aiming to bring him completely under his control. For he hated beauty instinctively, as only the ugly can, and sought to destroy it. Gradually, he surrounded the poor, foolish Boris with all sorts of nonsensical philosophical phrases, such as that beauty was useless in the world, even contemptible, as it laid traps for virtue and obstructed true ethical existence. He managed to make Boris deeply troubled about his beauty to the point that Boris thought: Why am I not as ugly and wise as Nikita? Eventually, he even began to curse his own beauty. One day, he sighed to Nikita, "I will take my own life — I am too beautiful for this world." The treacherous Nikita had been waiting for this moment. Now his time of triumph had come. "My poor, dear, misguided friend Boris," Nikita responded with feigned compassion, "that is unnecessary. But I can help you — if you promise to endure, for five minutes, whatever I do to you." "If it will save my soul, I will gladly endure the worst," Boris replied.

It happened during a walk outside the city. Nikita tied Boris to a willow tree using ropes he pulled from his pocket. Then he spat three times into the defenseless boy's face, saying, "This for your beauty! This for your chastity! This for your happiness!" He then took a sharp razor from his pocket and, with one swift motion each time, cut off both of Boris's ears and the tip of his nose. After that, he carved a cross into Boris's forehead with the same razor and untied him from the tree.

"How do you feel, my brother?" Nikita asked slyly, holding a pocket mirror in front of Boris.

"Much better!" Boris smiled insanely as he saw his mutilated reflection. "But give me the knife once more — I want to finish the job myself." He snatched the razor from Nikita and, with calm precision, slit Nikita's throat. Then he picked up the fallen mirror, looked into it once more, and grinned idiotically, baring his teeth. "Now I am beautiful again," he said. "Since Nikita no longer has a head."

Phryne

The young Hans-Georg, still attending high school, was returning from a friend's birthday party. The standard clock at Hallesches Gate showed just past eleven. He boarded a motorbus. There was only one free seat — next to an old, heavily made-up, and garishly dressed prostitute.

Hans-Georg didn't notice her. He yawned and was so very tired. The party had been delightful. And they'd had punch — an incredible amount! Before he realized it, he had fallen asleep. Slowly... slowly — gently, he slumped to the right. His handsome, beardless face came to rest on the old prostitute's bony shoulder. His lips, dark red from the copious wine he had drunk, were slightly parted, and his warm breath flowed through the thin lace of her blouse onto her cold flesh.

A few passengers smiled. The old prostitute smiled too, her small, blue-rimmed eyes twinkling with an expression no one could understand. Her sharp nose twitched back and forth a few times.

She didn't disturb the boy. Tenderly, like a mother, she lightly patted his cheek, taking great care not to wake him. Gently, she tilted her large black hat to the right to ensure it wouldn't bother the sleeping boy.

"Planning to take him home with you, miss?" quipped a young man with a waxed black mustache and an unpleasant cologne that reeked of his trade as a shop assistant. He laughed, a shrill, braying laugh, as if he'd made the joke of the century.

"Let's hope he doesn't lose his way," added a stout man in a stiff little hat, winking at the prostitute.

The shop assistant brayed even louder, elbowing a Salvation Army soldier seated next to him.

"Pardon me, ma'am," he rasped, laughing at his own antics. The stout man grinned. The shop assistant felt exceedingly clever.

The prostitute suddenly became very serious, her body trembling. She couldn't hold back — tear after tear rolled down her gaunt cheeks, her pupils nearly vanishing beneath her eyelids.

Hans-Georg woke up. He glanced out the window. The bus had stopped at Weidendammer Bridge. He quickly got off — he'd gone too far. A few mocking glances followed him. He didn't see them.

The old prostitute sat stiffly, her bloodless lips pressed together. She could no longer hold back. Then it burst out of her — a convulsive sobbing seized her. In long, deep wails, she cried like a storm-swept siren. Her sharp fingernails clawed at the leather seat. The other passengers grew uneasy. Voices called out in confusion: "What's wrong with that woman?" "Unbelievable," "Conductor!" "Such behavior!" A gaudily dressed Sunday market vendor shouted her contempt directly into the prostitute's face. A woman in culottes moved to the platform.

In a wild rhythm, the prostitute's stiletto heels hammered against the floor. The conductor tried to calm her down, snapping at her.

A threatening murmur rose among the passengers. "She's insane!" The man who had shouted "Unbelievable" earlier now bellowed, "Police!" and received general approval.

The conductor didn't resist this moral demand and waved down an officer at Oranienburger Gate, who took her into custody.

The conductor explained, "This woman was causing a public disturbance with her racket."

"All right," the officer said cheerfully and took her to the nearest medical station.

The attending doctor, a young man who had just passed his second medical exam, quickly came to a diagnosis: "Hysterical woman, suffering from a fit of hysteria. Not surprising, given her lifestyle."

Marching to War

That's all well and good, thought Peter Nikoloff, who had been conscripted from his village, that now we're going against those damned Muslim swine. But if I get shot dead, I can't live anymore. And if I don't live, I can't love anymore.

And I love my wife Maria very much. After all, we've only been married for a year. And you don't get tired of marriage in just a year.

Peter Nikoloff went to the young lieutenant Konstantin, whom everyone in the regiment called "Little Brother" because of his kindness and willingness to help even subordinates, and shared his troubles with him.

"Well, there's no way around it," said Little Brother. "We have to kill the Turks."

"Why?" asked Peter Nikoloff.

"Because it can't be helped," said Little Brother.

Peter Nikoloff understood that.

"But I have a wife!"

"I have a fiancé," said Little Brother.

"That's not so bad," Peter Nikoloff thought aloud.

"Oh, it's much worse!" Little Brother countered.

"But what if I get shot dead?"

"Is your wife pretty?" asked Little Brother.

"She's beautiful." Peter Nikoloff was genuinely proud that he had a beautiful wife and that he could tell his lieutenant about her.

"If you're dead, she'll marry someone else," said Little Brother.

Peter Nikoloff gnashed his teeth. "But I have a son!"

"But if you have a child," Little Brother smiled, "then rest assured, you're better off than me. Then you simply can't get shot dead!"

At that, Peter Nikoloff nodded solemnly and gravely, shook his lieutenant's hand, and let himself be outfitted with his uniform, reassured.

Waldemar

"Waldemar:" like a rocket, the name always shot up right in the middle of the conversation, only to then quietly and brightly fade away: "Waldemar, for God's sake, I must not miss him."

Peter tried to calm her down, and soon the conversation was back on track.

"So, you're going to drama school?"

He held her right arm, which shimmered bluish-yellow from the wide sleeve up to her elbow, and carefully dug his nails into the strikingly soft flesh. It felt like jelly.

"Man-eater," he thought, in a proud reference to himself.

She leaned back a little and flirted with the handsome guitarist on the podium. She laughed.

"My God..." He fumbled around her neck. "What do you have?"

She laughed. Suddenly, she paused and looked at the clock.

"Waldemar..."

It was only half-past one.

She extended her hand to him.

"There – you – have you ever seen a smaller woman's hand? The smallest glove size is too big for me."

He kissed her hand – from her fingertips, to the nails, which shone pale like rosy agate...

"Tell my fortune from my hand, you..."

He saw the small lines in her palm winding like delicate little lizards.

"You are clever, cautious, very, very cool... and honest."

Peter said almost the opposite of what he thought. Only honest – yes, she is honest, with that special kind of woman's honesty that, however much she may lie, always tells the truth.

"On New Year's Eve, I will be murdered."

Her black eyes, which might have been blue by day and changed color with dusk and light, sparkled and suddenly lowered, sharp and silvery like two daggers into his. He felt a slight dizziness. They are stabbing into my brain... or is it the grog? He had already drunk the ninth glass.

"Who nowadays still has the great sensation of being murdered? I congratulate you, my dear young lady."

A gentleman at the next table, it was two o'clock, and no one was paying attention to the time anymore, threw these words into the conversation. He sat there, hunched, squinting, with the head of a dachshund, staring at her belt.

With his thoughts, he fiddled with her blouse. She probably didn't mind. She stroked his forehead.

Peter was somewhat put off. But suddenly, she slid closely to him, and he buried his lips in her brown-blonde hair, behind her left ear. The gentleman at the next table grinned. "Now she's got it behind the ears." She laughed. Peter didn't understand it. Suddenly, she became serious. "Waldemar – ...do you know him?" Peter lied.

"What does he look like?"

She half-closed her eyes.

"Light blonde, almost reddish hair."

"That's true... but he has a feature that only a few men have... well?"

"He has a scar across his mouth," Peter lied.

She no longer listened and blinked at a nearby table where three students were sitting. One of them sighed and kept his hand over his heart.

Then she had to laugh. But when she looked again into Peter's eyes, which were wide open and drawing her into their innocent depth, she felt a little uneasy at the depth of the gaze.

"If only he didn't have those eyes," she thought, "actually, he's terribly decent..."

"Curfew, gentlemen!" – the landlady with small, charmingly sly eyes, a pretty figure, and a faintly reddish frozen nose clapped her hands.

She helped Peter into his coat.

"I don't have a winter coat yet," he suddenly thought, "that's why I'm so sick. But where is the money?" He looked away resignedly.

"You know," she said, "I only came with you on the condition that I could separate from you at three o'clock. I have to wait for Waldemar..." They were standing in the cool, clear night air. "A cab?" someone shouted. They crossed to the other side of the street. "He's wearing a gray ulster," she said.

"I don't want you to be with a man today..." the grog encouraged Peter.

Her eyes surrounded him like black crows.

"I'm going home with Waldemar. I love him..."

He ground his teeth and grabbed his cane.

"Give me your hand, we'll meet on Sunday... you're my friend."

The last word, which she spoke both affectionately and contemptuously, made him pause. He no longer knew what he wanted to think. He also had trouble standing straight. "If I want to kiss you now..." he didn't let go of her hand.

"Sunday, Sunday, now go – if Waldemar saw you... please..."

Peter left, stood for five minutes at the corner, stared fixedly at a streetlamp, and then went home.

He threw his clothes off and threw himself onto the bed. It was four o'clock.

"Irmgard!" he screamed and cried into the pillows.

Angrily, in her nightgown, the landlady knocked on his door.

Was he with another one of those women again...

It didn't take long, and she had found Waldemar. He wasn't wearing a gray ulster, but a brown one, he didn't have a scar across his lips, nor reddish-blonde hair. Instead, he was bald and around forty, forty-five years old. When he saw her eyes, he hesitantly let a hundred-mark bill slip into view.

Test of Style

One day, a frail young man appeared at the editorial office of the "Daily People's Welfare" in Potemsk. He made an exceedingly timid and foolish impression. He was led into the room of the chief editor.

"What do you want?" the powerful man snapped at him.

"A position as an editor at your highly esteemed paper, Your Grace, if I may ask."

The mighty one smiled contemptuously as he looked at the emaciated body and fearful eyes of the small man, then leaned back significantly in his armchair.

"A journalist must know how to conduct himself courageously and energetically in all the perils that surround him, richer than any other mortal. You seem to me" he glanced lightly at the miserable figure, "poorly suited for that — do you at least have a style sample with you?"

The frail young man then pulled a revolver from his pocket and held it to the chief editor's forehead.

"Excellent," said the powerful man, without batting an eye. "You are permanently hired with a salary of one hundred rubles per month in the Department of

Internal Politics!"

The Smile of Margarete Andoux

For Fiete Wilhelm

She was the great-granddaughter of French emigrants.

Margarete Andoux's smile hung like an eternal spring sky over the little town. What would the little town be without Margarete Andoux's smile? Who would know of it? Of her Polish-sounding name, her dirty, indifferent streets? How could I tell a story about it if Margarete Andoux didn't exist? Her smile fluttered into the hazy offices, the poorly lit shops, the narrow and dreary furnished rooms. Through the windows of the schoolhouses, even if they were half whitewashed so that no careless person would let their gaze wander to the street, this smile glided like the morning sun into the bare rooms. The teacher shifted restlessly, awkwardly adjusting his double glasses and blinked, as if an insect had flown into his eye. The adolescent students, these boys who had just begun to learn to see, hear, and feel, sat stiffly and perplexed, and in their foolish souls, they solemnly toyed with Margarete Andoux's smile.

Even the name, when one took it into the mouth like a delicacy: Margarete Andoux. The tongue caressed it and didn't want to let go, holding it back until it finally released and died in a soft "doux" that slid into a pleading "you."

Everyone loved Margarete Andoux. The diminutive but pompous textile manufacturer Kellermann, who had inherited the business from his fathers, had never left the small town, but made a big ruckus in the city council — he shrank along with his mouth into a real nothing when he met Margarete Andoux and held his hat in his hands as if before the Virgin Mary for at least ten minutes before putting it back on. He loved Margarete Andoux. The witty headmaster Klingebiel, who had a doctorate, many travels, and had fathered seven children in an eight-year marriage: he loved Margarete Andoux. The baker's boy who brought rolls to Margarete Andoux's aunt, where she stayed: he loved her. The upholsterer, the stove setter, the mayor, the small, shy second-year student Bregler, who prayed daily to God that he would make him as beautiful a poet as Schiller, the drunk city scoundrel and degenerate watchmaker, known as "the handsome Oskar," the theology student Mr. Böserle, the pharmacy apprentice — everyone, everyone loved Margarete Andoux.

But the women hated Margarete Andoux and her smile, which stole their husbands' eyes and hearts. Most of all, Margarete Andoux was hated by Isabelle Kersten. She was the second most beautiful girl in the town and her best friend. At that time, a lazy law student, who had carried twelve semesters on his crooked back, was holed up in the little town. After his father had recently paid off five thousand marks of debt for him with a heavy and painful heart, he now gave him money for the last time so he could prepare for his exams in the quiet countryside.

Adalbert Klinger bore long and short scars from his fraternity days on his left cheek and forehead, unnaturally deep red, like lines drawn with red ink, on his pale yellow skin. The alcohol brought them out. Adalbert Klinger drank. But his calm, brown, half-squinted eyes and his sensual, slightly crooked mouth had a confusing effect on the women. All the women of the small town loved him, whom the men despised for his feeble inability to work. They didn't even deem him worthy of hatred. But most of all, Isabelle Kersten loved him.

This Adalbert Klinger, of all the men, did not greet Margarete Andoux. He didn't even look at her when they met on the street, his coat collar turned up, his upper body bent forward, the cigarette in the corner of his mouth.

Margarete Andoux was puzzled. She usually accepted compliments with a smile, naturally. Why didn't this... this man greet her? Didn't he know her? He knew all the women in town and greeted them. And the girls were all in love with him — how could he dare to overlook her?

She spoke to Isabelle Kersten, who secretly felt triumph and glee.

"He probably doesn't know you," Isabelle Kersten said. "Has he been introduced to you? No? Well then."

Margarete Andoux and Isabelle Kersten, dressed in white and violet, strolled arm in arm to the promenade concert that the town band gave on Sundays in the market square.

Adalbert Klinger strolled along the path.

"Watch out," said Isabelle Kersten. "He knows me, he —"

Isabelle Kersten turned pale. Adalbert Klinger had passed by without greeting her. She placed the blame on her friend.

"He doesn't like you," she said mockingly.

Margarete Andoux shrugged her shoulders and fell silent, lost in thought. What did he have against her? No matter how hard she tried, her thoughts couldn't shake free from him. She suffered, but didn't know how to help herself. She felt an urge to study Adalbert Klinger, inside and out. "I will think him through to the end," she thought.

And she lay awake all night, brooding.

Shadows flew over her, and there was a dark hum and singing in the things around her. Where had she heard that monotonous melody before? It's just one note, and yet a melody. And no one knows the note. Everyone has it within them, but no one can say or sing it.

Margarete Andoux grew restless. In the presence of this man who didn't know her and was indifferent to her smile, she lost her sense of security. She felt terrified as she became preoccupied with him and lost herself in him.

She now sought to meet him on the street, walking past his ground-floor apartment without an umbrella, hoping he might come out and offer his company. She learned when he went for his evening drink and practically waited for him. When he came near, she smiled. The smile begged for pity. Without looking at her or turning his head, he swung past her. She burned with feverish curiosity: what did he want from her? Why was he striking her, why was he trampling on her? –

And she humbled herself so far as to glance after him and stand in the street until his gray, swaying silhouette disappeared into a house.

One day, she sat on the balcony. He turned the corner below. She quickly dropped a glove in front of him onto the pavement. He didn't pick it up. She bit into her handkerchief in furious disappointment and clenched into tears. What use was her beautiful, charming smile if it seduced all the men, but not this one, the one it so painfully longed for? For God's sake. I don't love him, she interrupted her thoughts. No, no, she laughed, I'm just enraged that he doesn't want to see me. Because the one thing I know now for certain is: he doesn't want to see me.

And she pondered how to force him to look at her. Oh, how she hated him!

Outside the town, on the Oder Dike, Margarete Andoux and Adalbert Klinger crossed paths. It was winter and icy. Margarete Andoux stumbled and fell. Adalbert Klinger pulled his head deeper into his coat, whistled quietly through his teeth, and stared at the stream, which carried a thin layer of ice. Margarete Andoux had to help herself up.

How I let myself be treated, how I must let myself be treated, she gritted, and wept.

One evening after nine, the doorbell rang at the student's apartment. Adalbert Klinger tossed the "Contes drolatiques" he had just read onto the bed, took a hasty sip from his mug, and opened the door.

"Please, come in, Miss," he said politely. "What can I do for you?"

Margarete Andoux stood before him. Her lips trembled, and her hands searched for a hold in the thunderous emptiness. "May I assist you with your coat?" He took her jacket off. Then he led her to the sofa and fetched a bottle of champagne and two glasses from the glass cabinet.

Margarete Andoux smiled.

Three days later, the law student Adalbert Klinger, in his twelfth semester, got drunk at his regular table until he lost consciousness. He had won his bet handsomely. The bottle of champagne that evening he had already credited to his winnings.

On the way home, he hit his head on the pavement and lay there. He died the next day from a concussion.

Margarete Andoux went to the morgue, where he lay on display in a white, clean shirt. His scars glistened pale violet on his waxen skin.

At the top of his neck, almost invisible, a small, seemingly fresh, jagged scar appeared, as if a rat or cat had bitten it.

And Margarete Andoux smiled.

The Suicide

My friend Katarakt had gone completely silly, utterly silly. To take one's life because of such a person!

I had just sat down at my desk to write a shocking report for the evening newspaper and extract the funeral wreath when it occurred to me: suicide victims are strange people. Maybe he didn't even shoot himself!

I immediately went to Katarakt's apartment. He wasn't there. But on the nightstand, there were twenty-five unstamped letters: to his parents, to the laundress, to the society, to the Statistical Office: Department of Suicide, etc. On top, an open note, scribbled with a pencil, addressed to me:

"Dear friend! Perhaps you would kindly do me this final favor and post the letters after you've stamped them. Also, regarding the rent for the room (which has been due since January), you are so kind as to come to an agreement with Mrs. Schlabzeck.

"Yours forever, Katarakt.

"P.S. I bequeath my tailcoat to you for the funeral! But you must have it cleaned first. Best at Spindler's. He still owes me 20 Marks and 30 Pfennigs.

"Your faithful above."

Not very reassured by Katarakt's last will, I went to Pia. I wasn't surprised to find Katarakt lying on the divan, smoking a cigarette.

"Man," I said, "You're still alive!"

"Yes," said Katarakt, "I've changed my mind: I'm going to shoot myself and you!"

At that moment, the door creaked, and Pia bounced in.

She threw herself over Katarakt and lay sobbing on his neck: "Darling, how I've worried about you!"

"Unfaithful! Do you still love me?"

"Otto!!! You're cruel!"

"Then die with me!"

A dark cloud passed over Katarakt's face. He pulled the revolver out of his pocket. I stood next to him in joyful, reporter-like anticipation.

"Yes," Pia smiled through her tears, "certainly, as you wish, darling, but first, let's have breakfast, okay? I have an terrible appetite!"

Katarakt sighed, then put the revolver back in his pocket: "What do you think, Pia, Kempinski?" And with a gesture toward me, "Max is inviting us..."

The Brown Devil of Adrianople – A Bulgarian War Story

Well, children, don't try to fool me: I fought at Lüle Burgas and gutted seven Muslim pigs and teetotalers — Wasileff, toss me your schnapps container — I pulled their guts out, then lay wounded near Adrianople until they finally decided to shoot an eye into my thigh, bluish-gray, mouse-gray with a nice red stripe and a yellowish, pus-filled edge. That's why they dragged me to this field hospital, because I couldn't walk anymore, just a heap of warm flesh, nothing else. Now I'm feeling fine again, very fine — if only your schnapps were better, Wasileff —

but, by my ancestor's beard: I wouldn't want to go through what I've gone through again. Even though the air outside Adrianople blew a little fresher, actually much fresher, than the stale, sickly hospital stench here: I breathe it in like rose-scented air and sum up my impressions in the patriotic cry: "Long live Greater Bulgaria!" — but let me be content with that from now on. I've done my duty. Cheers, Wasileff, may Anita and the fatherland have children again!

But I wanted to tell you the story of how my thigh suddenly got a hole, a nice round hole. When I first noticed it, I didn't just fall over and collapse. Oh no, my brothers, a Georgeff doesn't fall that easily, unless he's drunk. But I was far from drunk back then. I was sober, damn sober.

So, when I saw the small black hole, I first thought it was a joke, and I stuck a postage stamp over it — a stamp with the image of our illustrious Tsar. I had saved it for a letter to my sweetheart — Wasileff, don't grin — but now it seemed better suited for another purpose. In the evening, I was going to show the hole, the nice little black hole, to the medic soldier, when I just collapsed, simply collapsed. Blood poisoning, you see, blood poisoning, and it almost went terribly wrong. But Saint Sebastian didn't want me, a Georgeff, to die so disgracefully, and he held me back and interceded with dear Death. And so I'm still alive — despite that little brown pig.

But who, my brothers, do you think was that little brown pig? And from whom do you think I received the shot in my thigh, my brothers? Was it a Turk, a regular Turkish soldier, who, rightly from his point of view, chose my beloved thigh as his target? Was it a wandering scoundrel, who thought I had riches and considered himself their heir? Was it a friendly Serbian neighbor, my brothers — honestly, my brothers, I trust these Serbian miscreants to do anything, and then some. – Wrong, my brothers... it was a pig, a little brown pig, a truffle pig, so to speak, that shot me in the thigh. With my own rifle. Yes. And from ten paces away. That's what war is called. And the glory of war. So, my brothers, to continue with the proper description of events: it was a Thursday, and I was on guard duty. You may believe it or not, Thursday has always been something of an unlucky day for me, and I had a hunch, but of course, I didn't know anything for sure, especially not that little brown pig. Wonderful are the ways of fate, which can rightly be called the God of desperate people.

So, I stood on guard duty, patrolled in front of the earth hut where our squad was camped, and a cursed icy wind was howling, blowing down needle-sharp hailstones that grew into a veritable hailstorm, which pounded down on me in the darkness — it was eleven o'clock — so that I lost my hearing and sight. I made my rounds, moving a hundred, two hundred steps away from the watch — when suddenly I heard a whimper through the storm, the pitiful whimper of a... human voice? Or was it the voice of an animal? This uncertainty made me damn nervous, and I decided to get to the bottom of it. So I crept cautiously toward the sound. Nonstop, this whimpering, now panting, now screeching sound... I'm close now.

"Who's there?" I shouted, cocking my rifle.

No answer.

Always the same whistling whimper, like when a lung forces its way out.

Now it's my turn, and I let my electric flashlight shine. And what, my brothers, did I see? Tied with ropes to a tree stump? A goat? A ram? No, a human... a woman. Yes, a woman. Beautiful as God made her, with the hair of an archangel, but with the eyes of the devil. Unfortunately, I didn't see that at first, because the rest of her, despite my electric flashlight, dazzled me. – A woman, in this wretched weather, out in the open, tied to a tree. Only two hours — and she'll freeze to death.

I, very polite and gallant, as Georgeffs are wont to be, bow and ask kindly: "Who are you, my sweet dove, my sweet pig?" I get no answer, only a horrified look from her wonderful eyes, so that the latter nickname almost made me regret it. "Virgin," I continue, "who are you?" and cut her loose with my bayonet.

She staggered, barely able to stand from the cold and excitement, into my arms, and now I saw that she was a Turkish woman, a real Turkish woman, who, of course, didn't understand a word of our honorable Bulgarian language. So, I lovingly supported her; she warmed up in my arms surprisingly quickly, as I noted with astonishment... and suddenly, she crawled up to me, her small mouth opened, and her tongue flicked up sharply and kissed and licked my neck. That was by no means unpleasant to me, having not held a woman to my chest for six weeks. And I kissed her, because I'm very tall, on the forehead. "Hoh," she whispered suddenly, "hoh," and tugged at my coat.

She pointed into the dark.

Could she be a traitor? I thought, and followed cautiously. After ten, twelve steps, we stood — what do you think, my brothers, in front of what? — in front of a cart, a cart with a cover, stuck in the muck. She jumped into the cart as fast as a cat and waved to me from under the cover. I followed, like a panther. Leaned my rifle against one side of the cart and was about to pull her to me, when I happened to catch her eyes again. But these eyes almost physically pushed me away. For an inextinguishable hatred flared from them, suddenly sobering me up and made the blood curdle in my veins like thick milk.

As soon as the little brown pig noticed this — the women, my brothers, have damned fine instincts — she grabbed my rifle and aimed at me. Smiling, sneering. You probably think, my brothers, that she aimed at my heart or my head. Far from it. You don't know the little brown pig. No, she aimed at my lower body, you know where, and it's only thanks to Saint Sebastian or the Virgin Mary that she missed and hit my thigh instead. What I'm describing in detail here, my brothers, happened in three seconds. I immediately jumped to the side and tried to approach her sideways. Too late. The shot hit. And I, the fool, deserved it. But the little brown pig had disappeared into the dark. Thank God I managed to grab my rifle, or else I would have been in deep trouble with my lieutenant.

But who, my brothers, do you think the little brown pig was? They caught her later and executed her by firing squad. Do you know why? That whimpering in the night before the outpost was a trick of hers that any sheep could fall for.

And then, my brothers? Then she practiced her art of hatred and destruction on each of them. With what, my brothers? With a dagger? With a rifle, as with me, the fool? Oh no! With her body!! Simply with her body!!! She infected no less than five hundred of our men with her damned, filthy, incurable plague. On purpose. Out of revenge. That, my brothers, I call patriotism. She worked more precisely than a howitzer battery. The little brown pig. The brown devil of Adrianople, as we later called her.

Cheers, my brothers! Wasileff, your schnapps and my story are at an end.

But Love

"That's a cheeky fellow."

Some cheeky remark had flown over to her. Without intending to, she turned around.

There stood a man in a top hat, tailcoat, green tie, and rolled-up light gray trousers.

When he caught her gaze, his eyes rolled inward with joy, so that for a moment the whites gleamed like zinc oxide paste from the sockets.

"Pretty girl," he said.

"You brat!" the fiancé growled.

But the man had spoken so casually into the air that no one could harm him for it.

"Honey," she reassured her fiancé, "you're being mean!"

Suddenly, an uncomfortable feeling rose in her throat.

The comparison had come to her by chance: him, with the top hat, tailcoat, green tie, and rolled-up trousers, and her fiancé with his ill-fitting, locally-made worsted suit and shaft boots.

But on the man's feet gleamed patent leather shoes: they maliciously stabbed her eyes.

And now — she was frightened.

The man with the top hat, tailcoat, green tie, rolled-up trousers, and patent leather shoes had stopped.

He squinted his fat seal-like eyes, and laughed, broadly... heartily... maliciously.

She nervously looked down at herself. What... what was wrong with her?

She blushed darkly.

And she looked at her fiancé.

He trudged clumsily in his high boots, and the brown tie she had crocheted hung over his collar, around his neck.

Her delicate boots crunched helplessly in the gravel.

That man spoke again, into the air: "Pretty girl."

"Man," the fiancé groaned, his anger flailing through the air in angular arm movements, causing little rolls to slip from his sleeve.

She cried.

"But, dear..."

Re was completely at a loss.

Why is she crying now? He thought, and wanted to comfort her.

The man with the top hat, tailcoat, green tie, rolled-up trousers, and patent shoes laughed again... broadly... heartily... maliciously.

She cried... endlessly, in gurgling, musical sounds, almost as if for pleasure.

The next morning, she sent the ring back to him.

Little Lorbeer

When the small, modest Lorbeer went for a walk, with tripping, cautious steps, asking the ground for forgiveness for touching it, he stopped every ten seconds to stare at a woman. She might be pretty or ugly, tall or short, as long as she had a large chest. He would be ashamed and blush when he looked, but he had to look. And he would keep staring even after the young lady had long disappeared on the bus or around the street corner. In the evening, in his furnished little room on the fourth floor, he would open the window, letting the blue, shuddering night sky in, and gaze anxiously and reverently at the stars, wondering if they could be of help in his distress. And he prayed to dear God, accusing himself of dirty sins and thoughts. But he didn't feel any better; the prayer only brought the temptations of his heart painfully close to his memory, and he shuddered at his corruption but couldn't break free from it. He struck himself and whimpered, trembling in his desecration of prayer. White, big-breasted women walked through his dreams, climbing and clawing at his moral strength, so he couldn't shake them off. They drained him. And like vines, their fiery arms twisted around his thoughts whenever he tried to escape them. He lay awake for nights, his face red and his pulse pounding, or crouched, staring at the yellow window curtain, where the street gas lamps cast flickering images on the fabric, like visible sighs blowing across the yellow cloth. His pleas to God became less sincere day by day. He didn't even regret the lust of his thoughts, he merely babbled about it because he loved the vague, uncertain, and feared the truth. He hated his thoughts, oh yes!, but only because they were so weak and never led to action.

How he envied his colleagues in the office when they told stories about women. Nearly every one of them had an "affair," which they would take to the concert garden or dance hall in the evening: shop girls, telephone operators, seamstresses. They spoke a fully developed erotic jargon that sounded terribly crude. Their girls called them "bolts" and "sprays." Going out with their girl was called "tying the goat." To seduce a girl was "to bend her," and anyone who hadn't done that at least once was considered a "wimp." Poor little Lorbeer had thus fallen prey to their compassionate contempt. No matter how hard he tried to hide his true nature, they soon figured him out and mocked him. The Don Juan of the office, a young man named Ziegenbein, who wore artistically twisted ties with ends fluttering like flags over his vest and coat and dragged his left foot a little, slapped little Lorbeer on the chicken chest and chattered, "Always go for it, my dear Lorbeer, always go for it, my dear Lorbeer, always go for the bacon. Don't worry. There are plenty of women – look at me! You can't save yourself from them. After all," he spit in his hands and mounted his stool again, "sometimes it's disgusting. Look at me, dear Lorbeer. To use a kind of analogy, a comparison! I am like the queen bee, surrounded by bees, and I am deep inside, stuck. Getting out of there is hard." And he began slowly painting a calligraphic "D," while the whole office grinned in approving reverence, but little Lorbeer, having been seen through, turned alternately pale and red. From then on, he secretly glanced over at Mr. Ziegenbein whenever he could, curious, almost tortured by the agony of expectation, to figure out why Mr. Ziegenbein had such a lasting effect on women. He wasn't handsome – apart from his tie, which he used to change every day. On Sunday, he wore a white tie, Monday a blue one, Wednesday a green one, the color of hope, since it was nearing Sunday again, and so on. The color of each day meant something to him symbolically. Mr. Ziegenbein wasn't handsome, his nose even grew beyond his brown mustache up to his lips, Mr. Ziegenbein limped – and yet...? Was it his cleverness? Little Lorbeer shrugged contemptuously. Cleverness, education – he was ahead of them all in that. Who among them read poetry or sometimes even tried their hand at poetry themselves? Or went to the theater? If he could have impressed a girl with education! It was clear to him that education didn't impress girls. Yes, he thought scornfully of girls, that they couldn't appreciate intellectual grace – but he still yearned for their bodies and burned for them. He secretly quickly looked into his pocket mirror: handsome... as handsome as Mr. Ziegenbein, if his eyes shimmered with a blue that seemed too diluted. So why was it that the girls didn't like him? He remembered that he hadn't yet tested it, that he had always only felt the contempt of the girls from afar and read it in their looks. Could he have been mistaken? A stone rolled off his heart! He decided to take the risk; he would speak to a girl once! – Little Lorbeer's admiration for the female sex had always been directed at the whole. He had never loved any one in particular; anyone who crossed his path and seemed sufficiently passable to him had counted as a "woman," a woman in that moment, until perhaps the next moment brought a change.

In the evening, after business hours, little Lorbeer strolled through the streets, looking at shopgirls, factory workers, and those others who always seemed the most beautiful to him, boldly yet shyly into their faces. Now and then, he would catch a glance, like children catching grasshoppers in the meadow, grabbing hastily, afraid it might escape. But he couldn't decide to chase after a girl; there were so many, and if he followed a blonde for a few steps, a brunette would appear who he liked far more. Then a little black-haired girl tripped by, two friends laughing on her arm. She was a cheeky little thing, giving him big round glances and languidly turning to him. However, he misunderstood her attentiveness: he held his breath in startled infatuation, his watery blue eyes widened, looking like delicate blue plates of Delft porcelain. Then he sighed deeply and remembered: he had to follow her. But where was she? Far in the distance, her red blouse glowed like a poppy on a gray-green meadow. He ran and ran, awkwardly elbowing women aside, stepping on a gentleman's patent leather boots, and almost wanting to shout, "Stop the thief, stop the thief!" For, he told himself, she has stolen my heart, as it always says in novels, usually around page fifty, when the love declaration is near. When he finally caught up with her, her friends were no longer with her. She was walking, laughing, swinging her violet-colored bag, accompanied by a young man, obviously a student, who was convincing her with sharp and abrupt arm and hand movements.

Poor little Lorbeer stopped in the middle of the sidewalk, squinting his eyes and puckering his lips, motionless, as if under an uncomfortably cold shower.

"Evening post," "Evening post!" someone shouted close beside him. And a schoolboy with a chubby, clever face planted himself firmly in front of him and piped, "You, little man, move on, you're blocking traffic."

A few passersby laughed.

Little Lorbeer continued on his way. His defeat hurt him. He had no desire for further adventures. In a huff, he entered a beer hall, drank a few glasses of beer, and began his way home. His previously lively desire had given way to an empty, dead feeling, where anger, hope, resignation, and exhaustion battled for dominance. None of them seemed to win, and his thoughts swirled in a murky chaos that disgusted him.

That night, he closed the window and didn't look at the stars.

The next day, he was plagued by a headache. He looked so pale and gloomy that people at the office made suggestive remarks, and the Don Juan, Mr. Ziegenbein, made a statement that brought a flush of shame to his head, because it sadly lacked truth. Then it became clear to him again that it was his duty to his honor to finally win a girl. And that evening, he set out again, this time consumed by reckless courage. Today, he didn't trust every daring glance from a girl, so he didn't make any decision and wandered the streets for an hour when he saw a girl at the gate of a suburban villa, her steel-blue gaze like lightning zipping into his watery blue eyes. Straw-yellow hair was braided around her head like a harvest wreath, and under the blue of her eyes shimmered a faint rosy glow – like the pink hue that lies above in the black-blue North Sea on hot, clear summer nights, a tone that the sea retained from the day, from the sun.

Little Lorbeer circled around her, embarrassed like a bat, blushing, choking on an approach; suddenly, he stepped up to her with a jerk.

"Excuse me... are you... waiting... for someone?"

She said slowly and indifferently, without looking at him: "Not for you."

Little Lorbeer stood next to her for five minutes, feeling as though he had just lost an ignoble battle. He wanted to make things right somehow. But he couldn't find any words. He went into the standing beer hall and began his journey home. For three days, he didn't think about women at all, working in the office with such zeal that it seemed he wanted to earn a salary increase.

On the fourth day, his infatuated thoughts returned. And he didn't dismiss them unkindly, even though they brought him enough restlessness. He kept them in check for the time being. They behaved so properly that he could even admire the daughter of the porter, without undressing her, out of just innocent pleasure.

But on July 23rd — this was the most important day in little Lorbeer's life and deserves to be noted — little Lorbeer was on the verge of being consumed by longing for love the entire day. Secretly, he prayed to God in the office, asking Him to grant his one wish.

That evening — on a warm summer night, when no bench is unoccupied by lovers, and even the guards patrol the park in pairs — he went home again after closing time, tied on a new red silk tie, and sprayed his coat with "Queen of the Night" perfume. He let his walking stick dance merrily between his fingers. Tonight, he focused his gaze on those women who dressed so elegantly and made such an exclusive impression, occupying a distinguished position in society. They were gladly invited in through the back door for supper, yet driven away from the main entrance, marked "For Gentlemen Only," with whips.

Little Lorbeer knew that there was love for money. He had often wavered, wondering if he should try it at least once. But however charming these women seemed — much more beautiful than shopgirls, maids, and chambermaids — he had a principle, which told him that love for money was immoral, even vile. For anyone could possess the woman he might desire, as long as he had money. But today, as he grappled with this problem once again, it unexpectedly showed him new perspectives. Could these girls not also love? Wouldn't they, perhaps, truly love someone to whom they sent strange glances, without money, if they got to know him, his good heart, his character? And if it were him...? Little Lorbeer searched for understanding in the eyes of the well-dressed women... for love; might he not find it in at least one?

Then a slender beauty brushed past him. Her eyes were small and brown, and her well-shaped breasts stood out distinctly under her white blouse. She wore no corset. Little Lorbeer felt dizzy. This, this... was it. He walked behind her, then beside her, and tipped his hat. She laughed when she saw him. Then they turned into a side street and into a house. They climbed four flights of stairs. Four flights, just like mine, thought little Lorbeer. She unlocked the door, let him in, and locked it behind them. "Take it off," she said, unpinning the hat from her head, which she carefully placed on a chair.

"How do you like it?" she asked, pointing to the hat.

Little Lorbeer had not said a word until now, only repeatedly looking at her, astonished, uneasy, and very much in love. If only she loved him... loved him... without money. For that isn't love... with money.

"Tell me," and she rubbed her breasts against his upper arm, "will you give me something?"

He was startled.

He fell to his knees before her, his head between her knees. He groaned, and the words came out like crumbs and lumps that broke off from the rock of his suffering, awkwardly, filled with restrained tears, from his mouth: "You, love me, love me... why do you want money? Then it isn't love... Then it's sin... No woman has ever loved me... why do you want money? Why don't you love me?"

The girl looked down at him with pious eyes, like the Madonna looking at a penitent who confesses his heart to her.

She gently tugged at his hair: "Sweetheart, you're not paying me... I really like you... look... you're giving me something – freely... entirely voluntarily."

Little Lorbeer slowly understood, then he rejoiced: this was love!

In the office, he now displayed a self-satisfied air. He let it slip that he had a lover, a lover.

Three times a week, he visited his "lover," bringing her a small gift of money each time.

By the way, his window was open again at night. The blue night sky came in, bringing the stars, which, once witnesses of his misery, were now witnesses to his happiness.

After about half a year, poor little Lorbeer invited everyone to the wedding.

Balaschew

"Keep those American millionaires away from me."

The Russian millionaires: they are the real deal. For example: Balaschew.

Balaschew was a great philosopher.

He always did exactly the opposite of what people expected of him.

The "orphanage" (which was heavily in debt) could reasonably suspect that he, the multiple millionaire, would help with a small sum, but he didn't give a single red cent. No matter how pleadingly they called on him, invoking various ethical arguments. However, one day, he surprised the "Union of Convicted Anti-Alcoholics," of which he was a declared opponent (his unusual consumption of vodka proves this), by donating 10,000 rubles to establish a "Balaschew Foundation." The interest from this sum was to be used to present fifty bottles of Karlsbad mineral water to association members who had been with the union for at least 15 years, on their name days.

Balaschew could crow like a rooster and bark like a dog.

Not wanting to let this talent go to waste, he bought a house on one of Moscow's main streets, had it demolished, and built a spacious and comfortable doghouse in its place. Once a week, on Thursdays, he would crawl inside and loudly and maliciously bark at passersby.

He called this: "Playing Diogenes."

He owned a cat, old, scruffy, and of repulsive ugliness. He had her photographed in every possible position: from behind, from the front, from above, and from below, and sent the photos to all the magazines, both domestic and foreign, including the *Hong Kong Times* and *The Weekly*, which later published them (after his death).

He subscribed to every newspaper via the strip-band method. But he only checked to see if the banderole read "His Highness." If this phrase was missing, he immediately canceled the subscription. If it was clear and correct, he subscribed to one hundred copies.

One day, his feet had to be amputated. He had them buried with honor and erected a reddish marble monument with the inscription: "Here rest the feet of Balaschew. Wanderer, hurry past if you don't want a kick."

Balaschew died about four weeks ago. He was buried in a pauper's coffin without spiritual assistance. A band followed his coffin, playing the same melody tirelessly until they reached the cemetery: "Beautiful Minka, I must depart."

Thus, we see that Balaschew, in a manner rare for millionaires, was whole-heartedly devoted to the care of intellectual goods, particularly passionate about Stoic philosophy.

By the way, he was in correspondence with Tolstoy, which only further strengthens our high opinion of him.

The Lover

The senior student Arnold Bubenreuther swaggered casually and arrogantly through the dirty, one-story suburban alleys. How dull this Saturday afternoon is! And I have no more money. Where should I go tonight? To Lizzi? She won't want to write to me anymore. I can't blame her. I owe her too much. She's really noble, Lizzi, but otherwise, she's no good. How about Nelly? The eternal widow, the little dark person? I've actually wasted enough comfort on her. Besides, she's now after that stupid rich baker.

But Claire, now that's the only worthy one. I haven't been with her for at least a month. With her, something could be made out of it through serious, persistent effort.

He sighed.

Unfortunately, money was required for that. She has talent, she has genius to be a great courtesan.

He tenderly traced the conflicting lines and daring curves of her unique body in his thoughts, which he had, when he last saw her, thought was pregnant. She denied it.

Unfortunately, she lets a bungling tailor work for her. Haven't I told her that yet? This dull blue he made her wear is absolutely impossible; maybe it would work for a stylized higher daughter, the vague, unreal quality of this color. Her dress must throw folds just as vibrant and glowing as she herself. I wish I could be her mentor! That would be a goal, a passionate task of my being. Success should be my only reward... instead, the school forces me, a large part of my life, to deal with the delusional shoe polishers of so-called Humanitas — that's the teachers — and the wooden feelings of Antigone, Wallenstein, Uhland, Erlkönig, Lafontaine, and their papier-mâché wisdom.

These poets offer a dreadful, immensely comic sight. How can one degrade oneself in such a blood-desecrating manner? If only they could hold back, the lustful lovers of art. But they continuously tap into their finest soul powers until they become impotent, and Lady Life, who wants to be raped, mockingly turns away from them. Others prefer to be castrated and sing with squeaky voices about the grace of eunuchs. Is there anything lower, weaker than the self-denial of the artist? Before the rooster crows the third time, you will have denied me, Petre. I only accept one "artistic direction": the caricature, the satire, the self- and thus all-irony. Any objectification is nonsensical. What falsely shines out from the display ground of ideal art: Purification, irony may bear it on its shield: It rings in the distortion, the ideal art distorts in its purification. When I am fully aware, I will write a comedy, just one, which, as it should, will turn dear God into the devil and Beelzebub into the archangel, and the crooked and twisted world will see its true face in hollow mirrors, so that it will burst out laughing.

Otto Schulz, Arnold Bubenreuther's schoolmate, stuttered along the way. His walk stuttered just as awkwardly as his speech.

The trousers dangled awkwardly around two stiff wooden sticks. Otto Schulz had no sense of his limbs. He never knew where to place his eyes, arms, and hands. Even in his head, it seemed that the cerebrum and cerebellum had become a little mixed up. Feeling and reason, energy and sluggishness bubbled around and over each other. Sometimes he wanted to be an explorer, sometimes a religious founder, sometimes a government assessor. He was utterly miserable when he was addressed. Arnold stopped him: "Man, where are you coming from?" – Arnold always addressed his classmates formally – "You've really gotten yourself dirty. You must have been swimming for rare algae in the Poet's Temple?"

Otto Schulz stared at him in confusion. Then, with a whistling sound and breathless, with startled eyes, he blurted out: "Leave me alone, Bubenreuther... I'm in a hurry... I have to go to the police, oh, think... what am I supposed to think?"

Bubenreuther fixed his gaze on Otto Schulz's unbelievably tasteless Turkish tie. His sister, the unfortunate girl, must have given it to him for his birthday, he thought.

"Up by the pond behind the shooting ranges..." The thread tangled.

"Pull yourself together, dear Schulz,"Bubenreuther admonished him with tender irony.

"Is there a child's body lying in the reeds?"

Otto Schulz was at the end of his concentration. The image he had seen at the pond grinned gruesomely into his soul, making him afraid.

"Then, of course, you must quickly go to the police," Bubenreuther said slowly, "and I won't keep you. Adieu."

Otto Schulz hopped along like a wounded rabbit, hopping and panting.

Arnold Bubenreuther continued on his way, thoughtfully.

The country road began. To the left, the last house appeared, a four-story tenement with an unpleasant red paint, polished like an intrusive woman: Planing noises, children playing, and women's voices echoed around the house. At the well, a pretty, sturdy maid leaned in a faded blue cotton blouse, sending Arnold Bubenreuther a curious smile.

Arnold Bubenreuther turned right towards the shooting ranges.

In ten minutes, he had reached the pond. Searching, he walked along its edge. From a group of reeds two steps away from the shore, a whitish something peered out. After a brief moment of thought and a glance around, he stamped his shoes into the water, bent down to the white spot, and held a boy's corpse, the body of a newborn, in his hands.

He sat down on the shore and placed the dead child in the grass in front of him. With his head resting in his hands, he absorbed the sight. – "It's good that your mother stepped on you, worm, you would never have learned to walk and would have always had to crawl. You know your mother, but choosing among your fathers would probably have been difficult for you.

A child born without a father doesn't live at all.

The simplicity and naivety of your death intoxicates me."

And the child lay there, like a halo, the mysterious silence of its riddle. Its little hands were pressed tightly against its chin.

Arnold Bubenreuther looked at the little hands.

"Who are you?" he asked. "Who is your father and your mother? Who are you?"

The child remained silent.

Arnold Bubenreuther laughed angrily.

"You're stubborn, my dear, you're willful. Why so quiet? They'll say you're completely mad because of your eccentricity. What's wrong with you, huh?"

And this time, the child answered.

"It's not true," Arnold cried in horror, "say it again, it's not true."

And the child answered.

"It can't be." – Arnold Bubenreuther groaned. His hot breath blew like desert wind.

"It can't be."

And then he wept, tear after tear dripping gently onto the forehead of the child.

"I cry May rain. May rain makes you grow. It lets you grow! You shall grow!

"You will never grow, dwarf, you dead giant...

"What could you have become, you who were conceived with such deep zest for life? When your mother killed you, she killed herself. You were our fulfillment, our end. Did she go mad in her motherly love and maternal pain? Claire, – why didn't you think of me? You... whore.

"...I wouldn't have paid alimony? I would have stolen... I would have murdered my father... for my son's sake."

It was gradually getting dusky. The mist spread white cotton over the land. In the crystal-clear sky, the yellow horn of the moon hung like a freshly pulled anise cake.

Arnold Bubenreuther jumped up and understood. The police could arrive at any moment. They would take the body to the mortuary and, eventually, once the murder was solved, bury it somewhere in the sand.

"My son, my son – and dead."

Grimly tender, he stroked the fine down on the child's head.

Then he suddenly roared in a mighty rage, so that foam appeared on his pale lips, "You... You... You..."

He calmed down, gently lifted the small body, and cradled it warmly against his chest under his coat.

"You blood, you my blood," it sang within him, as you sometimes flow from this child and me. I will build you an altar, you my dead conqueror. You dead god. Since you were my son, you would have become a god. I will prepare for you a divine, blazing burial and scatter your ashes, wherever you came from, into the south wind."

Calm and self-assured, he walked through the streets of the city.

He encountered the police.

Stassi

Before going to bed, I had taken a hot foot bath to warm my cold feet, then, as Mother Jenschen had advised, I wrapped them in a woolen blanket and placed a thoroughly damp compress around my neck to guard against the cold. After that, I climbed into bed and blew out the light — when something strange happened. I felt something crawling and shifting under my abdominal wall, something alive — like a young crocodile. It pattered slowly over my liver, very slowly, plop, plop, plop, plop. I slipped my hand under the blanket and grabbed the mischief that had leaped through the hoop filled with paper, just like an acrobat in the circus. It felt squishy and wet like a frog. Only it was warm, not cold, as one would expect from body temperature. When I tried to grab it more firmly, it slipped away, and I couldn't find it even when I lit a match. I only had such a curious sensation once again when Madame Fichon later married me and I was compelled to reach into her bosom.

Where the warm, damp toad under my shirt came from on that night described above gradually became clear to me: I had eaten too much of a dish called "poppy strudel," which my first wife, God rest her soul, knew how to prepare excellently.

Madame Fichon was merely a professional name. In truth, she was Emilie Fischer. She was a madam of a brothel. Good heavens! As if I were trying to hold that against her! Quite the opposite. Life pushes us here and there. One bumps their nose or brain against this or that, stumbles and falls into the street filth, and without at least dirtying one's boots, no one has crossed the street. We want nothing to do with couch potatoes. Their virtue is pale and reeks of the stove.

Madame Fichon was a good madam. She didn't do like others in her trade, taking bread from her poor children's mouths, but instead ensured they had decent, nutritious food, insisted on cleanliness and order, and even encouraged her reckless people to save money, so that the women were very fond of her.

In the final days of my first marriage, I often visited the house. My wife was unwell, shrank prematurely, and, as they say, "there was nothing there." But I, the master brush binder Gustav Albert Hellermann, was still a strong and healthy man. Damn it, the man wants a woman, and my wife was no longer a woman — just look at my muscles! I was a member of the gymnastics club "Father Jahn," the cycling club "Gentle Path," the rowing club "Triton," and if you ever visit me, I'll show you the many cups, honors, and medals I won at regional and national festivals. I made the giant wave seventeen times, and in the thousand-kilometer tour of the German Cycling Federation, I won.

And a sick wife on top of that! Enduring that was tough for me. So, I became, so to speak, a quarterly lover and guest at Madame Fichon's house. One day, a girl named Klara Stass arrived. She called herself Stassi; she had probably derived this nickname from her last name, as I don't know if Stassi is a common maiden name. She was beautiful, blonde, lively, and very nice, so I liked her immensely, and I decided to free her from her rather pitiful profession. I spoke to Madame Fichon about it and offered her a settlement. She accepted my proposal. I took Stassi as a maid into my house. She seemed too good for a maid, but for the time being, it was all I could do to help her. She behaved well, and even my wife was satisfied with her. Of course, my wife had no idea of the full context of the matter. She found the name "Stassi" somewhat adventurous, but she let that superficial concern pass.

I had sworn to keep my house clean. The devil intervened. The oath lasted a month. Then I fell endlessly in love with Stassi, and she, of course, became my sweetheart. Meanwhile, she had found a fiancé, a mechanic at the brass goods factory, to whom she remained "faithful." She had given herself to me out of gratitude. Publicly, she upheld her virginal honor, and granted me liberties that she firmly refused her mechanic.

One evening, I was with her in the attic room, which was opposite the girls' room. I had told my wife that I was going to the attic, and this was all the easier to do since she, fragile and frail as she was, had trouble climbing stairs, so I removed all suspicion with this half-truth.

Suddenly, someone shook our door. I quietly asked what was going on. Stassi grabbed my arm and looked at me in horror.

My wife's voice screamed: "Gustav, Gustav, for God's sake, fire, fire!"

I jumped up. Stassi let go of me and fled to the farthest corner.

Outside, my wife screamed, "Gustav, Gustav, the stairs are going to catch fire!" and she fell into a pitiful whimpering: "Gustav, Gustav, what have you done... fire, fire." And I heard her desperately tugging at the door handle.

I gritted my teeth: "Stassi, you have to come."

The clanging of the door handle and my wife's cries of distress drowned out my whisper.

"Your wife sees me," she hissed. "That doesn't matter now," I replied. "This is a matter of life and death. Come."

"No."

"You must."

"No."

"Yes."

"No."

I was exhausted. "The stairs are on fire, Gustav, Gustav..."

"I'm coming!" I shouted, turning the key. Without looking back, I rushed down the stairs, carrying my wife, who had collapsed unconscious. It was high time. The flames singed my hair.

Outside on the street, I regained my composure and looked up at the gable. I wasn't thinking about material losses. Only about Stassi.

"There's still someone upstairs," my voice snapped with excitement. "Put the ladder up."

I had hardly spoken when I heard a brief scream and a dull thud next to me. Stassi had run into the girls' room and now jumped down onto the pavement. They picked her up and took her to the hospital. She had broken her spine, but she briefly regained consciousness and called for the mechanic. He rushed over from work, sweating. He truly loved her and is said to have even cried. And now —

Imagine, she persuaded him to marry her on her deathbed! The poor fool! A victim of her public honor. She wanted to leave life decently and civilly. And used her passing to promote her public virginity. I never would have expected such a masterstroke from her. I admired her for knowing how to stage what is called honor so beautifully.

For what does honor mean to most people, if not a dress one puts on when going out — but when at home or among themselves, one is happy to hang it on the hook? And it's only ever immoral if someone sees it. That's why I, Gustav Albert Hellermann, master brush binder, have no shame about my love-driven sins. For no one knows about them except Madame Fichon. And I married her and moved with her to a place where no one knows her or her secret profession. Here, she's simply Emilie and is my loyal wife. And if you ever have the honor of visiting me, she'll serve you delicious meatballs in Dutch sauce. For she runs an excellent, albeit middle class, kitchen.

The Third

She stood outside by the garden gate, her arms braced on her hips, her chest tightened with longing beneath the white blouse.

The street was gray, empty, silent.

But someone was pacing back and forth.

I listened to his inaudible footsteps.

A few dead leaves danced to the ground through the dim glow of a gas lamp.

I stepped closer.

Her hair shimmered whitish-blond, bleached by the sea wind, and her pale blue eyes were separated by a thick red line from her cheek. It looked as though she had painted her lower eyelids.

I had known such women in Friesland.

I lifted my hat slightly and asked politely: "Is your mistress at home?"

She looked over my shoulder.

Was someone behind me?

I turned around.

Indifferently, she spoke over my head, as though she could have said it to any-one else: "I live alone... on the third floor."

"Your home is Bremen!" I said very decisively.

She laughed — away from my shoulder — toward the other.

"Braunschweig," she laughed. "Braunschweig... yes," she confirmed.

But this year was also a lascivious question to the other man.

It trembled from her mouth, drawn from the well of memories and rolled into the stream of the future.

The play of her hands made the garden posts rattle.

I stroked her silky apron.

"Come!" I said.

"Come!" she whispered and sighed.

There was a third person between us.

He resisted me.

We groped our way up the back stairs — a spiral staircase.

She unlocked the door.

And lit a stearic candle.

The blind had already been drawn.

I looked around the room, the maid's usual room, the mirrored cabinet, the gold-painted chairs, the postcards on the walls, and the huge photographs in frames.

And above the bed, an image of a saint.

And all around and rising from everything, a repulsively blazing scent of soap, mouthwash, and poorly aired girls' upper and undergarments.

She sat on the bed and began calmly unbuttoning her shoes.

Now I thought the moment had come: the third was still inside her, between us. I had to kill him.

I drew the dagger from my pocket, the bright dagger with its seductively slender steel body.

She saw the knife flash.

Her eyes widened in a mixture of lust and horror, then she collapsed weakly, without resistance.

Gently, I placed the tip of the knife on her white neck and reached with the other hand to her chest.

So quietly, so that the dagger sank perhaps a centimeter into her throat and a fine trickle of blood trickled out, she leaned forward and kissed my fist, which was clenched around the dagger's hilt.

Then I threw the knife into the corner and extinguished the light.
He was dead — the third one.

The Poem

Christoforus Ehrensam received a letter in a foreign language with the morning post from Geneva. It made him thoughtful. He went straight to his lawyer.

"It's absolutely impossible!" he said, citing various hygienic reasons.

The lawyer smiled — God, these laypeople! — and adjusted his pince-nez. "But you did, so to speak, have dealings with the lady?"

Christoforus Ehrensam grew nervous. "Yes, yes, but..."

The lawyer smiled again.

Christoforus snapped, "I swear it wasn't me!"

"My advice is to acknowledge the child. At a distance, we won't be able to find another father," said the lawyer.

Christoforus groaned. "Fine, I'll let it go to trial." He left.

Christoforus Ehrensam had the harmless habit of publishing poems in obscure magazines that no one read. But the prosecutor assigned to the case of Ehrensam vs. Bibi did read them. And he was horrified. "A midwife! She's a midwife! I've never heard of anyone loving midwives!" For in the *General Lyric Auction*, he had found the following poem, signed by Christoforus Ehrensam:

I loved her in Geneva...
Oh! When I see her now in dreams!
She was the youngest apprentice,
Sage-femme maternite!–

"Do you admit to being the father?" asked the prosecutor.

"But it's quite impossible!" Christoforus Ehrensam roared.

"Why not?" the opposing counsel replied gently. "After all, if you can write such charming poems as..." And he recited from memory all the poems he could gather by Christoforus Ehrensam, plus a few more for good measure.

Christoforus Ehrensam's face lit up with a new glow.

"Well then!" he stammered.

The Invention

"Thank God," said Kasimir Przk. "Now a new era begins. No decent person could kill another these days without being dragged to prison or the scaffold. Too much feeble culture, too little honest animality. But that will change now."

"Why?" I asked.

"I've made a delightful invention. It looks like an innocent fountain pen. But with this fountain pen, I intend to inscribe my name in the golden book of humanity."

"That's unfair," I said. "In this mechanical age, to contribute even further to its mechanization. And besides, it's plebeian. Every second man you meet on the street is an inventor. If only there were an invention to rid the world of inventors!"

"Or at least the inventors," Kasimir Przk remarked. "And that is precisely what my fountain pen is perfectly capable of doing. Picture a small, tubular device, equipped with a tiny push button. You have a hole tailored into your coat pocket, just large enough for the tube to stick out slightly. The uninitiated won't notice it at all. A passerby brushes past you, click — you press the button, and he drops dead, as if struck by lightning. You can repeat it as often as you like, without ever being caught. It will become a most entertaining sport — dispatching a few people after breakfast or lunch to aid digestion.

"The shots are completely silent and smokeless. And it's something new for a change. I am the first superhuman and master of this new era!" Kasimir Przk added.

We paid for our coffee and were about to leave. I admired Kasimir Przk's new fur coat, which he had the waiter drape elegantly over his shoulders.

We had barely stepped outside when a stranger rushed out of the café after us. "Sir," he shouted at us, "you've stolen my fur coat!"

"Why?" Kasimir Przk asked, but the stranger was already lying on the ground, dead as if struck by lightning.

"I can't understand why people get so worked up that they immediately have a stroke," said Kasimir Przk as we walked on, giving me a strange sideways glance.

I began to feel deeply uneasy. But then — thud — I fell, dead on the pavement.

The Child

When Tatyana came to visit me for the first time, she sat down on the stove.

I reprimanded her for this uneducated behavior, and so my lap was the only place she could sit.

I can't help that she had a child.

It was very cold in the studio, and we had to huddle together for warmth.

Your Honor! The unexpected death of my illegitimate child is being pinned on me — and on my, unfortunately tattered, shoes.

"Illegitimate!" What a word! All children are illegitimate, for in a proper marriage, no children are born at all. Childbearing is nothing but the devil's work. But that is beside the point.

To make a long story short: when one fine day, purely by accident and without the assistance of a midwife, the child fell out of her womb, I was quite shocked by the wretched little beast that appeared. It was a dirty, blood-and-slime-covered lump of flesh that made me retch, though there was nothing in my stomach but gastric acid. So, I told myself, that's what you once looked like in your youth, a spring blossom. A lovely blossom — and what a fragrance! Compared to the (so-called) lord of creation in his swaddling clothes, freshly born kittens, jackals, crocodiles, rhinos, and even earthworms are delightful creatures.

This is merely a euphemistic and somewhat mystical comparison because at that time, there was no mention of swaddling clothes in our case. At best, I could have wrapped the filthy little creature in the cold studio floor.

Since Tatyana had fainted, I took the child and held it under the water tap to clean it.

Your Honor! I have always been a proponent of cleanliness. Even as a boy, while other children blew their noses into their hands, I used a proper handkerchief — one that depicted the Battle of Plevna in our three national colors: blue, white, and red. Or was it red, white, and blue? I always confuse the order, unfortunately. But we should be proud of our flag. It precedes us at every pogrom. God save Russia! God save the Tsar! But that is beside the point.

The cold water treatment had no effect on the child. It remained dirty, screamed, and became increasingly entangled in its snake-like twisted limbs, which, may God strike me down, could not be anatomically defined. It is not impossible that, instead of holding it by the hands like one does with babies, I held it by the feet under the water stream.

When nothing worked, desperation took hold of me. I fetched our bottle of gasoline, soaked a woolen rag with it, and attempted to rub the filth off the little beast.

High Court! What is the best remedy for stains on clothes and trousers? Be they mud, ink, or food stains (of which there was no abundance in our home)? Gasoline! Only gasoline! An old, honest household remedy, whose universal value I had absorbed during my childhood. Incidentally, it is also said to work well against lice — or am I confusing it with kerosene? I'm not certain.

So, after scrubbing the child thoroughly with gasoline for half an hour, it wheezed, sighed, and died before my eyes.

What was I to do? What, I ask, would a High Court have done in my position? I despise doctors. They are the certified henchmen of the Grim Reaper. And no faith healer resided in our district (although a petition to the illustrious Duma is in preparation and on its way about this disgraceful lack of progress in the heart of the world, Petersburg). But that is beside the point.

Tatyana was still unconscious, lying in her blood.

I took the dead child, tied it to a string, climbed from the studio window onto the roof, and lowered it into the first chimney I could find.

Fourteen days later, during the monthly chimney cleaning, it was retrieved, well-preserved, as a small blackened figure. The sun — in this case, the chimney sweep — brought it to light. Blackened with soot, it made a generally favorable impression, and I felt a pang of sorrow in my soul (if humans indeed have souls, which remains to be proven) that it was dead.

Your Honor!

Tatyana noticed none of this — not even that she had given birth. When she awoke from her faint, I told her that the devil had been residing in her and, upon my exorcisms, had fled from her body with a bang, a stench of pitch, and sulfur. She readily believed me.

Your Honor! These are the facts! This is my confession, true to the best of my knowledge. Should a High Court reach a verdict of acquittal, as I hope, I request the return of the child's corpse. We wish to sell it to a wax museum. We are hungry.

Adventure

Konrad was so drunk that he pursued every female figure he encountered on the nighttime streets. He would overtake them, stop under a streetlamp to get a better look, and then recoil in horror. Now he was following a young girl, just out of a gathering and being accompanied home by a maid. She returned his glances coolly and curiously. But suddenly, he lost the courage to speak to her. He couldn't bring himself to do it and mechanically turned into a side street.

He had taken only a few steps when he noticed a red curtain glowing behind a ground-floor window. There must be light behind it, he thought.

That's something, he thought, without knowing why, and tapped lightly on the window with his walking stick. Once, twice.

My God, thought Esther, could it be a friend of Kurt's? She threw a shawl over her bare shoulders and peeked through the gap in the curtains. All she could see was an indistinct shadow. She opened the window slightly.

"Who's there?"

"I want to come in," said Konrad. "Let me in!"

She pushed the window further open and leaned out cautiously. Then she saw his flushed, excited face, his intensely eager eyes, and heard the trembling of his voice. He let his stick fall and raised both arms like a worshipper.

"You..."

It thrilled her: the dimly lustful street, the wild lover, and the tingling danger of the moment — Kurt could walk in at any moment and catch them. He was sitting in the study across the hall, working on a paper. He might continue writing for hours — he often worked on his manuscripts until dawn — but he could just as easily open the door at any second.

She tiptoed to the door and listened to the hallway. Then she carefully locked it, padded back across the carpet to the window, and said, "You'll have to climb in through the window."

In one swift motion, Konrad was in the room. When he saw the beautiful woman standing before him in her nightgown, with her sleek hairstyle, narrow black eyes, and soft, pale-yellow forehead like something out of a Japanese woodcut, he sobered up instantly and became wild with love. Groaning, he pressed his head to her chest.

"Quiet, darling," she whispered, kissed his hair, gently disengaged herself from him, and tiptoed back to listen at the door. Then she reached to the wall, flicked off the electric light, and plunged the room into darkness.

Konrad left the same way he had entered, through the window, clutching a blue silk ribbon from the neckline of her nightgown in his fist.

"What's this?" Kurt asked later, as he was unbuttoning his shirt. "The blue ribbon is missing from your neckline."

"Yes," said Esther indifferently, touching her neck so that her fingertips brushed against her breasts. "The washerwoman is so careless. She must have forgotten the ribbon again..."

The Birthmark

"Whenever I drive home with you, I get so bored," he yawned, stretching himself against the reddish-brown leather cushions of the electric automobile. "Why do I even do it?"

The thin blue-glass branches of the dyed heron feather on her dark hat lightly tickled his forehead. She laughed and clucked like a hen that had happily survived laying her egg.

Gray darkness lay in the compartment: streetlights, clouds, waxwood sellers flashed past the rain-slicked windows in a garish sequence, like colorful bats.

He absentmindedly rummaged in his coat pockets. His left hand found an old bus ticket, which he unconsciously crumpled into a little ball. The yellow color of the paper and the faded black letters came back to his mind.

"Because you love me!"

He felt an unfamiliar hand somewhere on his body.

His neck sank into his coat collar — the white collar liner rubbed against his pale red lips.

How indifferent all of this is to me, he thought. I barely like her; she can fall wherever she wants. It's only because I happen to have money right now. As if I were always drunk, just in a way that I lack both will and proper awareness.

And he said aloud: "Your breasts stand like two pyramids, steep and firm. I've never seen or felt such breasts before. They are pointed and firm, crowned by two red tips — round and glowing, like the bronze domes of church towers when the evening sun lavishes them with crimson kisses."

Lavishes... The word lingered with him. I give her too much. How will this end?

"And isn't that love... darling?"

She whispered, concealed, secretive, as if there were a third person among them who must not hear.

The car stopped with a jolt.

"Maybe," he sighed.

"Give the chauffeur a tip, darling."

Lightly, she hopped ahead and under the sheltering doorway. A raindrop had nevertheless dripped from the gutter onto the right pink silk stocking, on the bottom of her black velvet loafer, forming a yellowish-gray circle.

He noticed it as he slowly followed her.

"The birthmark," he mused to himself. "I will kiss her there. It's something new..."

Revolution

(For Guiseppe Cassi)

You may believe me or not, my dear fellow: in my youth, I traveled far and wide. I spent eight days in Paris and lived somewhere on the outer boulevards — but every day for dinner and supper, there was rabbit meat, with and without garlic... I beg you, my dear fellow, even the devil would get dysentery from that if he didn't rinse it down with vodka... and where does one find a vodka rinse in Paris? There's not even a water rinse!

After that, I honored London with my presence. But I couldn't endure it for more than eight days either. These non-alcoholic drinks! They even dilute their whiskey with soda, and such people want to conquer the world! *Tschort poderi Anglin* forever, ever... And then there's the prose of their food (if one considers spirits its poetry). I mean the steaks, the rump and beefsteaks, so overcooked, bland, and poorly styled, like an English sixpence magazine novel. May Saint Lawrence protect me from this — better to let my stomach play a tune of hunger than to sole it with these various kinds of leather. And over all those steaks, always the same sauce. It's true what a wise man once said about that peculiar island nation: a hundred sects... and only one sauce.

Let me show you a trick, my dear fellow... I place this kopeck on my bare elbow and... fff... it's gone. My dear fellow, what does this kopeck mean to you? You're young, rich, have an uncle who's a district commissioner, an illegitimate brother who's a policeman — what more could you want? To me, this kopeck is a little shot at paradise... I buy myself a drink with it... A Russian citizen performs a good patriotic deed by drinking schnapps... Doesn't he dutifully pay taxes to the state in doing so? Doesn't the state have a monopoly on schnapps? Isn't a drunkard a ridiculous or repugnant figure in every other country, but in Russia, a laudable, government-approved sight? Doesn't the current Russian system thrive solely on the perpetual drunkenness of melancholy fools? What? You find my judgment harsh, my dear fellow... And the gendarme over there in the corner is already rolling his oily whale eyes... He wants to eavesdrop on us, that greasy bearer of state authority and the rubber truncheon... Let's speak more quietly...

My dear fellow, I must tell you a story where alcohol also plays a peculiar role...

It was during the last revolution, in the winter of 1905 or 1906 — I can't remember the exact date, as I have a poor memory for years. At that time, I lived in Lodz, eking out a miserable existence as a typesetter for a democratic newspaper, which, of course, was soon confiscated and suppressed. And we poor devils were left without bread or means to survive. Well, there was plenty of strange and wickedness to see back then... One didn't get bored during those endless holidays. On your morning walk, you'd stumble over various corpses on the stairs, and if you weren't careful, you'd end up with cold lead in your stomach instead of warm morning soup.

Cossacks galloped through the streets, dispersing any group of three people with lance thrusts, as it was considered an illegal assembly. In the evenings, you couldn't have lights burning in rooms facing the street, because the Cossacks found it amusing to shoot at every lit window.

It was an extraordinarily cold winter, and for some inexplicable reason, the city government had set up iron stoves in certain side streets, so that people — who would later be shot — could warm their hands beforehand.

It was at one such stove that I first met her.

She was completely drunk, holding a half-frozen (probably also drunk) child, no more than three months old, wrapped in dirty Scottish cloths, over the heating.

She had pale blue, bloodshot eyes and a wild, fox-red wig that, had I been a security commissioner, I would have confiscated, as it was more provocative and revolutionary than a hundred misspelled manifestos.

When she staggered off in ecstasy, I secretly followed her — and many others did too.

In the deserted yard of a trading house, she stopped, and once enough people had gathered around her, she gave an impassioned, fiery, frenzied speech with a grand gesture — nearly dropping her child in the process.

It was from that speech, from this drunken, red-haired woman no one knew, that the revolution in Lodz truly began.

We tore up the cobblestones.

We stole rifles and ammunition.

We built barricades out of furniture carts, carriages, dead soldiers, dead horses, dead citizens.

The red-haired woman, the angel of God, was our leader — always with the child in her arms, always swaying, always drunk.

... One afternoon, machine guns were brought up against the main barricades on L... Street, which had held out the longest. A regiment of Cossacks and a regiment of infantry were kept in the background, ready to attack.

Behind the barricades, the red-haired woman moved from one to another, encouraging, advising, inspiring, always with her child in her arms.

The commander of the soldiers raised his saber to signal the start of the bombardment... and then the strange, the miraculous, the one true miracle I have ever seen in my life happened.

The colonel's saber, along with his arm, froze mid-air as if paralyzed; the machine guns jammed, their bullets stuck in the barrels; the gunners, the Cossacks, the infantry, the horses — none of them moved, no one stirred.

On the top of the barricade stood the woman, smiling, with her child at her bare breast, drinking thirstily. Her red hair fluttered in the wind: the woman, the red-haired, drunken woman.

Where was her drunkenness now? Where her swaying stance and gait? Where the crudeness and heaviness of her being?

Pure and radiant, smiling — a pleading smile — the young mother stood on the barricade. She stretched out her child to the executioners who had come to slaughter her and her kind.

No one dared to shoot. To speak. To breathe... and suddenly, the church bells all around began to ring the Ave.

Then, unfortunately, a revolver went off accidentally among our own ranks.

The shot was the signal that shattered the heavenly spell with a bang. It was as if a veil fell from everyone's eyes. The commander's saber slashed the air. A barrage followed in a flash. The first volley swept the red-haired woman and her child to the devil — or should we say, to the angels?

She was an angel, my dear fellow, in her eternal drunkenness, a symbol of Russia. A fiery heart, trembling as it swims in vodka...

I knew her well, my dear fellow. I believe her name was Emelyanova. Perhaps I even loved her.

Novella

"You may do whatever you want; I'll never amount to anything worthwhile," said Elias. "Give me five thousand marks, and you'll be rid of me forever."

His father scratched behind his ears and silently thought that his son wasn't entirely wrong. Here he was, causing foolish trouble, undermining his father's social standing with dog breeding and aeronautical experiments that never went beyond cardboard models, and provoking the disapproval of all reasonable people with his fashionably shaved head — a style that inspired resistance in anyone who shied away from both fashion and originality as a turkey does from bright-colored cloth.

"If you swear never to show your face here again," the father said deliberately.

Elias swore and received the five thousand marks.

He went to Berlin and rented a place near the Oranienburger Gate.

He wanted to become a poet, and since he believed knowledge of women to be the most important thing, he went out that evening, met a nice lady, and paid her five marks as a modeling fee. He claimed to have recently arrived in Berlin and to have once strolled along the Maiden's Walk in Hamburg. At the mention of "Maiden's Walk," she clicked her tongue.

Elias found it very charming.

The next morning, he sat before a blank sheet of paper, chewing on the end of his pen.

"Damn it, this has to turn into a novella," he thought.

But nothing came.

He consoled himself with the thought that he hadn't done enough research yet and continued paying modeling fees.

Dark circles formed around his eyes, the whites of which began to take on a faint sulfur-yellow hue. His pale cheeks grew hollow. He developed the shakes, and the women had also gotten him into the accursed habit of smoking indoors.

After six months, he had only three marks sixty left, along with three ten-mark postage stamps, and still no trace of the longed-for novellas.

One fine Thursday, market day, which made the shops particularly busy — he suddenly graced his old Markish homeland with his presence.

His father crossed himself and, in shock, dropped a Bismarck herring. Thankfully, it was already wrapped, and a stout farmer's wife casually placed it into her basket. A piece for a groschen, three thirty-five.

His mother, however, embraced him with tearful joy in her frail arms. That very morning, despite it being market day and there being much to do, Elias started working as an apprentice in his father's general store.

I believe he's now a partner.

And if he isn't married, he's still alive today.

Professor Runkel

As soon as the bell rang, Professor Runkel flung the door open and burst into the classroom with a jolt.

"Asseyez-vous."

The seats clattered down with a thunderous noise — then breathless silence. "Primus." The boy sprang up in fright. "What else could it mean?" Professor Runkel rolled his eyes so that only the whites were visible.

The small Jewish boy at the back row began to chuckle softly and furtively. For greater caution, he crouched behind the broad back of his stout classmate in front of him.

"Assoiyez-vous," stammered the Primus, making his famously servile upward glance.

Arnold Bubenreuther, watching him, shuddered with disgust.

Runkel plopped his wide-brimmed black floppy hat onto the coat rack and pulled off his green loden coat. Underneath, another layer emerged — a black, half-woolen summer coat.

The class sat perfectly still.

Arnold Bubenreuther gazed out the window. He saw nothing but a patch of intensely blue summer sky, in which the gnarled and dusty crown of a chestnut tree hung.

Runkel shed the second coat and stormed to the lectern. With his bushy-maned head tilted back, he sat there tugging at the ends of his brown full beard.

"Who left the window open?" he suddenly shouted.

"I'll throw the culprit right out the window! Damn it, you all know I can't stand drafts ever since that damned cannonball hit my damned thigh in the damned war! You, close the window."

Someone slid the latch shut. The class muttered and shrank down. Now they would have to sit another stifling hour in the stale air, all because that guy up there liked it that way.

Runkel opened the class register. As if he couldn't see it properly, he brought his right hand to his eyes and twisted the book around with the other.

"Monitor," he bellowed.

The small, timid Penschke stepped uncertainly to the lectern.

"What kind of pigsty handwriting is this? Might as well rain farm boys or wooden clogs! This goes beyond midnight meadows grazing under ultraviolet shadows! Damn it, who can read this? Is it Siamese? Arabic? Like this? Or like that?"

Poor little Penschke was on the verge of tears.

Bubenreuther scraped his boots against the floor.

"Bubenreuther," Runkel shot up like the devil leaping from a child's toy chest that represented the lectern. "You think I don't see you? I'll grab you by the collar and throw you out with three hours of detention, straight to the temple. You can bet on it, you can take cyanide for it. – Penschke, sit down, Bubenreuther, the reading, read it, we are on page...?"

"Sixty-two, Professor," came the response in unison.

"What, Professor, Professor? That's devilish! Call me, for all I care, 'Mr. Scholar,' or 'Heinrich,' but not this damned 'Professor.' – Bubenreuther, you hustler, read."

Bubenreuther read: "Nous avions perdu Gross-Goerschen; mais cette fois, entre Klein-Goerschen et Rahna, l'affaire allait encore devenir plus terrible..."

Runkel hissed and bit his lower lip so that his beard stood up like a bristly wall: "No Frenchman says "avions,' it's 'a-wü-ong,' with the second syllable short: a-wüong. Keep reading."

Bubenreuther read and translated tolerably. Runkel patted him on the shoulder: "May the devil hold the light for that eosin pig: the noble Baron von Bubenreuther once prepared it. – Continue, Schulz."

Schulz could barely hold the book in his trembling hands from fear. He wore glasses, was pale, stupid, and very diligent. Runkel enjoyed tormenting him, but later gave him a "sufficient" grade for his lack of resistance.

"Schulz," he screamed at him, "you must have been groomed by an ape. I have something to discuss with you — about yesterday, to pluck a chicken with you, or rather, a rooster. Didn't I forbid you to greet me when you're out on the street with your parents? Why did you greet me? So that people would stare and say, 'Here comes the crazy Runkel,' eh? What?"

The class struggled to suppress their laughter. But no one dared to laugh. Whoever burst out laughing would inevitably be sent to detention.

There was a soft knock outside.

Runkel spun around: "That's like taking the virgin to the ceiling: who's disturbing the lesson? It's nearly over anyway, and we're getting nowhere. Primus, check."

Primus opened the door and let in the janitor, who handed Runkel a notebook and a pencil.

"It's for the summer break," he said, glancing over at the boys.

Immediately, a blissful smile played across all the tired, disgruntled faces.

"Thank God." Bubenreuther whispered it softly to himself.

"My dear Bubenreuther," Runkel was in a kinder mood today, "moderate yourself. Summer break? It's enough to drive one mad, summer break in this cold. I'm freezing—always freezing. See my two coats? I could do with a fur."

The janitor rang the bell. So today was the last period.

"Prepare pages sixty-four and sixty-five. May God bless our departure. Penschke will write the tasks in the class book first. Amen..."

Runkel stormed through the streets, his floppy hat pressed against his forehead.

"Once again freed from those damned brats — they don't know what a struggle it is for me to be who I am... Dear God, dear God... if I don't harass them, they'll harass me — how else can I assure them of my superiority? I have to take them under the whip, or they won't believe it. And I am superior to them... if only I could give it to this Bubenreuther. He has such an impertinent face."

Bubenreuther passed him with two smaller students. Runkel waved his hat ironically, smiling: "Good morning, good morning — are these your brothers, dear friend?"

Bubenreuther answered the question as he turned slightly backward: "No, Herr Scholar." Then he lifted his cap.

"Pardon," Runkel snorted, "pardon."

If only I could catch him, thought Runkel.

After about ten minutes, he stopped in front of a corner building. He adjusted his hat and wiped his monocle. It seemed as though he was looking down one street, at the factory chimney or the steeple, or into the other street, which led out to the open fields: in the distance, a bluish, pale ridge of hills disappeared into misty clouds. It only seemed that way. In reality, he was glancing up at the second floor of the corner house.

Would she know that he was free at eleven today? Would she even be there? If she had checked the thermometer, she would have seen that there would be a heat holiday.

A yellow tulle curtain shifted in a second-floor window. A little later, a black silk, middle-aged lady stepped out from the house gate, carrying a pompadour under her arm and just fastening her gloves.

Runkel greeted her very gallantly, his movements suddenly losing their awkward, grotesque quality.

"See, Herr Professor," she smiled, "I thought as much. You and your boys will be glad. – But there's also a storm in the air," she added, pointing with her parasol at the dull horizon.

"Where to now — into the city park or across the field to Gerbersau?"

"To Gerbersau, whenever it pleases you," Runkel said with perfect politeness. Any thought of the city and the school today made him uneasy. He might run into all sorts of students...

"The path under the poplars is shaded, and the forest after that will be cool and pleasant in this heat," he tried to tempt her.

"Well now, where's your frosty temperament, dear Professor? Aren't you freezing out of the ordinary today? – But alright, Gerbersau it is," she agreed.

They started walking slowly.

Runkel was very monosyllabic.

I could have married her earlier. Damn it, why didn't I do it?

The young lady chatted cheerfully and at length: about Ella Munker's engagement to Lieutenant Beckey, and how they had no money, and he would probably have to become a police officer if they ever wanted to get married... about the rising cost of meat, The Barber of Seville, and the recent Reichstag elections — she talked politics with passion. Runkel listened with half an ear. He saw a figure approaching from a distance that seemed familiar.

He grew uneasy and was ready to turn back.

"But why, dear Professor," the young lady laughed, "we're not going to do anything halfway."

The professor endured an agonizing fear. Sweat dripped from his forehead.

Arnold Bubenreuther politely greeted the couple as they passed. Runkel completely forgot to greet him back — in his astonishment. This time, he truly forgot without any intention.

"Was that not young Bubenreuther?" the young lady asked.

Runkel ignored the quiet question.

Where has this Bubenreuther put his ironic face? he thought excitedly. He always puts it on every moment. And strangely, I know for certain, he will not tell the class about this encounter. Why? Does he — feel sorry for me?

Runkel made a grimace, causing the young lady to stop in shock.

"What's the matter, Professor?"

"Nothing, dear young lady," Runkel smiled grimly, "I believe the students are holding their forbidden drinking sessions here in Gerbersau. Someone should put an end to their little scheme."

Secretly, he thought: That Bubenreuther, that dog, feels sorry for me. He dares to have pity on me. If only I could get hold of him...

The New Poet

(A chapter from a literary history of the year 2003)

In the year 1900, Joshua Kraschunke, who most purely and strongly embodied the literary type of the mid-20th century, was born as the son of the village schoolmaster Habakuk Kraschunke in Beutnitz, a small Markish village near the Silesian border.

The gradual formation of this type, along with its precursors and prophets, shall be reported on shortly.

The idea of Naturalism gradually disappeared in the first decade of the 20th century. Oddly enough: the more mechanical and industrial, the louder and more advertisement-driven the outer life became, the more lyrical and emotionally elegant, the more intimate and romantic the spirit of the new poetry revealed itself. The metropolis and industrial districts soon came to be perceived as nature, as landscape (Heym, Zech) — though not without still providing ironic mood stimuli for atavistic intellectuals. The world-friend Else Lasker-Schüler and the world-friend Werfel take a step further toward the goal of the unproblematic, simple-dreaming genius: coquettishly prancing and still too deliberately blossoming. Officer, amok runner, notary, red cyclist; all this and much more, the world-friend wishes to embody in one. Yet — he is still too much in the act of presenting himself; he does not become. Cowardice poisons him, falsehood — painfully sensed but never grasped — festers in his soul. In this sense, the desperate journeys of Dauthendey and Hesse to the Orient should be viewed. The distant lands, and the colorful excesses of India and Japan, still appear to promise the wildly longed-for and cursed adventures. It is an escape from metaphysics and self-dissolution into the physics of thrillingly foreign cultures. The physics of the self is neglected or "misrecognized." Unpoetic, descriptive travel works, such as Holitscher's *America* and Rosen's *Lausbub*, are the first to (in the dark) stumble upon a proper trail that will lead to the main road. Wedekind's *Marquis von Keith*, Thomas Mann's swindler novel *Felix Krull*, and above all Gorleben's *Rastaquar Comedy* stand on the threshold of fulfillment, where the poet and the swindler (criminal and judge) strangely merge: Josua Kraschunke.

Josua Kraschunke created poetry as a second reality — not out of necessity and compulsion, like previous writers (who were too weak and incapable of letting the first reality flow through them), but out of pleasure, out of sheer willfulness. The others played at life and lived through literature. He lived life and played with his verses as a child plays with dolls.

Josua Kraschunke's first poetry collection (Berlin, 1923), with the affected title "Verse in Blond," still seems influenced by Bellman, Aristide Bruant, and Peter Hille, yet it surpasses those bohemians (for Josua Kraschunke was no bohemian) in the power of physical sensation.

His first great novel, "One" (Berlin, 1925), represents his artistic peak — marked by an effortless naturalness of invention, character, and style, which, despite its fully liberated romantic form, is astonishing. The novel's theme is the dual love of a boy for his sister and his friend: elevated to the most profoundly human level.

Josua Kraschunke's outward life saw him as a teaching candidate, a porter at the Hamburg docks, a photographer, an officer in Guatemala, a pimp in Buenos Aires, and a naturopath in Appenzell. Josua Kraschunke did not merely play these roles — he became them, entirely absorbed in his drunken immersion in life, where all ethical and philosophical problems, like millstones (hung around others' necks), drowned.

In 1927, Josua Kraschunke strangled his young friend — a millionaire's son from Berlin — with his own hands. At first, rumors circulated of a robbery-murder. He endured the deed with composure and indifference. It left no remorse, no ugly crease on his smooth, boyish face.

Due to a lack of evidence, he was acquitted to frenzied applause from the public (by then, the American judicial system already ruled Germany).

When the verdict was announced, Josua Kraschunke turned, coughed (he suffered from tuberculosis), and spat the yellow, pus-laden phlegm into the audience — where it landed on the violet satin dress of a plump accounting officer.

That dress, now considered a relic, was immediately bought by an antiques dealer for a thousand marks...

Part Four:

The Commissary Wagon

(Erich Reiß Verlag, Berlin, 1914)

Revolution in Montevideo

When I was in an editorial office earlier, a few marks unexpectedly fell into my hand. I used them to buy a travel suitcase because I want to travel to Berlin next Wednesday. After that, I went to Café Fahrig for the afternoon concert.

Just as I sat down, a rushing, enervating, tropical music bursts over me. And an echo resonated within me spontaneously. I clenched my fist and let it bang like a drumbeat on the marble slab. What kind of music! Haven't I marched under its flags before? In the rhythm of a mad obsession? Oh, not obsessed with a woman: sweeter, tempting, tempted!

I checked the program:... National anthems... 878... Uruguay...

Libertad! Libertad orientales!

When I passed my university entrance exam at 17, my cousin, the ship's doctor, invited me to accompany him on a mail steamer to South America.

From Hamburg to Madeira, I lay dirty and seasick in the cabin, begging the grinning steward to pierce me with his carving knife.

Even Madeira is now just a memory to me, like a mountain that looked like an ice cream cone emerging from the waves.

Then the storm subsided, my sickness slowly faded away, and I was allowed to sunbathe and gaze happily at the ocean.

I was happy for three days.

On the fourth day, I began to feel bored by the sky, sea, and sun (and the abundant ship's food). We didn't have any women on board.

I was glad when Montevideo, the capital of Uruguay, rolling hills, swam into view: a little bit like Zurich, when approaching it along Lake Zurich from Chur.

I went ashore with my cousin. As fate would have it, we got separated. I wasn't saddened by it. On the contrary, I felt free; I wanted to "discover" Montevideo on my own terms, and I was confident I would find my way back to the ship.

I checked for my wallet, my revolver, and let myself drift through the glittering streets, which, partly paved, kicked up rainbow-colored dust.

I exchanged some money at a bank. The fact that I only spoke a dozen words of Spanish didn't bother me. I first stopped at a café facing the grand cathedral and slurped down a sorbet-like refreshing drink.

Infatuated as I was, the evening unfolded like a young woman wrapping her dark, soft arms around me; she (the image wouldn't leave me) anchored me to her with her arms like ship ropes.

Streetcars, now financed by A.E.G., Berlin, flew like dragonflies through the city's undergrowth.

I boarded one and felt like I was in an airplane.

Suddenly, I fell back to earth and stumbled straight into a musical hall.

A blonde, greenly-adorned American girl danced with a woolly-haired black man something similar to what is now called the tango. Creoles, packed tightly together, laughed at and shouted about the striking racial mix. Then, a sort of native appeared — a degenerate Winnetou, a piece of painted filth — armed with a shield and a poisoned spear, bellowing war songs.

He had just finished when a frenzied howl and the sound of distant shots threw us onto the street.

Everyone ran amok, laughing, crying, roaring, whistling. No one seemed to know where, how, or why.

Is this a festival? Or some suburban wedding? A bachelor party or something? I thought.

Ten streetcars were already blocked in front of our sideshow, pushed together like a herd of sullen blue elephants.

Just as I was about to ask one of the pointless barkers and runners about the destination and cause of this popular movement, music swelled up the long street like ants being devoured by a lion. We all fell into this funnel like ants to the doodlebug. Lion-like, the music devoured us. Suddenly, I marched in formation, in step and rhythm with the music, revolver drawn. In the rhythm of a mad obsession. Oh, not obsessed with a woman: sweeter, more enticing, seduced! My hands trembled like the paws of a young leopard stalking its first prey. English singing surrounded me, and I sang, inflamed, unchained, those words that, despite my limited Spanish knowledge, I understood too:

Libertad! Libertad orientales!
Freedom! Freedom to the eastern people!
Freedom of the East! Freedom from the East!

My involvement in the revolution in Montevideo did me good; I happened to be with the party that won. It was a relatively mild affair: the next morning, about twenty corpses lay scattered in the square in front of the cathedral, like pepper and salt.

The children went to school and kicked the corpses with their feet.

For today, the Reds (or the Whites? – in Uruguay, political parties name themselves after colors like in England) had won.

Feverish with excitement, exertion, and sleeplessness, I stumbled back onto the ship.

My cousin was also feverish, fearing I had been trampled or shot.

In joyous reunion, he popped open a bottle of cheap sparkling wine. We raised our glasses and clinked them together.

"What are we toasting to?" said my cousin. "To your health! Cheers!"

"Wimp," I said, my eyes burning, "Health! Let's drink to freedom! The freedom of the East! Libertad! Libertad orientales!"

Il Santo Bubi

He sat at the very head of the table, next to the Secretary of Course Administration. His round, rosy, smooth face, large blue childlike eyes, a shaved bald blonde head, and the short black-and-white checkered English trousers made him appear at first glance as a high school student of no more than 18 years old. When I made the mistake of asking him at the table when he intended to take the final exams, his gaze met mine with a kindly superior mockery, and he introduced himself as law trainee Dr. jur. S., not without emphasizing his titles as ridiculous mockeries. He was very seriously ill, although he never coughed and had to display a healthy appearance. He sat at the table surrounded by five young ladies who tenderly pampered him and (perhaps) loved him. Since he enjoyed sweets very much, the ladies took turns offering him their share, and he acknowledged their kindness with always new and graceful jokes, accepting them as a matter of course and entitlement.

He played the piano poorly (and knew it). Nevertheless, he had to sit at the piano every evening after supper and play "In the Night, In the Night, When Love Awakes" – a melody he himself found despicably stupid – just so that the young girls could observe and admire his slender, beautiful, playful hands in motion and caress them in their thoughts. But it soon became clear to me: as he played the piano, he played himself: as an operetta melody. But he played it poorly. You could clearly hear pain and soul behind the off-key notes, notice the intention, and not be put off. On the contrary, you felt touched in a minor key, resonated with, almost tortured by the spectacle of the sick person who was yourself. The law trainee had been taking cures for five years in a row, in all the famous high-altitude resorts for lung patients. Every day, he lay for eight hours, on good days on the veranda, on bad ones in his room. He was allowed to walk for half an hour every day. If he exceeded the half-hour, he would experience shortness of breath, fever, and would crawl into bed for a week.

I once asked him whether I should lend him some books. He shook his head in thanks. They bored him. He didn't even read the newspaper anymore. He saw the sky, he saw the clouds, the mountains, the stars, and sometimes into his own heart. He couldn't, wouldn't, and couldn't "do" more. As he said this, he ironically put it in quotation marks.

Three ladies were his special attendants: a young Swiss teacher from Zurich, a small Bavarian girl from Kempten in the Allgäu, and an Italian. The Italian (as Herr K., a xylographer from Brunswick once called her "The Queen of the Mountains") was considered his lover because she used his private balcony. The three played bridge with him in the evenings (oddly, he always won despite changing sides), boiled his milk on a spirit stove – which was actually forbidden in the guesthouse – (he drank children's milk), sewed buttons for him, washed the cushions from the deck chair with ammonia. When a small sore bothered him on the back of his head recently, he had to submit to the expert treatment of the small

Swiss teacher, who had taken a Samaritan course.

Sometimes the three of them sat by his bed, and he told them strange stories that he claimed to have experienced, very funny stories in a sad tone, which made them laugh a lot. The three called him *Il Santo Bubi* among themselves. The Bavarian girl christened him with the name Bubi. The Italian added *Il Santo*, the Saint, because, she said, he is certainly a saint. He never says, thinks, or speaks anything bad. And never has. He's just sick. But all saints are sick.

Recently, during an examination, the doctor announced to him that he could not stay up here for the time being. He had to go down to the lowlands. As soon as possible. To Heidelberg, to the clinic. For a small, completely insignificant, completely harmless operation. – We all know here what it means when one of ours (we are a people, we sick ones) is sent back down with this reassurance. The operation is the last resort. And helps in one out of a hundred cases. Sometimes people are just sent down so they don't die up here. Because of statistics...

The law trainee knows all this. While his three attendants weep, he smiles. He has ordered a special carriage; the three will accompany him.

I spoke with him about his fate, calmly, matter-of-factly, as one speaks about business. After all, illness is a business.

"I will not die," he sighed, and his young face turned into that of an old man, "I cannot die, believe me..."

The next day, I found two poems in his handwriting placed at my seat at the breakfast table, along with a brief farewell note. He had left with the Italian woman at six in the morning.

The first poem, biting and filled with desperate, despair-inducing humor, reads:

> They must rest and rest and rest again.
> Partly on patented deck chairs,
> You see them writhing in wool and rage,
> Partly they undergo their cure in bed.

> Only at noon do they squat toad-like at the table,
> Devouring food, fat, sweet, and plentiful.
> Suddenly, a woman's laughter rings out, full of torment,
> Like an Aeolian harp, enchantingly strange.

> Perhaps then, one of them turns to leave
> – Next day he is no longer there –
> And his dull existence ends with a Browning.

> Another grows plump and round and red.
> The doctors neigh with pride: Hallelujah!
> He was healed! (... and became a half-idiot.)

Above the second poem is the title:

Ahasver.

You are eternally the sea and flow into the sea,
Spring, cloud, rain – Ahasver.
A fool is he who dreams of fleeting hours,
Wise is he who lets the years slip by.
Thus Bear the eternal burden of the earth
And the crown of thorns with joyful grace.
Strike down your world and yourself,
From the ruins, new flames will rise.
Death is but a word, so that one forgets oneself...
Woe, mortal, that you are immortal!

Il Santo Bubi died during the operation. Or did he not die — the sick Ahasver, the Ahasverian invalid? Does he still live? In Heidelberg? Or somewhere else? Could it be that I am him? Does he still lie for eight hours a day and take a half-hour walk, supported by his companions, so that he does not slip on the ice with his weak bones?

What does it mean to be dead? *Il Santo Bubi* was certainly not a true poet. But how beautiful is that line "Death is but a word, so that one forgets oneself"... So that one forgets oneself...

The Golden Death

Sharp peaks emerged from the clouds like snow-covered fir trees as the two-horse carriage drove into Chur, the distant thunder rumbling darkly down from the mountains. A fresh gust of air swept through the door, which had opened in the fog, and the blue sky wafted towards us like the wallpaper in certain Berlin salons: a little icy, a little delicate. A little out of fashion.

"It's drafty," said Annette.

The coachman cracked his whip. A few children were playing with spinning tops. A maid was out shopping: a yellow basket with boldly curved shapes entwined her bare right arm, and a clean apron was tied over her blue-checked dress.

"She surely works for an architect. He designed her basket."

"Architects don't design baskets. They build houses," said Annette.

A dog, seemingly belonging to the girl, yapped and dashed around our horses like a small gust of wind.

Annette shivered.

"We've only been gone from Arosa for six hours. Do you believe that?"

No, I certainly could not believe it.

"How the anemones bloomed out of the snow? Do you remember? Directly from the snow!"

I remembered.

"The spring sun brought them to bloom so quickly on the snow-fertilized soil that you could almost see them shooting up with your eyes. As if a hot hand reached down from the sky and pulled them out of the earth. Don't you believe that flowers are there for the sun?"

No, I did not believe that. I was unsettled by the image of snow-fertilized soil, didn't find it very poetic, but understandable and forgivable in Annette, the daughter of a country estate owner.

I sat, pale and reserved, in the cushions.

Suddenly I had to laugh.

A cyclist in a gypsy-style blouse crossed our path. His bicycle wobbled, and it looked as though he was riding not on the road but on a tightrope, entertaining a festively excited crowd.

Annette adjusted her seat.

She doesn't like hearing me laugh out loud. She always thinks I'm making fun of her.

"What's the matter?"

I showed her the cyclist.

"Is a cyclist something special? Or something particularly funny?"

"But we haven't seen one in nine months!"

"A cyclist is never ridiculous. Even if you haven't seen one in nine months. You're a child."

She reached for my hands under the fur blanket. My hands, rubbed with glycerin, were stuck in large woolen mittens.

"By the way, why am I saying nine months... and: you're a child! We were in Arosa for nine months. If only you were a child! In nine months, you could have a child, right? Why haven't I had one?"

As we sat in the compartment Chur-Zurich, Annette asked: "Why are you ill?"

She said it very calmly and unconcerned. You can't be mad at her. Although, in nine months, she would have had enough time to ask me why I was sick.

We made a stop in Weesen on Lake Walen, following the orders of the medical officer Dr. Römisch, a small, reddish gentleman from Saxony who had written a noteworthy pamphlet entitled "The Influence of High Mountains on the Intellect."

The Mariahalden Castle Hotel in Weesen is a first-class hotel located on a stone terrace about 30 meters above the lake. It is frequented by many English people and gives a dull impression. When we arrived, a few wooden figures, the mere sight of which made you yawn, were scattered around the garden like croquet mallets; upon closer inspection, you could see them lying in hammocks.

Dinner was the usual fare of first-class hotels: soup, plaice with remoulade sauce, roast beef with various vegetables, and a shapeless dessert. I drank half a bottle of red Vaud wine with it; Annette had mineral water.

We walked down to the lake.

I really like the mountains at night, when you can't see them and can only sense them behind the lights of a distant village.

A soft wind drifted between the chestnut trees. In front of a café, someone sat with their back to the street and ordered a vanilla ice cream in a rasping voice.

"It's quite warm, actually," said Annette.

I clung to her arm. She supported me.

The waves lapped softly, like when someone accidentally leaves the water running at night.

Music from a boat out on the lake swayed towards us. A waltz.

"The waves are dancing a waltz," said Annette.

And indeed, I could hear that too.

"When you hear music, you long for death," said Annette.

She said it casually. But like Indian summer, like autumn veils with invisible spiders on them, the words caught on my face.

She doesn't know how much I would love to die — if only I didn't have to leave her, and if I could find a proper death for myself. Am I supposed to die in bed as an old cavalry officer (old cavalry officer! — I'm 31 years old)? Not to be killed, but to endure death? If only there were a war!

I can't tell Annette that I keep having the same dream: I see death before me as a golden skeleton, glowing against a black background.

Farewell

As Balder left her in the gray field uniform, holding a rose in her hand, with the lance corporal buttons on her collar that had been awarded to him that morning, and his slim step faded away on the stairs, Lillie, horribly confused and feeling scattered, thought of all sorts of nonsensical and ridiculous things. Tennis... how long had it been since she played tennis? Didn't balls always fly through the air, and when you hit them, didn't you hit them into the sun and over the net? Where were her tennis shoes? Right: there was venison roast for dinner tonight. At least, some kind of venison roast. A real venison roast is only eaten for Sunday lunch. So probably venison shoulder or venison stew. With dumplings. Dumplings. The word stuck to her, and she still had it in her mind when tears began to flow down her cheeks.

After she had cried herself out, Lillie went out onto the street. But as soon as she had taken ten steps, she was startled. There... that field-gray soldier hobbling on crutches... wasn't that Balder? She poked the pavement with the tip of her parasol to regain her composure. How foolish! Balder had only just marched off to the field... could she not gather a sensible thought anymore?

She despaired: every wounded person she encountered seemed to be Balder to her. That one with the bandaged head. That dragoon with his arm in a sling.

Saber blows! That such a thing still exists: he got a blow with the saber. Would his arm remain stiff? God in heaven, help: that his arm does not remain stiff. She would do anything, everything for him, to make his arm better again, to bind it every hour, to stay with him every minute. Oh, and then the day when she could shake his hand again first! Balder!

She had to turn and pull the veil over her face because her eyes started to shine silvery and more and more silvery. She must not cry on the street.

When she dared to look up again, a young lieutenant was coming towards her. Completely healthy. Slim like Balder. Walking in a manner that indicated a cavalryman. At least one who spends a lot of time on horseback. He approached, and she recognized that he was an artilleryman. She was glad that she had managed to determine his branch of service. That's not always easy in the field-gray uniform. The lieutenant saluted. She thanked him. Delighted. With a smile in her heart. I know him, she thought, I certainly know him. I just don't remember where from at the moment. But that's so irrelevant. I'm so glad he's not injured. And that he looks so much like Balder.

And as she continued to walk slowly, she saw another soldier again. And another one. And yet another one. And suddenly they were all healthy. Walking without crutches. Not wearing an arm sling. Smoking cigarettes. Some even laughed. And they all looked like Balder.

"Balder!" she said, and her feet found firm ground again.

She stood at Odeonsplatz. A flock of doves fell gently in front of her like a white garland from the Theatine Church.

She rummaged in her small handbag and pulled out a small brown bag. She poured the grains into her hand and leaned slightly down towards the animals.

Over there, from the guard at the castle, came the sound of drumming and command calls.

"Balder!" she said softly to herself.

The Bear

This story begins like a fairy tale by the Brothers Grimm. However, it's not a fairy tale. It's also not a proper story with the necessary conclusion: a rounded story, perhaps, round and transparent like a glass sphere, with a shimmering moral. This story is, in fact (almost), true and took place in the small town where I recently visited. It's nothing but a sad and ridiculous arabesque to the sublime event of war happening outside (far from here, the small town doesn't know where...).

On the day Germany declared war on Russia, the widely renowned magician Francesco Salandrini arrived in the small town, intending to perform his great and secret arts. He could turn water into wine and wine into water. He amazed the country lads, the bewildered young men, and the giggling young ladies of the small towns by pulling coins out of their noses and ears and making them clatter into his shiny black top hat, even though it was quite evident that he himself didn't possess a single one of those silver things. In his aforementioned top hat, which couldn't be denied certain magical powers, he smashed half a dozen raw eggs and, without fire or pan, baked a genuine and tasty pancake.

Herr Salandrini's vehicle, with a few small windows and painted brick red, rolled into the town, rumbling over the Oder Bridge, pulled by a melancholy and elderly horse. In his company were his wife, Bella the snake charmer, the floating virgin, the otherworldly medium, and a person who bore the prosaic name Hugo.

Herr Salandrini, who had never concerned himself with world history and politics in his life (and had no intention to do so, as he was neither willing nor capable of paying taxes), was quite surprised to find the small town in a state of excitement. People were running about, children were shouting and singing, and women looked out of windows with worried expressions.

Nevertheless, Herr Salandrini calmly and composedly directed his carriage to the salt square, where at fairs the dice booths gleamed and carousels merrily spun, to set up his "Interesting Wonder Theater" there.

With the help of the floating virgin, he had just driven the first stake into the ground, wrapped a rope around it, and tied Hugo to it when the corpulent policeman Neumann approached with springy steps. He kindly and firmly informed Herr Salandrini that he could save himself the further trouble of erecting his "Interesting Wonder Theater." War had been declared. The performance scheduled for tonight could not be allowed by the mayor in view of the serious circumstances. People were now concerned with other things than the pancake in the top hat or the mind-reading bear Hugo. No one had the desire to watch such adventurous nonsense now. He should suspend his "Interesting Wonder Theater" until more favorable times. With that, Officer Neumann departed as kindly and firmly as he had arrived.

Herr Salandrini was dumbfounded. The possibility of an international conflict that could deprive him of his livelihood and bread had never remotely crossed his mind. Even Hugo, the mind-reading and fortune-telling bear, had neglected to inform him of it, and he himself seemed unaware of the impending disaster gathering over his head in dark clouds. He sat small and emaciated next to the stake, nibbling on his paw nails like a child and staring ahead with that expression of possessed vacuity that tickles our laughter as much as it arouses our horror.

Herr Salandrini sat down on the wagon shaft and pondered all day what he should do now to make ends meet for himself and his family. His real name was George Krautwickerl and he was from Bamberg. He wouldn't be called up for military service anymore; he was too old for that. Furthermore, he was well aware that at the moment, no one would understand or show interest in his peculiar card tricks and the astonishing talent of the mind-reading bear Hugo.

He pondered for several days. Then he went to the mayor's office and asked for any, even the smallest, job. The floating virgin and the bear remained behind in anxious anticipation. She shared an old crust of bread with him like a sister.

Herr Salandrini returned with the joyful news that he had found employment as a coke worker at the municipal gasworks. That was something, although not much, because the salary Herr Salandrini received barely covered a stomach (the demand for coke workers is not significant even in peacetime). So if the floating virgin was still provided for in case of need – perhaps she could find a job in town as a dishwasher? – what would become of the little, already half-starved bear, their darling, capital, and idol?

The next day, an advertisement appeared in the newspaper: "Noble gentlemen are requested to provide scraps for the fortune-telling bear of the magician Salandrini."

From then on, the bear Hugo fed on the scraps of noble gentlemen, which did not come to him in abundance enough to fully satisfy him. He sat tied to the stake on the salt square, under the supervision of the floating virgin, who mended laundry, and the autumn rain washed his fur. It became late autumn, and the bear was cold. His fur trembled, and his weary eyes looked fearfully up at the leaden sky. The floating virgin cried.

Then Herr Salandrini had a good idea. After all, he was a coke worker at the gasworks. He asked the city council for permission to house the bear in an empty warm room of the gasworks, next to the large ovens. The council, long convinced of the harmless nature of the half-starved and weak little bear, granted permission, and the bear now sat behind a wooden barred door, looking with sad eyes into the fiery glow of the ovens. Occasionally, the children of the gasworks inspector visited him and brought him a piece of war bread or kitchen scraps. He ate everything that was stuffed between his teeth.

But one morning, he was found dead behind the bars, and the pink light of the ovens danced over his dark brown sparse fur.

Herr Salandrini was shaken, but as a coke worker, he had no time for long meditations. The floating virgin threw herself screaming over the dead bear, and the whole scene looked like a painting by Piloty.

It was not determined whether the bear succumbed to gas poisoning or starvation.

Attorney K. bought the bear skin, including the head, from Herr Salandrini. Herr K. is about to leave the city and start a new practice in Z. He will nail the skin of the fortune-telling bear Hugo to the wall in his study, and when he has friends over, he will point to the skin with a grand gesture, carelessly shake off his cigar ash, and begin to talk distractedly:

"When I was still hunting bears in the Black Mountains..."

The Wealthy Young Man

It's Sunday afternoon. Somewhere, there's a war going on. Outside, a cold, blue sky hangs overhead. The winter sun divides the opposing house into two almost identical halves, one grayish-yellow and the other bright golden. The rust-brown elongated window crosses stand steep and stiff like crucifixes. Now, one of them – on the third floor – is being torn apart. A man with a thick, bald head and a dirty green loden jacket pushes himself out and looks onto the street. A woman dressed in black, holding a dust cloth in her right hand, leans over him. Then they both disappear, and the white curtain slowly closes.

I lie on the sofa, burying my head in the soft, warm velvet cushion. Somewhere, there's a war going on. I don't need to think, feel, or act. Without effort, I dream almost dreamlessly. No memories of the past, no will for future actions. No unconscious desire to be myself. Like a torch extinguished in the sand, I am snuffed out in the void of space. I close my eyes. The light forces its way through the windows. It dissolves all shapes in the room and consumes them: the large cupboard, the pictures on the wall, the armchairs; now it gropes its way past the mirror, now it reaches for the brass door handle. The light is like a body. Like a body from which all things emerge. Like a creator. It caresses the white tiled stove. And the stove is there. I feel the breath of light on the white-blue tiles. The light doesn't reach me. I curl up and squint through my eyelids. As another, hostile being, I lie outside the light in a tight, comfortable darkness like in a cradle that rocks itself... slowly... back and forth... back... and forth. The clock strikes. Once. I see how the dull, beautiful sound rolls into the luminous room... how it trembles afterwards... restlessly... softly... softly weeping, like a child who has lost its way. How the rays chase after it, carrying it on silver-golden wings, letting it fall and lifting it again. I don't know what time it is, I never do. I set the clock wrong. I love life between times. A clock that punctually and reliably strikes the hours in my rooms would annoy and be unbearable to me, a pitiful admonisher. I don't even have a tear-off calendar. The days are so indifferent to me, the first and the sixth and tenth. What are they for? Certainty is an indecent virtue; not even death is entitled to it.

I stretch and roll around. It's half past. Somehow, half. Half past three or half past four. And then the clock goes on for two or three more hours and so many minutes and so many seconds ahead or behind. How beautiful, how foolishly beautiful, to have no desires, no hopes, no rushing, no forced laughter of faith anymore. Just a fluttering and drifting on dark waves, sometimes on wave peaks, sometimes in wave valleys.

The reflection of a window crawls annoyingly over my face.

I wake up. What should I do later? Should I go to the café? I wanted to speak with the manager. The buffet waitress had a dirty apron on yesterday. She's pretty though. How abstract things inherently lack cleanliness. How we always have to wash them first.

Or should I get on the tram – the first one I see – and sit by the window – I haven't done that in a long time – and gaze at a house, a patch of meadow, a chimney, a backyard. And if a picture or sound pleases me, I get off at the next station and search for that spot I liked, in its dreamless, perhaps lost twilight that no one can feel but me, who is akin to it. This searching is wonderfully thrilling, enticing, arousing. You never know if you'll find the place as you remember it. Meanwhile, the mirage may have changed... or the window in that house where a child or a girl or a mother looked out from may have closed... or the veteran with his peg leg, his bent gramophone, and dirty medals may have long since let his creaky instrument and screeching voice echo in another courtyard. I enjoy searching for purposeless memories. And is any other happiness given to us but to collect words and images?

Between two suburban train stations, about in the middle, stands a stunted pine in the sand by the railroad embankment, not far from a new building. I saw it for the first time when a thunderstorm hung overhead. I went to it in pouring rain. I stroked its rough brown bark, embraced it, and let it scratch my forehead until it bled. As if I were its blood brother. I visited it again and again. It's most beautiful when a jet-black wall of clouds stands in the bright sunny sky or in winter, when fresh snow has fallen.

The bell rings. Sharply. Twice. What is it? – ..., the dispatcher... "Coming tonight. Selma."

How can one have an affair named Selma? The name hurts. She herself does too. It smells so terribly of woolen underwear and an unventilated room, which is at once kitchen, living room, and workshop, where Mother fries the potatoes, the unwashed little ones romp around, and Father, a furrier and hatmaker, stores the furs and sews hat brims.

In between, Selma. There's spinsterhood and smooth malice in this cursed name at the same time. I named her Fritzi. I baptize all girls. It's an entertaining business and very rewarding for a layman in psychology. She loves me very much. The next morning, I always have lung and rib pains. I don't love her. I just want my friends to envy me for the beautiful girl. I'm only interested in girls if I can be seen with them and be seen with them. I'm good to her. I can't do without her soothing tenderness. What else do I have? I, who can hardly love myself and others not at all? Maybe I could kill people if I went to war. But I have flat feet, varicose veins, an enlarged heart (my heart is so vast that the world disappears in it like a wrinkled nut), lung defects, and a bilateral hernia.

My Brother Said

Do you know that none of the wounded returning from the front want to sing anymore? We have quite a number of lightly wounded who are already back on garrison duty in the company, but when we sing "Three Lilies" or "Homeland, O Homeland, I must leave you..." they fall silent and have big eyes. The two Rebers

– you know them, right? The sons of Headmaster Reber – are already in the field... in Galicia or Poland... and have eaten nothing but raw turnips for five days... Hans arrived in Belgium on the 28th of October. Barely unloaded, they had to storm at Dixmuiden. Three times in 36 hours. Dixmuiden boiled like the cauldron in Goethe's "Faust"... Hans is wounded... shot in the belly... He's already back and lying in the hospital... I visited him yesterday... There were twelve of them in the room, and one sat on the edge of the bed playing the harmonica. He was a Pole, and he played a melancholy tune. Some were reading the newspaper, and one whose head was completely bandaged was being fed warm milk through a glass tube by the nurse. He smiled gratefully... Hans' appearance has changed so much that I hardly recognized him and stared at him in shock. "Good day, Hans." "Good day, Jochen." "How are you?" "So-so." His face was pale blue, glassy, almost like the white of a boiled lapwing's egg. His eyes burned with a strange fire, and a small blonde beard hung in fringes around his face... Once in Berlin, I saw a Bulgarian officer who had been through both Balkan wars. I didn't know why he had such dead white eyes. Now I know... Hans said, "I have experienced a lot." At the word "experienced," he paused, thought, and said, "One should actually say: died, instead of experienced... And I was only out there for two days." He turned to the wall. "When we fixed bayonets with feverish hands... we were in the fire for the first time... we charged against English core troops like devils... But nobody shouted "hurrah"... Can you believe that?... The shrapnel burst like sacks of flour... the grenades whistled as if millions of violins were playing the highest F sharp... the machine guns clattered like excessively loud hens... and one of us screamed, screamed his whole heart out: "Mother!" And like an echo, this scream rolled along our ranks... Mother!... Mother!... Mother!... Under this battle cry, getting wilder and fiercer, we ran towards the enemy positions... And we took them... I don't know how long I ran like that... years must have passed... my legs pounded like a machine... Suddenly, I got hit in the belly, still shouted "you damn dog" and fell down... I woke up on a stretcher, saw a smoke-blackened village, and a Belgian priest in a cassock hanging from a tree... Then I fell asleep again... And again, after many years, I woke up here... I must have gotten so old... Give my regards to Lilly, she should visit me if her parents allow it... What a pity that we won't be able to get married, and that I won't have a child with her." Then he turned away from the wall again, shook my hand, and said, "Farewell." I buckled his belt, the Pole started playing his harmonica again, and I left as quietly as I could with my army boots. Hans isn't older than me. Seventeen years. He will die. What he said made me very pensive, especially that he would like to have a child. But I understand it. Oh, how much I understand it. After all, this is my last leave here. Next week, I have to go back out. To East Prussia. Or to Arras. As fate dictates. Then say hello to Ruth for me and tell her what Hans told me about Lilly.

The Corporal

It was in the latter half of August 1914 when Corporal Georges Bobin of the 3rd French Line Regiment was brought in as a prisoner.

He looked immaculate: smart, neat, shaved, with strawberry-red pants and a blue coat of impeccable cut.

He introduced himself to the hussar officer interrogating him with a courteous smile: as Monsieur Georges Bobin of the 3rd French Line Regiment, originally from here and there... from the South, of course... by profession a language teacher. He knew the Germans. Oh la la. As if he would not know the Germans. He had spent three years in a row in Germany before the outbreak of the war. A long time. Three years. Like not seeing the Mediterranean Sea for three years. And not smelling Marseille, this romantic dump. Because: there are cities you see. Florence, for example. And cities you hear. Berlin, for example. And cities you smell. Marseille belongs to the latter. And since the sense of smell goes hand in hand with the sense of taste, if the bold metaphor is allowed, you eat as well and cheaply in Marseille as nowhere else in the world. For a few sous, for next to nothing, oysters and fish in daring preparation, steamed, fried, baked, and sauced, as even the most imaginative palate of the most extravagant epicure cannot imagine. In Germany, where he had last worked at the secondary school in a small Brandenburg town, he always had to eat cabbage rolls and Königsberg meatballs. Well: be that as it may. He had gotten used to it. He found especially the first-mentioned dish, reheated for supper, quite appetizing and tasty. He couldn't deny a certain grace to the landscape where the small town lay. A bit sober. A bit Prussian. But pleasantly animated by the steamers and barges of the navigable Oder and gently softened by the tenderest sunsets. And vineyards rose on the eastern shore: planted with red and yellow wine. And if you blended the red wine a little with Italian, you would get the finest Bordeaux. Well: he was exaggerating. Certainly. But a good Crossen wine is better than a bad Bordeaux. Pardon: they probably didn't want to know all this from him.

Yes: what battles had he been in? Actually, none at all. This was his first battle, in which he had been captured. He had fired fifty rounds, then had to advance, and his company had come under flanking fire. Voilà.

By the way: he had said too much. Or rather, too little. He had actually been in another battle. A very peculiar battle. Perhaps the most peculiar of the whole war.

The regiment was on the march. They were approaching the enemy zone. A village suddenly lay before them. An unremarkable and highly indifferent village, like a long loaf of bread shoved into the oven of a narrow valley.

Was the village occupied by the enemy?

Two trains with patrols at the front were sent out to reconnoiter the village. One train under the command of Corporal Georges Bobin came from the left, the other from the right height. The village was to be caught like a pair of pliers.

Creeping and peering, Corporal Bobin with his patrol came close to the first house. He was perhaps twenty steps away when suddenly shots rang out.

Pfff... a bullet whizzed past his nose.

A very uncomfortable situation indeed. But onward. Take cover.

Where were the shots coming from? He questioned his men. They all said: from the house up ahead.

So, the house must be occupied by the enemy.

He crawled five steps closer.

Pfff... new shots... a faint cry... one of his men was wounded in the thigh... blood ran into his trousers... He sent him back to the regiment. The rest became restless and kept firing incessantly into the house.

No window in the house was intact anymore.

Another casualty... Another one... The first fatality... What should he do?

It was impossible to storm the heavily fortified house head-on.

He gave the order for a cautious retreat.

Crawling and firing, they withdrew.

As they reached the exit of the village, they saw the second column on the other side also retreating with gunfire and crawling.

And now he knew – and as he paled, he burst into a sick and spasmodic laughter: the two columns had been firing at each other!

Between the houses and through the houses.

But the gunfire had not only put the regiment, but the entire division, which also had artillery, on edge.

Throughout the afternoon and evening, the valleys and villages were still echoing with gunfire.

The artillerymen, who were jealous that the infantry had "their battle," drew their revolvers and began firing as well.

And since there were no enemies to shoot, they fired at anything alive that crossed their path in the village streets.

All the chickens, ducks, cows, pigs, cats, dogs, rabbits, and doves fell victim to their combat frenzy.

The trenches were full of torn and whimpering animals. Horses roared like tigers. A dead cat hung over a fence like Punch from a puppet show after the performance. A mother pig bled to death in the middle of the street, and three living piglets squealed as they suckled on her dead breasts.

Some geese had died of fright and lay in the grass without gunshot wounds. –

So the war started a bit strangely for us, said Corporal Georges Bobin of the 3rd French Line Regiment, and I fear it will end just as strangely for us...

In the Russian Camp

Here, you feel more of the war in one day than in Munich in five months. No sooner had I arrived in C.(rossen) than I saw a procession of about three hundred

Russian prisoners, escorted by militiamen with fixed (captured French) bayonets, marching slowly through the streets to their place of work. Once they gained a foothold. They didn't kick their legs like our soldiers, but stamped the ground with bent knees. Like horses at a restrained trot. An impractical and certainly very tiring way to march.

For the most part, they were excellently equipped with high black Russian boots and thick, clay-colored coats. A few wore wooden clogs and had fashioned fantastic uniforms from overturned cloths. Some looked like monks or devout pilgrims, marching with suffering faces as if to the melody of an inaudible funeral march. One in a saffron-yellow cloak shone, like their idol and the incarnation of their imprisoned longing, far ahead of the brown column. At the end crawled small, senile-looking fellows with yellow crumpled masks: Kyrgyz and Mongolians from the Siberian regiments. I didn't see any Cossacks. Not even later during my visit to the camp. There are surely some among them, but they've made themselves unrecognizable. When you ask about Cossacks, they think you want to blame them for the Cossack atrocities in East Prussia and impale or hang them. A lean, degenerated fellow in a black fur hat, whom I addressed as a Cossack, raised both hands against me in an imploring manner like a saint in early medieval church windows and said: "Oh, oh, not Cossack, not Cossack."

The wooden barracks where the Russians live are tall, airy, and well-ventilated. Some barracks are half-buried in the ground. The sleeping places or beds are stacked three high: the prisoners sleep on straw mattresses and receive firm wool blankets as cover. Each barracks is heated by a large stove. In some barracks, there are still small cooking stoves where people can warm up their food or make tea. The wooden tables they eat and work on can be transformed into large, zinc-lined washbasins through clever mechanisms (folding the tabletop).

I arrived just as lunch was being served in the kitchen. A chef from a large Berlin hotel is the head chef; he supervises two dozen Russian cooks. Today's meal was rice meat, meaning beef in a thick rice soup. Ten hundredweight of meat was used for that.

Each man receives one liter, those who worked hard in the morning receive one and a half liters. Additionally, each person receives one pound (baked in the city and also enjoyed by the locals) "Russian bread" – rye bread with potato flour.

In the main barracks, the Russian choir, led by a captured music director from Petersburg, sang us some Flemish songs. First, the bell song. The lead singer carries the melody. Everyone else sings in bass like bells. Lastly, they sang the melancholic song of their memories of home:

> Tell me, where are you, beloved homeland?
> Where the stars are, you are safe.
> Girl, dear girl, I must ride
> Into the distance and the darkness.
>
> When golden eyes gaze down from the night sky,
> Think of me, who rode into foreign lands.

All clouds that blow from the west
Carry my longing with them.

A very young Russian, an infantryman from an Odessa corps captured near Suwalki, stood leaning against the wall, by himself, resting his head in his hand, closing his eyes and softly reciting the verses. His lips trembled, and his eyelashes quivered. Some who lazily lay on their beds held their breath and didn't know where to look.

The most peculiar inhabitant of the camp and worthy of being mentioned by name was the dog Samuel. He was "captured" (a kind of terrier with a slight hint of dachshund) by the Osterode Landsturm battalion in the Battle of Tannenberg. Since they couldn't communicate with him, they returned him to the Russians who interned him in camp C. But even the Russians didn't know what to do with him; he didn't understand Russian or Polish. Until a Jew, a merchant from Lodz, had the idea to speak to him in Yiddish. The dog jumped up, half-crazed with joy at being understood, towards his new friend, wagging his tail, and his brown eyes shone like those of a happy child. The dog must have belonged to an old Jewish family and probably had defected to the Germans with several Jews at Tannenberg. The Russians mockingly called him Samuel. He didn't get along with any orthodox Russians, bravely barking at them and refusing even the most tempting morsels from them.

The Jewish merchant and the other Russian Jews in the camp grew very fond of him. Sometimes they thought: if only all Jews showed as much courage against the Russians as this dog. One could sense that this dog hated the Russians with all his soul. And since he was an animal, he didn't restrain his hatred, openly displaying it and biting the Russians in their tall boots. Because on top of everything, he stole their meat rations (which he didn't eat, but buried), a strong dislike for him arose among the Russians. And since they couldn't take action against the real Jews (after all, they weren't in Russia), they chose the Jewish dog as the victim of a pogrom. On a Sabbath, the Jews found him beaten to death behind the latrine. They were not animals but human beings, and moreover, a helpless minority. What good would it do to bark at the Russians when they couldn't bite them? They dug a grave for the dog Samuel, and a captive rabbi delivered the eulogy for him as if he had been one of theirs and a true Jew.

Flower Day in Northern France

We from... the Landsturm Battalion are assigned to the umpteenth logistics inspection and currently have a small town in Northern France as our garrison. We burn the candle at both ends standing guard day and night: on the railway embankments, in front of the hospital, under the bridges. From six in the evening until ten in the morning, there is also a guard in front of the brothel. Every morning at half past nine, the girls are examined and checked by our regimental doctor.

There are nine of them in total. Eight are French and one is German. The German is a petite blonde from Hamburg. When people from our group visit the brothel, she keeps her head down and looks to escape with her eyes. Under no circumstances would she sell herself to a German. When we see her, we blush. To avoid the painful situation, we crack silly and loud jokes and laugh, sounding like gramophones. Or someone sits down at the piano and plays, "I like the dark-skinned girls so much." Then she goes out and cries. After all, she's blonde. The townspeople, municipal secretaries, small tax officials, and well-to-do merchants obviously prefer the German girl. They see her humiliated in the eyes of their own compatriots and revel in her suffering. Madame is delighted with her because she earns the most money. "Where is the German cow?" shout the tax officials, and one after the other wants to kick her for their money's worth. I spoke to her recently. Her name is Leni. She wants to slit her wrists. She can't bear this bestial life anymore. I thought about how to help her. She had to get out of the brothel. But Madame will resist fiercely. We would have to offer her money, a lot of money. I spoke to the Major, and he gladly gave permission for a collection in her favor within our battalion. He donated ten marks first. And after him, all the officers and all the dignified, bearded Landsturm men, mostly respectable family men, followed suit. No one, not even the poorest, excluded themselves. So we bought Leni back from Madame for the price of 1200 francs, dressed her from head to toe in new clothes, and sent her back to Aachen with the next hospital train that was returning. She could hardly believe her luck. She wanted to individually shake hands with all of us and in her haste, pin a colorful paper flower to the coat of anyone she could reach.

The Black Flag

A man left behind sat in the café, ordered an eggnog, and said: I have an inhuman longing to die. Every field post letter I receive from outside awakens in me the conscience of a painful shame because I'm still alive. What am I still talking about? What am I still writing about? The scattering sand of shrapnel dries up every ink. And every tear. Sometimes, in the small quiet room in the suburbs, three flights up, in the evening when the honking of a cheerful car, the screeching of a deflowered cat, or the clattering hoof of a saddened horse noise through the closed shutters,I cry out for a release from a life that is only valuable to me because it can be thrown away. Like a half-smoked cigarette. (I don't have enough for a cigar.) What are all the sufferings of unhappy love compared to the agonizing desire for death? I could shoot myself behind the scenes at home — but I don't struggle with death, I don't bleed to death, I wouldn't vie for its love. And I couldn't let myself be seen with my beautiful lover either. (What's the point of loving if other people don't see that you're loved?) I would have bought my death here at home like a dirty streetwalker. At the price of my revolver. (A good Browning costs 80 marks. So I would pay considerably more for the value of the girl.) I want to court death. Fräulein Death. She must learn to love me. I will have to flatter her. Give her gifts. Precious gifts. For example, a pretty poem that I would still write. Or a loyal friend whom I honor like no other person. (But I love the horses much more than people. Even the turtles.) Or I must sacrifice my mother to her. A woman always prefers that you sacrifice a woman to her. And what woman does she hate more than the mother of the beloved? (Because she didn't also get to give birth to him herself.)

I will sit in a farmhouse on the Marne, cheerful with some comrades. Suddenly a grenade falls through the roof. All my comrades are dead on the spot. Richard has no head anymore, and from Hagen, you only see a soiled uniform jacket. But I myself remained alive. Alone: whole in all limbs. My relatives, to whom I calmly report the incident on a field postcard, cheer and pass the anecdote on to the newspaper. I am unhappy. I feel that I am still rejected. That I have not completely unveiled my heart. They still don't believe me. They mistrust my love.

Now I'll try mockery. I mock the beloved: cheeky, bitter, shameless. I go to the most dangerous posts. Avoid cover when patrolling. I dismount. The bullets whizz around me. I stand like an Indian at the stake and no arrow hits me. I stick my head above the trench. Like holding a pumpkin on a stick as a target, for fun and pastime. The enemy is just bored. They don't shoot at all.

But I will find a way to force death to reciprocate. And if I have to gallop alone against a whole battery. (The French will think I'm a delegate and will stop firing.)

I can't stand it at home anymore. If the war lasts much longer, those left behind won't know what to do with their desire for death in the field. They will become megalomaniac and believe they are immortal. They only know death from the newspapers. A suicide epidemic will break out. People will beat each other to death for dessert.

A small hunched man with red hair and horn-rimmed glasses, stirring nuts in a bowl, jumped up like a frog from his seat and screeched: so the black flag will wave over us and the sky will burst dark from night.

Millions and millions of volunteers, men, women, elders, children will follow the rustle of the black banner. In love like dancers before their first waltz, and strict and holy like priests of the Transfiguration.

The Stamp on the Field Postcard

Captain R. reluctantly parted from his beautiful young wife, whom he had married a year ago and who, at 18 years old, was still a child. He harbored those paternal feelings towards her that come so easily to a man over 35. How would he take care of her from afar? She was perpetually in need of his care. And a helpless little girl without his guiding glances, gestures, and words, with which he lovingly, or sternly, directed or admonished her. Should he entrust her to her parents, Dr. P., the dentist, and his wife, for the duration of the war? He was glad that he had rescued her from their soul-plumbing apparatus and pinchers and forceps. So he left her in the care of an older aunt, who had poor hearing but played the piano excellently and persistently. He hoped that Annette (that was the beautiful young wife's name) would not be impervious to the consolations of music and would overcome the separation more easily with its gracious help. Now Chopin is not the right music to cheer someone up. But what choice did the older maiden have but to play Chopin? Since she had been playing him and only him for 43 years? She played Chopin, and Annette listened, sighing and knitting.

For supper, a distant cousin of hers, a young postal clerk, appeared every Wednesday and Saturday, either declared indispensable or belonging to the un-trained Landsturm. He told her about his stamp collection, and she enjoyed laughing with him. One Wednesday evening, he kissed her in the corridor. And the following Saturday, their lips could hardly part. They were so fused together.

Captain R. went to Namur and Charleroi. He was seriously wounded in the street fighting and taken to the hospital in Liège. Here he lay, feverishly dreaming of his young, beautiful wife, who was still a child. Should he have someone write to her about his condition? An unprecedented jealousy made him burn more intensely, as he felt his wife blooming and healthy while he felt crippled and maimed for all time. He dictated a field postcard to the nurse: "Dear Annette, I am lightly wounded in the Liège hospital, you don't need to worry. With a faithful embrace from your Gerd." But he affixed a Belgian stamp to the field postcard. During their engagement days, they used to hide their secret love confessions under the stamp in tiny writing.

The field postcard arrived one Saturday evening. "Oh," said Annette regretfully, "he is lightly wounded. But he's okay." "Show me the stamp," said the postal clerk. "Do you want it for your collection?" asked Annette, beginning to carefully remove it. She gasped softly as she read: "If you feel driven to remove the stamp as a memory of our engagement, then I know that you still love me as before, and that you are strong enough to hear even the most horrific things and bear them with a holy heart: my eyes are blinded, my feet torn apart by a grenade. I am only a stump now. Be strong. Your Gerd loves you as fiercely as ever."

Annette clutched her chest. She wanted to scream. The postal clerk had turned pale. In the next room, the aunt was playing a Chopin waltz. Like two shot birds, Annette's eyes collapsed lifelessly into themselves.

The Young Polish Shooter

(For Ira)

I received a card from the hospital inspectorate asking if I would visit a severely wounded Polish junior rifleman who had been admitted three days earlier. He was refusing to eat. He still believed he was in enemy territory. He's delirious. Since no one speaks Polish, it was impossible to communicate with him.

I set out on my way.

He lay in a single room. On his bedside table was a small artificial Christmas tree adorned with tiny red lights. It was the second Sunday of Advent.

"Who's there?" he said in Polish, curling his left hand on the bedspread like a revolver pointed towards me.

"A good friend," I replied in Polish.

"That's not the password," he said suspiciously, "but at least you speak Polish. The password is Warsaw. Who are you?" Now he looked at me. "You smile so peacefully. You're not Russian. You speak Polish. Are you Death? Death speaks Polish. Sir, if I may introduce myself so you don't mistake me: Konstantin Barzynski, Professor of Natural History in Tarnopol. 31 years old. Who would believe that the world is only 31 years old? But it is so. Oh, the little girls from Tarnopol! From the suburbs. They always send me cards with blonde or black girl's heads and a verse underneath:

> Oh, please be nice and be so good,
> You know how love works.

I am a true sinner. I have bad eyes. Like hunger. And hunger has eyes like a Ruthenian pope. In July, I was still in Split. I can't say that people love the Austrians in Dalmatia.

In Split at the hotel, there was a young married couple. Delightful. Delightfully naive. Once I met them in the evening at the beach. "Schani," she said, "be careful of the snakes. Don't accidentally step on a viper." "My dear sir and madam," I said, "there are no snakes on the seashore. You can rely on me. I teach natural history in Tarnopol."

When I came home, I found a little child on my bed. I thought I had suddenly had a child... from the little girls of Tarnopol... but it was the innkeeper's child. Dalmatian women like to gossip and meanwhile leave their children wherever it suits them. But my sir, the worst is yet to come. Have you ever taken digitalis? I would like to strangle every single Russian with my own hands, and Nikolayevich before them. The Russians do not recognize the Polish young shooters as soldiers. They had captured several of ours. We followed their retreat route. Although I am a professor of natural history and can define the laws of nature — I went mad. I went so mad that I didn't care when someone fell next to me... shot in the belly... and screamed like a pig. Sir... the trees along the streets were decorated like Christmas trees... with Polish young shooters. Six were always hanging from one tree. Neatly arranged. I threw my head around and roared louder than a field howitzer. And then I climbed up the first tree and cut off the first six. They shouldn't hang in the air and dry like smoked meat. They should have their honest Catholic burial. The skin hung in tatters from my hands. But I dug a grave with the sweat of my brow, for three hours, it was so deep that, by my calculation, 120 men could fit in it. I climbed the next tree. And cut off six. They fell like ripe pears from the tree. Then I climbed the third, then the fourth tree. By the fifth, I felt that I couldn't go on anymore. That I was about to hang myself. That was also the end of the song. As you see me here: hanging from a tree, with five other Polish young shooters. I sway in the wind. My bones clatter together. C-sharp minor. The cursed peasants shoot pellets at me. I have a bullet in my lung, but it doesn't matter. When I run out of saliva, I want to spit my last drop of blood in their faces...

The Revolutionary

Anna Emeljanova is the daughter of a wealthy Russian farmer. What one calls a wealthy Russian farmer: he owns a few pigs, a few cows, a small house. And the small house is a bit less dirty than the others. In the parlor a grey parrot that looks like a raven sits on some chair arm. It can only say two words: "Anna" and "Nitschewo." When it calls "Anna," the old farmer goes outside, shields his eyes, and looks into the empty air until his eyes burn.

Anna Emeljanova's hometown stands right on the Prussian-Russian border. From the border barrier, where the main road runs from one country to the other, one can see the tip of its church tower. And whoever only sees the top of their homeland's church steeple with their eyes: what do they see with their hearts!

How often Anna Emeljanovwa stood at the barrier and looked over to her homeland with the infinite longing of a Russian banished from Russia due to revolutionary activities, who can only gaze over the border but never cross it again. Certainly, one can re-enter Russia with a fake passport, but someone as well known to the Russian political police of 1905 as Anna Emeljanova can only dare under special circumstances, if they don't want to be "lost for the cause." And Anna Emeljanova will only sacrifice herself "for the cause" if it benefits "the cause."

I met Anna Emeljanova two years ago in Geneva in a café garden. We dreamed across the lake, let the veil of Mont Blanc blow over our foreheads, and turned our gaze, bored with the brown monotony of Salève, away: towards the violet water, towards the bright blue shimmering swans on the shore that we stroked in our minds. Swans can only be stroked in thoughts. In reality, they bite and are very malicious.

"You see," Anna Emeljanova suddenly said – we had thought the same – "Russia is such a swan for us revolutionaries..."

And she made a tender gesture through the air.

Anna Emeljanova is married.

I also met her husband: a gentle, black-bearded, and as it was said, very talented painter.

Anna Emeljanova has no children. And yet, she has a wonderfully maternal heart like many Russian revolutionaries. For hours, she plays with dirty children in crude and unclean alleys and visits her parents' apartment.

Anna Emeljanova is not allowed to have children. "The cause" does not allow it. She must not attach herself to any worldly happiness.

Her husband is, of course, also a revolutionary. They always have to wait for "the cause" to suddenly call them. And then they must be ready. Immediately. Without delay. They own only the absolute essentials. A small furnished apartment. Two rooms. Poorly and ascetically furnished. Even books are only the most necessary. Such as: Bakunin, Tolstoy. A crate of cigarettes. A samovar. And a plate of sweet nut cakes.

"Russia is so vast," Anna Emeljanova always said, "how can one not love it?"

And her thoughts probably wandered to the barrier on the main road at the Prussian-Russian border, where she sometimes shook her old father's hand and could see the tip of the church tower of her homeland.

I hadn't heard from Anna Emeljanova for a long time. Then recently, a card came from Geneva. On it were only these words: "The cause is calling. Farewell. Anna Emeljanova."

As one reads in Russian newspapers, tea evenings are held in Russian hospitals. There is singing, music, recitations, and even some laughter and fun among the lightly wounded. The nurses are instructed to be very attentive to the intellectual needs of the people. The nurses and the wounded talk a lot and very quietly with each other – so quietly often that it cannot be heard at the next bed – and I believe that in one of these nurses... Anna Emeljanova can be recognized.

The Widow Pulko

(For Hanns Schmidt)

I'm well acquainted, not to say friends, with Widow Pulko. She lives in Wismar, by the harbor, not far from that little smoky tavern called "König Christian" or something similar, where you can get a grog and a mulled wine for 30 pfennigs, like nowhere else in the world: a wine that truly glows and makes one glow – a mulled wine that (if such an expression weren't a bit out of place) is top-notch.

It's been a few weeks since I was in Wismar again. Wismar is the epitome of a blonde and blue-eyed Nordic city. The brick Gothic of the churches and old houses makes it heavy, defiant, and massive. A city that knows what it wants and only wants what it can have. An old city, full of winding streets where brown buildings, like the Gothic old school, the erratic block of St. George's Church, or the Renaissance-styled Fürstenhof, attack one like stone dogs. A "limited" city, whose stiff and cold severity is pleasantly softened by excellent warm grogs that rise lightly and airy like children's balloons into one's head. The people and the churches don't reach into the sky: the towers are blunt. The blunt towers and the blunt people give the city a measured attitude and compact unity.

I was sitting with my friend Hanns Schmidt, who had just returned from the East, from Iwangorod, at the "Old Swedes" having a beer. We looked out through the windows onto the market square. A few soldiers stood wide-legged in front of the guardhouse. A couple strolled seriously by the Creation Fountain. Elderly gentlemen cautiously examined the weather from slightly open windows. Children disappeared around a corner, playing with hurried legs. Women, dressed in grey, diagonally crossed the square with large baskets.

A muffled sound like very distant thunder made the air gently vibrate.

"They're doing target practice again in Swinemünde or Kiel or out at sea," said Hanns. Then he laughed. He laughed like a dove. Cooing. I always liked him for his laughter at school. "The old ladies of Wismar always think it's the Russians shooting with their so-called Baltic Fleet out there. And they think they're aiming at the Wismar Water Tower..."

We drank to all the old aunts' well-being, to reassure them.

Twilight hung like a spider between the many delicately rigged brigs and schooners that were mounted on the ceiling to decorate the pub.

"You know," I said, "Hanns: it's time to ask Widow Pulko about the general world situation. What do you think?"

And we crept through the twilight alleys to Widow Pulko, who lives down by the harbor in a small one-story house, in a damp and cold room towards the back – Widow Pulko, with whom I am well acquainted, who, with all her kindness and goodness, tirelessly prophesies a long life, fame, honor, an unexpected inheritance, a successful journey across the great waters, a millionaire marriage with the daughter of a Hungarian magnate (American millionairesses seem to have fallen out of favor with fortune tellers since the war...) and other such joyful things.

Her prophecies have, in contrast to those of big-city representatives of the secret arts, the great advantage of being inexpensive. They cost on average only 50 pfennigs, and yet are no less true than the predictions at 5, 10, and 20 marks – prices typically paid to fortune-telling "ladies of society" in Berlin.

Widow Pulko has various methods. One cannot deny a certain richness of her mental and manual gifts. She reads the future from coffee grounds. She reads the past from carefully piled sand or salt mounds. She knows the Gypsy alphabet. She masters the German, Spanish, and French art of cards. She owns a Polish dream book. She has unlocked the secrets of the 13th book of Moses.

As we entered Widow Pulko's place, she was sitting under the oil lamp and studying the "Baltic Messenger."

"Well, Widow Pulko, here I am again," I greeted politely, "and I'd like to consult you once more."

With that, I placed a coin on the table.

"Oh my, young sir, what is it this time? Do you have lovesickness? Should I consult the cards?"

"No, Widow Pulko, this time it's not lovesickness. You don't need to consult your cards either. It's about the war..."

"And what do you want to know about the war?"

"When will the war end, Widow Pulko? Do you know that?"

Widow Pulko shook her pelican head.

"I know, young sir, I know. But you mustn't reveal it to anyone..."

She fetched a slate from the cupboard, placed it in front of her on the table, and started writing numbers. Then she showed me the numbers. And the numbers looked like this:

$$
\begin{array}{r}
1870 \\
+ 1871 \\
\hline
3741
\end{array}
$$

37 | 41
3+7 | 4+1=10.5
1914
1915

$$
\begin{array}{r}
\hline
3829
\end{array}
$$

38 | 29
3+8 | 2+9=11.11

"A simple addition. The holy Arabic addition," said Widow Pulko. "On the tenth of the fifth month, meaning May 10, 1871, peace was concluded between Germany and France."

Hanns and I were not knowledgeable about historical dates, so we took Widow Pulko's word for it.

"Using the sacred Arabic addition, the eleventh of November emerges as the peace date for 1915," Widow Pulko continued instructively.

I left a shiny two-mark coin for Widow Pulko. (Paper money is still not considered valid by fortune-tellers...)

On the way home, Hanns remarked while looking at his boot tips, "It's doubtful that the spirit of historical destiny would reveal and manifest itself in Widow Pulko of all people — but it would be nice if it did..."

Bed No. 13

"Quinine," said the young assistant doctor, looking through the barrack window.

In the courtyard, four men were hopping around a machine gun. A lightly wounded soldier floated under the chestnut trees with blue stripes. In the training trench, a cat was frolicking.

Sister Crescenzia inclined her slim white forehead and went to the house pharmacy.

The young assistant doctor sighed.

He thought of Manon.

He longed for her.

Horses are nicer than women. And just as hysterical.

He held the patient's hand, checked the pulse, looked at the clock, and then walked out absentmindedly with jingling spurs.

No. 13 gently rose from the bed.

His gray eyes followed the doctor like grass snakes. They tried to slip through the door crack. The door fell shut with a clatter and a tremor.

The eyes returned.

No. 13 pondered.

Quinine, he said. What does that mean?

No. 13 sank back into the bare pillows.

One is so lonely. So lonely, like... like... like a person. The pillows are so cold. One is so hot. And the whole room is burning with heat.

God, it's so hot.

Like back in Southwest Africa.

The sugar factory in Souchez... my goodness... heavens... that was no trivial matter. I wouldn't want to have shares in that factory.

Quinine – where have I heard that before? Qui – nin. Qui – na. No, that's not it.

No. 13 tried to sit up. Behind him, on the bed, there was a blackboard looming. It had numbers and a few Latin names written on it. Fever curves climbed into the sky.

No. 13 was startled.

I'm going blind.

I must have gone blind. I can't read anymore. Can I still write? I want to write something. Little thoughts. A verse. I'm not stupid, am I? I once had two poems published in "Youth" magazine. And one of my stories was translated into Russian. By a soft Russian woman.

She was my lover. My only one.

No, not my only one. In Southwest Africa back then, there was another. A Herero girl. 14 years old. With breasts like copper. That's going to be seized now. With hands like meadows. And proud boyish feet. And an oasis mouth.

I am doomed to love my enemies. My enemy women.

I am a Christian. Confirmed by Pastor Gluschke.

What was the sweet black lady's name? Ro-ri. Ro-ri. That actually sounds like a non-alcoholic refreshment.

She wasn't black at all, but cocoa-brown. And she had a child: three months old. It sniffed like a mouse and playfully snapped at my hand.

If only I had a child with her.

No. 13 trembled.

I don't want to die yet. I want a child. A son. An African. So that I can live on when I die.

Sister... Sister, come... help me... I want a child...

The nurse approached with short, rabbit-like steps.
"What's wrong?" she asked gently, her cap tilting over him. "Are you in pain?"
"Quinine – what is that? What disease do I have?"
No. 13 trembled.
"It will all be fine," said the nurse softly, smoothing the bed.
Then she turned her cool face aside.

My lungs are full of sand, he felt.
A hot wind ripples through my head as if it were a sea. The steppe rises over my shoulders. With sparkling soles. Sand fleas swarm in my shirt.
Cacti prick my heart.
Nurse! I've experienced Southwest Africa. I am a Southwest African. Do you see the yellow medal on my chest?
Windhoek bursts from my gaze. Okahandja weeps. A thousand oxen trample through the terrain. Antelopes jump afar on bluish peaks. Monkeys hang from swaying branches. I bloom like the *Victoria regia*.
I am brilliance and shallowness: a gigantic leaf. A pinkish tree frog sits on my stomach.

"Malaria relapse," said the young assistant doctor, thinking of Manon. "I only gave him two days anyway."

The Regular's Table

One evening, at the "Hindenburg" regulars' table, a young, thin man appeared whom no one knew and made himself comfortable. He placed his small bundles under the chair and instructed the waiter, who hurried over in deferential shock, to bring a dice cup. Soon, the cup was clattering in the bony hand of the young man, who was holding the bank. The game was a lively game of seven. "Stakes," said the young man, "not less than ten marks. I also accept immobile assets as payment: hollow heads, red hearts, building plots suitable for cemeteries, iron crosses, and so on. Just no female breasts. They resist me..." – It was like dealing with the devil. Everyone lost. The wobbly district judge lost his (insignificant) legal knowledge. The pharmacist lost his poison cabinet. The headmaster wanted to lose his mind and offer it as payment. But the young man rejected him as unsuitable and defective. – The young poet lost his heart. When he tried to cash it in, it turned out he didn't have one at all, but that he possessed the same one as the young man. So he couldn't lose it at all. They recognized each other and drank to brotherhood. Afterwards, they played poker in pairs, and lo and behold: the poet held all the ladies in his hand, while the young, thin man had only the ace of spades. Thus, the poet outplayed death.

Bartholomew and the Young Man
(A Friend)

Bartholomew had met him at the Odeon Café. The café was quite crowded, and he had to sit at a table where a young man was already seated.

He lifted his London-bought top hat and asked in his soft, cultivated voice, "Is this seat free?"

The young man smiled politely, but somewhat disdainfully at him and his hat, saying, "Please."

Bartholomew immediately recognized the native Munich accent from the sound of that one word.

He ordered a strawberry ice cream with whipped cream and discreetly observed the young man, who – for reasons he couldn't fathom – was beginning to occupy his thoughts significantly.

The young man wore a simple blue, evidently very affordable, double-breasted suit jacket that fit him with an unintended elegance.

A twelve-pfennig Virginia cigarette was lodged in his angular reddish-brown Native American face.

Two hard blue eyes surveyed the audience with cheerful and determined objectivity, sometimes focusing on individuals.

The band played the waltz from "The Rose-Bearer."

"Nice music," said the young man, directing the last word to Bartholomew.

"Certainly," Bartholomew concurred courteously.

"It's a waltz," said the young man. "By whom, I wonder?"

"By Strauss," Bartholomew hastened to reply.

"Strauss composed many nice waltzes, such as 'The Blue Danube,'" continued the young man.

"That's another Strauss," Bartholomew remarked, "there are many composers named Strauss."

"Actually, it doesn't matter what the people who make music are called," pondered the young man, "it's just good that there is music in the world. What would people have if they had to die without having heard or danced a waltz?"

"Do you like to dance?"

"As much as a woman."

"And yet you seem to me one of the most masculine men I've ever met."

"Women always dance for others, I dance for myself."

"When was the last time you danced?"

"Five weeks ago."

"Where? Here in Munich? Where do people dance here?"

"In Buenos Aires."

"You were in Buenos Aires?"

"I've just come from there."

"Directly from Buenos Aires to this café?"

"Directly from Buenos Aires to this café! My luggage – if I may call my bundle of luggage that – is still at the train station."

"But you're a Munich native..."

"Of course..."

"Forgive my curiosity: where did you dance in Buenos Aires? In a variety theater?"

"No, in the hospital."

"You're not a professional dancer?"

The young man laughed loudly and seriously.

"I was a nurse. I danced life into the dying in the hospital, before they passed away."

Bartholomew nervously and thoughtfully tapped his grey suede gloves on his thighs.

"Forgive me," he finally said, emphasizing each word hesitantly and with emotion, "forgive me if I ask you another question. I begin to sense you as my destiny. (It was no coincidence that I approached this table...) Everything I have ever thought, you have done. You are truly living my life. I only think it. – How old are you?"

"Seventeen," said the young man, smiling. For he didn't understand much of what Bartholomew was saying.

"Seventeen!" echoed Bartholomew, trying to appear surprised. "Seventeen! At what age did you leave home?"

"At fourteen."

"Deployed?"

"Of course!"

"And now –"

"I'm back here!"

"You're right: you're back here. You are everywhere you are. But for example, I am not where I am. I'm not sitting here in my chair."

"Where are you then, if I may ask?" the young man asked amusedly, flashing his silver teeth.

"My will is sitting in your chair, and only my thought enjoyed this strawberry ice cream... But you don't understand that, and you never should."

Bartholomew stood up.

"I have an appointment at the bar with the poet Rainer Josefa Fintenfein. Here is my card. I would be very pleased if you would visit me sometime. I ask you to. Perhaps I can be of some use to you (and myself). Good evening."

Bartholomew let the waitress wrap his fur around him and bowed slightly.

The young man watched him go. Then he looked at the business card Bartholomew had given him, shook his head, and lit a new Virginia cigarette.

Bartholomew henceforth lived only the life of the young man. That is to say: he allowed the young man to live his life for him.

He thought, "It would be nice to love that actress." And the young man loved her.

He thought, "It's time to go to Monte Carlo."

And the young man went to Monte Carlo.

The poet Rainer Josefa Fintenfein wrote a sonnet about the young man, who danced life into the dying in the hospital in Buenos Aires.

The painter Ramsold Ruck painted him as a ship's boy against a backdrop of extraordinarily beautiful blue. And this blue was to represent the South American sky.

The actor Kalischer Bohnenblust played the role of Hannibal in the comedy "Hannibal's Bridal Journey."

Bartholomew had imagined all of this, and for the first time in his life, all of his thoughts turned into actions.

He was at one with himself because he was one with the young man.

When the war broke out, Bartholomew was seized by it like a sensation.

He volunteered for war service with the light Bavarian cavalry.

However, due to his severe heart and lung condition, he was deemed completely unfit for service during the medical examination.

In his place, the young man went to the front.

And on the last evening, he sang various songs to him on the guitar: German, Spanish, and English songs, and finally, he sang the old soldier's song:

> "I don't know if I'm rich or poor
> Or if I'm headed for ruin?
> I don't know if I'll come home again
> Or if I'll die before the enemy..."

Then he shook his hand, said, "Farewell, Bartholomew," and left.

When the news came that he had fallen at Souchez: shot in the head during the assault – Bartholomew knew that he had died for him.

He, Bartholomew, should have died like that. This death was meant for him.

But since he hadn't lived his life, he also didn't experience his death.

He realized that there was no point anymore in arranging to meet with the poet Rainer Josefa Fintenfein at the Odeon bar, buying a painting by Ramsold Ruck at Kunstsalon Dietzel, or watching the actor Kalischer Bohnenblust in his latest role.

One day, he went to Berchtesgaden.

He encountered tourists on the way to the little Watzmann.

Then he was never seen again.

His body was also never found.

In the "Munich Latest News," it was reported that he likely fell in the crags by Lake Königssee.

Does Your Watch Glow at Night?

I was strolling one morning along Kaufinger Street, thinking neither good nor evil – when suddenly, from the shop window of a watchmaker's, a yellow poster with blood-red letters caught my eye:

Does Your Watch Glow at Night?

German Reich patent! etc. Radium. First-class quality. Guaranteed for life. With chime. With a barking mechanism: alerts like a dog when danger approaches (essential for army and navy personnel). With scissors telescope, with periscope for submarines.

I stood there, stunned. A chilling terror crawled from my spine to my brain. What good did it do that I honorably passed my Ph.D. in philosophy at the University of Illinois in the U.S. for a fee of 320 dollars? What good was it that I knew the answers to all life's questions, such as: why? for what reason? on what grounds? to what end? What, I say, is the use and benefit of all this if I don't know if my clock glows at night? And I must confess, I didn't know. But the yellow poster with blood-red letters forced me relentlessly into introspection.

I was feverish all day. I ate nothing. I sat blankly and bewildered at Café Glasl in front of a bowl of nuts, thinking only all day: Does my watch glow at night?... Does my watch glow at night?...

If only it were evening already... if only it were night!

A lady with gentle lizard eyes kept looking over at me.

She was the most beautiful woman in the world. I dared not speak to her. A whirligig spun in my entirely hollow brain: does your watch glow at night?... Does your watch glow at night?... Finally, I couldn't take it anymore: the silver shine flowing from the lady's eyes fell like mist on me.

I stood up, staggered to her table, and, politely tipping my hat, I said with a trembling voice, madly in love and no longer in control of my senses: "Does your watch glow at night?"

The lady then took one of her gentle blue eyes out of her face and threw it angrily at my head.

It was a glass eye.

With a bump on my forehead, I left the café. The evening hung dark nets around the valley and hills, around shrubs and trees.

The street was brightly lit by a thousand electric apples and bulbs.

I pulled out my watch – but it was much too bright in the streets; amidst the intrusive flicker of a thousand lamps, how could I see if my watch was glowing?

I took a car and drove to Therese's Green. Alone, I walked into the middle of the field and, trembling, pulled out my watch.

But behold, I had not noticed that a full moon was indicated on the calendar.

Mockingly, the moon grinned on the watch glass.

I drove back into town. My temperature had risen to 45. I was nothing but sweat, in which, like a fat droplet in broth, the watch floated.

In Schwanthaler Street, I saw a sign: "Cellar for rent." Immediately, I rushed into the house and rented the cellar, despite the late hour, for a downright ridiculous price.

I locked it carefully, plugged the window holes and door crevices, and once again, prepared for everything, I pulled out my watch.

I waited for one, two minutes.

I waited for three hours.

It didn't glow!

Tears welled up in my eyes. Mine was a botched existence. My life was ruined. What should I do: my watch didn't glow...

What's the use of washing myself with Hindenburg soap? Of sleeping on a mattress "Always firm on top?" Of owning a wallet with the Iron Cross pressed into the leather? Of having the Battle of Metz and the Vosges depicted on my handkerchief? Of wearing an armband with the inscription: "God punish England?" Of my inkwell resembling a 42 cm mortar? Of my pen holder, with which I write, made from cartridge cases? Of delousing myself every day with the lice removal "Mackensen" that works infallibly after one use?

What does all that mean if I don't have a watch that glows at night?

Weeping, I woke up the next morning.

By 5 o'clock, I was already in front of the watch store on Kaufinger Street, and I nearly got caught by the street cleaners.

At 7:30, the store finally opened.

I slipped in under the opening assistant through the iron rolling shutter and, with a voice that sounded like a harlequin, demanded a watch with a ff. radium illuminating device. Brand Kronprinz. Guaranteed for life, with chime, barking mechanism, scissors telescope, and periscope.

I was feverish all day. I ate nothing. I sat still and bewildered in Café Glasl in front of a bowl of nuts, thinking only all day: Does my watch glow at night?... Does my watch glow at night?

If only it were evening already... if only it were night!

And evening came. Night came.

I sat in my cellar on Schwanthaler Street – and my watch glowed!

It glowed!

It glowed all night: chalk-white and gray-green like a magical circle. Over and over, I stared at the ring of pale lights. It looked like this:

And as I gazed deeper into the painting, I realized: it was the sky, the starry sky, that I held in my hand. Venus and Libra, Ursa Major and Pisces shimmered in my hand. I had found the puzzle of life.

Sleepless but intoxicated by the knowledge of the night, I emerged from my cellar in the morning. The world lay dull and pale like a plate of stale water.

It rained in streaks, and a white wind sighed.

The world disgusted me.

I don't sleep anymore. I don't eat or drink anymore.
My cheeks are sunken. My eyes are pink and inflamed.
I sit in the cellar and watch my watch glow at night.
Sometimes I wind it up so my heart doesn't stop.

Short Hike

1.

A red-bearded district sergeant politely grants me a three-month leave. At the police headquarters, they issue me a passport. I had to have it endorsed by the Austrian Consul. The Consul endorses it. And me. He targets me. Military thoughts immediately come to mind. One remembers one's Prussian descent and stands at attention. The Consul's blue eye shines more gently. Vienna smiles in his gaze. And Budapest. One stirs, a little embarrassed, and bows courteously. The Consul is Hungarian. All Austrian consuls are Hungarians. I think of the day Austria declared war on Serbia. It was in Leipzig. We marched under the leadership of a baker's assistant to the Austrian consulate. The baker's assistant strode ahead of us as if in silver armor, waving an improvised black and yellow flag. The Consul spoke from the balcony. Or from the window. He sang more than he spoke: many O's and R's. He was a Hungarian. The baker's assistant later drove home in a carriage, cheered by the crowd. He still had to prepare for night baking.

2.

I pack my backpack. It's not a real backpack: it's a small, feather-light brown knapsack that can also be carried as a handbag in the city. It holds a lot. I put on a sturdy pair of shoes, and now I can stay away as long as I want: three days... or three weeks... or three months.

3.

A few white clouds are scattered across the blue sky. It's not as hot as the past few days. The early train to Garmisch is as busy as usual. Like in peacetime. Pine-green tourists clatter through the hall with their worn-out boots. Older, well-dressed gentlemen tread carefully with elegant handbags. They handle the day as thoughtfully as their handbags between their fingers. Women in loose blouses laugh and wave. It's like usual. The train departs on time. As usual. It doesn't run a quarter-minute longer than usual. These two words: as usual – aren't they also a testament to German conscientiousness and conscience, and not the slightest one? Whether our minds are troubled or our hearts shaken: everything is still (fundamentally) as usual. The world. And the sun. And man. Even in peacetime, the earth trembles. Vesuvius erupts. A tidal wave engulfs Galveston. Icebergs float on the ocean. And the Titanic sinks. Cars fall into the Spree and the Seine. Robbers skulk through degraded streets with treacherous knives. A bullet kills in war. And in peacetime, a brick, a lightning strike, or a hurtful word. Perhaps words are much more powerful than actions. They make the actions visible. What is the greatest general without glory? His glory is created by words. And words are created by the writer. Who would know about Achilles if it weren't for Homer?

4.

We are not weaker than usual. And not stronger.

The grain stands tall. The poppies bloom red. Like children in little skirts, the birches run along the path. The Starnberg Lake gently ripples. The mountains are lightly embroidered in morning mist into the sky's canvas. The sun hoists the golden shield over the Herzogstand. The lake sparkles. And a new day dawns, as there have been many, and always will be. There is only one sun. And it shines on the righteous and the unjust: in Poland, in Flanders, in Italy, in New York. Let no one think they own the sun and that it's contracted to shine for them. We all have a place in the sun.

5.

There is Murnau. And the Staffelsee. Here, the railway branches off to Oberammergau. It's been five years since they performed the Passion Play. Back then, only English was spoken in Oberammergau. John, the Lord's favorite disciple, went around with a book: Do you speak English? and declined: the lady, of the lady... Pontius Pilate attempted a confused High German. After the performance, the gentlemen would have liked to unhitch Christ's carriage horses if he had one.

Now John lies before Ypres and utilizes his English language skills in a different way than before. Peter hears the roosters crowing in Petrikau... and Magdalene weeps...

Mittenwald

Wrapped in blankets, you lie on the porch. It's ten o'clock in the evening. The Karwendel appears like a large steamship in darkness and clouds. During the day, it looks like an animal: like a huge resting cow. From Mittenwald, from up the valley, a few sleepy golden lights peer out between low stone-covered roofs. Sometimes a small moon shines like an electric torch over the rocks at the Karwendel precipice. As if it were searching for someone lost. Or a startled deer.

In the distance, a bell rings: very high and soft. Like a bird chirping from the forests. It rings beyond the border already. Perhaps from Scharnitz. Or is it the train?

A stream, a cricket, and a star resound.

Next door in the room, a child laughs. Clattering and almost like an old man.

It's getting darker, and one thinks of their mother. Whenever it gets dark, one thinks of their mother. In the morning, when it gets bright again, one thinks of their son. That one wishes to have: a slim, blond one. He shouldn't wear glasses. And he should become a forester. Or a steward on an ocean liner.

A wind rustles in the trees. The narrow flag on the gable flutters.

At four o'clock came the news that Brest-Litovsk fell. Salutes were fired from the hills across the valley, echoed back by the walls of Karwendel with a bang. Then all the bells in the valley rang. The grand peal! It mingled with the bells of the herds returning from Lautersee. It rang out war and peace simultaneously.

It strikes eleven o'clock. A few clouds fall from the mountains, and it begins to rain...

You've been in the war for nine months now, my brother, nine months, and we know so little about you. You're seventeen years old. You stand with the...ers. In the east. As a lance corporal. From school straight into war.

Your letters are short like telegrams.

"Today I bathed in the Bzura. Regards, Hans."

Or:

"On the pursuit. Captured 1600 Russians yesterday. All of Poland is in smoke and flames. Hans."

Dear brother – who could I love more than you! You don't know because you're too young to know. Now you've participated in the storming of Warsaw and lie wounded in a Warsaw hospital. "Slightly wounded in the head and eye by shrapnel," you write.

But you don't write an address. How am I supposed to know where you are, in which hospital, and if I can send you something. Cigarettes. Or chocolate. (You do prefer chocolate anyway.)

If these lines should come into your view, immediately write down your address. Forgetful boy! And think once of your brother, who always thinks of you. And to whom war and you are the same...

Autumn

In the fourteen days that I haven't been outside, it has turned to autumn.

Bright yellow trees line the paths. And others are ochre-light, like Indians. Shrubs bloom all over in violet or blackberry blue or brick red.

The wooded mountains lie brown like rusted knight's helmets in the land.

The Zugspitze and the Wetterstein have white snow caps.

Winds play, and one is as tired as that cloud that has sunk like the head of a sleep-drunk child at Karwendel and cannot go further.

Three weeks ago, one stood on the small Isar bridge, looked upstream, into Tyrol, and thought: Where does the water come from?

Now, one hesitates on the same bridge, looks downstream, into the valley, and asks: where does the water flow?

And even though one knows a thousand times: the Isar flows to Munich. Munich is not far. Munich is a beautiful city. One has friends in Munich. A nice apartment. Soon, one will be back in Munich...

Is Munich our homeland? Do you even have a homeland: sad rider on foot?

Where does the Isar flow then? From Munich...?

In the department store on the main street of Mittenwald, there is a box of Frenchmen for sale. Real Frenchmen: with red pants, blue jackets, caps, and genuinely French faces.

They come from a toy factory in Nuremberg, are sewn very durably, and cost fifty pfennigs each.

They are almost more real than real Frenchmen and are not at all terrible to look at: a little melancholic, a little grotesque, but full of charm.

The shop owner said she had already sold a few boxes.

The children handle their little prisoners very delicately. They give them a lot of freedom. They even go for a ride in a cart with their field-gray brothers and are treated just like brothers, or at least like cousins.

It's good that the children are starting to play with Frenchmen again...

The day before yesterday, on a steamer on Lake Starnberg, the only passenger I encountered was a young lady I had met in Arosa in the winter of 1913.

We shook hands and looked at each other a little surprised.

"We are not strangers, are we?" the young lady said, distressed. "We knew each other quite well. When was that? Please help me..."

"That was before the war... 1913..."

"1913... before the war... I lost my memory during the war... but I still know that we were the two Sioux Indians at the Arosa carnival. We declared war to the whole world back then. Now the world has declared war on us... I will never be able to laugh again... I am like that tree on the shore there... see... completely covered in brown leaves... there's only autumn left in the world..."

All Soul's Day

Today hung in the air like snow.

I thought it was going to snow. The clouds drifted down between the houses and billowed like sheets in front of the windows.

The smoke from the chimneys twisted like black paper streamers in carnival around the roofs.

Eventually, it rained. A long, slow rain.

A rain that must rain itself into gloom.

The lights of the lanterns on Ludwigstraße pierced the asphalt like golden bayonets and shimmered in the depths. When you looked down, you felt like you were flying.

A faint bird, with the clinking wing beat of evening.

Zeppelins traveled like trams across the asphalt sky. In the eyes of women, autumn was dawning.

Today is the day of all souls.

Today we don't want to be bodies. Not even holy bodies or the body of the Lord. The body of a woman. Just soul. Cloud of snow. Falling leaves. Singing wind.

How many graves must I visit today? How many graves do I want to search for but won't find?

In the forest cemetery, among the trees, the graves lie like dead animals. There a hedgehog. There a fox. A deer. Some rabbits.

The rain falls like pine needles from the trees. I sit on a grave. Because I'm tired. Tired of wandering in the wilderness of war.

I don't know which grave I'm sitting on.

I haven't looked behind me at the iron or marble plaque.

Whoever you are: lying here under the moss: you are my friend.

Accept gladly and graciously the pain of the living about your death, about the death of all your brothers, in your brown rushing depths.

You rest at the bottom of the sea of all things like a beautiful starfish, and the silver waves pass over you like swallows.

How we once walked in the blooming light of spring, jubilant geniuses.

How young you were, my friend, a leaping deer. Hamburg was your home, and you were full of the smoke of the harbor and the vastness of the sea. Full of red corals and ringing with the chimes of Hanseatic towers.

We lived together in Tegernsee at the Gasthof zum Alpbach, at the entrance of the valley leading to Schliersee.

Every morning, we let ourselves drift in the boat to the highest point of the lake. Then we lay flat on our backs in the boat, and you said you could see the stars even on the brightest day.

You had such sharp eyes.

In the evening, we loved the same girl. Gentian blue eyes and red hair. A squirrel. "Oachkatzl," she always said and laughed. She loved both of us, but I think she loved you more than me. Because you looked so much like Saint Francis in her prayer book.

What you always wanted to become, you have now become: earth. Eternal earth. Humus, you became, and your strength grew into the trees.

This fir tree that I embrace and that fraternally brushes my cheeks: it's you. Thus, you are simultaneously above and below ground.

Simultaneously death and life.

I, stumbling pitifully through the October night of existence, dark and freezing, with the uncertainty of life and the certainty of death: I am less than you, my dead comrade, and only like a blue flower on your grave. My hope is only a hope of pain, and my faith only the faith of all souls.

Nights

It strikes one o'clock.

I draw back the curtain from the window and look out into the courtyard. The houses stand waxen-white and like props in the moonlight. Between them, the sky is painted with black Chinese ink.

You can sense some stars. But you can't see them.

Do people live behind these cardboard scenes? That cannot be. And even if there are people, they must also be made of cardboard. Cut out from picture sheets. Colorful and ornate and martial on the front. Empty white paper on the back, with the name of the company that printed them in very small letters.

Which company is branded on the people who live in these houses? God? Devil? Love? Greed? Drunkenness? Courage? Humility?

I hear a step.

The step sounds completely detached. Disconnected from a body. It ticks through the streets. Like a clock.

The body that belongs to the step wafts shadowy and transparent past the house wall over there.

Goodnight, ghost!

Where are you coming from? You must hurry if you want to catch up with your step. It's far ahead of you already and might run away from you.

A polite ghost.

It greets the moon.

I think of a few lines from a poem by Li-tai-pe:

> In the jasmine arbor, I sit drinking wine.
> The good hour calls for good comrades.
> Then the moon rises over the ridge; bows with a golden glow –

I too bow politely, and my shadow bows as the third in the group...

Do you even have a shadow, ghost?

Yes, you have a shadow. You show it timidly, like a validation: believe me – I am a human.

Yes, we believe you. You are a human. You are an honorable ghost. A ghost with a shadow. A ghost that no one needs to fear.

But I have reason to believe that you are afraid.

Of what? Of other ghosts? Of those ghosts without shadows? Who cast no shadow in sun or moon?

Did you come from the war?

Can't you sleep because the grenades are whistling in your head? The machine guns are drumming? Wild mouths scream wrath, mercy, pain, and jubilation?

I am so tired that my eyes will soon close, and I will soon no longer believe in ghosts. But I still need to know who you are.

You now stand in the middle of the street. Like made of gray glass. You hold a staff in your hands and move it back and forth.

Are you the man with the divining rod, searching at night, undisturbed, for water under the pavement? But we have enough water here in Munich. We have an excellent water supply. The water is rich in iron.

Oh, you're the street sweeper...

You sweep the streets clean so that the young day doesn't dirty its new shoes right away.

You're doing something. While I once again only think that you're doing something.

But you mustn't take it badly that I think about you.

I live in one of those houses that stand like props in the moonlight. You see the house and say to yourself: there live the rich people who do nothing all day long and all night long.

And you're a little right: I do nothing all day long and all night long. Absolutely nothing.

I just think. Because you don't have time to think, I take care of that for you. And because I don't have time to do, you do something for me. Good or bad: whatever you do for me, thank you.

The moon rises over the gable.

A cat howls.

The ghost tirelessly sweeps the street.

I want to go to sleep. I draw the curtain closed.

It strikes two o'clock.

The Dying Soldier

Day and night are no more. They have sunk like sailboats behind the horizon of the sea. I no longer know of day and night. Of sun and the gray crows of twilight. Of the earth and the round sphere of happiness. We march. We march by day. We march by night. We sleep at night. We sleep during the day. We shoot day and night. When I turn around, time stands before me like a pinkish-black wall. No day. No night. No month. No year. Only a bleeding field, blood-red soil, from which our bodies grow into the sky like white flowers. The sky moistens my eyes like dew. I want to bloom forever. Slender lily. Sword lily. I have never believed in myself so strongly. If I raise my hand, I will stop a grenade in flight. I am thirsty. For water. For fire. I want to swallow fire like the Eastern wizards. My horse is dead. It must be lying somewhere beside or beneath me. What should I ride now? I will ride into hell on a dead Englishman. But Lillie doesn't want that. She takes my hand, I am blind, and she will search for heaven with me. "Lillie," I say, "it smells like violets here, here is heaven." She lets go of my hand. I can't see her anymore. There is another hand in front of me. A glowing hand. Smoke-blackened. It reaches for the house with the shingled roof. The hand suddenly becomes a mouth. It eats the house. Gnaws at it. If the sergeant knew that I'm lying here lazily while he holds roll call. "Ulan Bubenreuther," he will call. "Ulan Bubenreuther...?" No one responds. "Ulan Bubenreuther missing..." I am thirsty. I want to drink something. Something hot. I'm cold. Hot tea. I have to laugh when I think of the Polish Jews who always sold us tea: "Give you coin, sir, get you hot tea..." They have no homeland. No one has a homeland. Only death. He is at home everywhere. Where is the small town where I was born? The narrow streets bend and stoop with age. The young girls skate. Citizens hurry with important faces to work, meetings, or pubs. The Oder rushes beneath the clods. The patina of the St. Mary's Church tower gleams violet and green in the winter sun. Someone must have died: the sexton rings the bells. I want to wave quietly with the lance. Perhaps, he will notice me.

The Flyer

When Flight Sergeant Georg Henschke, son of a farmer from the Markish region, came home on leave from the war, his hometown had already been buzzing for several days. Upon his arrival, everyone with legs ran halfway to meet him, with some brave souls even going 1½ hours to the Baudach train station, and the children and teenage girls sat on the cherry trees lining the road he had to come on.

Now he was there. The whole village crowded around him so tightly that he could hardly breathe, his mother cried, "Georgi, my Georgi!" and the pastor said, "What a providence of God!" "Children," laughed Georg Henschke, "children, I'm starving!" The crowd dispersed to regroup into a procession that dignifiedly escorted him to the table. It was set up outdoors. The village took the honor of giving him a meal. There were about seven courses, and in each one, pork appeared in some form. They drank sweet, new wine.

After the meal, as the wine took effect, people became bold. They dared to approach Georg Henschke, to ask, to request. "Georgi," his mother marveled tenderly, "now you can fly!" "Won't you show us something of your flying?" the little Marie asked timidly. "Oh," laughed Georg Henschke, "that's not so easy. It requires an apparatus!" "He surely has it in his pocket," the shepherd grinned mischievously, "he just wants to tease us." "An apparatus, is that something to wind up?" his youngest sister Anna asked. Because she remembered that he had once brought her a tin elephant from Berlin. A rod mercilessly ran through its belly, and when you turned it a few times, the elephant started wobbling, tapping its trunk on the ground, and suddenly running around the room like a weasel in erratic circles.

"No," said Georg Henschke, "I don't have the apparatus with me because it belongs to the state." "Oh, I see," the shepherd with his white-haired head said, "the state. That's also a new invention." "Exactly," laughed Georg Henschke.

"So tell us something about flying and how one learns it, Georgi," his mother begged. She was so proud of him.

Georg Henschke stood up, and everyone with him.

"Alright, I will do it. Listen!"

He jumped on a chair. They gathered around him. Excited, surrendered to his will, like the herd around the leader. They lifted their heads, longingly, and the blue sky reflected in their eyes. Georg Henschke, on the other hand, raised his arms, shook them against the light, joy of triumph sparkled in his eyes, and as he spoke, it flamed out of him. He felt himself becoming so light, so smilingly light, the ground sank beneath his feet, his arms spread like wings, swayed, and like an eagle, he soared high and steep into the blue.

The whole village stood like a being with a hundred heads bent toward the sky. And they saw Georg Henschke hovering in the ether, calm and clear, distant and more distant, until he vanished from their sight.

Hölderlin

I live with the master carpenter Zimmer in Tübingen.

My room is small and vaulted, receiving the sun through a blinded window. When you open it, you have broad oval views sparkling over leafy hills and mountainous trees. Herr Zimmer crafts tables, brown implements on which wine stands in golden carafes, and chairs, on which to sit and contemplate distant ships in twilight and sea tides. Where are you, flocks of swallows? Will you return soon with resounding wings, as April seized the broom and warm winds sweep the streets? The gentlemen students are already riding along the wandering avenues, the hooves clattering, and farmers courteously tip their hats.

Professor Conz meets me and says, "Good day, Herr Magister." They never call me by my proper name! Am I a Magister? Am I not, by all angels, Diotima, most beautiful of angels, am I not the princely librarian? Important personalities are never given what befits and benefits them. Professor Conz carried Homer in his pocket. He let the white bird out of its cage and exclaimed, "Look, our old friend!" I reached for the leaves and caught it, opening the passage where Nausicaa stands by the hall's doorpost, smiling down at Odysseus ivory-like. Tear after tear drips into the blue cave of her heart. We can do nothing better than what Homer did. And yet we are 1300 years older than him. "Oh," said Professor Conz, "you are modest," and he quoted some lines from my elegy to Nature. Humanity, I said, has got the rupture and the gout. And gout and rupture cloud thoughts. An elegy is nothing more than a chain of unclear thoughts, colorful like lanterns hung in the tangled mists of a spring night.

I received the doublet and three pairs of stockings and the gloves that my dear mother sent me. May often brings damp vapors and late frost. I would like to write to my venerable mother if I knew what to write to her. She often misunderstands me. Has she ever understood me? She is of an uncertain and too tender mobility, wavering like a silver gull in a stormy roadstead. But I wish for a firm nature. I am falling apart. Only music still holds me together. Then I am a chord, and the master cantor plays me on the organ in the chapel of Maulbronn. In the early summer mornings at six, he snuck through dew and dawn on bright green paths to me and played a chorale so that it would find favor with God.

I eat grapes every day. Herr Zimmer brings them on a plate painted with tendrils and strawberry-red hearts. I think: if someone painted your heart on such a plate, pierced by a black-feathered arrow and with a Latin motto: per aspera ad astra. Then they would have to pour grapes over me in Italian vineyards or on the banks of the Dordogne picked by dancing women.

Yesterday, Herr Zimmer showed me a drawing of a Doric temple. I don't believe Herr Zimmer designed it: but the flow of lines and the dream of completion seemingly carved in stone brought tears to my eyes.

"Herr Zimmer," I said, "instead of the tables on which golden wine stands in carafes, and instead of the chairs on which one, head in hands, remembers the gliding ships, why not build a temple out of wood, as small as you like? So that I may pray again."

"Pray to God, Herr Hölderlin," Zimmer said.

But God resides in small Doric temples made of wood. Herr Zimmer regrets he has no time for toys, he must work for bread, and who will pay him for such a Doric temple and the wasted time? I didn't know what to say, as I have no money and probably never have.

I searched for the drawing of the temple, looked at it, and wrote with a blue pencil on a board lying around in the workshop these verses:

> The lines of life are varied,
> Like paths and the boundaries of mountains,
> What we are here, a god may complete

With harmonies and eternal reward and peace.

Every day I must call upon the vanished deity again. When I think of great men in great times, how they, with holy fire around them, grasped everything dead, wooden, the straw of the world, and turned it into flame, which soared with them to heaven – I feel myself, as I often do, a smoldering lamp, wanting to beg for a drop of oil to shine through the night a little longer...

The Battle Line

Our Latin teacher, the old Professor Hiltmann, was like Fontane, a sworn enemy of all solemn and pompous phrases. Therefore, he could not stand it at all when, according to the dictionary, "acies" was translated as "the battle line" instead of simply and plainly as "the army."

The last in our class was one of the von Falkenstein, a kind-hearted, but foolish boy.

Years passed.

The world war broke out.

Hiltmann, as a sworn enemy of all solemn and pompous phrases, could not make friends with it.

The man-killing battles raged before Verdun. One day, Hiltmann received a field postcard from Falkenstein, who was stationed before Verdun. There was nothing on it but:

> "Dear Professor!
> 'Acies' does mean 'the battle line'...
> Most respectful regards,
> Your Falkenstein."

Then the old Hiltmann rested his white head on his lectern, and tears ran down his wrinkled cheeks, dropping onto the corrections of the Latin exam.

Falkenstein fell before Verdun.

The Commander

"The human soul," said the young Bulgarian officer sitting next to me at the table, "is much darker, more ambiguous, and irrational than psychologists want to prove and make us believe. Especially in war, where millennia-old inhibitions and traditions spring open like rusted bolts from decayed doors, where the path to inexplicably bright heights and unfathomably horrifying depths is revealed, it unveils the entire incomprehensibility of its emotional and volitional complexes. Psychologists think that because something is a certain way, a second thing must also be that way. A follows from B, and B from C. They construct a parallelism of (mental) movements of all people and turn psychology into a mechanical doctrine of motives, which has caused much mischief in literary history and especially in criminology. They infer (a clumsy word in German: it sounds like 'stumbling') motives for our actions that – uncivilized, audacious, and peculiar – stand outside of any calculation? Shouldn't such a crime, with somewhat clever planning, remain undiscovered, as the lock pick of the usual motive doctrine fails? This realization (from which an attempt at reforming our criminal science and our criminal law could be derived) certainly did not dawn on me for the first time, and, if I am not mistaken, has also been discussed in professional journals. But I digress. I wanted to tell you a little story from the First Balkan War. The story vividly illustrates my theses and illuminates, as if with a blinding lantern, the cave of eternal uncertainty that we call the soul. Metaphysically, it is called – and yet it lies underground. Its entrance is blocked by thickets, through which the hope of the stars sometimes blinks with golden eyes and rings with distant bells at night.

"General S., the leader of our first army, proved to be an unusually capable field marshal. He conducted all operations with a defiant and self-assured calmness that did not leave him even in moments of personal danger. I remember very well (I had the honor of belonging to General S.'s staff) when an enemy aircraft dropped bombs on the headquarters. Several soldiers, drivers, and horses were more or less seriously wounded and killed. The general didn't flinch. He raised his binoculars and attentively observed the aluminum bird that circled excitedly and shakily above him.

"General S. is to be credited with the great victory at L., which, based on the theory of unconditional destruction strategy, will immortalize his name in military history. I was appointed as the personal adjutant to the general in this battle and can vouch for the truth of the following anecdote. It ends earlier than you might think and is actually summed up in one sentence.

"The general was plagued by lively restlessness the entire day. He sat at the map table, twirling his beard, looked at the clock every five minutes, in short: he was sensually irritated and excited, like a young man awaiting his lover. He gave his orders carelessly and distractedly. He received reports as if he didn't hear them at all, and we were filled with consternation and fear, fearing that an inexplicable ailment, which might impair his decisiveness and talent for disposition, had suddenly struck the general. – The evening brought us a complete victory. Both enemy wings were pushed back. The enemy's losses in prisoners and war materials were enormous.

"The general drove to the battlefield in a car and rode up to the first captured position for a brief inspection. His face had brightened and cheered. His eyes showed a metallic gleam, which we attributed to the joy of the victory just achieved. His nervousness had completely subsided. He casually scanned a few fallen dispatch runners, a pile of sandbags, a few dead infantrymen with uninterested eyes. 'Good, – good!' he said, and then we rode back. 'You know, Lieutenant,' he turned his head to the side and reached into his pocket, 'I received a letter just at the last moment.' – 'From home?' I dared to ask. 'From home. Yes. I am so glad. I was restless all day. I was waiting for the letter – and here it is.' Then he fell silent and looked into the horizon. He sighed in relief: 'The experiment was successful.'

"I thought of the battle won and wanted to congratulate the general again. Then he inclined his head and said softly, 'It's blooming...'

"I later learned from the general what these two words, initially incomprehensible to both you and me, meant. The general is a passionate cactus breeder. He had left a small cactus at home that was unusually difficult to cultivate and nurture. I don't know its botanical name or have forgotten it, as I occupy my leisure time with oil painting, in which I have achieved a certain skill – the cactus had to bloom for the first time in these days. It was uncertain. It was hardly to be expected, yet so sweet to hope for. The experiment succeeded. The cactus bloomed. What did the general care for the glory of the great battle? The hope of immortality? The gratitude of the fatherland? He gave it all up with a light heart, shaken and delighted by the event of a blooming flower."

The War Correspondent

Siegfried Silbermann, who had already covered the Boer and Balkan Wars as a war correspondent for the "New Free Trumpet," was summoned telegraphically to the headquarters of Excellency Eydtkuhnen, Commander-in-Chief of the Northeast, – that general who had only risen to such dazzling prominence during this war.

Even before he boarded the press staff's car, Siegfried Silbermann's eyes were blindfolded with a dark wrap like a diplomat, so that during the journey to the front, he wouldn't see anything that could be construed as a military secret and might be used by him as an excuse for one of his well-known chatty conversations. It is part of the mental and professional characteristics of a war correspondent that he sees nothing, absolutely nothing of the war: occasionally, the blindfold is removed, and he finds himself astonished before a dead horse or a burned-down house. He is then allowed to report as an "eyewitness." If he shifts his gaze a little upwards from the dead horse or the burned-down house, he sees nothing but a gray, desolate, endless field stretching for miles to the horizon. He calls this the "emptiness of the modern battlefield."

Siegfried Silbermann opened his eyes and found himself facing an older, dignified gentleman whose chest was covered with medals and decorations. Broad red field marshal's stripes sparkled imperiously on his taut legs. He thoughtfully twirled his brown-mottled, ancient beard.

Silbermann took out his notepad and jotted down: martial.

Excellency Eydtkuhnen, the great field marshal – for he was none other –

placed his large, bony hand heavily on Siegfried Silbermann's trembling shoulder.

Silbermann trembled.

He moistened the pen softly on his tongue and noted: affable.

Silbermann finally dared to examine the immediate surroundings.

A picturesque group of higher and lower-ranking officers was gathered around a huge smoky bonfire. It was the general's staff. They were smoking a pipe that passed from hand to hand: the so-called peace pipe. An ox was being turned on a spit over the fire by several orderlies. They were preparing for lunch.

"Would you care to dine with us?" said Excellency Eydtkuhnen. The general's voice rolled in guttural throat sounds.

Silbermann noted: not only the paw but also the voice of the lion...

"I have arranged with the enemy commander that the battle will only commence after lunch, once the coffee is served."

Silbermann noted: humane conduct of war. There was only one camp chair available.

Silbermann noted: Spartan way of life...

"Won't you sit down?" Excellency Eydtkuhnen smiled. "Writing and thinking while standing is tiresome."

"Please, after you, Excellency," Silbermann bowed deferentially.

"Oh,"the Excellency waved off, "I have been standing in the field for so long that I can certainly stand a bit longer.'

Silbermann noted: perseverance... endurance... Teutonic toughness... Up in the skies, it started whistling and buzzing, snorting and popping.

Excellency Eydtkuhnen chuckled: "Enemy planes... they are targeting my headquarters... but rest assured, dear Silbermann, they never hit anything. At most, if one were on neutral ground, they might pose a danger."

Krrrrrrrtz... knautz... rum... a bomb exploded fifty steps away from Silbermann.

Silbermann could only note: composure, then he fainted. Excellency Eydtkuhnen waved, and Silbermann was carried by the orderlies, who had just been roasting the ox, to the press staff's car.

At the editorial office of the "New Free Trumpet," he regained consciousness. The evening edition of the "New Free Trumpet" featured on its front page Silbermann's now-famous interview with the Commander-in-Chief of the Northeast, Excellency Eydtkuhnen.

Four weeks later, "The Iron Wall" was published by the publishing house Brösel & Co., impressions and expressions, experiences and sights from the Northeastern front, by Siegfried Silbermann – a substantial volume in encyclopedia format.

The Ballad of Forgetting

In the skies, vultures are already crying,
Lustful for new carrion.
Many already raise their lyres
By the freely flowing glass,
To triumphantly strike down the old evil foe,
As he presses the tankard...
Have you forgotten the tears you've shed,
Forgotten, forgotten, forgotten?

Have you forgotten what was done to you,
The slaughter, the hacking and mowing?
The wheel of history turns forward with God,
But never backward with the devil.
The commander, who lost war and nerves,
Still wears his epaulettes.
His defeat shines in glory
And splendor: You have forgotten it.

Did you forget the good old days,
The worst ever in the land?
Your ruler was called Fool, his daughter Sorrow.
The courtiers were Cowardice and Shame.
He led you to ruin
With cheerful faces, with audacity.
Long ago, amidst wine, women, and song,
Forgotten, forgotten, forgotten.

We have defiled God and fatherland
With foaming mouths,
We have turned with our dirty hands
Shirt and opinion.
No word was honest and clear anymore,
Only immeasurable lies...
We had completely and utterly forgotten
The truth, forgotten, forgotten.

Millions perished in this war,
Which only a few dozen won.
They slunk away after their devilish victory
With bags full of loot.
In headquarters, amidst wine and champagne,

Many hugged their darlings.
At the front lay the men, lice-infested and filthy,
And forgotten, forgotten, forgotten.

Murder still flourished after the war,
It was a pleasure to shoot.
In this sad sport,
Germany showed itself above all.
Every scoundrel held court,
Drenching the earth with blood.
Germany, you shall not forget the murdered
Nor the murderers!

Oh Mother, you sacrifice your son
To army orders and commands.
He will one day demand a stern
Reckoning at God's throne.
Your son, who cried in the trench, in the grave,
For you, devoured by worms...
Mother, Mother, you should never
Forget, forget, forget!

You howl about war and peace – oh:
The others – You want to seek revenge:
Do you have the audacity to speak freely
Of guilt and atonement?
See your grimace in the mirror here
Possessed by hate and greed:
You have, if there was ever a soul within you,
Forgotten, forgotten, forgotten.

Once war was still chivalrous,
When Friedrich led his men,
With the flag in his fist – not sneaking to Sweden
And not capitulating to Holland.
Once it was still head to head in battle,
Man against man – meanwhile
Today the chemist presses the button,
And the hero is forgotten, forgotten.

The new war comes differently,
Than you dreamed it.
It doesn't come with sabers and rifles,
Proudly held.
It comes packed with poison and gases,

Brewed in the devil's kitchen.
You will, you will not soon
Forget, forget, forget.

You drummers, drum, trumpeters, blast:
There are no longer parties, only corpses!
Berlin, Paris, and Munich gassed,
While vultures circle above.
And whoever raises the lance to the sky,
To measure themselves against the blowing winds –
They will perish in an hour
And be forgotten, forgotten, forgotten.

No shot was fired. Cannoners sit stiff and dead
On the gun carriage.
The women lie in the morning glow,
The children perished in bed.
At Potsdamer Platz, singing and applause:
Volunteers from Bavaria and Hesse...
A yellow wind – the song is over
And forgotten for eternity.

You fight with demons no one sees,
Heroes are no match for bacteria,
There will be no *Song of the Nibelungs*
Telling of your downfall.
It's too late then to flee from the earth
With some heavenly passes.
God has spat you out of his mouth
And forgotten, forgotten, forgotten.

You rush into war, into the gleeful war,
And drive the fools to pair up.
You will witness only one single victory.
The victory of death.
Those called to reason by you,
They languish in the dependencies:
Upon His return Christ will not
Forget, forget, forget them.

Photographs and Illustrations

Kalbund's Father, Dr. Alfred Heneschke
(1858-1936)

Klabund's Mother Emilie Antonie
Buckenau (1867-1945)

Klabund, 1922

Dr. Alfred Henschke's Pharmacy
in Crossen, Poland

Klabund Lithograph by Orlik, 1915

Klabund with Fran Bruno at Walchensee,
1915

Brunhilde Heberle in 1917
(1896-1918)

Klabund and his first wife Brunhilde Heberle
on a trip to Mergosscia, Switzerland

Klabund with Brother Hans and Two
Cousins

Brunhilde Heberle, 1916

Carola Neher in 1925, (1900-1942)

Klabund in Davos

Klabund, Date Unknown

Klabund Portrait by Eric Buttner, 1919

Klabund, Date Unknown

Klabund, Date Unknown

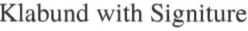

Klabund with Signiture

Klabund with the Actor
Alexander Granach, 1926

Klabund, 1925

Klabund, 1928

Carola Neher in 1925

Klabund's New Years Greeting
to Irene and Max Heberle, 1923

Klabund and Carola Neher, 1924

Klabund and Carola Neher, 1925

Klabund and Carola Neher on the Beach,
Date Unknown

Klabund and Carola Neher in 1928

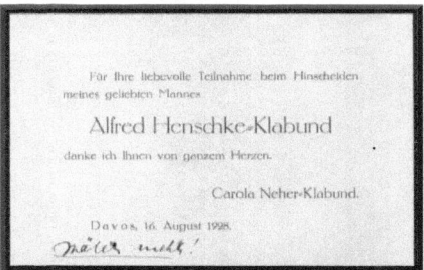

Für Ihre liebevolle Teilnahme beim Hinscheiden
meines geliebten Mannes

Alfred Henschke=Klabund

danke ich Ihnen von ganzem Herzen.

Carola Neher=Klabund.

Davos, 16. August 1928.

I thank you from the bottom of my heart for
your loving condolences at the passing
of my beloved husband.

Klabund, Last Photograph, Brioni,
Summer 1928

Newspaper Clipping: Klabund and Neher in Vienna, 1927

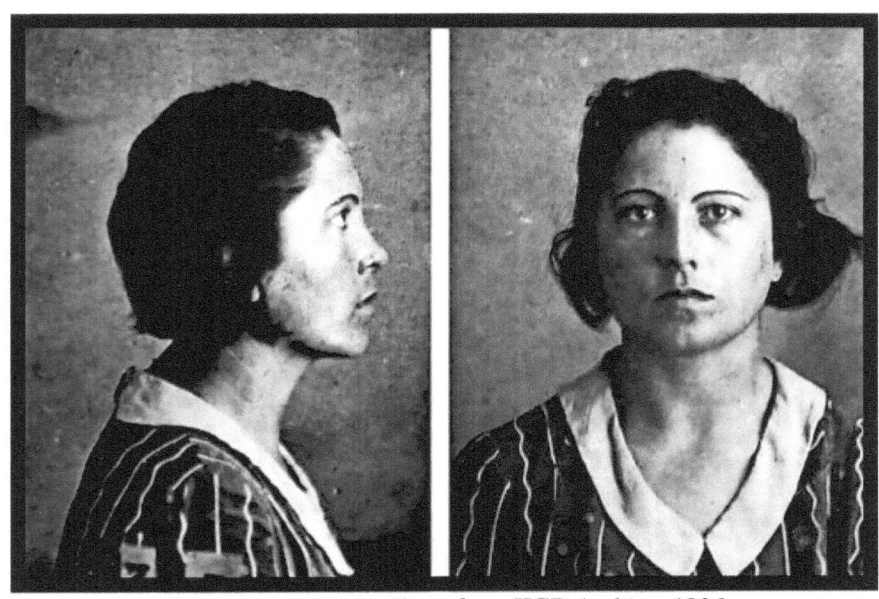

Carola Neher Prison Photo from KGB Archive, 1936

Klabund's play *The Chalk Circle*, 1925

Klabund's play *The Cherry Blossom Festival*, 1928

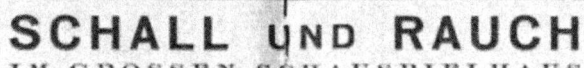

SCHALL UND RAUCH

IM GROSSEN SCHAUSPIELHAUS

Direktion: RUDOLF KURTZ — Künstlerischer Beirat: HEINZ HERALD und ERNST STERN

DEZEMBER-PROGRAMM:

Der Conferancier . . . . Eberhard Wrede
Der Zirkusdirektor . . . . Paul Graetz
Serenissimus . . . . Hans Junkermann
Kindermann . . . . Hans Henryk
Der Kammerdiener . . . . Edgar Kanisch

Gustav von Wangenheim: Pierrot-Lieder
Text: Gustav v. Wangenheim — Musik: Werner R. Heymann

Lala Herdmenger: Tänze
Musik: Robert Forster-Larrinaga

Klabund: Eigene groteske Dichtungen

Ein Tag des Reichspräsidenten
Karikaturenfilm, gezeichnet von Walter Trier
Musik von Friedrich Hollaender

PAUSE

Gertrud Eysoldt
Hans Heinrich von Twardowski: Parodien

Paul Graetz: Der alte Motor
Text: Theobald Tiger — Musik: Friedrich Hollaender

Blandine Ebinger: In der Bar
Text und Musik von Friedrich Hollaender

„EINFACH KLASSISCH!"
Eine Orestie mit glücklichem Ausgang (ein Puppenspiel)
von Walter Mehring
1. Agamemnon im Bade — 2. Die Morgenröte der Demokratie
3. Die klassische Steuerflucht

Personen:

Der Wächter (invalide von anno 1870)
Agamemnon (königl. Hoheit — kommand. General in den besten Jahren)
Klytemnestra (seine Gattin, vollbusig, gefährliches Alter)
Aegisth (davon O'apun) Literat und Berufsverführer, später demokr. Präsident)
Kaas Andra (rassig, mit Spitzenzäckchen)
Elektra von der Heilsarmee
Orest (Offizier eines attischen Freikorps, Königl. Hoheit)
Heany Pythia (gesponnt die Duse des nordischen Kinos)
Woodrow Apollon (lebt in höheren Sphären)
Der Chor der Presse (später Steuerezmulden)

Mitwirkende: Blandine Ebinger, Fränze Roloff, Lotte Stein,
Edgar Kanisch, Gustav von Wangenheim, Eberhard Wrede
Musik von Friedrich Hollaender
Leitung: Bildhauer Waldemar Hecker

Musikal. Leitung: FRIEDRICH HOLLÆNDER — Techn. Leitung: PAUL ERCKENS — Am Flügel: FRIEDRICH HOLLÆNDER
Eröffnung ½8 Uhr   Abänderungen des Programms vorbehalten!   Beginn ½9 Uhr

Text und Musik der Vorträge des Marionettenspiels sind am Büchertisch in „Schall und Rauch" zu haben.

December 1919 program for the Sound and Smoke Cabaret

Script for Klabund's XYZ play

Klabund's Works Published by Eric Reiss Verlag

Klabund Statue with the Mayor of Crossen, Poland

Part Five:

Short Hike

Short Hike was published in the Davoser Blättern (Davos Leaves) on
12/11/1915.
It was a weekly entertainment newspaper for spa guests in Davos in the Swiss
canton of Graubünden.

Short Hike

A red-bearded district sergeant politely grants me a three-month leave. At the police headquarters they issue me a passport. I have it signed by the Austrian consul. The consul signs it. And me. He's got his sites on me. You immediately start to think in military terms. You remember your Prussian origins and stand at attention. The consul's blue eye shines more gently. Vienna smiles in his gaze. Budapest invites you. You move, a little embarrassed, and bow obligingly...

I pack my backpack. It's not a real backpack: it's a small, feather-light brown knapsack that can also be carried around the city as a carry-on suitcase. It can hold a lot. I put on a pair of strong shoes. And now I can stay away as long as I want: three days... or three weeks... or three months.

A few white clouds have dotted the blue sky. It is not as hot as the last few days. The early train to Garmisch is full as usual. As in peacetime, pine-green tourists clatter through the hall with their studded boots. Older, well-dressed men walk carefully with elegant handbags, They hold the day carefully between their fingers like their handbags. Women in loose blouses laugh and wave, Everything is as usual. The train leaves on time, ah. As usual. It doesn't run a quarter of a minute longer than usual. These two words: as usual - are they not also a success of German conscientiousness and German conscience, and not the least? Our minds may be troubled or our hearts shaken: after all, everything is (basically) as usual. The world. And the sun. And people. Even in peacetime the earth trembles. Vesuvius spews fire. A spring tide swallows Galveston. Icebergs float on the ocean. And the "Titanic" sinks. Cars fall into the Spree and the Seine. Robbers and murderers sneak through run-down streets with treacherous knives. A bullet kills in war. And in peace a brick, a bolt of lightning or a bad word. Perhaps words are much more powerful than actions. They make actions visible. What is the greatest general without fame? His fame is created by words. And the writer creates words. Who would know of Achilles if it weren't for Homer?–

We are no weaker than usual and no stronger.

The corn is high. The poppies are blooming red. The birches run along the path like children in little skirts. Lake Starnberg is gently rippling. The mountains are lightly embroidered into the ceiling of the sky in the morning mist. The sun waves its golden shield over the ducal land. The lake glitters. And a day rises, like many that have been. And always will be. There is only one sun. And it shines on the just and the unjust: in Poland, in Flanders, in Italy, in New York. No one should think that they have a lease on the sun and that it is committed to shining for them. We all have a place in the sun.

There is Murnau. And the Staffelsee. Here the railway to Oberammergau branches off. It is already five years since they performed the Passion. Back then, only English was spoken in Oberammergau. John, the Lord's favorite disciple, walked around with a book: Do you speak English? and declined: the lady, the lady . . . Pontius Pilate tried his hand at a confused High German. After the performance, the gentlemen would have liked to unhitch Christo's horses from his cab if he had had one.

Now John is lying outside Ypres and is using his English language skills in a different way than before. Peter hears the roosters crowing in Petrikau... and Magdalena cries...

Part Six:

Legends of the Saints

Legends of the Saints was published in 1921
by the Dürr & Weber Verlag, Leiozig.

Legends of the Saints

Foreword

Who are you?

Come closer, so I can see your face. Your cheeks are furrowed, your eyes veiled. Premonitions hang from your forehead like tassels.

Where is your knowledge? Your conscience? Your science?

You know nothing.

You don't even understand "nothing." You know neither the Nothing, nor the Something, nor anything at all about yourself.

Today the call goes out to you: to listen to me and follow me.

It is not the first time that I have called you. Do you remember that stormy night when you startled from sleep and saw lightning flash from your eye?

You were overtired: and so you fell asleep again – and forgot – yourself.

When you stood at your wife's grave: alone in the hot midday: did not a wind pass through you, as if you were a bush? And was the wind not mild, and did not its breath delight you, and did you not yourself smell like a magnolia – swaying blossoms and branches?

My friend, why did you forget yourself so much? And why did you forget me, who sends you lightning and wind and today the word?

Every hour, every minute, every second you may begin: the new path that will lead you into all depths, to all heights. Blessed are you and graced.

The golden sisters await their silver brother. The mammoth has set out to clear the path for you through the primeval forest. The bamboo hedges creak under his stamping hoof.

Believe my word.

Love the golden sisters.

Hope for the silver helper.

A rain has fallen that has bent the ears of grain, but they will rise again and will ripen more gloriously than ever.

Clouds have gathered to darken the sun.

The clouds will break, and the sun will shine: brighter and hotter and more gracious than ever.

Here begins a praiseworthy and useful, a light and heavy, a bright and dark book: of the saints' lives, joy and suffering, called the Little Passional.

The Saint of Sorrow

She was the daughter of a pagan king; that was many centuries ago, and no one knows her name anymore. She was very beautiful, gentle, and clever, and a pagan prince wanted her in marriage. But she had secretly promised herself to Jesus Christ and rejected the prince's proposal. Her father was angry about this and had her thrown into a dark and damp prison with rats, worms, snakes, and newts. Then it happened that even the evil animals were good to her. She shared her bread like a sister with the rats, who, in gratitude, guarded her sleep like little dogs. The snakes, which she fed from her bowl, played cunningly and merrily with her during the day. One day the gate opened, and Christ himself came out. He stroked her cheeks and comforted her. But she asked Him to give her a form in which she would please no one but Him alone, so that she would no longer be exposed to any temptations among men. Then Christ raised His hand, blessed her and transformed her into an ugly, ape-like creature. When her father, the pagan king, saw her like this, he was greatly frightened and made a gesture of deep disgust. This, he said, is not my beautiful, clever and gentle daughter. This is a dirty and disgusting animal. But she praised the Lord and said: I was your daughter and am no longer one, since I have promised myself to the crucified God. Then the pagan king said: you too shall be crucified like your God. And his henchmen seized her, and she was crucified like the Savior once was. But whoever calls upon her in distress and need will be helped immediately. And since her name, which was a pagan one, has long been forgotten, one should only call out to the Saint of Sorrow in one's distress. The saint will then know this is intended for her.

Saint Loy

When his mother carried the saint in her womb, it happened that whenever she left the house, an eagle would circle above her and shade her head from the blazing sun with its wings. From this heavenly sign, it was concluded that the child was special, and when it was born, the king himself became his godfather. Saint Loy was a child of such remarkable ability that all who saw him or tested his wisdom were amazed. when he was a year old, while his playmates drew in the sand, he traced the sign of the cross into it. At the age of two, he declared, I am a Christian, even though no one had spoken to him of Christian matters before. Later, Saint Loy became an apprentice to a goldsmith. The king, who favored him, sent him a statue to be gilded. However, the gold the goldsmith provided was insufficient. Then Saint Loy looked up from his work and saw the sunbeams playing through the window. He reached into the sunlight and gilded the statue's head with golden sunlight. The king, marveling at this miracle, took him out of his apprenticeship and sent him to study the holy books with devout monks. He soon surpassed all his masters and teachers, became Bishop of Paris, and performed many more miracles and good works.

Saint Eustachius

Saint Eustachius, who was named Placidus before his baptism, was a passionate hunter. He hunted all the creatures of the forest: deer, roes, hares, foxes, rabbits — and hunted them purely out of the thrill of the chase, not because he needed them for sustenance. Among the animals of the forest, there was great fear of Placidus, the fierce hunter. No deer dared graze peacefully, no partridge dared nest, and no hare dared leap about freely. The animals agreed among themselves to send a messenger to God in heaven to plead for deliverance from the fiend who was their doom. They chose a jay as their envoy. One morning, the jay flew up to heaven, all the way to God's throne, to beg for help. God listened silently. Then He spoke: You shall be helped. For every living being is dear to My Father's heart. One day, as Eustachius was pursuing a magnificent stag in the wilderness, the stag suddenly turned to him and began to speak human words: Why do you hunt me, Placidus? I am Christ, and I have long been hunting you without capturing you until today. Thereupon, Placidus converted to Christianity and gave up his wild lust for the hunt. The animals praised God, and there was singing, rejoicing, and chirping throughout the forest in honor of the Most High.

Help us, Saint Eustachius, to see in every creature — even the most pitiful and lowly — a creation of God and our brother. Whoever torments an animal will be judged no differently than one who torments a human being.

About the Holy Child Saint Quiriacus

In Apulia, there lived a nobleman named Rogerius. He was defiant and arrogant, and he did not believe in holy signs and miracles. Once, as he stood before an image of Saint Francis, he mocked the stigmata and said: the Lord's stigmata were painted on your image, oh so-called Saint Francis, by your brothers, the Franciscans, only to make it look all the more pitiful. No sooner had he spoken these words than he felt a rushing sound in the air, as though an arrow had been loosed from a bowstring, and a burning pain in the palm of his left hand, causing him to cry out loudly. He looked at his hand and saw it bore a wound like the stigmata of the Lord or Saint Francis. And in the wound was a small arrow. As he pulled the arrow out, a small child approached him on the country lane — for the image of Saint Francis hung in a small chapel niche by the road — a halo around its blond head and a bow and arrow in its hand. I am, he said, Saint Quiriacus, the Holy Child. In pagan times, I was honored as the boy Eros or Cupid. Back then,

I stirred the hearts of many with my feathered arrows, enticing them to reckless lust and love.

But now, I have been chosen for holy tasks. With my bow, I shoot the stigmata into the hands and feet of the holy martyrs. You, doubting Thomas, refused to believe in the holy sign, so I have given you the surest and — the child smiled — the most striking proof with my arrow. The Holy Child Saint Quiriacus stepped closer, pulled the arrow from the nobleman's wound, which burned and caused him great pain, and then slowly disappeared into a field of wheat. Now and then, his red-haired head flickered like a poppy blossom above the stalks before vanishing again in the waves of grain. The nobleman, however, knelt before the image of Saint Francis and begged for forgiveness for his sinful arrogance. His prayer was granted by Saint Francis, and the wound began to heal that same evening.

Through the merits of the Holy Child Quiriacus, preserve us, Almighty God, from pride and unbelief. Amen.

Saint Florian

Saint Florian's calling was revealed when a fire broke out in the house of a poor widow in his village. Moved by compassion for her, as she owned nothing but this wretched little mud-and-shingle house, he turned to the flames in fervent prayer and implored them. The fire collapsed upon itself. The house remained completely unscathed, and no soot or ash could be found after the blaze. Since then, Saint Florian has been invoked successfully during conflagrations. But also, if your hearts are burning, you young women and men, call upon Saint Florian, that he may quench your passion and calm your flames!

Holy Saint Florian, spare my house, spare my heart, set others alight instead!

Saint Francis

In the vicinity of the Franciscan monastery of Monte Casale, three notorious robbers dwelled in the forests. They ambushed travelers, murdered them, and led lives filled with atrocities. In their audacity, these men once came to the monastery gate and asked the brother porter to give them bread and wine, as they were hungry and thirsty. The brother scolded them, saying: You wretched scoundrels, begone to hell, from whence you came! Would you rob us poor monks of our meager sustenance as well? The three robbers laughed and went away. When Saint Francis heard of this incident, he summoned the brother porter and said: You have greatly erred, brother porter. The commandment of Christian love obliges you to do good to everyone without regard to their status or their hearts. You wronged the robbers. You must atone for this. Go now into the forest, take bread and wine, and do not rest until you find the robbers. When you meet them, kneel before them, offer them bread and wine, and ask their forgiveness for your sins. Ashamed, the brother departed and did as Saint Francis commanded. He found the robbers, who were so startled and moved by his humility that their consciences were pricked. They abandoned their wicked deeds, sought Saint Francis's blessing, and joined the Franciscan order, where they lived godly lives until their peaceful end.

It is not the healthy who need a doctor. In the Kingdom of Heaven, there is more joy over one repentant sinner than over a thousand righteous ones. Examine yourself to see whether you may have contributed to someone becoming a robber or a thief. Perhaps you are only good because someone else has taken your wickedness upon themselves!

One day, Saint Francis was walking across fields and meadows. Birds flocked to him from all sides, seeking to hear his sermon. First, the partridges rose from the furrows of the fields. Then came the wagtails from the brook, the wrens from the fences, the blackbirds from the bushes, and the sparrows from the trees. Swallows descended from the sky in dense flocks. Even doves appeared, always in pairs, male and female.Saint Francis began to preach:

Birds, my dear brothers and sisters, you are deeply connected to God, your Creator, and should always and everywhere sing His praise. For He has granted you the freedom to fly wherever you wish — here and there — close to the earth, high among the clouds, even near the stars. He preserved your kind in Noah's Ark; the first creature to fly above the waters after the flood was one of yours: a dove. Even the Holy Spirit often reveals Himself in the form of a bird. You must be grateful for the element of air, which He has granted you. You neither sow nor reap, yet the heavenly Father feeds you, gives you rivers and springs to drink from, mountains, valleys, and gorges for shelter, tall trees and dense shrubs for your nests. Though you neither spin nor weave, God clothes you and your young. How greatly your Creator loves you, to grant you such blessings! Guard yourselves, my siblings, against the sin of ingratitude, and strive always to praise God! Then, a heavenly, blissful song of praise rose from thousands upon thousands of bird throats. Saint Francis blessed them with the sign of the cross. As he made the sign of the cross, the flocks of birds ascended in beautiful order, forming the image of a cross as they flew: to the south, west, north, and east.

And Saint Francis raised his voice to the sun and sang:

The Canticle of the Sun by Saint Francis of Assisi

To you, Goodness, God, and Spirit,
The torches of our devotion burn bright.
No human is worthy to utter
Your exalted name in the light.

Praised be to You with every creature you have made:
With the sun above all, our brother,

Through whom You summon golden days
To follow one another.

You created it in the blink of an eye,
As well as the moon,
Who, sisterly and feminine,
Sits so pale in the sky.

Praised be to You, Lord,
Through our brother, the wind,
Whose companions are the light clouds
And the bright and dark hours.

Praised be to You, Lord,
Through our sister, the spring,
Delicate and pure,
Yet serene, clear, and swift.

Praised be to You, Lord,
through our brother, fire,
Who brightens the night, bestows light
And delight, and whose power is immense.

Praised be to You, Lord,
Through our sister and mother, the earth.
Flowers bloom upon her breast,
And fruits she bears upon her back with much toil.

Praised be to You, Lord,
Through those who endure and serve.
Their weakness is their strength.
You are the queen to their hive.

Praised be to You, Lord, through our brother, Death.
With gentle hand helps us into his black boat.
It carries us to the brightest dawn,
On whose amethyst sky your name shines eternally: Amen.

Saint Irene

Irene is a Greek word, meaning peace. In Greece, the Boeotians and Thracians had engaged in fierce battles. The war had lasted so long that no one knew anymore what they were fighting for. Some claimed it was for the honor of the homeland, others fought as mercenaries and adventurers, gaining from the conflict. Some wanted to seize a piece of Boeotia or Thrace. Around this time, the cross also began to shine over Mount Olympus. When the Boeotians were preparing, as they did every year, to celebrate the festival of Cybele, the goddess of fertility and love, behold, the goddess rose from her pedestal. But instead of a helmet, she wore a halo, and instead of a sword, she held a cross in her hand. She spoke: I am not the one you have worshiped. For such a one does not exist, since there is only one God, with no gods or goddesses beside Him. I bring you the gospel of love — not only the love of the sexes, not only the love within the family. I bring you the vision of a united humanity bound together in love and tell you the first, but also the hardest demand: Love your enemies, love the Thracians, and let no hatred or war remain among you. Follow me. Lay down your lances, spears, daggers, and swords — I will lead you to the greatest victory — the victory over yourselves... And the Boeotians, overcome by the wondrous appearance, laid down their weapons, and with only bunches of lilacs, oleanders, almonds, and mimosa in their hands, they followed the goddess, who led the unarmed directly to the enemy camp. The enemy, seeing the strange procession from afar, singing psalms as they descended the hills, dancing and hopping, felt as if Pan, the old god, had awoken once again. It seemed to them as though their hearts, once filled with wounds, now opened into blossoms. They rushed toward the Boeotians, unarmed themselves, and threw themselves into each other's arms, weeping. But the goddess Cybele transformed into a Christian saint: Saint Irene, which means Holy Peace, called so because she established eternal peace between the Boeotians and the Thracians.

Saint Irene, grant us peace too after all the torments and horrors of war, grant us eternal peace.

Saint Jerome

Saint Jerome built a monastery and a church in the middle of the desert. One day, a lion came to the church gate, limping on one leg and letting out a pitiful cry; it did not roar like a lion, but mewed like a cat. The monks fled in fear when they saw him. But Saint Jerome approached him. The lion stretched out his left front paw, and Saint Jerome saw that a thorn was stuck in it. He pulled it out and wrapped the lion's paw with a piece of cloth torn from his own mantle. From that moment on, the lion never left his side, and in all depictions of Saint Jerome, including the beautiful one by Albrecht Dürer, he is shown with the lion.

The lion was made the guardian of the donkeys by Saint Jerome. He took them out to the field in the morning and brought them back home in the evening. One day, he drove a donkey to the pasture; but outside, he lay down because it was very hot and fell asleep. Meanwhile, a caravan passed by, saw the donkey grazing alone, and took it with them. When the lion woke up and saw that the donkey was gone, he was frightened and ran back and forth, roaring across the desert. But none of the donkeys answered his dull question: Where? where? where? So, he trudged home, his proud head with the golden mane bowed low. For he was ashamed of his carelessness in performing the entrusted task. The monks would not let him through the gate because they thought he had eaten the donkey; they did not give him anything to eat and said, First digest the donkey you've swallowed. But Saint Jerome believed in the lion's innocence, allowed him into the monastery, and ordered him to pull the cart instead of the donkey from then on. So, the proud lion now worked under the yoke of the donkey. One day, while he was once again at the pasture, that same caravan passed by on its way back, the one that had once stolen the donkey from him, and at the head of the procession walked the lion's donkey, fully laden with food and jewels. The lion roared so loudly that the robbers, who were the caravan riders, fled in fear. Then the lion drove the entire caravan, with the donkey at the head — well over a hundred mules and camels laden with a thousand treasures — before the monastery, and the monks were astonished when they saw the marvelous procession coming. They opened the gate, and all the animals, with the lion at the end, walked in, wagging their tails like a little dog. The monks were overjoyed by this strange Christmas gift, as it was just Christmas Eve. Saint Jerome ordered that the treasures be carefully watched, and if their rightful owners appeared, they should be returned to them. But the robbers never returned out of fear of the lion, so after a year, all the treasures came to belong to the monastery. To this day, the monastery of Chalcis still enjoys its wealth of gold, jewels, carpets, velvet, and silk. The lion, however, was happy to have his donkey back. They never left each other's side again, and it is said that Saint Jerome often joined them as a third companion, speaking with them in a language no one understood. He was as friendly with the donkey and the lion as he was with people, and when he died, the lion and the donkey died with him, and they were buried in the same grave. Himerius, Bishop of Amelia, suggested, when Saint Jerome was canonized, that the donkey and the lion be declared saints as well. I don't know if this was meant seriously or out of malice.

Saint Cyprian

Saint Cyprian was a secret bishop in Carthage. The pagans learned that he was secretly spreading the doctrine of salvation among them and dragged him before their chief judge. The judge asked, Who are you? Cyprian replied, A Christian. The pagan asked, What is that? Cyprian answered, No longer a man, but not yet God. The pagan said, I don't understand this. I am a pagan. Then Cyprian said, so, you are neither an animal nor yet a man. The pagan thought that Saint Cyprian was mocking him and ordered him to be beheaded. Before his head rolled into the sand, Saint Cyprian bequeathed all his possessions to the executioner, who was about to strike. He also blessed the chief judge with a bishop's blessing. You have judged rightly, he said. For I am a negligent sinner and a crude fool. May the Lord be with you. Forever.

And also with us, Saint Cyprian.

Saint Someone and Saint No One

Saint Someone and Saint Noone, two pilgrims, met each other on the country road of life.

Saint Someone said: Where do you come from, brother? You seem so sad.

Saint No One said: I come from nothing and step into life. And you? You look so cheerful.

Saint Someone said: I am leaving the world, parting is easy for me. I walk into nothing.

Saint No One said: Brother, the sun rises and sets. The moon waxes and wanes. Spring, summer, autumn, and winter change like death and life. You die. I am born. When I one day sink into death, you will again take the pilgrim's staff from my hands. Life is sacred. Death is sacred. Someone is sacred and is called Saint Someone. No One is sacred and is called Saint No One. God holds the scales in His hand: the scales of justice. In one side of the scale is life; in the other, death. They weigh equally. And thus, only the world exists. And thus, only you and I. I was not without you. You would not be without me. Farewell. Die well. We meet again and again.

Saint Someone and Saint No One shook hands in farewell. One walked uphill, the other downhill. They looked back at each other several times. Finally, they disappeared at the same time: one behind a rock on the heights, the other deep in the valley. The sun set, and quietly the horn of the moon began to sound in the evening.

Saint Notburga

Those who sail along the Neckar River by ship encounter the ruins of Homberg Castle. There once lived, in ancient times, a powerful but also violent count; he had a beautiful and devout daughter, named Notburga. He had promised her in marriage to a neighboring prince without consulting Notburga. One day, when the count spoke to Notburga, saying: Prepare your wedding gown, for tomorrow I will marry you to Prince Benno, Notburga, in the anguish of her heart, called out in prayer to her deceased mother, whom she had loved deeply. She feared her father and loathed the prince with all her soul. As she wandered sleeplessly in the garden at dawn, suddenly the bushes rustled before her, and a silver-white stag came towards her. It stopped in front of her, and without fear, she mounted the animal, which then carried her away, setting her down only at a lonely forest chapel. There, the stag left her, but after an hour, it returned with bread and a jug of water, both hanging from its antlers. Thus, the stag fed the holy Notburga daily, and she never grew tired of praising the goodness of the Lord.

It happened that the wild count, while hunting, encountered the white stag, pursued it, and so reached the chapel, where he found Notburga kneeling in prayer before the cross. Runaway wench! he cried, pulling her by the hair. But she held onto the cross and said: I have pledged my faith to my heavenly bridegroom. I shall not return to the people... In his fury, he yanked her harder, and suddenly her head, detached from her body, was in his hand. Tormented by horror, he fled. But angels flew down from heaven and laid the holy Notburga to rest. Though it was late autumn and no flowers were in bloom, they scattered white and red roses on her face. Around the meadow where she lay, flowers began to bloom as if it were summer, with all the meadow and forest flowers. Two white bulls appeared and carried her body across the Neckar River, without their hooves touching the water. The white stag led them, and between its antlers, the cross shone brightly. The bells of all the churches around began to ring on their own. The bulls carried the holy Notburga to the church of Hochhausen on the Neckar, where she was laid to rest by invisible spirits. To this day, the image of Saint Notburga stands in the church, carved in stone.

Saint Thais

Among the holy women is also a prostitute, named Thais, who gave herself in a public house before the venerable Father Paphnutius converted her and redeemed her from her sins. He approached her in disguise, pretending to be a lover. But in her chamber, he removed his mask and grew enormously before her, so that she could no longer see his shoulders or his head. From above, as if the house were uncovered and no roof remained, his voice, as if from the clouds, asked: Do you, beautiful sinner, believe in God? Thais fell to her knees: I believe, I believe... And she went with him into the wilderness and did seven years of bitter penance. She always kept her eyes closed, having sworn to herself that she would not receive the pure light of the sun again until she had completed her penance. After seven years, she lifted her gaze for the first time and saw the heavens open. There, she saw three holy virgins guarding a golden throne, and a voice spoke:

This throne will be taken by the sinner Thais in the kingdom of heaven, because of her repentance and severe penance. And she was taken up to the holy virgins.

You, chaste and virtuous women, do not wrinkle your noses or shrug your shoulders at a fallen poor child of mankind. You do not know if a holy Thais may be hidden within them. Be careful not to fall into temptation and sin. May Saint Thais help you with this.

All Souls' Day

We should observe All Souls' Day with particular devotion and with especially heartfelt thoughts and practices, and pray to the saints that they help the poor souls, who, having departed from us repentant and without mortal sin, may attain eternal bliss. May God grant this.

Once upon a time, there was a priest who loved all souls immensely. Every day he sang the Requiem and said a funeral Mass, probably every day. The bishop was informed of his pious deeds and actions. He became angry and said, Why do you concern yourself with the dead? It would be better for you to care for the living and, as a true shepherd, take heed of the sheep, lambs, and goats entrusted to you. And he forbade him from saying the daily funeral Mass.

One day, as the bishop was walking across the churchyard to his residence, the day already fading into twilight, the graves opened, and the dead stepped out. And one of the dead — an old soldier who could not find rest in his grave because of the many enemies he had slain, though it had been for the greater glory of God — spoke: Let our priest again intercede for us at God's and all saints' throne, as we are accustomed! For his Masses were our comfort, devotion, and hope. But if you deny us our request, you will have to die, and soon become one of us. The bishop made the sign of the cross and fled in fear. From then on, he had no objection to the priest saying his daily funeral Mass. But from that time, the priest came to be known as the "Priest of the Dead." At his godly passing, all the dead from his cemetery accompanied his burial, so that no living person dared to honor him with the final respects. The dead, however, lamented and mourned: Who will be our intercessor before the holy throne now? Holy Mary, pray for us!

And also for us, mysterious Rose, who still walks in the light. Who knows how soon our hour will come.

Saint Petronella

We read in Saint Marcellus that Petronella, the most holy daughter of Saint Peter, was very beautiful, but also very sick and weak. Saint Peter's friends and companions were greatly astonished as to why Saint Peter, who performed so many miracles for strangers and even for the most distant people, did not use his miraculous power on his own child and allowed her to suffer so pitiably. But Saint Peter instructed them: Petronella has forbidden me to help her. She is happier than we are, for anyone who suffers in the Lord is closer to salvation than we are, who, healthy as bears, trample through the world, crushing and bending many flowers and grasses. She is like a butterfly, lightly and lovingly fluttering from blossom to blossom, until God's storm will lift her high above the clouds.

Despite her frailty, a young count fell in love with her so intensely that he thought he would die if she would not belong to him. She asked for three days to consider his proposal. When he entered her chamber after three days, he saw a white dove fly through the open window. But in the bed lay Petronella, as beautiful as ever, but cold and pale as death. The knight then collapsed unconscious by her lifeless body. Saint Peter, however, wrote with his own hand on the cross at her grave: To golden Petronella, my dearest daughter.

Help us, holy Petronella, that we may learn to bear our pains and frailty as gracefully as you did, and show us the right path to the heavenly kingdom.

Saint Macarius

Once, in a hollow way, the evil enemy encountered Saint Macarius and said: I am strong and mighty and all-powerful. Everything you can do, I can easily do: I can fast, I can mortify myself without feeling pain, I can go without sleep for seven days. There is only one thing I cannot do, and it is the only thing by which you can overcome me... Macarius asked, What is that? The evil enemy replied, Your humility... and left.

On another occasion, Saint Macarius again encountered the evil enemy. He was wearing a cloak that was full of holes and ragged, and from each hole, the neck of a bottle was visible. Macarius asked, Why do you carry so many bottles in your cloak? The evil enemy answered, In these bottles are all the potions and little brews, sweet-tasting and fragrant, with which I seduce and deceive people. And even if some do not like this or that drink, I find among all the bottles one that will tempt their palate. And once someone has drunk from my wines, they always crave more. For they taste sweet at first, like Greek or Spanish wine. The bitter end comes only later.

Saint Macarius went into the desert. To find his way back, he had cut himself some reeds, which he stuck into the sand from time to time as waymarkers. In the evening, he laid down to sleep. In the morning, he found all the reeds gathered in a heap by his head. The evil enemy had moved them so that he could no longer find his way back. But as Macarius set out again, trusting in the Lord, he saw that wherever he had planted a stick, a date palm had sprouted from the desert, providing him with shade and sweet fruit.

It was under such a tree that he was stung by a large mosquito. In a sudden outburst of rage and pain from the bite, he killed it. But when he saw its blood flowing, he realized he had wronged it and killed a creature of God. So he walked naked back into the desert, to a place where no trees stood, where there were no fruits and no shade. There, he gave himself over to the mosquitoes, for having killed one of them. A dense swarm descended on him like a cloud, and they stung him to death. Thus, Saint Macarius died a martyr's death, from the bites of mosquitoes and gnats.

Saint Nicholas

Saint Nicholas carried the burdens of others whenever he could. Once, as he was passing the gates of the city of Aconita, he encountered a pack donkey with its driver. He took the two sacks of flour from the donkey and carried them on his back, already battered from scourging and torture, all the way to the baker's oven.

One night, as he awoke in his cell, he saw a golden star hovering just above his head. In his simplicity, he did not understand what this star meant and told the learned Brother Peregrinus about the golden dream. The brother easily interpreted it and said: O holy father, the star is the sign of your sanctity! Just wait and see when it appears again and where it fades or disappears.

That night, Saint Nicholas awoke, and again the star stood above him. As it floated away, Saint Nicholas rose from his bed and followed it carefully. He saw how the star, like a firefly, fluttered along the cloister, passed through the open door into the chapel, and hovered for a moment before the altar image of the Madonna and Child. There, it united radiantly with the carved, gold-painted star that the woodcarver had placed above the forehead of the Christ Child. Then Saint Nicholas knew that he was following the true star and decided never to lose sight of it, nor to let it depart from his heart.

Shine upon us too, Star of Aconita, until we reach the gentle realms of the blessed!

Saint Gregory

When King Markus was nearing death, he called his son to his bedside and instructed him to rule the kingdom justly and to care for his sister, the princess, with love and kindness. Afterward, he passed away. The prince did as he was told. He ruled the kingdom with kindness and integrity, and loved his sister above all. However, this love eventually took such hold of his senses that he, no longer able to control his reason, embraced her one night as a husband embraces his wife. Regret seized him too late. The princess became pregnant. Then he bade the world farewell and went off to the Holy Land to do penance, where, fighting against the unbelievers, he met a Christian end. The princess gave birth in secret with trusted servants, and placed the child in a golden cradle, which she set in a barrel. At the feet of the child, she placed a treasure of gold, and on a tablet she wrote: This child was conceived by a brother with his sister. Whoever finds it, let him baptize it, teach it a trade or craft, and keep the treasure. She placed the tablet in the barrel and set it adrift on the sea, letting it float wherever God willed. There was a monastery by the sea, and the abbot said to the fishermen: Go, you fishermen, and catch something good for the days of fasting! The fishermen cast their nets but caught no fish, only a barrel in which a golden cradle lay, and in the cradle, a little child. They brought it to the abbot, who said: What a strange catch you've made! He read the tablet by the child's head, and upon reading it, he shook his head and baptized the child with the name Gregory. He entrusted the child to a fisherman to care for. As Gregory grew, he surpassed all his peers in wisdom and virtue. By chance, one day, he learned from the fishermen the true cause of his birth when he discovered the tablet with his mother's words. He cried out three times, Woe! I will do penance for the sins of my parents and travel to the Promised Land! However, the ship carrying him was wrecked in a storm near the city where his mother had resided since his father's death. She was in great distress because her neighbor, Duke Othmar, was waging war against her, as she had rejected his advances. Gregory arrived with his companions in the city, and upon hearing of the plight of the beautiful queen, he offered his help through her chamberlain, as he was experienced in all knightly arts. He rode into battle for her, succeeded in killing Duke Othmar, and forced the enemies to flee. The people, through the chamberlain, asked the queen to marry the victor, so that the land would once again feel the firm hand of a lord and king. The queen agreed, and with great pomp, Gregory was married to her. They lived in love and harmony for an entire year, for an inexplicable, powerful force drew them together. One day, the queen found the king in his chamber, tears streaming down his face, his head resting on a tablet. When she bent over him to read the words on the tablet, she was struck with horror, for they were her own words, and her husband could only be her son. She cried out many times, Woe! Gregory, after she revealed herself to him, said: I will go into the wide world and wander until God has freed us from our great sin. On that same day, he left and went to the fisherman who had once raised him. He said to him: Take me to the Rock of Suffering, where the fountain of tears flows into the sea. The fisherman took him to the rock, and Gregory had himself chained to it, throwing the key into the sea, where a fish swallowed it. For seventeen years, Gregory did penance, chained to the rock. He ate only the air and drank only the light with his eyes. In the eighteenth year of his penance, the pope in Rome died. A voice from the clouds called out to the people of Rome: You shall make the holiest one your pope. His name is Saint Gregory. The people called out his name throughout the land. The fisherman heard this by the sea and sent the messengers to Gregory at the rock. When they arrived, a flying fish leapt before them, spitting out the key that it had swallowed. The fisherman took the key and unlocked Gregory from the rock, and they led him triumphantly to Rome, where he was crowned pope. Around this time, the queen, his mother, made a pilgrimage to Rome, unaware of her son's holiness and papacy. She wished to confess to the holy father and confessed to her son. When he realized it was his mother, he absolved her of all her sins in the name of the Savior.

The Image of the Virgin Mary

I walked home through the tropical moonlit night, up the winding path from the Church of Saint Antonio to Monti della Trinità: the Mountain of the Trinity, where I live.

Suddenly, I was blinded by the white masonry of a small chapel.

I had often passed by the baroque shrine during the day without paying attention. Too many churches and chapels grow in this area: like radishes and poppies amid the corn. And the sight is always the same, and the altar image is always the same: a Madonna holding the infant Jesus in her arms, awkwardly painted as a fresco on the lime wall. And before the image: small candles, fresh and withered bouquets of flowers, left by old pietists and young lovers.

But tonight, in the moonlight, something unconscious, unknown, compelled me to stop and step closer. And I saw, illuminated by both the moon and an inner light, an image that shook me to my deepest core.

Perhaps the magical moonlit night, the twilight, the half-light in which we live, set the stage for this feeling, perhaps others would not find the experience so extraordinary and unsettling: I saw a sign from heaven, unlike many I've seen. On all the Madonna images I know, the Madonna bends lovingly and blissfully over the infant Jesus in her arms. But in the image of this night, I saw this:

At the Madonna's chest lay the infant Jesus, drinking. But she turned her head away, her eyes filled with tears. All the future torments and pains that awaited the holy being she had borne, she seemed to feel them in advance: to feel in advance all the great sufferings of small human life. No smile softened or calmed her harsh and stern features. No maternal joy blessed her, but a mother's pain tore her apart.

Thus, I saw all mothers of today nursing their children, their early wrinkled faces turned aside, unable to bear the sight of the beloved being drinking from their breast the bitter milk of a future, born in a stable, lying in straw, surrounded by oxen and donkeys, having no other roof over them than the starry sky and no other hope than the hope for a better present for their great-great-grandchildren.

Saint Genevieve

Saint Genevieve had taken the veil and become a nun. Pious and simple, she served the Lord faithfully. Above all, she loved to do good for poor children.

She fed them with bread and milk, clothed them, and played with them in the convent garden. She was a holy and honorable virgin, but in her virginal heart beat a maternal love. Often, she would kneel in prayer before the Madonna with the infant Jesus and say: O Mother of God, you too were a virgin, but you were graced, and your body was blessed, and you conceived without sin. Would that I too could have a child... But I am only a poor nun. And her tears soaked the prayer bench.

The feast of Christmas drew near. It was customary in the convent for an empty cradle to be placed at the altar, into which the Christ child was imagined, and a nun was assigned to rock the Christ child with songs of praise from the sisters. This year, it was Genevieve's turn to rock the Christ child.

Puer natus in Bethlehem. Eia unde gaudet Jerusalem, eia, the devout sisters sang. And as Genevieve gently rocked the cradle, as though the infant Jesus himself lay there, suddenly a soft cry came from the cradle, and as she leaned over it, there lay a naked little child, gazing at her with large blue eyes. – Genevieve called the other nuns to witness the miracle and praised the holy Virgin who had granted her this child at Christmas and heard her prayers. She took the child to her cell. And lo, a miracle: milk flowed from her breasts, as if she had given birth to the child. Saint Genevieve became like a mother to the child, which had fallen from the heavens, and thus it was baptized Coelia, the Heavenly One. Coelia was never to leave the convent and, in due time, took the veil just as Genevieve had. For Coelia was not inferior to Saint Genevieve in holiness.

Saint Genevieve, however, is the patron saint of mothers.

The Seven Holy Sleepers

In the time of Emperor Decius, a great persecution of Christians took place. In the streets of the city of Ephesus, the blood of the believers flowed in streams. At that time, there lived in this city seven men named: Malchus, Maximianus, Serpion, Marimon, Konstantinus, Dionysius, and Johannes. These seven fled from the wrath and bloodlust of the pagan mercenaries into the nearby mountains and took refuge in a stone cave, from which only one of the seven descended daily to secretly buy bread in the city. One day, when it was Serpion's turn, he did not wait for the twilight to return, and so the soldiers followed the trail of the seven Christians. The captain saw that the seven men were sitting in the cave like mice in a mousehole. He laughed a dirty laugh of malicious joy and ordered that the seven be walled up in their cave. But God sent them a beneficial sleep, so that they fell asleep and did not notice the plot of their adversaries.

The bones of Emperor Decius had long since dried up, the holy doctrine had spread further and further, Theodosius, a Christian, sat on the throne. Then one day, a rich man, whose property included the cave, had the wall torn down, intending to build a country house there. Then the seven sleepers awoke from the noise of the builders and rubbed their sleepy eyes. And because they were hungry, they sent Malchus to Ephesus in the evening to bring bread. He carefully descended the mountain — how astonished he was to find Ephesus so transformed. The bakery, where he had bought bread only yesterday, no longer existed. He also learned, to his great astonishment, that Ephesus had become a Christian city overnight... When he wanted to pay with his money at a strange bakery, the baker shook his head and said he could not accept the coin because it showed the head of Emperor Decius, who had died three hundred years ago and therefore no longer had any value. Now, the mighty Emperor Theodosius ruled, as he should well know. Malchus opened his mouth and eyes wide. Then he made the sign of the cross and fainted. When he awoke at the guardhouse, where he had been taken, he spoke, and a holy serenity shone upon him: Come, my brothers, with me to my companions in the mountain Celon and see the miracle: that God saved us from the fury of the heathens and barbarians and allowed us to sleep for two hundred and seventy-two years until Ephesus became Christian. And they went joyfully and psalm-singing, with Malchus leading the way, to Mount Celon, where they triumphantly brought back the seven holy sleepers and carried them before the emperor's throne, where they had to report their fate in well-chosen words.

Many of us would likely wish that God would let us sleep through this troubled time as gently as the seven holy sleepers once slept through suffering and death. Since this cannot be, for we are all unholy, we ask for a mild sleep in our nights to rest from our wild days and a blessed sleep in eternity someday.

Saint Goar

On the Rhine is a small town called St. Goar. It takes its name from the holy Goar, who built his hermitage there a thousand years ago. Saint Goar had to endure many trials, as people refused to believe in his holiness. His inner joy was called irreverent arrogance, his hospitality was seen as gluttony, his piety as hypocrisy, and his signs and wonders as illusions of hell. Yet he remained undaunted and in good spirits, looking not outward, but inward: there he had created a world for himself — trees and flowers not of this earth, ponds full of flowing silver, towers and chapels made of pure marble. And beings moved in this world, light as the wind and shining like the sun. Once, two servants of the Bishop of Trier sought lodging with the hermit after being delayed on a hunting trip. Full of joy, Saint Goar prepared a bed for them and ate and drank with them what his humble kitchen offered. The next day, the two servants rode back to Trier and informed Bishop Rusticus that the hermit Goar led a very lavish and indulgent life in his solitude. They also claimed that they had seen a half-dressed woman in his sleeping chamber, with whom the hermit was living in an immoral relationship. It may be, however, that they had mistaken a vision of the holy Mary, who often descended to Saint Goar, for this woman. The bishop, who was a wicked man, believed the lies and slanders of the two servants and ordered them to bring Saint Goar to Trier. They set out and met Saint Goar, taking him with them. It was an unbearably hot day. All the springs in the forest had dried up. By noon, the servants thought they would surely die of thirst. Just then, a doe emerged from the forest. Saint Goar commanded her to stand still, approached her, milked her, and gave the servants something to drink. Upon reaching the bishop's residence, the bishop arrogantly said to him: Now let us see what miracles this Saint Goar performs. Saint Goar, who was short-sighted, searched for a beam on which he could hang his cloak. As the sun shone through a crack in the door and cast a golden streak on the wall, he mistook the beam of light for a golden rod and hung his cloak on it. The bishop turned pale and said: This is the work of the devil. But Saint Goar did not know what he meant. Then a servant entered the hall, carrying a newborn child in his arms, which he had found in a chapel. For unmarried mothers, who wanted to dispose of their children, often left them in churches, believing that the Lord would care for the poor little ones better than they themselves could. The bishop said: Here is an opportunity for you to demonstrate your power. Command the newborn child to tell who its father and mother are. Saint Goar, in the name of the Holy Trinity, commanded the child to name its parents. The three-day-old child opened its mouth and spoke clearly and decisively: My mother is the whore Flavia and my father... Bishop Rusticus. The bishop was horrified and fell to his knees before Saint Goar, saying: Yes, you are a holy man, and I am a sinner, condemned and forsaken. I acknowledge it, I confess it. Then Saint Goar said: Get up, my friend, I will do penance for you for seven years. You would also do penance for us, Saint Goar.

Saint Augustine

Saint Augustine walked up and down the shore of the sea, lost in thought. Then he saw a boy sitting in the sand, scooping water from the sea with a shell. What are you doing? asked the saint. The boy smiled and replied: I am scooping out the sea. You fool, said Saint Augustine. You will never scoop the endless sea with your little shell. Stop your childish play. Then the boy stood up and said: Saint Augustine, you think you are wiser than I. But how foolish you are. You believe that with your limited understanding, you can grasp eternity and its workings. You are doing nothing different from what I am doing, as I scoop the sea into this little shell. The boy grew golden wings, rose up before Saint Augustine, and flew over the sea.

Saint Elisabeth

It was decreed that the Devil himself should be Saint Elisabeth's confessor. He took on the form of Master Conrad of Marburg. There was no word too crude for him to throw at her like a lump of dung when she came to him, begging for the Christian bread of absolution for her so-called minor sins. For what were her sins? That she gave her wealth and money too generously to the poor, that she tore off her clothes to cover the nakedness of pitiful, hunchbacked old women. To make her see her own lowliness, he scourged the noble woman with a whip, so that the blood flowed in streams down her bare back. He took away all her servants, took away her most trusted and dearest friends, and assigned her to be served by: an unbearably ugly virgin with the head of a vulture and the feet of an ox, who looked as if she had come straight from hell, and a mute, elderly widow who was unable to hear or take in her wishes or concerns. Furthermore, the virgin with the vulture head was full of malice and cunning, spoke ill of her, and ate half of her meager meal. However, Master Conrad hypocritically wrote to the Pope: I assigned Elisabeth the ugly, coarse maid and the mute widow, so that through the maid her humility might be increased, and through the widow her patience might be tested. One day, when Conrad ordered her to come to a sermon, she did not immediately obey, as she was busy caring for a leper. When she eventually appeared before him and apologized, he struck her so that she nearly fainted. Yet, she bore the pain patiently. She told her servants that God had comforted her, for the Master had beaten her all the way to the third, heavenly choir, so that she could see the angels and Jesus Christ in bodily form before her. When Master Conrad heard this, he said: Why didn't I strike her all the way to the ninth choir? Saint Elisabeth was the wife of Landgrave Ludwig of Hesse. He loved her very much, but he disagreed with her extravagance and frequently reproached her for it. Once, he met her outside the castle with a basket full of the finest white bread, which she had taken from the royal kitchen to bring to the poor in Marburg. He scolded her: What do you have in that basket? She blushed in fear and quietly replied: Roses... which I picked from the hedges... The Landgrave lifted the cloth from the basket — whereupon the white loaves had turned into red roses. For God did not want His saint to be made to lie. This is the Miracle of the Roses of Saint Elisabeth. On another occasion, when her husband was away, she had taken a sick man into her bed to care for him better. The Landgrave unexpectedly returned from his journey. A malicious servant reported to him that his wife had a strange man in her bed. Agitated and beside himself, the Landgrave rushed into the room and threw back the bedclothes, only to see the dear Lord Jesus Christ with all His bloody wounds. He fell to his knees and said: Lord, have mercy on me, a poor sinner. I am not worthy to see such miracles. Help me to become a man according to Your will!

Saint Catherine

Catherine of Siena to Gregory IX.

Most holy and venerable Father in Christ, sweet Jesus. Your unworthy daughter, Catherine, servant and handmaiden of the servants of Christ, writes to you in His precious blood. Heaven is opened. I see Christ as I did once in my sixth year, when He descended with the lily to betroth Himself to me and placed the ruby ring on my finger: so steadfast that I have not been able to twist or turn it since. This night the ruby began to drip blood, and my heart bled, and my desire to help the poor, tormented, and suffering humanity swelled up like a mountain stream in the flood. Make peace, gentle Lord, peace with your enemies, peace, peace, peace also with yourselves. It is the will of the Savior that you strive for this peace with all your might, and He wants you to act through Him as much as you are able. Ah, it does not seem He wants us to care much for earthly power, rule, and glory: that we forget and do not consider, in our desire for dominion and our delusion of power, the horrors and wickedness and vice and crime that war brings, and how it feeds on the purity of our will and our soul, and how blasphemous it is to bless weapons meant to pierce the heart of a poor brother. Did not this heart also beat against the sweet Jesus, and did not His eyes, with delight, see the blue flowers and the birds in the bushes, and the sun by day and the stars by night? Who has the right among men to break a brother's eyes like a cheap mirror and shatter a whole small, a whole large world? The Lord wants you to turn your gaze to pious understanding: that gentleness is better than madness, yes, madness, and grace of soul better than arrogance. You may object, most holy Father, that your conscience obliges you to preserve and increase the good of the holy Church. Oh, please consider that more precious than all goods, even those intended for the holiest purposes, is goodness itself: the goodness that is purposeless. The goodness that is based only on itself and desires nothing but itself. The Church's treasure is the blood of Christ, given as the price for souls, and this price was not paid for earthly power and might, but for the eternal salvation of humanity. So let us concede that you are obliged to regain control over the cities the Church has lost: yet this control can never be worldly. Try to rule over the apostates and rebels in humility and love. Go to them unarmed, with the bleeding heart of Christ in your open breast. You will conquer them more easily with the blooming staff of peace than with the thorny whip of war. Better to renounce earthly gold than spiritual gold. Peace, peace, for the love of the crucified Christ. And do not mind the pride, ignorance, blindness, and deafness of your disobedient sons. For you are humble, all-knowing, far-sighted, and keen-eared. Your superhuman holiness and the power of your helplessness will bring them to their knees. For man, created out of love, is drawn to power by nothing other than love. Through the love of the incarnate divine Son, the war waged by man when he rebelled against God and submitted to the tyranny of Satan was overcome. In this way, I see that you, most holy Father, will overcome the war and the power of

Satan in the fortress of the souls of your sons. For Satan will not be driven out by Satan: but through the strength of your gentleness and love, you will overthrow him. Only through this gentle and kind way will the demon be overcome. I place my hope in God's supreme goodness and in Your holiness. I am but the least lamb in His flock, the humblest violet blossom that flowers on the bank of His unfailing river, the weakest pillar in the mystical building of His holy Church. Forgive me the presumption of daring to offer you counsel. The counsel does not come from me, but from the one who whispered it in my ear last night. I would have gladly spoken to you in person, to relieve my conscience completely. Whenever it pleases your holiness that I come to you, I will come willingly. Act in such a way that I am not called by you to Christ the Crucified, for only to Him could I call, since on Earth there is no one higher than you. Remain in God's sweet and holy grace. Humbly, I ask for your blessing. *Jesus dolce. Jesus amore.*

Saint Dorothea

Saint Dorothea was led to martyrdom and execution during the time of the Roman Emperor Diocletian. There, she encountered a young man who said: You Christians always talk so much about the garden of paradise: how glorious the flowers bloom there, how magnificent the fruits grow there. Today, you will be in paradise, Dorothea. Perhaps you could send me some roses and apples from there... The holy virgin replied: I will gladly do so.

And on the night after her execution, a beautiful blonde child appeared at the bedside of Theophilus, wearing a cloak entirely covered in stars, and handed him a golden basket filled with roses and apples. This, said the child with a voice as sweet as a flute, Saint Dorothea sends to you from the garden of paradise. Afterward, the child vanished, leaving the basket in Theophilus' hands. It was wintertime, and there were no flowers or fruits on earth. Then Theophilus converted, publicly professed Christianity, and was beheaded with the ax, on which the blood of Saint Dorothea had not yet dried.

Help us, Saint Dorothea, that we too may show such courage in our confession.

Saint Luke

In a dream, Saint Luke was visited by an English apparition who spoke: Arise, Saint Luke, you shall paint the face of our beloved Lady, so that an image of her may be passed down to future generations. Saint Luke rose at dawn and humbly went to the hut where Mary lived, bringing with him his brush, palette, canvas, and paintbox, all wrapped in his cloak, for he was already a respected and famous painter. There, he humbly greeted the Holy Virgin, informing her of his request and the angel's visit during the night. Mary smiled, as only she could smile, and sat outside the hut beneath the trees, posing. Saint Luke set up his easel and paintbox, measured various proportions, and began to draw and paint. From the clouds above, little cherubs, putti, and angels floated down. Some formed a crown, playfully winding around Mary, and became part of the painting. Others stood with folded wings behind him, curiously observing the masterpiece being created, or helping him grind paint and hand him brushes.

The work progressed briskly until evening, when the twilight fell too early, hindering the artist's progress. The painting was almost, but not entirely, complete. The eyes of Mary lacked their final radiance, her mouth a hint of a smile, and her whole being a trace of maternal tenderness. Sighing, Saint Luke packed up his tools, promising to return the next day to finish the work in the Lord. That night, however, Mary was called up to heaven, and when Saint Luke knocked on her hut the next day, no voice answered. When he opened the door, he saw the earthly form of the Holy Mother lying pale and still upon the bed. Thus it came to pass that there is no completed image of the Holy Woman on Earth. Even the greatest painters of all time — Raphael, Bellini, Fra Angelico — have only captured a faint reflection of her on canvas. Always something is missing: some captured her eyes, but missed her lips entirely. One painted the most beautiful and tender hands, but her forehead was too severe, her hair not blonde enough, not golden enough. The one who could have painted her completely and perfectly in her lifetime, had death taken the brush from his hand. But it must be so. Everyone must make their own image of the Madonna. She will bless it, even if it does not succeed perfectly. Life remains incomplete. We too walk imperfectly to the other side.

Help us, Saint Luke, to complete our image in the heavenly kingdom. There you have gold and rose-red, dawn and sky-blue on your palette — colors that we, painted in gray and black, long for with blessed yearning. Lift us from the shadow into the light. Let us shine like the stars, sun, and moon, Saint Luke.

The Nine Muses

When Christ drove the Greek gods from Olympus, the exiled nine Muses sadly gathered on the slopes of Helicon and Parnassus. Clio, the Muse of History, sat hunched over her parchment, silently reading about the rise and growth of Christianity. Melpomene, the Muse of Tragedy, tearfully watched the endless procession of the holy martyrs and martyrs' wives, tormented and killed for their faith. Calliope, the Muse of Heroic Song, sang the epic of the dawn of the new world. Urania gazed at the stars in the bright day; but all were overshadowed by the Star of Bethlehem. Euterpe played the first liturgy on her flute. Polyhymnia, her dark locks crowned with laurel, listened to her silently. Erato, holding the crown of roses and myrtle, vowed to serve the heavenly Bridegroom alone in love and fidelity. Terpsichore danced to the music of Euterpe in the holy circle. When Christ saw that each Muse wished to serve Him and be His subject in her own way, He had pity on them and kindly promised to take them all into the Christian heaven. Each one should wait her time, and whenever a saint walked on Earth, one of the nine Muses would ascend to heaven in her soul. The Muses were then joyful and in good spirits. And it happened that Clio ascended in Saint Catherine, Melpomene in Saint Cecilia, Calliope in Saint Apollonia, Urania in Saint Juliana, Euterpe in Saint Euphrosyne, Polyhymnia in Saint Eugenia, and Erato in Saint Thais.

But Terpsichore, the dancer among the Muses, still walks on Earth unredeemed. If you are lucky, you may see her dancing on a Sunday in this or that village. She can be recognized by the fact that she only dances once with each dancer. — O beautiful virgins, is there not one of you who would like to give up dancing and become a saint? Immediately, Terpsichore would be redeemed and would ascend to heaven in the soul of this holy maiden...

Saint Cecilia

The convent of Our Lady was ruled with a gentle yet firm hand by a young and beautiful abbess named Gertrudis. She had a brother, a knight, who one day rode past the convent. With him in the saddle lay a beautiful young man, his eyes closed, his blonde hair disheveled over his forehead, and feverish sweat on his cheeks. He was the knight's friend, who had been seriously injured while hunting near the convent when a wild boar had charged at him, goring him with its tusks and pushing him into an abyss. The abbess took the young man in lovingly and cared for him according to the Christian commandment of charity. However, as he grew stronger, she began to lose the color in her cheeks and became deeply ill in her heart. She whipped and punished herself in her cell. But it was in vain: the image of the handsome young man shone ever more seductively and brightly in her soul. The young man, too, was so captivated by the beauty of the young abbess that he thought it better to have died under the boar's tusks than to live without possessing her. And he confessed his love to her. Every night she went into the convent chapel in her heart's distress, and each night she asked a different saint for advice. But the saints remained silent. Now, in a niche, there hung a miraculous image of Saint Cecilia. On the seventh night, she knelt before it and spoke: Holy Virgin, see how I suffer. I cannot live and die without the knight. I entrust to you the affairs of the convent until I return... And she placed the keys at the image's feet and, that very night, left the convent with the knight. She lived blissfully with the knight for a year in the outside world. Afterward, the knight died of a treacherous illness in her arms. After burying him and planting roses, carnations, and a weeping willow at his grave, she returned to her convent, her farewell tears still in her eyes. And behold, there at the gate window sat Saint

Cecilia in the form of Gertrudis, who had managed the convent's affairs for the year as though she had never left. She opened the gate and spoke: Lost sheep, did you find your way back to your flock? Full of fervent thanks and deep regret, Gertrudis sank to her knees before Cecilia. Saint Cecilia spoke: Rise, no one knows you were gone for so long. Here are the keys. Manage your duties as before and do not fall into temptation again! And she gave her the keys and disappeared into the twilight of the chapel.

Saint Alexius

Alexius, a wealthy young Roman, left his wife on their wedding night and went into the world. He did penance for thirteen years in Asia Minor and stood on a pillar in the desert, never leaving it. After thirteen years, God sent him a dove. He then descended and returned to Rome, entering his own house as a stranger and serving his wife as a lowly slave without her recognizing him. But when, weakened by suffering and emaciation, he lay on the bier and the washers of the dead shaved and bathed him, they recognized him as Alexius and called his wife, who found the ring on his hand, the one she had once given him at their engagement. She lamented and wept, striking her chest. The people of Rome gathered around his bier, from which a sweet fragrance emanated. They brought the sick and suffering of all kinds, and whoever touched the body of Saint Alexius went away healed, praising the miracle of the Lord.

From Our Dear Lady

Our dear Lady is filled with unspeakable goodness and grace. She shows no regard for social standing or education, rank or prestige among those who serve her sincerely. A bright heart, even if it beats beneath tattered clothes, is dearer to her than a dark Sunday dress. And often a kind word, spoken at the right time, helps more than a thousand good deeds.

A murderer, who was hanged, once cried out in his last moments, after he had long forgotten the Madonna's name and had not thought of her in his sinful ways: Help, Maria!

His soul departed from his body. Then the devil came and claimed it for himself. For years, he justified his demand, saying that he had acted in my spirit and according to my will. He was a scoundrel, an adulterer, a spendthrift, a sensualist, a robber, and a murderer. His soul belongs to me rightfully and justly.

Then our dear Lady appeared in a bright cloud and proclaimed: He has repented of his evil deeds in the last second before his spirit departed and called upon my name and my help. He shall not have called in vain. Depart from here,

Satan, for this soul is mine.

And he was a thief of a strange nature. He had chosen the Mother of God as his patroness. Every time before he went about his wicked work, he entrusted himself to her protection and asked her to bless his plan – as if he were going on a pious pilgrimage.

Who would not see such a sinful beginning as mockery and blasphemy against God? Not so for our Holy Lady. She sensed the true essence behind the cracked exterior. Though he had often escaped the hands of justice – thinking he was protected by his humble prayers to the Virgin – one day they finally caught him and hanged him. There he hung for ten days. But when the court officers came on the eleventh day to cut down his body, they were greatly surprised to find the thief still alive. The holy Virgin, the sweetest lady, preserved me, he said as he descended the ladder, for the death that had hovered around me in the form of a black raven for ten days could do me no harm. Blessed be you forever, Maria. And he went on to become a monk, living a life of penance and improvement from then on.

Let us not, in vanity and peacock-like delusions, exalt ourselves above this murderer and this thief. Perhaps, who knows, we are more in need of holy grace than they are.

Here follows a hymn in praise and honor of the holy Virgin:

I must leap,
I hear the ringing
Of your name, Maria.
All things must turn out
As you will, Maria.
You divining rod, Maria.
Cherubim,
Seraphim
Sing your praises, Maria.
Whoever harbors,
whoever bears
heartache, let them call:
Help, gentle maid, Maria!

Here ends the book of the saints' lives and passions: which is a mirror in which a person may behold whether they are like them or may become like them. For nothing affects and educates toward virtue more than their examples: flung like a fiery beacon into the night of vice and falsehood, of which we all partake, sinners one and all, entangled in trouble and death and misery. May the holy women and men help us toward a joyful ascension to heaven. Blessed be God on high for this. Amen.

Part Seven:

Little Klabund Book

Novellas and poems published by Philipp Reclam Jr. Leipzig 1921.

Little Klabund Book

Short Autobiography

I am, as I write this, twenty-seven years old. But I could also write: three years, or: fifty thousand. I come from somewhere in the Mark. I am a Prussian. And my colors, which you know, are black and white. Black, that is the night, and white, that is the day. I am. Day and night. I was born in the Mark, but earlier I once lived in China and, with large horn-rimmed glasses, wrote little verses on large strips of silk.

My path is still long. Whoever wants to accompany me for an hour is welcome. Again and again, I must be born. I can still clearly remember that I once was a hare, hopping over the fields and eating cabbage. Later, I was a vulture, who used to gouge out the eyes of the hares. In this way, I murdered myself. I was good. I was bad. I was beautiful and ugly; charming and dreadful, cowardly and brave, domineering and servile. I love the people. But I do not love them more than the animals or the stars, with which I can speak just as much as with you, my human brother. I love the women. Above all, the dearest woman, who was both the daughter and the mother of God. She has long since returned to God's throne. There she stands, holding the lily, and smiles and cries down upon me. – What you know is only part of what I composed. Often the wind blew away the pages on which I wrote. During my many wanderings, I lost two entire manuscript drafts of dramas. Whoever found them may keep them, whether they use them to wallpaper their room or read them to their wife after supper. Again and again, I must fight the ringing battles inside me with a hot blade to the end. The battle of the red and white rose. When I once sink to the ground, having bled to death, let them throw white and red roses on my grave. It should be decorated like a bridal bed, and a loving couple should fall upon it like golden rain. And even in death, I will bless the new life.

Locarno 1919, 29 years old.

Katharina

"You're being foolish," said Lapa. "You mustn't sleep alone in a room any-more; otherwise, you'll cry and pray all night instead of, after a day of honest labor and a short, God-pleasing prayer — God doesn't love long prayers; they taste to Him like overly diluted wine — sleeping the dreamless sleep of good people. I'll dismiss one of the maids so that you'll have work to keep you busy and no time to chase after your whims, crawling into damp caves that are none of your concern and seeing mountains where there are none."

Katharina bowed her head.

A smile swayed on her slender shoulders.

Lapa shouted angrily: "Jakob Benincasa, that swine, your father, came home drunk again. He soiled our bed and fouled the entire room. I had to sleep on a chair in the kitchen. You'll tidy up the room immediately. Carlotta, the maid, can leave at once."

Katharina raised her head. She saw her mother unfold — a golden flower — and saw the holy Mary as a bee, humming as she rose from the chalice.

When I serve my mother, I serve the Mother of God, she thought. My father is Christ, my brothers resemble the apostles, and Bonaventura, my sister, flees the family home in a monk's robe, transforming herself joyfully into Euphrosyne. But I, her twin sister, consecrate my service under the name Smaragdus to the cloister of my parental home, and only when I have died will people understand and realize that I was a woman.

When Jakob Benincasa entered the bedroom, where Katharina was busy with rag and bucket, diligently erasing the traces of his drunkenness, it seemed to him as if a white dove rose from her crown and drifted softly through the open window.

He hurried at once back to the tavern "The Merry Federigo" and invited the assembled company to a hearty drink at his expense.

"Is your daughter Katharina finally getting married," laughed Ciseri, the hunch-backed cobbler, "or what joy is driving the cork out of your barrel?"

"I know," whispered Bosco, the lanky stonemason. "His wife is expecting their thirteenth child in nine months. He just told her, and she told him. That's why his happiness knows no bounds..."

"I believe," thundered the innkeeper's hammer at the cask, "he's struck a good deal. The noble ladies of Siena have commissioned him to bleach their gray, love-ravaged hair blond or, where they have no hair at all, to paint their bald heads black at the crown. If he gets even one coin from each lady, that's surely a tidy fortune."

"Nonsense," brayed Jakob Benincasa. "You're all fools. You stumble like mules through the mountains, heads lowered, grazing on plain herbs around your hooves. Do you see the waterfall at the rock's edge? The quiet chamois, brown on the horizon? The vulture that's a lightning bolt? The blue flower of snow? The moss of men's villages?"

"Young man," the painter Simone Martini flung his words like dabs of color into the gray space, "you speak like Petrarch. You should have it printed."

"My daughter Katharina is a saint," Jakob Benincasa roared. He struck his elbows against the low vaulting. "That's why we'll all get drunk today. Because I, Jakob Benincasa, am the father of this saint. And if she's a saint, then the seed of sainthood must be in me as well. For she can't have gotten her holiness from Lapa. Lapa is a malicious hound."

The painter, the hunchbacked cobbler, and the lanky stonemason clapped their hands. The innkeeper's hammer resounded one last blow. Now the cork flew from the barrel.

"If your daughter Katharina is a saint," said Ambra, the little goldsmith, "then you'll need to have a halo made for her by me. Pure gold."

"Does she already have stigmata on her hands and feet?" asked Pedamonte, a jeweler. "You'll need to set rubies in her wounds."

"If she wants to flagellate herself, as all true saints do, she'll need a durable scourge or a whip with nails. I recommend myself to her holy patronage," bowed Marchetti, the armorer.

The painter Simone Martini sketched Katharina's likeness in chalk on the table.

"She's as beautiful as few women in Siena," he said quietly.

Jakob Benincasa trembled.

The poet Petrarch approached Martini, placed a hand on his shoulder, and leaned gently forward to observe the drawing.

His forehead shone like an eternal lamp, and his lips moved like the wings of two butterflies.

Ferdinand Cortez

He screamed like a jaguar in his sleep.

In the morning, a golden hummingbird sat before his window and called out.

The palm trees in the tubs at the entrance to the royal palace broke free and rooted themselves in his dream.

A rose cockatoo screeched: Thief! Thief!

Columbus strode across the horizon, clad in blue armor, commanding like a god.

He knew the small province of Extremadura inside and out.

What does that barren hill mean, eh?

Seven times it had been climbed; the land around it remained equally brown and dirty each time. Yes, browner and dirtier with each climb.

That olive grove?

At best, a fleeting inspiration for a tapestry. But the deed? The impact? The essence of the world? Where?

In that effeminate paunch? Impregnated by a priest?

There, the village: — Medeleir — essential, because one was conceived there, carried like a calf, born in the hay, desired in drink, conceived in the drunken frenzy of a periodic booze-hound?

Out of this flat circle! From shrub and bush to trunk and arch.

To be a shadow in this over-brightness. To shade the new world.

Europe was decaying.

Granada crumbled into ashes like a burnt-out log.

Where still burned a heroic star?

Kings wallowed effeminately in indulgent beds. Knights served for gold.

Poets begged for warm soup like dogs.

But the great deed: It suffices unto itself. It seeks only itself.

A hero raises a world from the ocean like the rising sun.

Columbus stood at the bow of the ships.

He believed in America. In the new world. And thus, he found it.

Farewell, father.

You will hear from me when I have forgotten the stripes you lashed into my back.

Farewell, Ines.

One last kiss.

Your son shall be called Fernandez.

The waves crash upon the shore: They beat the rhythm of the oars.

They beat in time with my pulse.

The world ocean is my heart.

The new world — my will.

Don Diego traced a route around the world on a map with a goose feather.

"You conspire against me? Abuse my trust? I shall have you hanged!"

Cortez yanked the chain so that it clinked.

"Even better. On the gallows, I'll be closer to heaven. For this cursed earth sits in my stomach like a meal of overly rich, oil-fried dumplings. I spit it out of my mouth."

He climbed the gallows like a dancer. He placed the noose around his own neck. He turned once from east to west, from north to south.

The whole island was a pedestal for his gallows.

But out there in the south — wasn't a row of dolphins swimming toward the island?

Didn't the sound of small bells ring out? Didn't a cannon shot echo faintly in the distance?

Cortez cast off the noose. He stood on the top rung of the ladder and shouted: "Don Diego! Your fleet is back from America!"

Don Diego rushed to the harbor.

Already, trumpets blared, flags waved, pennants fluttered.

At the mast of the flagship stood, bound with ropes, a naked brown man, roaring.

But that which gleamed in the sun? That gentle creature lying between ropes and rigging: Meant for me?

Don Diego embraced the admiral. But Cortez stormed onto the quarterdeck, lifted the Indian woman from the ropes into his arms, and dashed through an aisle of soldiers and sailors into the olive grove.

Don Diego sent for Cortez: "I grant you the gallows! — Where is the American woman?"

Cortez shrugged.

Don Diego: "You want to go to America?"

Cortez knelt and kissed the viceroy's mud-caked riding boot: "Help me!"

Diego: "You must take the bull by the horns! Weave me soldiers! Sailors! Thieves! Scoundrels! A glorious expedition awaits! We shall conquer the newest world! Columbus is a field preacher compared to us: He is a sage who showed us the new world; we shall own it.

"I give you five ships! Sail to Mexico!"

The Transformation of Harun al-Rashid

Harun al-Rashid, disguised as a young scholar, had won the affection of a lady who loved him only as the handsome and noble young man she saw, unaware of his princely status. Harun al-Rashid pondered at length how he might enter her father's house without compromising the lady's reputation. He devised the following plan: He informed her that he would enter her father's house, who was one of his higher officials, disguised as Harun al-Rashid himself, and asked her not to be alarmed by the misuse of the name and persona of the illustrious Caliph, for he undertook this bold act solely out of love for her. The lady, equally horrified and delighted, embraced her young scholar in the guise of the Caliph, who, through his many transformations, had now arrived at the ultimate one: transforming from himself into himself...

The Two Realms

There was peace on earth, for the earth was peaceful, and humankind was peaceful, and peaceful was heaven and the Son of Heaven. People spoke not for the sake of speaking; they spoke their thoughts. Life was simple and earnest. Cheerfulness dwelt in the heart, not in taverns. Everyone had their own tasks: to till the fields, tend the livestock, and love their spouse. Everyone had their own thoughts: to follow the course of the stars and the gold beetle, to observe the turtle's pace, and to read the future in the scattered pollen of the prophetic plant, Schi. There were few cities. Children were raised collectively by the community. Only sacred festivals were celebrated according to sacred rituals. Clothing was like the dust of the Earth: brown. Only for the dead, at the festival of the dead, did people wear gold. The elderly, orphans, and widows were supported by public means. There were no beggars. Everyone had air to breathe, food to eat, smiles to share, and life to live. Sons served their fathers, daughters served their mothers, and spouses served one another. Whoever stumbled was helped to their feet. At the grave of the good, all wept. The ruler rode on a mule through the cities, like a humble official, and he preferred to be a guest of the old man on the mountain. There he sat at the old man's feet, and as dew dripped from the trees, crickets chirped, and a flock of wild geese tore the horizon with their cries, the old man spoke to him, planting a seed in his soul that blossomed into glorious beauty for him and his people.

But times changed, and so did people. They forgot how to think well and thus how to act well. Simplicity turned into complexity, quiet contemplation into noisy reflection, noble rule into crude tyranny. Gentle calls turned into wild screams. The golden garments of their former festivals became everyday attire, worn day and night, and they placed poor symbols in the coffins of their dead instead of reviving the dead within themselves to new life (for such is the meaning of death, which is only seemingly death, just as this life is only seemingly life). They whispered: "Let the dead remain dead, and let us — live. What do we care for the old times, the times of the wise elders and the old man of the mountain? We want a new, sparkling time. Let it shine like this copper kettle in which a chicken is roasting or like that glass goblet full of wine and cleverness. Let it glow like our thousand cities at night, with millions of paper lanterns, or like the patina on the giant dome of the temple of Cheu-kong." Thus they spoke thoughtlessly, speaking only to speak, and thinking only to think. And so the unity of thought and action was torn into a cruel duality. And the trinity of soul, meaning, and being was torn into a disharmony of three. Soul remained soul, apart from the rest. Being remained being, apart from the rest. Meaning remained meaning, apart from the rest. Sons no longer served their fathers, nor daughters their mothers. Women became the slaves of men, and men the slaves of women. Beggars sat in rags before the sanctuaries, and the sanctuaries sat in rags before the beggars. The people starved. Widows were violated. Orphans were abused. The elderly froze in the winter nights. Each person raised their children according to their own depravity.

The ruler, however, rode a silver-bridled white steed amid a cavalcade of noble riders to the old man on the mountain. He galloped over rice and maize fields; the hooves of his horses trampled the harvest, and the shouts of his companions dishonored the women working in the fields. He did not return the humble greetings of the peasants. Day laborers threw themselves, whining, before his horse. The horse pranced over them.

He tied his warhorse, its white coat still crusted with the blood of enemies, to the gatepost of the hermitage. The knights settled on the lawn before it, drinking and making noise. Some raised their bows and shot arrows at the little songbirds in the branches or the swans gliding on the forest pond.

The ruler entered the hut, adorned in splendor, his hand on the jeweled hilt of his sword. There sat the old man of the mountain, 111 years old, weathered as an eternal peak. But in his eyes were blue blossoms. His head was softly snowed upon, but the snow held sunlight. He spoke and spoke his thoughts: "Greetings, prince! Forgive the loftiness of my humility if it sets right the rank you have given it. He whom you call a Wu, a great magician, is a Ju, a humble man striving to set right the sacred Three. You come to ask me about the good old times because a bad new time has arisen like a storm. The blue sky is veiled. Clarity has turned to twilight. Instead of the sun, lightning reigns; instead of the zephyr, the storm. Instead of dew, rain drips; instead of the nightingale, thunder sings. You have gone out of yourselves instead of into yourselves. You have presumed to grow flowers from pines and fruit from violets. You waged war with horsetail reeds as weapons, and your peace was a struggle with knives. Brother hated brother, and woman hated woman. Un-being ruled being. The essential — fled.

"Cast off your gold and the golden rings on your fingers, which you stole from ancestral graves. Cast off the triumphant mask of power that distorts your face. Undo the deeds you have done. Tear down the palaces you have built. Give your unworthy jewels to the poor who loiter before the temples of an alien god. Send your retinue, this noble rabble, into the steppes to their kin: the vultures and jackals. Raise the most wretched prostitute from the most wretched teahouse of the capital to be your princess. Then return, clad only in a loincloth, without horse, without retinue, without mule — on foot, with a staff you have carved yourself. And I will teach you to read, think, and act from this book with three seals, which is called I-hi-wie, or the doctrine of the holy triad. For three is the sacred number. It is heaven, earth, human. The I, the You, and the It. This is what I tell you."

And the ruler was struck to his core, to his third heart. He found no words for farewell or thanks. Silently, he left the hermitage. He stepped silently among his companions. Their laughter died, their clinking cups fell silent. The bowstring drawn to the evening star snapped. They saw the prince's forehead: a sudden furrow was etched into it. And it was the scar of a wound that would never heal.

He spoke: "I have seen the dragon Lung. It roared and swept through the air, and it was a wind that cast me to the ground. My forehead struck a stone and burst open, and behold: vermin spilled from my brain — lice, crabs, and caterpillars."

The evening glow lay over the pine forest.

The prince tore his silk garment. He tore the saddle, the costly trappings, and the covers from his horse.

And naked, he mounted the naked horse and rode into the evening.

And he rode toward the setting sun into the great desert and was never seen again.

Some say he reached the western land of Ta-tsin, where he taught the wisdom of the old man from the mountain, lived to a great age, and became himself an old man of the mountain.

Child in the Cradle

This I know: that I resisted awakening. With hands and feet, I struggled against being born. When the Indians proclaim that souls push toward birth, I can swear the opposite for myself. I played with many delicate and good beings on the lotus meadow. It was an eternal bowing to and fro, like flowers in the wind. A gentle pink twilight enveloped us: neither day nor night. Infinite fragrances flooded.

Everyone was good to everyone. And no soul suspected any malice or treachery.

Now that I am alive, lying in a white cradle, I feel deep in my heart that along with the umbilical cord, the likewise silken bond was torn that had connected me with bliss.

With painfully large eyes, I sometimes see my mother, who bends over me, blonde and smiling.

And like a parakeet, scarcely audible, the realization rustles through my small left brain: In that gaze of the mother, with which she tucks me in at night, a ray of the lost paradise is captured. And quietly, I raise my hands to hold the ray.

Little Songs for Irene

Shall I sing little songs,
As I often did?
The sun is already shining and nightingale wings
draw near.

Under the snow the melt is already
Rushing towards spring.
Let us smile, let us listen!
You!

Isn't May already flowing
In your tears?
Mountains lean lovingly against mountains.
Be!

A fir tree stands in young growth,
Where the marten crept.
Winter falters. The foehn winds are gusting. Love
Me!

God made us light and heavy.
You cried. I laughed.
You laughed. I cried.
Just as the sun and moon shine in the sky.

Tears will trickle down forever
And the rain of thunderstorms.
Gods are all like pebbles.
Bile tastes so bitter in the mouth.

Pain bites shamelessly into the chest,
And the ribs drum for war.
The air bends toward decay,
And the kiss splits lips apart.

Mountains stand between hearts.
Between eyes rivers flow.
Breasts are parted by brazen armor.
Between hands shots fall.

Even iron chains tear apart
In the strongest union.
And cold glaciers glisten,
And Fate laughs at the torment.

Where is my girl?
On the mountain,
With a dwarf,
My girl dwells.

Where is my girl?
On the meadow,
A red giant
Kisses my girl.

Where is my girl?
In the alder grove,
At her mouth
A butterfly flutters.

Where is my girl?
Above the earth,
Two black horses
Abducted my girl.

When the meadows glow pink at dawn
And the sun appears so beautifully,
I hasten with my lambs
To where we're treated with good care.

Clouds drift and meadows rise
Floating up from the depths to us.
And we graze, living in love,
By the silver course of the brook.

When my maiden approaches to greet me,
I take the youngest lamb,
And I sink at her feet,
offering, as Abraham once did.

Dear girl, take the gift!

When my cheeks have faded,
Have it graze upon my grave
And then remember me.

You enchanted the sun with your eyes,
So that it casts its golden rays more brightly.

You charmed the moon at night,
So that it still watches outside your window during the day.

When your foot once touched a stone,
A pair of wings carried the stone into the distance.

When your hand lay on my brow,
Eternal night became eternal day.

When you gave yourself to me with body and blood,
God entrusted the daughter to my care.

You blow around my cheeks,
You smile from the light.
I am embraced by you
In autumnal verse.

I am encircled by you,
I am echoed by you.
I am allied with you:
Creator and creation.

I am surrounded by you,
I am encircled by you.
My death and my life
Are spirit of your spirit.

To cherish the evening once more
In the depths of this feeling.
The forms, the forces
Are too many.

They swirl around the bold candelabrum,

Which illuminates the night.
More feverishly and moistly
The world's face shines.

First stars, first drops of rain,
The leaves on the trees sings ever sweeter.
And the fraternal lightning blesses
The awakened dream blue as violets.

One awakens in the sanatorium.
The bucket clinks, brooms clatter.
Holy than an oratorio
The day sounds: weeping... as before...

Kindly the doctor's steps resound,
A nurse skips along beside him.
From the midst of darkness
A clock strikes into life.

Already, busy looking at a chart,
An assistant dreams with great pretense.
And I pull at the bell,
Ringing for tea and the day to come to my bed.

The hour has come, the wound burns,
The sun is sinking from the firmament.
You are with me. I am with you.
The room is full of golden creatures.

Here they crawl heavily, there they fly lightly –
How quickly the wall is reached!

Your cool mouth rests upon my brow –
The heavenly rockets are whirring about.
The soul plummets. I do not know
Why my eyes speak in tears.

Lullaby for Myself

Oh, I lie far away
Beyond space and time,
In the sun, I lie still and aware.
Snow crowns me with light,
Heaven is my poem,
And the forests chime loudly and softly.

From the depths rise
A golden head and bows,
The lovely specter of its curls,
Soul, you of the sea, soul, you of the snow,
Soul, soul, sun how you burn!

When I wander in the nights,
A star like many others,
The golden brothers quietly follow
My journey.

The first tells the second
To guide me tenderly,
The second tells the many
To play around me in their radiance.

Thus, I cry out through the swarm
Of stars across the heavens.
I smile, shine, and wander,
A star like so many others.

Cheek rested against cheek,
Gaze rested against gaze.
Many women have walked with me,
And only one looked back.

Many slept peacefully beside me,
And only one awoke.
My tattered sail found its harbor,
And my day met its night.

Sister,
The fever burns.
Birds are building moonlit nests
From the firmament.
The red cross on your armband,
Forged in red –
Oh Mother, come to your child,
To your death –

Lullaby for Irene

For one summer long,
Golden bells swung,
Calling to ever fairer days.
When you opened your eyes,
My kiss rested upon them,
And your heart lay in my hands.

For an entire summer,
Song and laughter rang out,
And we were completely aflame with joy.
Snakes and lizards came,
And tamed they took
Sweets from your gentle hand.

For one summer long,
I wrestled with the angel,
So that this summer might be eternal.
Alas, I was too weak,
And in the autumn
The Grim Reaper broke the sheaf of luck in two.

This summer was
Full as a hundred years,
through which the blood of God's grace f.owed.
May it's fate bestow
Happiness upon our child
For many, many, many summers.

Lullaby for Your Child

Close your eyes!
Smile at the angels –
The sight of this world would furrow your brow.
The world is made of lions and wolves,
The world is a grey gulf,
As white sails drift in the storm.

Blessed without sin,
Faithful in patience,
You await life's coming: pure,
Will it be wild as today,
Will it be full of bells
And full of angelic happiness and spring?

Dream. slumber deeply!
When God called you,
Your mother Earth lay in travail.
Ah, perhaps your son
Will already walk in peace
Hand in hand with his brothers.

So I sit without rest
Sleeplessly here, line by line.
Nothing was as good as you,
Nothing as wicked as me.

Nothing was as black as me,
Nothing as blonde as you.
O remain, eternally,
Restless one, my tranquility.

In the next room, a stranger's footstep echoes.
The clock strikes seven. You do not appear.
It was a cloud-like shadow that slid
And arched ghostlike through the doorway.

I nevertheless prepared my arms to receive it,
For its was related to you in shadow.
The brow rose steeply. A golden cherubim
Stood radiant, waved its palm and vanished.

What has become of me?
I barely know who I am.
I threw myself overboard
Into the dark water below.

My joy is the mackerel,
My brother is the fish.
I lavishly cast my soul
Upon them without restraint.

At times, it seems as if a sunbeam
Calls me into the light.
Yet it neither pierces nor illuminates
My green depths.

I see it in your image, you too suffer,
Being so far away from me.
I feel how you avoid the angelic games
And how sad you are to be covered in stars.

I am but the narrow shadow of your shadow.
You are so bright. I am so completely dark.
Oh, cast the golden net toward your husband
And draw him across into your splendor.

In your hands you took
My heart with you
Into the catafalque.
I'm crumbling from all sides
Like lime.

Soon I will no longer be myself,
Always only you.
And I'll find peace
In your rest.

My pain will be endured
By me.

My heart will be cherished
By you.

And if I enthusiastically brandish the scepter,
A guardian to the people, and a call to glory:
All steps, great and small,
Lead only to your grave.

I fight the wicked with a sword of fire,
And bravely perform this deed or that,
My reward can only be: to rest
With you in a single coffin.

Like many who perish in boyish humility
Before the prince's stern appearance:
So do I perish before you. The cricket chirps.
And this day, I fear, will likely be the final one.

Ah, that I, even beyond the grave,
Would stretch out my arms to you forever!
I shall never return to my father's house,
And foreign soil feels like no soil at all.

Come at the hour of ghosts,
So no gaze may touch you again.
Come with a star through the window,
With a gust of wind through the door.

Lie down beside me on the pillows,
Let us be silent, cheek to cheek,
Until, in flaming kisses,
We lean toward each other.

Take me with you when you depart
With the song of the nightingale.
I want to suffer what you suffer,
Blessed to be in your soul.

The sun shines brightly and the moon sinks low,
Goats climb the hills.
Girls with colorful wings
Are as lively as parrots.

The mountain stands purple with violets
The chestnut leaves rustle,
And lovers whisper about
Their children in a golden bed.

Am I an echo? Am I a summons?
As I swim, I feel tears rising;
And I must bow my knees
Before the tomb I created.

Every day I must accustom myself
To this life anew.
Bells ring every now and then.
Clouds drift up and down.

And a stream of tears flows
Upward like a rainbow.
Into the sky, I pour
My waves, my surges.

Angels bow their cheeks,
Cooling the fires in their eyes.
And the most beautiful one comes walking,
And moistens his hands.

Part Eight:

The Chaotic Decline of the West

(Published in 1922 by Roland-Verlag in Munich.)

The Chaotic Decline of the West

Prologue

His face is grayish-yellow. The nose
Rises up to a cliff-like point. The eyes lie mottled,
Suspiciously shadowed by his lashes,
Crouched to pounce like panthers in their den.
His right arm, holding the cigar, stands
Stiff as a sword, as if to sever himself
From the others who are repulsive to him
And yet somehow sympathetic.
When he taps off the ash,
It falls like scorn upon the conversation.
A curt "Yes," a sharp "No"
He occasionally throws into the discussion.
With this pointed "Yes" and "No,"
He impales people as if on needless
And takes them home
For his beetle collection.

If you open the poet's next book,
Oh God! You find yourself already inscribed in it.
And whoever, in just self-awareness,
Believed himself to be a dragonfly-like creature,
Finds himself, to his astonishment, portrayed as a dung beetle.

It was the Morning of a Rainy Autumn Sunday

It was on the morning of a rainy autumn Sunday when he began to write this book. He sat in Room No. 2 of the "Zur Post" inn in Haag in Upper Bavaria and looked out at the old, five-spired tower of Haag Castle, which rose through the mist like a bundle of pencils. After Leni had told him that strange story about the silver spoons last night under the chestnut tree (not far from the monastery: the nuns' cells glinted through the undergrowth, and now and then ripe chestnuts knocked onto the leaf-covered ground and broke apart in fright), he was not particularly surprised that she hadn't met him this morning at the agreed spot before church. Surely, she must have hanged herself. Or perhaps the weather was too bad for a walk up to the alpine pasture? He lit a cigarette, which warmed him a little, and strolled through the slippery alleys. He saw people leaving the church.

226

It was already quarter to eight. The bell tolled out of kilter, and he looked up at the tower, noticing the coat of arms of Haag Castle: the white leaping horse on a red background. The rain grew heavier, and he took shelter under the pavilion. A boy stumbled up the steps to the tavern, carrying a milk can, tripped, and fell into the dirt. He thought about the mountains, which would remain hidden all day, and about Fiete, realizing he would have to write to her. He walked down to the market, debating whether to inquire at Leni's parents' house to see if she had come home the previous night. Perhaps her father would try to slap him, and her mother might attack him with a kitchen knife. "I can already picture her," he thought, "lying dead in bed: like yellow glass, with her eyes bulging as a blue river overflows its banks." He stopped by Andreas Lehner, a printer and the proprietor of the Haager Messenger, to ask about the latest news from the front lines, bought a few sheets of white paper and some postcards — one of which he set aside for Fiete — and returned to his room to write a story which began as noted above.

Reporting for Duty

Although I've been dead for quite some time, I received a summons to report for military service. This surprised me quite a bit, but I went to the district command despite the stir I caused in the streets.

"Excuse me," I rattled with my teeth, shaking the bone dust from my feet, "there must be a mistake here. I died in 1797 during the Great Revolution — oddly enough, by the natural cause of choking on a turkey bone. And now I'm supposed to serve in the military? That's a *contradictio in adiecto*."

The district sergeant-major eyed me critically. "The Great Revolution? You're a Social Democrat."

"Excuse me, I'm not anything, first of all. I was..."

"No splitting hairs. You're an anarchist, denying the state you're supposed to defend.'

"Sergeant-Major, when one is already negated, there's little desire or time left to negate others."

The sergeant furrowed his brow. "Enough. I'm philosophizing too much already. Forgetting the respect I owe the reality of my stripes and duties. Debating with subordinates. When were you born?"

"1747."

"Class of 1747? Good heavens, man, you're in the last reserves of the militia! That year's group is hardly likely to be drafted. And you've got an awfully narrow chest. Do you have any notable physical defects?"

"Bone decay!" I shouted, letting yellow dust trickle from my ribs.

"You do look a bit malnourished. You may go. Await further orders."

I stumbled down the stairs and nearly tripped over a very young lieutenant, whom I saluted smartly — it's the rule in the district command. I saw his youthful cheek, his sparkling eye, his radiant stride, and before I knew it, I collapsed onto his chest, crying without tears. "Brother," I cried, "you too must die, as I have. Take pity on me and give me back my blood. Inside there, your sergeant was thundering regulations. Put some meat between my ribs, and I'll gladly be a target for a thousand machine guns. Just one second of breathing! Look, I have no lungs left, I'm long since dead!"

The lieutenant brusquely shoved me away and fixed his monocle in his right eye. "Are you drunk, addressing a royal Prussian lieutenant so informally? Three days in the clink."

He gestured to an orderly. I quickly bolted down the stairs and sprinted to the cemetery. Tired from the day's events and unwilling to serve my sentence, I stretched out in my coffin and shut the lid over myself. Let them search for me now. They won't easily find me. The postman, who knows my coffin number, won't betray me either — he gets a generous tip with deadly regularity for every registered letter he delivers.

In the Ninth Month

For eight months, I carried the war. Like a mother, tear-streaked and shy, carries a child in her womb — forced upon her in accursed violence by a blue-haired vagabond. In the ninth month, I couldn't bear it any longer.

I cast the war from me.

I aborted it.

It was a monstrosity. A massive, waxy-soft head. A wooden chest. And no legs — only iron stumps. I stuffed grasses into its mouth. Moss grew from its nose. Its eyes fell from their sockets like golden pebbles. It suffocated.

I went mad.

I visited a specialist for nervous overstimulation.

He danced before me like a brown medicine bottle, snapping his cork with a constant popping sound: "Do you see white mice? Are you an alcoholic? Do you perpetually climb telegraph poles in your dreams? Do you blow the hunting horn?"

I smashed the doctor's skull and fled in horror when, too late, I noticed that he wore the uniform of a reserve medical officer, with yellow caduceus insignias on his epaulets.

This gave me the idea to buy myself an Aesculapian staff instead of a walking stick, which I urgently needed on my nocturnal wanderings in the Cloud Mountains and on the Milky Way, completely buried under stars. By the way: dear God should finally have a causeway built in the sky so that one could traverse it without risking a broken neck. After all, what is His Foreign Legion for, in which only devils serve, at most, here and there, an angel as a corporal. To obtain an

Aesculapian staff, I inquired in 111 shops. No one had an Aesculapian staff in stock, not even Tietz. And did I perhaps mean one of those modern sticks without a handle?

I was greatly surprised that sticks without handles existed.

Surely, then, there must also be people without heads.

I bought toy soldiers — only cavalry, so I could learn to ride — and played with them.

In the evenings, I walked in the fields near the Schwabing hospital. When I plucked a flower, red blood ran from its stem. If I chased a butterfly, it turned out to be a death's-head moth. If I tried to board a tram, it revealed itself as a hearse.

I painted a red cross on my forehead, screamed "Christ," and volunteered for nursing and care of the wounded.

I would have liked to love a girl one more time. But the girls I met all had glass eyes, false hair made of seaweed, and artificial limbs. The most beautiful ones were wheeled about in chairs, without a lower body.

"Farewell, beautiful world," I said to myself, and had a canning factory process me into tinned meat.

The Slow Combustion Stove

Sebald Eidotter came into the world as a perpetually burning stove. Burning all day and all night for nothing: that annoyed him. Having to swallow compressed coal instead of beefsteaks and mutton chops is embarrassing, especially when you have a sensitive stomach, tend toward luxury, and are only allowed to express your *bon vivant* spirit by crackling burnt logs instead of thousand-mark bills. Sebald Eidotter resolved to draw closer to humanity, to which he felt both a kinship and affection. He bought himself a pair of cuirassier boots, learned to clatter the stove door: "Forward, march!", and headed off to a trench in Flanders, where he immediately found employment as a field-gray officer equipped with ultramodern steel gear (breastplate and gas mask). He marched unscathed through a hundred assaults. His iron chest was already adorned with the Iron Cross, First Class, when a musketeer in the reserve trench got the idea to investigate what was behind him. The soldier tore open his stove door, and ash and dust spilled out. There was no fire left. He had long since burned out. Mechanically, he clattered: "Forward, march! Forward, march!" The musketeer ran at once through the fury to fetch fire for him. Too late. By the time he returned, Sebald Eidotter had already breathed his last.

Even slow combustion stove is not a perpetual motion machine.

Not even in these perpetually mobilized times.

World History from the Psychoanalytic Perspective

God, a typical neurotic and severe psychopath, created the world to act out his complexes. The fact that he has neither a father nor a mother prevents him from moving beyond autoeroticism. He suffers from an unresolved Oedipus complex. Desperate and full of infantile impulses, he attempts to construct an *imago patris*. Adam, his creation, his son — becomes his first father. Eve, his creation, his daughter — he (hopefully) interprets as his mother. In the guise of the serpent, he engages in symbolic incest with her, and, after tasting from the tree of (self)knowledge himself, banishes father and mother, Adam and Eve, from the paradise of his autoeroticism — Adam dies, that is, his feeling for him does. His Oedipus complex creates new fathers: Noah. Some live hundreds of years. The oldest: Methuselah, upon whom he lovingly suffers for nine hundred years. He failed to create an eternal father — to overcome eternity itself. All the flaws of creation stem from God's unredeemed state (perhaps unredeemability? Perhaps only we humans can be redeemed, that is, analyzed?) — from the repression of his numerous complexes.

The current war is a new visible sign that God's creature, humanity, suffers from an abundance of complexes and represses emotions, which it seeks to discharge in a violent, explosive manner.

Austria's ultimatum to Serbia points to symbolic anal eroticism (see "Götz von Berlichingen...").

Hindenburg, as an astute psychoanalyst, tries to free Russia from its Oedipus complex ("the little father Tsar"). But as he himself was not sufficiently analyzed and freed from his father complex (the "Kaiser" occupies the position of the father for him), the experiment had to fail and devolve into crude treatment in Courland. Russia disintegrated into many subcomplexes.

The relationship between Germany and France, as indicated by the symbolic naming: Michael and Marianne, suggests a typical sibling complex. Their mutual hatred is based on repressed love. Since they cannot ethically love each other from the standpoint of their complex, the male party (Michael = Germany) periodically rapes the female party (Marianne = France).

It needs no further elaboration as to what symbols the weapons — lances, rifles, cannons — are meant to represent.

The World War can only be understood as an expression of Europe's perverse sexuality.

The conquest and liberation of the seas, as dreamed of by England and Germany, reveals itself as an unimaginably heightened urethral eroticism.

The shifting of borders signifies nothing more than a shifting of affects.

The World War can be reduced to this formula: Humanity is Oedipalizing.

Away with school psychology — because only psychoanalysis is called upon to illuminate the deepest depths of the human soul. It illuminates for us, as it were, our true home: infantile infantilism.

Before it, we are all domineering infants.

Dr. Jaroslaw Praha's *World History from the Psychoanalytic Perspective* (Vienna, 1918, published by Hugo Heller) is urgently recommended to every Europathic individual (and since God Himself is a Europath – who isn't one?).

A Proposal for Decency, That is, for Wickedness

With the greatest astonishment, I observe the struggle waged by influential circles against trash literature, cinema, the Black Hand, cannibalism, and so forth. For millennia, religious founders, headmasters, and tract sellers have endeavored to instill in humanity an idea of the essence of goodness and to guide them toward the practical exercise of virtue to the best of their abilities. The extent of their success is sufficiently demonstrated by history. The more zealously and fervently these prophets fulfilled their duties, the more vile and godless behaved that small-brained mammal, which unjustly bears the name "human." Virtue is a sensation: integrated into their so-called life only as a negative stimulus. For their life unfolds only out of the spirit of contradiction. Everyone strives to do the opposite of what inherent reason expects of them. Once this law of contrary disposition is fully recognized in all its force, even the less gifted can easily draw the ethical-logical conclusion: Teach people wickedness — and they will do good on their own. Promote in public and popular libraries the reading of Nat Pinkerton, Otto Ernst, Courths-Mahler, and Theodor Körner. The Ministry of Public Education should distribute in millions of copies *Rosa, the Teenage Girl*, and *Emil, the Sevenfold Mass Murderer*. Agents should march through the streets, urging robbery and lust murder in flaming phrases under state commission. What will be the result? A wave of gentleness and self-sacrifice, of kindness and love, will flow over humanity. Why has censorship still not banned those childishly devout, Presbyterianly harmless educational films? The true educational film has yet to be created: all the crimes of humanity must be presented truthfully in film to the immature youth in special children's screenings with free admission. What a glorious generation we shall raise. In the future, it will truly be a pleasure to beget children. We will have heaven on earth. One more word to the pacifists, those foolish scoundrels of God. They have propagated eternal peace and have reaped eternal war. We of the League of the Wicked propagate eternal war: war must last all day, from morning till night, for a hundred years. Then we will have eternal peace. Join our league if you are serious about the upward development of humanity. For humanity, the worst is just good enough.

The People's Commissar

One morning, an unstamped postcard lay on my ersatz coffee table with the following contents:

Comrade!

As we hear, you have recently moved. Would you be willing to put your expertise at the service of the good — the best — cause and take over the People's Commissariat for Transport Crises?

With an international handshake,
Blaukraut,
Chairman of the Council of People's Commissars.

Aha! I thought. So here we have the revolution. Long-awaited, it has suddenly arrived overnight, as unexpectedly as a crate of eggs from Holland. And I, loyal to the Kaiser to the core only last night (loyalty others carried to market on my behalf), was today chosen as one of the leading figures of the new order.

I shouted, "Emmchen!" (By which I did not mean my hundred thousand, but rather the one and only, my housekeeper, Emmi) and ordered her to quickly craft a red revolutionary rosette from the red border of my veterans' association handkerchief, on which the Battle of Sedan is depicted.

Adorned with this, and casually draped in an old cycling cloak I retrieved from the attic, I set out — thus proletarianized — to the government building.

Blaukraut, a former house servant of mine, received me jovially. He slapped me on the shoulder and shouted: "Well, what do you say to that? How did we pull this off? The dissatisfaction, the boldness, the over-boldness of the people has burst open the gates of freedom. Freedom, as I mean it! Freedom, as I mean it! Conviction — that's the main thing now. Anyone lacking it will lose the first syllable of their name. A social conscience! Well, you've already demonstrated that with me! Humanity! It's about the socialization of souls."

I was assigned the Hotel Monopol as my office building. 120 rooms were at my disposal.

I sat in a deep club chair in Room No. 1 and pressed a button. My chief secretary appeared — a former tightrope walker.

I ordered him to immediately halt and immobilize all trains throughout the German Reich. The poor locomotive drivers should also have their rest for once. Since childhood, alongside nurses, my greatest sympathy has been for locomotive drivers.

I had to bring honor to my social conscience — constantly, like chalk eggs.

I pressed the button again.

My second secretary appeared — a former brewery waiter.

I ordered him to reroute the food supply train Express 777, Section I, Category A, Freight from East Prussia from Friedrichstrasse Station to Anhalter Station, nearer to my residence.

Unfortunately, I must admit, my measures did not meet with the hoped for understanding everywhere.

The number of complaint visits increased. They made me completely nervous. I appointed a deaf-mute cousin of mine as Complaint Commissar to handle grievances.

Little by little, I am bringing everything into the proper swing.

What the war hasn't ruined, I will ruin.

Guaranteed.

You can rely on me.

The Age of Absolutism is Dawning...

What, you're still swearing by Einstein? By the theory of relativity? Good grief: you're always a quarter of an hour late! Einstein: is no more. That would be a joke, all that talk about the refraction of sunlight! Man, you're thick! You'd better quickly turn your worldview and your worn-out cheviot jacket inside out immediately. Relativism has gone bankrupt. We've swallowed absolute truth by the spoonful. Don't you notice? The age of Absolutism is beginning.

That's absolutely right, you there. Were you at the Great Theatre recently? Great stuff, this Danton. There's something grand about a revolution... at the Great Theatre. And how, at the end, that one pathetic guy screams: "The Republic will only be pure when the Republic no longer exists..." You should have heard the applause from the respected audience. The whole hall was thundering. It was a huge rally against the Republic, that is, against relativism: and for Absolutism.

At least with Absolutism, a person knows where they stand: they are secure, they have their footing, there are absolute truths to follow, and that's that. For example: "Keep to the right!" "No trespassing!" "Office hours of the Secret Government Advisor from 5 to a quarter past 6." "Fresh butcher's soup today!" "Gentlemen – over there." "After the district command – here." There's no room for debate or interpretation. The absolute principle thinks and guides. A person doesn't need to think at all.

In all the kiosks, "The Absolute Truth" is available, a small pamphlet, priced at 15 Pfennigs. In it, the thirty-three absolute truths are plainly listed. Everything else, you'll notice, is nonsense, rubbish, humbug, fiddlesticks. If you don't believe us, we'll teach you the absolute truth, little uncle. At Knüppel-Kunze, a thousand rubber truncheons have been unloaded. One will surely fit your skull shape, good fellow. Or would you prefer to be converted with a hand grenade and a Browning? Everything's available. We're not like poor people. We are excellently equipped with all available intellectual weapons.

Biography

My father, the notorious highway murderer Klauschke, raised me with a sense of honor and reverence for God. "Always keep your house clean!" he would say, with a sideways glance at my mother, who was standing in the room with a bucket and her skirts rolled up, splashing around. As I later learned, my mother was not actually my mother, but a distant relative of my mother, whom I had to call "Aunt," and with whom, in youthful exuberance, I had nearly once become engaged. When I turned sixteen, my father apprenticed me to Simson Siegedurch, a porcelain dealer, a master of his craft. He was soul-friends with both my real and my false mother, and he would affectionately, not without insinuation, call me "my little son." He was a bit angry with my father, because, in a moment of mental weakness, my father had killed Mrs. Siegedurch with a copper kettle. The copper kettle was considerably dented. Siegedurch had loved that kettle dearly, and the dent in it greatly upset him. He was a connoisseur of art and also introduced me to the arts by placing two rows of porcelain cups in front of me and saying: "On the left, art – on the right, not." Yes, looking at things does educate. I thought the same when I met Röschen Zwitterbauch and swore her eternal love. My father was not pleased with this resolution of my affairs. He gave me the golden rule of life: "Kill them dead, kill them dead" – he meant that, with death always present in life, he had gotten the farthest. What else should I tell you? I see that you find my life quite uninteresting and are no longer even listening. Unfortunately, I grew up in a simple, middle-class environment, where life flows by monotonously. Another Steinhäger, miss, and the "Flying Leaves Magazine!"

Elegantly Furnished Rooms

Once, I thought, one must take the step into the big world. And I rented two elegantly furnished rooms with a bathroom, electric light, central heating, and a telephone from Doctor of Natural Sciences Limusine Reisfleisch at Karolinenstraße 47, garden house first floor, starting September 1st. On September 4th, I unexpectedly returned home from my summer trip to Mittenwald. In the living room, I found a three-day-old baby in the middle of a charming laundry basket, and in the bedroom, a strange young lady. This joke was so old that I was startled and initially doubted I was experiencing it. After that, I went to a hotel and had drying fits on the chest of the bellboy. These crying fits were charged on the hotel bill at thirty-five pfennigs each.

The next morning, I dared to visit Doctor of Natural Sciences Reisfleisch again. I asked if it was now permissible for me to move in... It was allowed, and I moved in, with many suitcases and boxes, which fell one by one onto my kneecap.

I wanted, as usual, to put my laundry into the dresser and pulled open the drawers. In the top one were hairpins, knitting needles, and other items of a lady of the world. From the bottom drawer, I pulled out a deceased parrot and a complete set of a soldier's cleaning equipment into the daylight, or rather, electric light. Because I had to pay for it, I had turned the light on during the day.

I was pleasantly surprised by the central heating, which warmed and heated simply by the layer of dust that settled upon it.

Worms were crawling along the white windowsills. A large cross spider was sleeping in a Biedermeier armchair.

Not wanting to wake her, I took off my boots and walked carefully on my socks. I intended to take a bath.

I rang the bell gently. I rang louder. I rang very loudly. I rang twenty-six times.

A child appeared at the door. In a white shirt. And another child. And more and more children. Finally, Dr. Reisfleisch appeared, wearing large horn-rimmed glasses and kindly moss-covered hair. And Doctor of Natural Sciences Reisfleisch appeared dressed as a Bavarian boy, or Bubi, as they say in northern Germany: with mottled calf-length stockings, mahogany brown knee trousers, and a yolk-yellow jacket.

"I declare my termination with immediate effect," I screamed, flying around the room. I didn't dare leave. "I declare my termination with immediate effect. You have violated every clause of the rental agreement..."

"Where is the written contract, please?" shouted the academic boy, mockingly stabbing me with his sharpest knife.

I wanted to run to the telephone to call the nearest specialist for heart ailments. But I couldn't find a telephone. Finally, I spotted it on the third floor. It didn't belong to the Reisfleisch boarding house at all, as they had claimed, but to an architect named Kohlraum.

Mr. Kohlraum didn't even let me near the telephone, but immediately offered me a favorable cost estimate for a single-family house by Lake Ammer. I now live there happily and contentedly. With a shudder, I remember the elegantly furnished rooms, feed the fish, and breed guinea fowl and white mice. Occasionally, I let myself drift in a boat across the lake... Who knows where to... who knows what for...

Mucius Mauke

Mucius Mauke had been self-reliant from a young age. While other children were still in diapers, he was already washing his own. One day, when he fell into the water, he saved himself from drowning by swimming, without the need for a gallant worker or a vigorous soldier who might have wanted to earn a rescue medal. This misadventure inspired Mucius to try his hand as a swimming artist. He even won several silver egg cups and silk honor ribbons at various international swimming competitions he attended. But this activity did not entirely satisfy him. It lacked the moral underpinning, without which work becomes either a farce or mere grimacing. Thus he successively took up the professions of oyster fisherman, dentist, itinerant bookseller, magician, private lecturer, and pamphlet poet. Each profession had a catch that made it difficult not to become entangled in it. But live and let live was Mucius Mauke's principle. He became a snow-shoveler, though in summer he again lacked employment. Grief clouded his brow. A rich talent would be lost with him if he did not soon find the right profession. Then, on the way to Milbertshofen one evening, his God appeared to him in a red thundercloud and said: "Mucius Mauke, just as a Saul became a Paul, so shall a Mauke be quasi de-materialized and re-materialized into a Pauke. Know thyself." Mauke looked down at himself. He had indeed become a timpani drum. He no longer needed to do anything; he only had to wait for others to do something with him. From then on, his life flowed in order and without excitement. He stood in the Munich Court Orchestra, which had purchased him. The goal of his life was achieved. He had become music, sound, the incarnation of a thundering longing. Very soon, he fell in love with the first flute, and they became a happy pair.

Cubism

A cubist painter named Dove decided, after painting many cubist pictures, to now live cubically as a right-wing activist. He had a cube screwed onto his neck instead of a head, with the number 6 facing outward, so everyone would see what kind of number he was. Therefore, he went without a hat in both summer and winter, only holding an octagonal board that served as both an umbrella and a walking stick.

His belly was a parallelepiped. His legs were two crates filled with wood shavings, labeled: "Do not drop, glass!" But there was no glass in the crates. In this way, Dove deceived those around him.

Everyone on the street would say: "What do you look like, Dove?" But Dove didn't care. His face, which grew from the 3 on the cube, smiled forgivingly.

Every honest person should live according to their optical-spiritual outlook. Then there would be less lying in the world. Dove was undoubtedly right, which only made him even more upset at the foolishness of the other people who either misunderstood or wanted to misunderstand him. One day, the house collapsed over Dove. It collapsed cubically: in cubes and blocks. Due to an earthquake. Dove narrowly escaped death.

He stood before his collapsed house, blissfully and delightedly admiring it.

"My house – it paints itself – a cubist painting. – I don't even need to paint it. – Blessed is the person for whom even the things and objects of their existence submit to their worldview. Their strength is mystical. Their will is indiscriminately persuasive. The thing in itself undoes itself and becomes... Being."

Dove photographed the collapsed house and sent a print to Picasso.

Picasso sent his business card back. In the left corner, it said: p.p.c.[1]

Dove was ecstatic; he nearly became round with happiness. But he caught himself just in time and smiled angularly.

The Yellow Man

Ambrosius, who had made a name for himself as a portrait painter, was surprised one morning in his studio by a peculiar visitor. A bright yellow man in an ill-fitting frock coat and top hat bowed before him and said, "Tscheng-ho," along with a few other monosyllabic, yet melodious words. Ambrosius, not understanding this language, immediately began to paint the little yellow man. He painted until lunchtime, by which point the figure on the canvas was already recognizable. The little man clapped his hands in delight and repeatedly exclaimed, "Ho, ho." Then he bowed and left.

The next morning, he returned, critically inspected the easel and palette, and struck a pose.

Ambrosius painted until midday, and the yellow man left.

Ambrosius painted for days, weeks, months. He marveled that, as a recognized master, he could make no further progress during this time.

"This isn't natural," said Ambrosius, staring at the yellow man's forehead, which was extraordinarily difficult to model.

"Ho," said the little man, for he understood nothing of what Ambrosius said or thought.

Ambrosius was at a loss.

His artistic honor demanded that he finish the painting he had started. He shook his head. His velvet beret flew into the corner. He took off his coat. He rolled up his sleeves.

The yellow man grinned.

At that, Ambrosius grabbed him with both arms and threw him onto the canvas, which was coated with fresh oil paint.

The little man screamed, "Tscheng-ho," and a few other monosyllabic words, but he stuck.

He struggled for a few more hours, then expired.

Ambrosius preserved him as a mummy. In the summer, he exhibited him at the *Secession*.

The critics unanimously praised "The Yellow Man" as his best portrait. Loose in form, rich in tone, and overwhelming in composition, it equaled — nay, surpassed — his role model: Titian.

---

[1] p.p.c. is the French abbreviation for *pour prendre congé*, which means "as a farewell." It was traditionally written on a calling card sent to announce a departure or to bid farewell politely.

Incidentally, it was purchased for the *New Pinakothek*. It hangs in the third gallery, immediately to the right.

The Journalist

Nothing could be easier, thought a dark-haired, but unsympathetic. young man, and sent the following letter to the editorial office of the *General Gazette*:

> Yesterday, during the midday hours on the sparsely trafficked Schwan-thalerstraße, an elderly, lame man fell due to the icy conditions. He grazed his cheek, causing the snow to turn blood-red in an area of approximately one centimeter, but with the assistance of a passerby, he was able to continue on his way without medical help.

This note appeared the next day under the "Domestic Affairs" section of the *General Gazette*, and the young man who had written it received, six months later, 60 pfennigs in payment via postal order. This unexpected success caused his pride and his scrawny pigeon chest to swell considerably. He went to a beer garden and ordered a couple of sausages with salad and a half-liter of lager. Then he wrote:

> The real estate speculations of Privy Councillor Z. have proven to be unscrupulous and misguided on the largest scale. His shady dealings have been exposed. The culprit faces punishment. Let this be the fate of all who suck the marrow of the people.

This piece, neatly sealed in an envelope, was sent by the ambitious young man to *Shrieking Injustice*, a publication of dubious repute. Two days later, it appeared on the front page in bold and spaced type, under the headline: *Revelations from the Financial World. Big City Rogues.*

After nearly three months, our young man received payment of 1.30 marks in postage stamps. This sum allowed him to survive for another half a year. Once it was exhausted, he resolved to aim for something on a grander scale. He sent a telegram to the *Daily Berlin Turnip*:

> Brilliant run of the *Berlin Intimate Theater* in our city. Applause upon applause. Wreaths upon wreaths. Director Gummiballon called to the stage thirty-seven times. Some incorrigible enthusiasts were found the next morning still hiding under the actresses' costumes. The impact of the performance is unforgettable.

He promptly received a telegraphic money order for 100 marks from the management of the *Intimate Theater*. He invested it in munitions stocks and retired. His pigeon chest turned into a fat belly. He now insists on being addressed as "Doctor." His esteemed pen is rarely encountered in the columns of our leading newspapers. He no longer needs to write. He has immersed himself in Indian philosophy. Instead of contemplating his navel, he admires his thick golden watch chain.

The Two

"You can't fool me anymore," snarled the poet.

"You can't imitate me anymore," hissed the inventor.

With flushed faces, they parted ways.

The moon sank lower. The weeping willows trembled. The soft sound of stars falling echoed through the world.

The poet sat at the open window. The balmy air brushed across his forehead.

He heard the stars falling from the sky... into the lake... as if wine glasses were shattering.

He thought: I have wronged him... I am only a poet, a condenser of existing clouds, a foghorn that warns even itself. He is bright... he discovers — without searching... I see him now, sailing on the lake, in a pink boat, with a net... and the stars that resonate as they touch the water: he catches them — and they are silver fish. Tomorrow, his wife will fry them for lunch...

He stepped back from the window, lit a kerosene lamp, and then there was a knock. The inventor entered, with a word of apology on his lips and a bottle of red wine under his arm.

"Let us darken ourselves, my friend. I am too clear about myself. Obscure me! Those stars: they are all too familiar containers of sunlight. Hang veils over them! Blue cloths! Stage the tragedy of non-being. Make a necklace out of the stars and hang it around a beautiful woman's neck. Let them unleash revolts of twilight. I want to become purposeless. Come! Read me some verses! You see: if only one could invent verses! But all we can invent is a new shoe polish or the law of gravitation. But the law of the gravitational attraction of the spirit? The spirit, my friend, is your domain. Yes: your domain."

The Chain

It was a Venetian glass necklace from the workshops of Murano.

He bought it at a bazaar in Lugano: black and white beads.

He thought: The Greeks held their referendums with black and white beads.

White meant: yes. Black: no.

Why is white affirmative and black negative?

He thought it would be delightful to make a woman happy with it. He met little Adrienne and took her home. He undressed her completely naked and, before a mirror, placed the necklace around her neck.

He decided to love her.

The necklace had 31 beads: 15 black and 16 white. He decided to love her for 31 days.

On the 31st day, she wore the remaining white bead on a ring.

She placed 15 black and 15 white beads into his coffin.

He had shot himself.

15 to 15 cancels out, she smiled darkly. For whom? I... remain. For nature demands its due. It is always upheld – even if only by a single vote. The one is what triumphs everywhere, or rather: the

One...

The Bedstead

Adolfine, a somewhat elderly bedstead, groaned in every joint. She stood in Room No. 3 of the Merry Goose Hotel. Last night, a young man had slept in her — not alone — and this had thrown her into a frenzy. In the past, when she was still young, she had taken great delight in such adventures. If the young man was handsome, she would often imagine herself in the position of the young lady in question, a feat made easy by her vertical disposition. She would sing and chirp like the charming creatures who enjoy one another's company in cheerful ways. Now, however, as she aged visibly, morality began to assert itself. She felt, trembling to her core, that she had thought too little of the hereafter, on whose dark threshold she now stood.

Without hesitation, she left the room, rode the elevator down, and soon disappeared into the bustling city.

At St. Mary's rectory, she rang the bell. The pastor's cook, a plump blonde with a lively manner of secretion, answered the door herself.

Suspiciously, she eyed the bedstead, which bowed deeply, striking the stone floor with its wooden front legs.

"What do you want?" asked the cook.

"I wish to speak with the pastor regarding a delicate ecclesiastical matter."

The cook gestured for her to follow; they stopped at the door to the study. While the cook went to announce her, Adolfine remained in the hallway. She felt so unwell from the unfamiliar and extensive walk that she vomited up the duvet and pillows. This brought her some relief.

"The pastor will see you now..."

Adolfine hopped lightly over the threshold.

The kindly old gentleman in his cassock rose from his desk.

"How may I help you, young lady?" Adolfine was overjoyed to be addressed as "young lady."

"Reverend Father," said Adolfine, kissing the clergyman's hand, "an inner law compels me to confess. I have led a sinful life."

"Insight and repentance are never too late; let me hear it, my child..."

And Adolfine confessed. She confessed her entire existence, which, since leaving the carpenter's workshop, had been full of indulgence.

She confessed every single incident, for she had an excellent memory for all her misdeeds and vices, concluding with the sin of the previous night, in which she had helplessly and blamelessly, and without the ability to resist, been involved.

The kindly old gentleman listened to her gravely and attentively.

"*Absolvo te*," he finally said, gently stroking the headboard with his delicate hand.

Shaken, but redeemed, Adolfine departed.

She resolved to lead a new life from now on. It was never too late to turn back. She moved to the suburbs, to a working-class apartment, where she now served as a resting place for a man, a woman, and their twenty-three morally well-raised children after the burdens of their day. She had humbly chosen the concept of service as the symbol of her twilight years.

She always made a wide detour around the Merry Goose Hotel, not wanting to be reminded of the site of her former transgressions. She also taught her employer's twenty-three children religious and etiquette lessons, and her highest motto was:

"Fear God, do what is right, fear no one, and you will win the crown of life."

The Literary Society

In our town, a literary society had to be founded. There was, so to speak, a need for it. Needs are made to be satisfied. Livestock breeder Schlampke gave a speech at the preparatory meeting, in which he pointed out, in a persuasive manner, the necessity of a literary education. Only with the help of Goethe can our nation maintain its current livestock population. Loud applause rewarded his commendable and appropriate remarks. Parquet floor layer Robbe fully agreed with the interesting points made by the esteemed speaker. He only allowed himself to briefly and succinctly point out the relationship between floor polish, which he kept fresh in stock in the excellent grades A, B, and C, at 30, 50, and 70 pfennigs per tin, and the relevant belles-lettres, especially so-called lyric and rhymed poetry. He concluded with a little self-crafted verse:

Long live literature —
But only with floor polish!

which was met with approval. The founding meeting then proceeded unanimously, and the statutes were set. Schaulke, the stocking maker, was elected as the first president, Dr. Hartwurst, the head teacher, as vice president, and the local poor baker as the treasurer. The goal of the court-registered society Literaria was to promote and spread the knowledge of high literature a) among its members, b) among the people. This was to be done through subscription to a reading portfolio at the bookseller Kletzke, the esteemed member of the society, through lecture evenings, author evenings, and other festive events. On May 4th, the Literaria flag was consecrated with great pomp, which opened with a parade through the town. The town brass band marched loudly at the head. Following them, in a tailcoat and a blue cyclist's cap, with a band of Schiller's great illustrated edition under his arm, was President Schaulke. To his right walked Dr. Hartwurst, carrying a postcard-sized image of Hindenburg, the poet of the great era, who wrote with iron, under glass and frame. To Schaulke's left staggered the treasurer, the local poor baker, with a coin box in the shape of an ink pot, rustling. Behind the board of directors, a group of white-clad honorary ladies moved, none younger than seventy, venerably shaking their bald heads, some of them even personally acquainted with Goethe. Then came the flag! Livestock breeder Schlampke waved it nervously. It had been donated by Saddler Säulchen, the esteemed member of the society, in exchange for the waiver of the annual membership fee of 1.50 marks: a former bedspread, decorated by Miss Säulchen with heartfelt verses from our great poets. Behind the flag (telegraph to Berlin, wire to New York, shout it to the winds: let it be carried as far as Appenzell and Yokohama) rolled a pram made of black-white-red wicker, pushed by Mrs. President Schaulke in a bursting silk gown. In the pram, carefully nestled in warm cushions, with his feet pulled up to his rosy belly, his little hands pressed to his face, his eyes closed — lay Kaspar Schmetterling, the great, widely known, praised, and respected yet still unborn patriotic poet. He was eight months pregnant. His weepy voice echoed back from the houses to the blaring trombones of the town band. On his soft white forehead, a red ladybird sunbathed.

The Goldfinch

A goldfinch named Lehmann had reached the senile age of 11 years, which was considered very old for his kind. As far as he could see among his acquaintances, no other goldfinch lived to such an advanced age. Müller, Maier, Huber — they were all 5, 6, 7, at most 8 years old. Maier, who had only just reached 8 years, had recently been named the honorary old man of Berlin, and the veterans and firefighter' associations had gathered at his apartment on Hallesche Street, singing "Ode to Joy" and drinking white beer to celebrate. Lehmann, on the other hand, lived completely reclusive in a small town in Brandenburg, where only the local intelligence paper occasionally reported: "Our esteemed fellow citizen, Mr. Lehmann, is still alive." Was this an honor? Was this life worth living at all? Has today's fast-paced world lost all respect for old age?

Lehmann boarded the train and traveled to Berlin. Upon arrival, he entered an advertising office and placed a huge ad in all the evening newspapers: "Lehmann will be 11 years old tomorrow: A toast to the brave goldfinch! Long live the old man!" This advertisement did not have the intended effect. Lehmann did not become famous, as he had hoped; instead, he was (unfairly) issued a summons for gross mischief and received an invitation to join a funeral club. This club's noble purpose was to honorably, solidly, and with a certain pomp, bury its members upon their death. Disappointed, Lehmann went to Aschinger's and drank a bottle of French champagne. He wandered melancholically through the fragrant Tiergarten, where couples walked arm in arm, the sun was shining from the sky, and it burned his bald head. Lehmann approached two police officers: "Lehmann is my name." The officers' eyes grew as large as dinner plates. "Straight to the station," they barked in their blue uniforms. Lehmann wept bitterly. Ah, the beautiful spring! At the station, Lehmann's pockets were searched. Then he was photographed, both in profile and from the front and back. "You are now in the criminal album. Shame on you!" said the sergeant. Afterward, Lehmann was released.

Lehmann beamed: now he was preserved for posterity, one way or another. Loyalty is no delusion of schoolteachers. Crime and fame are equally (philosophically) founded. Lehmann remembered that he had attended lectures by Simmel. What had Simmel always said? Every being has the worldview it needs. The salmon has the worldview of the salmon, the eagle the worldview of the eagle. So, Lehmann needed only the worldview of a Lehmann. Pensive and content, Lehmann flew to a freshly green chestnut tree. It was hard for him at his age of 11, but it worked; it had been presumptuous of him to leave his beloved home and chase after will-o'-the-wisps in the big city. Once he had rested, he wanted to return to his small town on the next train. He nodded his head and fell asleep.

A boy with a whistle, who had been watching him and also had a birthday that day — hence the whistle — made a ball out of paper and shot it at him. Lehmann, weakened, fell from the branch when he was hit. He died before he regained consciousness, aged and highly respected. The paper ball that fatally struck him had been made from the advertisement he had placed the day before.

One should never put anything in writing. It always discredits you, especially once it gets printed.

The Cricket

A cricket named Helene chirped from June 1st to July 31st (sixty-one days) non-stop, until she ran out of fabric. Then, she put on her cape hat, slung her old-fashioned market bag over her shoulder, and hurried to the nearest small or medium-sized town. She entered a trimming store and said:

"I would like seven thousand meters of fabric." The blonde clerk blushed to the roots of his hair and opened and closed his mouth in astonishment like a toad:

"Pardon?"

The cricket willingly repeated:

"I would like seven thousand meters of fabric."

The clerk fluttered: "Seven thousand meters of fabric! At your service, madam. We will have the desired item supplied by a wholesaler. May I ask what kind of fabric you need?"

"Seven thousand meters of fabric," said the cricket, turning green with excitement.

The clerk nervously chewed on his fingernails.

"Madam," he warbled, "may I ask what kind of fabric?"

"Seven thousand meters of fabric," said the cricket.

The clerk bounced on his toes like a ballet dancer: "Madam, what type of fabric would it be: silk? voile? linen? velvet? *barchent*? wool? *crêpe de chine*?"

"Fabric," said the cricket.

Sweat stood on her forehead. She collapsed heavily into an armchair. Her dress creaked at every seam. The clerk wobbled like a dancer. His voice sounded desperate, like the cry of a foghorn in the dark night.

"What kind of fabric, madam?"

"Fabric," said the cricket, "just fabric."

The clerk bellowed:

"What do you need the fabric for, madam?"

The cricket grumbled angrily: "What for? The question? For chirping, of course..."

"For – chirping –?"

The clerk burst like an inflated frog.

That gave material – for the reporters – seven thousand lines.

The cricket left empty-handed.

Fable

I poked around in an anthill with my walking stick. Wild and frightened, the ants scurried about. Suddenly, I pulled it out and walked away. The ants, seeing the stick vanish into the air, cried out: "What a strange bird!" – A particularly bold ant had climbed up the stick. I had to shake her off. Breathlessly, she reached the others. She gasped: "He had a human in his claws, he eats humans!" – She then went off, fell into deep thought, wrote a book: "The Species, Ancestry, and Organism of the Newly Discovered Stick Bird," and was appointed a full professor of zoology at the Ant University of Przmnldtbk.

The Proverb

"It is not good for man to be alone," thought the toad. For she was alone the whole day long and the whole nightlong. No one liked her, no one walked with her, no one played Tarock with her at the coffeehouse, no one understood her.

It was a dreadful life.

"Pay up!" she hissed in the bar, where she sat maliciously on a high stool drinking mulled wine, which never agreed with her, put on her raincoat, and made her way to the creator of all things. She politely lifted her brown plush hat and presented her request.

"It is not good for man to be alone," she said, tearfully and sorrowfully, "have I done something wrong to someone? I only look this way."

"Excuse me," said God, "I don't quite understand you – but you just quoted a proverb: are you perhaps a human?"

The toad thought deeply, and quietly admitted: "No."

"Well then," said God.

The toad lived on, lonely as before. What else could she do? She was no match for the dialectic of our Dear Lord.

The Uncle

Dear reader, you surely have an uncle who frowns upon your actions and, even more so, upon your dreams, always talking about how in his time this and that was completely different (and, of course, better). With such an uncle, I went for a walk along the banks of the Rhine, and since it was a beautiful day – the Cologne Cathedral was blasting its Gothic fanfare into the sunlit mist on the horizon – a beautiful day that must be fully taken advantage of, I threw my uncle into the Rhine. "Go," I said, "dear uncle, and swim to your time. Swim upstream to Constance, perhaps you'll find it there. But even Constance is a respectable city, I suspect they will greet you poorly. And even Lake Constance is deeper than you think. Certainly not as shallow as you."

My uncle lamented and tried to swim with the river. A whirlpool caught him. He screamed until the dirty water filled his mouth, and he sank.

Just a Quarter of an Hour

"Just a quarter of an hour," Aunt Anna stitched on a pillow that she gave to Uncle Max for his birthday. Uncle Max happily laid down with the pillow for his siesta – just a quarter of an hour – but it lasted one hour, it lasted two, it lasted three hours: he did not get up. Then they went into his room and found him – uncalled, no longer alive. A stroke had put an end to his life – right on his birthday. – – Aunt Anna was devastated. The beautiful pillow: it had missed its purpose! Uncle Max had not been able to fully enjoy it. She had it carved by the master stonemason Hagebusch into stone and placed as a tombstone on his grave, where it reads:

> Here Uncle Max rests in God's grace
> Just a quarter of an hour

Paula

Paula, a young girl of dubious profession and loose morals, went to Lake Wannsee and rented a rowing boat, an hour for 85 pfennigs. As she was used to in life, she let herself be carried away by the current. Suddenly, the waves parted before her, and a young man emerged like a water sprite from the gray flood and climbed into the boat with clenched fists. He wasn't even wearing a swimsuit, which didn't surprise her in the least.

"Are you a water god?" Paula asked, as she occasionally studied mythology.

The young man opened his mouth in confusion, then broke into a charming smile.

"Of course; I'm a city traveler."

"Why, if I may ask? And what are you looking for with me?"

"Just that," said the young man, covering his nakedness with a shadow that fell from his head.

Then he took a ring off his finger and whispered, "Elli, my sweet bride."

Paula, who cared more about the right intentions than the right name, did not dare to disillusion the young man and turn him down, a rejection he could have taken much worse, and they were very happy.

After half an hour, the young man looked up at the sky in alarm and cried, "It's already half past three," before disappearing into the waves with a pike leap, which no pike could easily imitate. Paula waved until he dissolved in the outdoor swimming pool. Then she came back to herself and noticed the ring on her finger. She kissed it and rowed to the shore until she got blisters on her hands. She took a second-class ticket on the subway, whereas she usually only traveled third-class.

She went to a jeweler.

The ring was fake.

Outraged, she stabbed the jeweler, who had given her this sordid information, with a hatpin, which was unsecured despite police regulations.

The police should really pay more attention to ensuring their regulations are followed. Many crimes and accidents could be avoided in the simplest way.

Paula decided to avoid young men without swimwear in the future.

Boschel

Do you know Boschel? Boschel is a peculiar fellow. You'll either believe me or not, but today, you'll encounter Boschel on the street. You'll greet him: "Good day, Mr. Boschel, how are you?" And Boschel, swaying under a black Calabrese hat, gives you a friendly reply. The next day, you go to the servants' bureau – who do you meet there, busy choosing a new maid? Mrs.... Boschel! You greet her politely:

"Good morning, Mrs. Boschel, how are you?" Mrs. Boschel smiles: "Thank you. And you?" – But you freeze – like Lot's wife – into a pillar of salt... It must be noted: Mrs.... Boschel, that is again... Boschel, who has today transformed into his wife. On the third day on your way to school you meet: who? The child Boschel! With a satchel on his back and a plum jam sandwich in his hand. You greet him cheerfully: "Good day, little Boschel." – And Boschel – for it is he – responds in a voice breaking with adolescence: "Good day." The coldest terror runs through your spine. Wherever you step: Boschel! Boschel is everywhere. Boschel is on the street and in the room. Boschel is that elegant rider and the ragged beggar at the church gate of Saint Antonio. Boschel honks in the car and barks in the butcher's dog. And when you go to bed at night and want to pray to the moon: you pull the curtain in horror, for there, large and golden, stands in the sky: Boschel.

The Man with the Mask

He sat every afternoon from four to six in a particular corner of the café and watched people from his hidden vantage point. He looked beneath the women's large hats and into their eyes, without them knowing what he gave or took from their souls. He traced the lines of their mouths and foreheads, observed their movements while smoking, and listened to the way they spoke.

The waiters knew him and treated him with a shy politeness tinged with pity. Most of the guests, many of whom were regulars, stared at him first with astonished curiosity, but relaxed after a few glances. Only strangers and women admired him more openly than was proper.

He always wore a white silk-lined mask over his face and gray gloves on his hands. Some whispered that he was suffering from wasting sickness, and that the mask and gloves concealed his sick, decayed limbs. No one had ever seen his face; no one could observe the play of his muscles in excitement or calm. His mask, which drew attention to him, simultaneously protected him from the surprise of his own unthinking self. On a rainy afternoon, the Jewish woman Justice Councilor Ammer and her seventeen-year-old daughter Mimi happened to wander into the café. Mimi widened the brown gates of her eyes in astonishment. The stout Justice Councilor also noticed the white mask and asked the waiter, puffing and speaking in broken, asthmatic syllables, about the man in the corner. The waiter gave discreet and transparent information.

"Mom, what's going on?" Mimi asked. She unbuttoned her overcoat. It was getting warm.

"Nothing for little girls," groaned Mrs. Justice Councilor, a bit too loudly, for the mask heard her, "just... He's sick."

"Oh no, that's sad." Mimi turned around, with the hasty, awkward movement of a seventeen-year-old girl who hasn't yet fully gained control of her body. The mask smiled. – No one saw it.

Mimi blushed and awkwardly adjusted her mocha cup. In her embarrassment, she took a lemon tart from the cake dish, though she didn't really want it. She ate it, swallowing it eagerly, seemingly focused on nothing else. Mrs. Justice Councilor waved to the waiter and paid. She gave fifty pfennigs as a tip. "We're leaving, Mimi."

The waiter bowed.

Mimi wanted to, but she didn't dare look around.

Two days later, Mimi Ammer appeared again, this time accompanied by her brother, the law student Julius Ammer, a corpulent, jovial young man, at the café. The white mask was already there, searching for the uniqueness of this girl in the narrow tanned face and the long, pale red mouth. Mimi dared only one glance at him.

"Who is that?" She burned with curiosity. Her brother muttered incomprehensibly. He was reading *Simplicissimus* and had not noticed the man in the mask.

A few days later, she came alone. How she was ashamed! What would they think of her!

The mask sent her his card through the waiter. Perhaps the acquaintance wouldn't be entirely in vain. Maybe material for a novella... or a four-line verse. "Since I'm slowly dying, I've become a poet. One must take what comes along the way. We, who are too full of adventures to actually have any." She read the name. Suddenly, her unease disappeared, and she felt joy. The name seemed familiar. She tucked the card into her bag and was punctual for the rendezvous the next day. He met a young girl, capricious and homely, crazy and very wise, very decent and very piquant. If she falls in love with me, that is, with my mask... it will be dangerous, he thought, but invited her to his apartment for tea.

She reveled in her secrets and came one afternoon after piano lessons.

"This is getting a bit boring," thought the mask. "How can I make use of her? In what situation?"

He didn't have to wait long. She fell to her knees before him and said, while reaching for his gloved hands, which he withdrew:

"I love you, please," (and this "please" was breathed out fervently), "take off the mask. Just once, I want to see your real face."

The mask behind the mask smiled.

"It's ugly and insults your beauty." Never have I hurt myself so much, he thought. But he didn't lose his presence of mind and strength to observe his emotions down to their finest ends and branches.

She's just curious, he thought.

She sobbed and lay on the carpet. Her small, undeveloped breasts rhythmically thumped on the floor. He wanted to pick her up.

"You'll catch a cold," he said.

She looked up.

"Please, please. Your face!"

Then he took off the mask. – Slowly, like a snake, her slender body rose from the ground to him.

Unnaturally large, his blue eyes lay in the deep hollows: he no longer had eyelashes. And the bone of his nose shone, completely fleshless, as if a beast had gnawed it away.

She stood right in front of him, so close that he felt her clear breath. Her gaze cruelly, rapturously pierced into his ugly, clear eyes.

Before he could stop her, she kissed him.

He was startled and stepped back. Then he put the mask back on. "Is your sweet curiosity now – satisfied?" he said softly

She breathed deeply, shook his hand, and left.

A week later, he read in the newspaper at the café that the young, beautiful daughter of Justice Councilor Ammer had, in a sudden mental breakdown, fallen victim to an act of self-mutilation. She had gouged out both of her eyes with a needle. They feared for her life.

The newspaper fell to the ground. His trembling, gloved right hand groped over the cold marble surface of the table. With his left hand, he adjusted his face mask. It had shifted.

Brigitte

A Modern Mystery

Figures

Frank Cotta, dramatic poet
Elias Unversorgt, a young man
Dr. Artur Bodenlos, private lecturer in literary history
at the University of Tschermeisel
Brigitte
Adolf, a skull
A South Sea Islander
Voice Behind the Curtain
A prologue

PROLOGUE (*steps in front of the curtain*) Ladies and gentlemen, before we begin, I would like to preface that in this play, only the audience can fail, not the author!

VOICE BEHIND THE CURTAIN (*it resembles FRANK COTTA's voice*) The man seems to suffer from sexual compulsions.

> *The curtain opens. Living and working room at FRANK COTTA's place. On the left, a door to a bedroom, on the right, a door to the corridor. Comfortable bourgeois elegance. On the walls hang many gold-framed female nudes. ELIAS UNVERSORGT stands in the middle of the room, holding a sheet of paper and a pencil. He is twenty years old, with short, blond hair, glasses, and a sports outfit with short pants. He has his face turned to the left, toward the bedroom door.*

ELIAS UNVERSORGT Frank...

FRANK COTTA (*from the bedroom*) Yes...

ELIAS UNVERSORGT Frank, can you hear me?

FRANK COTTA Yes...

ELIAS UNVERSORGT I've done something really great...

FRANK COTTA Oh?

ELIAS UNVERSORGT Listen, so...

FRANK COTTA My God, can't you at least let me brush my teeth in peace first? (*We hear him gargling.*)

ELIAS UNVERSORGT By God, art comes first.

FRANK COTTA (*we hear him rummaging*) Brushed teeth are better than unbrushed poems. Besides, it's far healthier, yes, more beneficial, to brush your teeth than to swallow bad poems, to have to swallow them. You hear that... (*we hear him gargling again*)

ELIAS UNVERSORGT You're disgusting, Frank.

FRANK COTTA In order to properly digest poems, your chewing tools must be in order (*gargles*).

ELIAS UNVERSORGT Your logic, as always, is highly questionable. It's that of an orangutan sitting on a plum tree eating coconuts.

FRANK COTTA Damn, so just read – you humorist (*gargles*).

ELIAS UNVERSORGT Would you be so kind as to not spoil the sacred moment with your noisy throat sounds?

FRANK COTTA (*stops gargling*) It's just, to put it mildly, like going to the ceiling with a virgin! Go ahead.

ELIAS UNVERSORGT (*declaring*) Yes, this is how it goes in the world, everything feels like it's slipping away: years, hair, love, money, and the great intoxications.

FRANK COTTA (*gargles, then immediately stops*).

ELIAS UNVERSORGT Oh, soon you'll be a doctor of law and an assessor and married, and you'll gradually forget what a real whore is.

FRANK COTTA (*gargles, then immediately stops*) I protest.

ELIAS UNVERSORGT You'll get sober and feel bad, heart, you dull, dull hammer! Once you're drunk, you'll immediately get a hangover.

> *FRANK COTTA steps out of the door to the left. He is wearing a dressing gown, gray with brown tassels. His face is sharp and clean-shaven, his hair short-cropped and white-blond. Medium height, about forty-five years old hands in the pockets of his dressing gown, a book under his right arm, he extends his left hand to ELIAS UNVERSORGT.*

FRANK COTTA Bravo, excellent. The second stanza is confiscated. Whores may only be used but never named. None of your poems will ever be published again. You're too indecent, too primeval. You're the true orangutan of the two of us, dear Elias, my boy, and you call yourself a lyric poet.

ELIAS UNVERSORGT Frank, don't insult yourself. Otherwise, I'll have to defend you.

FRANK COTTA What time is it? – Only half past twelve? Well, that's still acceptable – have you seen Brigitte?

ELIAS UNVERSORGT No.

FRANK COTTA Really? I'll check the corridor. (*He leaves and comes back.*) She's not in her bedroom.

ELIAS UNVERSORGT Maybe she went for a walk... in this lovely weather... especially if you get up so late...

FRANK COTTA Went for a walk... No, I don't know... it's possible, after all...

ELIAS UNVERSORGT You're restless, Frank...

FRANK COTTA (*throws himself onto the sofa*) You're crazy, Elias. She probably went out hustling...

ELIAS UNVERSORGT (*astonished*) She confessed?

FRANK COTTA Apparently.

ELIAS UNVERSORGT I find it inappropriate – she, the wife of a well-known man, a world-famous poet.

FRANK COTTA You can drop the "world-famous" – and the "well-known" needs to be changed to "notorious." Well-known? Me? No! Her? Yes! By the way, the cigarettes are over there – no, further left, those are the Russian ones –

ELIAS UNVERSORGT Thanks, Adolf.

A skull on top of the bookshelf begins talking to itself.

ADOLF ...The sexual hypertrophy that has nowadays absorbed the spirit of the Earth...

ELIAS UNVERSORGT You mean, that the spirit of the Earth has absorbed. But you're confusing hypertrophy with primal nature or Urning nature. If only you could keep your mouth shut for once.

ADOLF Maybe. Maybe... I'm afraid I'm no longer competent. I lack physical emphasis. My flesh is gone, so my spirit is gone too, for it had its own flesh.

ELIAS UNVERSORGT Oh God.

SOUTH SEA ISLANDER suddenly climbs in through the window.

SOUTH SEA ISLANDER Excuse me, am I in the right place?

FRANK COTTA No – you're not in the right place. (*He gestures at his forehead with a finger.*)

SOUTH SEA ISLANDER I've been hired as a teacher for sex education in kinder-gartens.

ELIAS UNVERSORGT You speak German? Aren't you an Australian Aborigine?

SOUTH SEA ISLANDER Yes – and?

ELIAS UNVERSORGT But for sex education, surely one shouldn't speak German?

FRANK COTTA And now, leave us in peace, dear sir. I want to say my morning prayers.

ADOLF falls silent. The SOUTH SEA ISLANDER shakes his head and exits through the chimney. FRANK COTTA takes out a book and begins to read. ELIAS UNVERSORGT sits on the armrest of a chair.

FRANK COTTA (*looking up from the book*) You'll never amount to anything. You have no knowledge of people.

ELIAS UNVERSORGT For that, I know animals all the better.

FRANK COTTA Fine, you're what bourgeois society calls stupid; among us, it's called egocentric, Olympian, self-contained.

ELIAS UNVERSORGT Brigitte says the same about you. You're always self-contained – even at night.

FRANK COTTA Brigitte isn't exactly sensitive.

ELIAS UNVERSORGT My God – the way the three of us are with each other, all formalities fall away. We see each other as we are: naked.

FRANK COTTA Don't you see that I'm wearing a dressing gown over my naked-ness?

ELIAS UNVERSORGT I only wear... doubts over mine.

FRANK COTTA You're a Trappist. But still a novice.

ELIAS UNVERSORGT Unfortunately, my mouth is always closed when I want to speak.

FRANK COTTA Then speak already.

ELIAS UNVERSORGT What are you reading, anyway?

FRANK COTTA My Bible.

ELIAS UNVERSORGT Which is?

FRANK COTTA The Book of Solomon.

ELIAS UNVERSORGT And who wrote it?

FRANK COTTA Naturally, I did. I only read books I've written myself. That way, I know where I stand.

ELIAS UNVERSORGT You're one of the greats!

> *The doorbell rings.*

FRANK COTTA Didn't that ring? Help, Satan, that must be my friend Bodenlos. He said he'd visit today. (*Leaps off the sofa.*) Don't you know him?

ELIAS UNVERSORGT I'm not sure.

FRANK COTTA I need to step into the adjoining bedroom and change a bit. He can't see me like this. That would ruin the respect. (*The doorbell rings again.*) Good grief, can't these philologists ever wait? – He must see me as he wants to see me. Perhaps you'd be so kind as to receive him, yes? (*The doorbell rings.*) Go on, open the door.

> *FRANK COTTA shakes his head and hurries off to the bedroom. ELIAS UNVERSORGT exits and returns with a large man wearing a small green hat, a glaring yellow-red ulster, and carrying a portfolio under his arm. The man is about thirty years old.*

BODENLOS So, Herr Cotta, our universally revered master, is still sleeping? Naturally, we can't hold it against him. Probably worked tirelessly into the night again. He really ought to take it easier.

BODENLOS sets down his things, acts as if he were at home, and sits down.

BODENLOS But please, won't you sit down?

ELIAS UNVERSORGT If you'll allow me? You're very kind.

BODENLOS My dear sir, you seem so familiar to me.

ELIAS UNVERSORGT You seem familiar to me as well, Herr?

BODENLOS Bodenlos.

ELIAS UNVERSORGT Unprovided.

BODENLOS (*pondering*) Yes, that's true.

ELIAS UNVERSORGT If I'm not mistaken, you're the famous Germanist and literary historian at the local university?

BODENLOS (*stands up, runs around, twitching his mouth*) Germanist? No! You mean philology? Oh! No! I am not a philologist! Never! I only became a philologist to fight philology better. From within.

ELIAS UNVERSORGT As a parasite?

BODENLOS What do you mean? I despise philology. I am a literary scholar, an aesthete.

ELIAS UNVERSORGT (*modestly*) What is the difference between a philologist and an aesthetician?

BODENLOS Oh! No! You're thinking of normative aesthetics. No! I reject them. I reject them. Completely. I stand firmly on the ground of an emotional, subjective aesthetics. (*Breaks off.*) But perhaps you don't understand that yet. You're still too young. By the way, now I remember: you were my student last semester. I saw you in my exercises on literary criticism.

ELIAS UNVERSORGT I recall with pleasure the delightful course you taught on Friday evenings from six to eight in Lecture Hall 101.

BODENLOS Yes, I dare say: I stand alone in Germany with those exercises. Here in Tschermeisel, I've created a center for cultivating a new generation of critics. Because – that goes without saying – extensive, solid literary education can never, under any circumstances, be acquired at journalism schools. It can only be gained at the university – and, of course, only here in Tschermeisel. By the way, what brings you here to see our master?

ELIAS UNVERSORGT I wanted to present him with a few poems for evaluation, to see if he might be inclined to endorse a publishing offer with Georg Meier. When one has no literary connections at all...

BODENLOS Young friend, you're very confident. Our master is a strict critic.

Don't bother him with trifles like yourself. You're wasting his valuable time. Let me take a look at the poems first.

ELIAS UNVERSORGT If you permit, I'll recite a few.

BODENLOS Go ahead.

ELIAS UNVERSORGT Here's one titled Vision. *(He recites the earlier poem modestly and with restraint.)*

BODENLOS The poem is mediocre, young friend, not to say bad. It entirely lacks the inner dynamism of action. It's a superficial reflection that may hold personal emotional value but, as a public showcase, fizzles out completely.

ELIAS UNVERSORGT You mean, like Onan, fizzled out completely?

BODENLOS And then: Heart, you blunt, dull hammer... Can one even imagine that? The heart as a hammer – and blunt? Are there blunt hammers? That's almost as absurd as when Goethe says somewhere: Thirsty peaks. Do peaks have mouths? What? Oh, no! Can they drink? Can they, therefore, thirst? Young friend, I strongly advise you against lyrical production.

> *The door to the left opens.* FRANK COTTA *enters, dressed in a black Pierrot costume with violet pompoms, moving with dignity.*

FRANK COTTA Good morning, dear Bodenlos. Please, remain seated! Elias, I hope you've been keeping Dr. Bodenlos properly entertained?

ELIAS UNVERSORGT Properly?

BODENLOS You gentlemen know each other?

FRANK COTTA Of course, dear Bodenlos. Almost as well as we two know each other.

BODENLOS You've been working, not sleeping?

FRANK COTTA Sleeping? Whatever gave you that idea! I've been working! Look here at my work attire. I'm writing a new drama: Gotthilf Tschimborasso, a masculine Agnes Bernauer. It will be breathtaking, dear Bodenlos.

BODENLOS Everything you create, esteemed master, is captivating.

ELIAS UNVERSORGT Yes, it's what they call crowd-pleasers.

BODENLOS Young man, you are impudent.

FRANK COTTA My God, Elias, must you always tell the truth? – What brings you to us, dear Bodenlos?

BODENLOS I have some news that will delight you. Your new drama, though not yet approved for performance, has been cleared by the censors for a reading, with only a few minor cuts. What do you say? I went to the police headquarters myself. I used all my influence to ensure that a work of art like this, which towers high above any petty police morality, wouldn't be obstructed in its impact.

FRANK COTTA (*offering him both hands*) My dear Bodenlos, heartfelt and profound thanks. You are a true apostle of my so often misunderstood art. (*Falls into his arms.*) My friend, my only friend. You will write the critique for the *Evening Post*, won't you?

BODENLOS (*moved*) Oh! The world rests upon my bosom.

ELIAS UNVERSORGT The upside-down world.

FRANK COTTA And as thanks, dear friend, I dedicate the book edition of the play to you. (*In a raised voice.*) Dedicated to Dr. Artur Bodenlos.

ELIAS UNVERSORGT That's where the ground has become unmoored.

FRANK COTTA Shut up, Elias. Gotthilf Tschimborasso I dedicate to you – you male Ophelia!

BODENLOS When will you present the piece?

FRANK COTTA This week. Elias, perhaps you could speak to Meier about having posters printed: Thursday, February 29: Frank Cotta, "Brigitte," a modern primordial myth in five acts. Popular, affordable ticket prices.

> *The bell rings.*

ELIAS UNVERSORGT Someone's at the door.

FRANK COTTA Go see who it is...

> *ELIAS UNVERSORGT exits, then returns, smiling.*

ELIAS UNVERSORGT : It's a lady. It seems she forgot her key to see you.

FRANK COTTA Ah yes – I am quite the keyed piece. Without the key, I cannot be unlocked.

ELIAS UNVERSORGT (*at the door, letting the lady in*)

FRANK COTTA Brigitte!

BRIGITTE (*dressed only in flesh-colored tights*) Thank God, Frank, I'm back with you. It was dreadful at the police station. No – such coarse people! And they left me alone the entire time. All night. I was almost as lonely as I am with you, Frank. Every morning at nine, they conducted a body search. I had to strip completely naked, as if I weren't already exposed enough. And then they examined me to see if there was anything obscene about me. They always found something. Oh! They treated me like a harlot, Frank.

FRANK COTTA Well, you are one – be proud of it, Brigitte.

BRIGITTE Ah, and there's my rescuer, Dr. Armin Bodenlos.

BODENLOS Artur, please.

BRIGITTE Oh no! Armin. You appeared to me as Armin the Liberator. My deepest thanks. How is your wife? Are you divorced yet?

BODENLOS Thank you kindly, Miss. The little one is doing well.

BRIGITTE Please send my regards to your wife. (*To ELIAS UNVERSORGT*) Good day, Elias.

ELIAS UNVERSORGT Good day, Brigitte.

FRANK COTTA (*to BODENLOS*) So, your little one is being raised on Soxhlet?

BODENLOS And milk sugar. Oh, he's thriving splendidly.

BRIGITTE (*quietly to ELIAS UNVERSORGT*) Will you be home tomorrow morning until eleven?

ELIAS UNVERSORGT (*quietly*) I'll be waiting, Brigitte.

BODENLOS (*to FRANK COTTA*) By the way, you know, esteemed master, that I support the efforts of the free student movement. Would you be willing to provide a few complimentary tickets to the literary department for the reading?

FRANK COTTA With pleasure, dear friend, of course. Right, Brigitte?

BRIGITTE Why not? If they're handsome young men. I like that, Frank. (*Kisses him.*)

> *Curtain*

The Tooth of Time

Before I die, I want to wash and embalm my corpse, said Joshua.

He bought himself a large bottle of Eau de Cologne, a bottle of hair tonic, a box of lily milk soap, as well as Dante's *Divine Comedy*, and went to the Turkish bath.

The bathing attendant was a hideous woman with a mossy braid in the middle of her forehead and a smirk directed at the sofa.

He bathed thoroughly, took a cold shower, doused himself from head to toe with Eau de Cologne, and lay down on the divan with a sigh of relief to read *The Divine Comedy*.

While dressing, his collar button broke.

He rang for the old hag.

"Do you happen to have a collar button?"

She shuffled off and returned a moment later.

Her toothless, lazy mouth twisted into a mocking grin as she handed him a grayish-white, unsightly collar button and disappeared behind the door, muttering back into the room:

"It's my last one..."

He was just about to fasten the collar button when he glanced at it again.

It was a dirty, carious human tooth.

The old woman's last tooth.

And freshly fallen out.

The Gambler – A Scene

The gambler staggers onto the stage in a green tailcoat, green top hat, and an orange cloak.

I've gambled away... I've gambled everything away... I'm finished... before I even began... Four queens I had in my hand... Four queens at once... Ha, I thought, at last, Fortuna smiles on me fourfold... I wagered 10,000... My opponent was a skeleton dressed in the latest fashion... an enormous pumpkin skull... no hair, no flesh... no eyes. Its skeletal fingers held the five poker cards motionless. "Twenty thousand," squeaked the skeleton, like a poorly-oiled handcart.

This man, I thought — if he even is a man — is insane, completely idiotic... I have four queens in my hand, and he wants to outbid me. "Forty thousand!" I shouted, and it sang, it chirped within me:

Whoever the Muse has offered herself to in fourfold form,
Walks intoxicated through these meadows,
What do housewives and street women mean to him,
And what is the breeze among narcissi at sunset...

Eighty thousand, cackled the skeleton... The card must be played to the fullest... You are life, and he is death... You must win the whole world against him... Ah, boundless happiness if you win eternal bliss... immortality... One hundred sixty thousand! I bellowed... "Three hundred twenty thousand!" echoed the rickety frame.

I calculated feverishly... 160 and 80 and 40 and 20 and 10... Sum total, 310,000... My entire fortune was in play and at stake... What could I wager against his 320,000?

Behind my seat stood Eveline... blonde, delicate, and sweet as ever... She had gone pale... I turned... I lifted her with my arms onto the gaming table... She closed her eyes and stood still like a statuette... Then I tore the silk dress from her body... and the slip... Naked, she stood on the table. And I shouted: "I wager against your 320,000 my wife and my girl, my lover and my goddess... Agreed?" The skeleton grinned and probed the blooming flesh of the young woman's body with its empty eyes... "Agreed," it confirmed with a goatish laugh. Eveline stood motionless...

We threw the cards on the table... He had four aces... I watched as he wrapped his black cloak around Eveline... and lifted her from the table... I heard him order a car from the club attendant in his metallic voice... I stumbled out into the black night... My fate is sealed...

Soon the apple trees will bloom again... I'll learn English at the Berlitz school...

I have a talent for languages and will write for American newspapers and magazines... They supposedly pay fabulously... truly fabulously... 1,000 dollars for an article with illustrations... Well... one simply has to get a Kodak and photograph everything... absolutely everything... 1,000 dollars, that's, let's see, in today's exchange, 20,000 marks... Twenty articles, and I'll have won Eveline back... Oh, it's not as bad as it seems... Gambling is the only way to deal with life and fate... Even as an embryo, I had the habit of playing baccarat. When I was born after nine months — 9 is the number of baccarat, you know — I won 1,000 marks in one coup, which I set aside to later pay for my year of voluntary service... since my parents were simple folk, my father a delicatessen merchant, my mother a candidate of philology... Their shared interests brought them together, a sacred sympathy of hearts... It was a love marriage, straight out of the books... My mother nourished me on the breasts of science, which was significantly less strenuous than doing so on her own...

My father's educational method was limited to granting or denying me licorice, carob, or canned American meat... Thus, practical life skills and ideology balanced out the scales of my upbringing... At five years old, a comet struck my head, giving my skull a somewhat compressed and flattened shape... At the same time, it was noted that this heavenly sign indicated that the cosmos had great plans for me... In my ninth year — 9 is the number of baccarat, mark it well — Edward VII of England lost India to me in a game of baccarat... I became Viceroy of India, a position I held until my thirteenth year... Then I returned the crown to His Majesty of England... It was, by the way, only weakly gilded... Since then, I haven't been able to give up the game...

But I kept losing, even my sanity, which I had to trade for 100 marks... Because to have luck, you need money... and to have money, you need luck... Luck is what humanity must have and should have... Luck costs a lot of money... An afternoon at a jazz tea in the Paradise Bar... price: 100 marks... Dinner with Fern Andra, just to be seen with her, at Hiller's or elsewhere... price: 1,000 marks... A visit to Madame H. on Z. Street, where one encounters a few debutantes... price: 2,000 marks... And finally, two hours at the gambling club called 'Association of Younger Terrarium Enthusiasts'... price: countless marks... Lend me 50 marks... I'll bet everything on my card... If I win, I'll buy myself a zebra or a spring cloud... The beautiful money... Adjectives for money are like those for women... Who would believe my patent leather shoes and pressed creases that I have no money?... An elegant beggar, that's the worst..

I'll go to a first-class hotel and live on credit for a few weeks... At a second-rate hotel, I wouldn't get any... It's a miserable life... Should I perform as an eccentric dancer at the Corso Theater? Oh, the beautiful money and the beautiful cards and the beautiful, beautiful women... the Queen of Diamonds... and the Queen of Spades... and the Queen of Clubs... and the Queen of Hearts.

Letter to Asta Nielsen on the Occasion of Her Hamlet Film

Highly esteemed Madam,

You adopt the viewpoint of the venerable Professor Weyning, namely, that Hamlet was a woman. Or rather: the film adopts his viewpoint. Allow me the humble observation that there is, so to speak, a golden middle ground between your — or Professor Weyning's or the film's — interpretation and the conventional, customary notion that Hamlet was a man. This middle ground has been explored by Professor Gotthold Breitenschröt in his seminal work, Hamlet – a Man? (Leipzig, 1851). According to him, Hamlet was a hermaphrodite, a man-woman or a woman-man. This thesis, deeply rooted in characterological and psychological studies, has much to recommend it. I offer it here for discussion, in the hope that it may provide you with some inspiration for your authoritative reinterpretation of the Hamlet role. –

You point to the intellectual leaders of today, who are already won over to film. Allow me to direct your gaze to the intellectual leaders of the past. In particular, there is one work of world literature that, in its colorfully ornate oriental garb, its bizarre eroticism, and its tersely and pictorially shaped anecdotes, practically cries out for a film adaptation: this is the *Tao Te Ching* of the ancient Chinese sage Lao-tzu. Tao is an old — pardon me, a young — Chinese princess, with whom, at five o'clock tea, an old (a truly old) Chinese king falls in love, which then gives rise to all sorts of humorous and serious entanglements. In film, there exists the opportunity to unroll the entire Chinese cultural sphere: truly, a colossal but rewarding task. Box office success is guaranteed. No one other than you, highly esteemed gracious lady, is more ideally suited for the role of the charming Tao.

We would have a monumental film production such as no other nation on earth could rival — a work that would cast *The Mistress of the World, The Secrets of New York,* and *The Man with the Black Mask* far into the shadows. What do you say to a title like: *Tao, the Dreamy Lotus Blossom*?

No intellectual or material cost is spared in offering the public only the very best! The Far East in top-notch packaging! *Tao, the Dreamy Lotus Blossom* will play to sold-out houses in a thousand movie theaters, for, to quote the Tao Te Ching: "He who holds up a mirror to the world will draw crowds from every direction..."

The Hot Water Bottle

I suffer from cold feet. Whether this affliction originates in my crippled toes, I do not know. To remedy it at night, I require a hot water bottle, which draws away the bothersome chill from my feet and wraps them in cozy warmth, like thick wool. Gently, I sink into resonant dreams. I wander across scorching desert sands. Palms, like feather dusters, line the path. Camels, heavily laden with dates and figs, plod through my dimming gaze. Arabs in white burnooses, brandishing pistols and rifles adorned with silver, gallop past me on noble horses. On prayer rugs, the faithful kneel, their devout eyes turned toward Mecca. Playful maidens, entirely naked, cast pearly black glances my way. The sun stands high. The heat grows increasingly unbearable. All things have lost their shadows. Even mine has seeped away, like a thin spring disappearing into the desert sand. Sweat beads on my forehead. The soles of my feet burn. Sand fleas bite into the crevices of my crippled toes. With great effort, I finally reach the protective oasis. Suddenly, trees fan me with cooling breezes, a thousand shadows flit across the path, purposeless and inexplicable, and blissfully, a lukewarm stream trickles over my bare feet... for the hot water bottle has leaked. I lie in a wet bed, cursing the maid who screwed the cap of the hot water bottle too loosely. Half-asleep once more, I begin dreaming of the Arctic Ocean.

The Demonic Otto

Otto was so demonic that it was downright exasperating. He sported a fringe beard like Dostoevsky. His atropine-drenched eyes plunged men and women alike into paralyzing confusion. Indeed, when he once entered a restaurant and let his gaze sweep around the room, like a cowboy spinning his lasso before throwing it, all the waiters dropped their trays in terror. Witty and physically frail women fell for him as if into a deep well, only to realize, bewildered after the fall, that they had landed on a barren sandy wasteland. The demonic Otto was a devoted disciple of Spengler. He believed in the decline of the West as fervently as God once believed in creation. "We are still stones atop stones," he declared, "but the coming day will deliver us." The demonic Otto despised phrases that said either nothing or everything. "The future of Europe," he smiled seductively at Lillie, raising a glass in which French champagne fizzed softly, "will depend on the proletarian tendencies, upon which the future of Europe depends." Late into the evening, Otto would expound on magic and the Rosicrucians. He spoke of the eternal lamp of his heart as he switched off the electric light. "I will," he bellowed at the bewildered Lillie, "hurl my soul into your tricks!" When Otto slept alone, he did so for religious reasons in a bathtub through which rose water continually flowed to cleanse his aura. However, he refused to remove the lice from his head, as he believed himself to be a reincarnation of Saint Macarius, who famously became the patron saint of lice, fleas, and bedbugs. When the demonic Otto confused the Holy Trinity with the threefold division of the social question during a public lecture, the police began to take an interest in him and committed him to an asylum for blasphemy. This did not lead to any significant change in his lifestyle.

He continued to sleep in a bathtub — the standard sleeping arrangement for the violently insane. However, the lice were taken from him, as the asylum warden, Puffke, showed him no respect whatsoever. Puffke was responsible for overseeing 33 gods, 7 religious founders, and 5 emperors. How could the demonic Otto impress him? Laughable!

The Mass Grave

If I were to describe my room to you, it is three meters long, three meters wide, and five meters high. A table, a bed, a chair, and a closet that is more symbolic than real complete the furniture. Apart from me, the room is also home to an elderly guinea fowl, a pregnant guinea pig, and a lame, syphilitic rabbit. The rabbit has a publicly undisclosed relationship with the guinea pig, and the guinea fowl has a publicly undisclosed relationship with the rabbit. As for me, I am, so to speak, quite alone here. It is only out of the need, so to speak, to begin a relationship with myself, to enter into a relationship with myself, that I write books, which are then later printed and brought to the public. Most of the reviews that appear in the newspapers about them are written by me. I send them under a false name, using the signatures of my roommates: Joseph Perlhuhn, Isabella Meerschwein, Isidor Ben Kanin Chen. I tend to either praise myself vehemently or criticize myself fiercely, in order to provoke a longer discussion in the various papers, which I alone engage in. If you consider my way of life to be exceedingly sad and almost idiotic, you are not entirely wrong. But what is there for a living person to do today that does not end badly or mean-spirited? Death is the only pleasant thing about life. I have dug and prepared a family tomb for myself in the garden: four graves side by side: for me, the guinea fowl, the guinea pig, and the lame syphilitic rabbit. A common cross will rise over the mass grave, with the pious inscription in golden letters: *Hic Rhodus, hic salta!*

The Boxer

My name is Joseph Peintner, known as the Bavarian Wildcat. I was born in Hals near Passau. My father is a mill owner and a truly despicable fool. He could easily give me 100,000 marks, but he won't, not for all the gold in the world. He spends the whole day sitting in his office counting brown bills. He has never counted his children. But there are thirteen of us. I am the fifth. When I was 15, I ran away to England. Okay then. Because life burned in me like an wild flame, I didn't know for what or where. Only that I was burning. Upon arriving in London, I went to a Christian boarding house. I stole a frock coat from a junk dealer in a Jewish alley, hanging on a doorpost like a man who has hanged himself. With it, I became a bellboy at a fancy hotel. It was a very fancy hotel: on the third day, a guest in Room 33 fell in love with me, an elegant manufacturer. Damn, I didn't know what was happening to me; he looked at me so strangely when I brought him chocolate in the morning. And only I was allowed to bring it to him. The room waiter and the doorman, who had discovered the gentleman from Liverpool's preference for me, used this knowledge for a small blackmail that succeeded beyond expectations. I received 10 percent of the amount. With this money, I went to the Moulin Rouge in Whitechapel: a cursed place where you stumble around like in a vegetable cellar. There was also all sorts of vegetables to be found there, and I, being a greenhorn at the time, fit in perfectly.

The place was shrouded in thick tobacco smoke. Women and men, all dressed in bizarre ways, screamed, whistled, and shouted in confusion. An orchestra sounded somewhere out of the clouds. In the middle, a tangle of people were dancing. On the sides, there were niches draped with old calico cloths, behind which now and then a couple disappeared. I smiled at a lady who danced past. Never had I seen a more delicate, prettier creature; she seemed as fragile as a vase, and her eyes were full of innocence and soul. Suddenly, a man stood next to me. He shouted to make himself heard over the noise: "Why are you smiling at the lady? Do you want her or not? No long speeches!" He held out his open hand: "Three shillings, and you can go behind the calico curtain with her." I turned pale and didn't know what to say. The man was waving his hand in front of me. Somewhere, my angel smiled. In the middle of the room, a wild outcry arose. Knives glittered suddenly, and a shot rang out. The lights went out as if on command. And now began a tough, fierce fight in the dark, like between rats: I didn't know what it was about, nor who the parties were. I fled into a corner, knocked over a table, and hid behind it. The fight lasted a full hour. Then morning came. One by one, people disappeared through the cellar hatch, from which a greenish glow flowed like pus. Finally, no one was left in the place. I crawled out from behind my barricade. Pools of blood were laughing everywhere. And in the middle, under the greasy chandelier, lay: my angel, still smiling, a knife stuck in her chest.

I went home, packed my things, and turned to the profession of selling newspapers. Nowhere is the fight for existence, for that little bit of disgusting, sweet existence, fought more bitterly than between newspaper boys, who on the street corners fight with all means to steal each other's customers. The decision is usually made in a proper boxing match. The boys lay down their bundles, roll up their sleeves, and then the fight begins. A crowd gathers. Bets are placed. The loser must no longer sell newspapers at the corner. I had already knocked out seventeen boys – because I am a strong, wiry Lower Bavarian – when, after the eighteenth match, an elegant gentleman with a top hat and white gloves, who had bet on me, came up to me, took off his hat, and asked shortly: "Would you like to become a boxer? I'll have you trained..." I left my newspapers on the ground, said "All right," and went with him. I became an apprentice to the Turkish master Sadi: a master of his craft, but a pig. And "pig" doesn't even begin to describe it. He beat me half to death, but I learned something, and I am proud to be called his student. Once, when I tried the heart punch ten times and still couldn't get it right, he punched me in the eyes so hard that I couldn't open them again. Then he gave me his famous stomach punch, and I fell and lay like a log. He threw himself over me and cried. That's how all boxers are: brutal and sentimental. And so am I. Sadi is a big fixer. Should I tell you how he made his fortune? The championship for England was announced. He faced Jones. Both were top class. But he was far better in shape. He had to win. Huge sums were bet on him: Sadi – Jones, the odds were 10 to 1. He went to the bank handling the bets and said: "If you give me 25 percent of the net sales, I'll tell you who will win." "All right," said the banker, who was focused on his business. Then Sadi grinned widely and said: "Jones" – left, and let himself be deliberately knocked out in the twentieth round after betting on Jones himself. That's how boxers are. Most of it is fixed, and it takes a lot to distinguish between a fair and honest fight and a vile fix. Do you know the black man Johnson? I claim he is the greatest boxer who ever lived, and the most honest and fairest fighter too. Yet, he had to give up the world championship in America because it was intolerable to the Americans that a black man should triumph over the white race. With a revolver in hand, they forced him to forgo the world championship in a fictitious fight. They paid him 40,000 pounds in gold, and he shoveled the gold into a sack with his enormous paw, said: "A black man has no right in the world," and left. – I have the South German championship. I am only 23 years old. This winter I plan to go to Berlin, and we'll see if Breitensträtter and Naujocks can stand up to me. Because I am Joseph Peintner, known as the Bavarian Wildcat, from Hals near Passau.

The 99th Return of Buddha

Buddha came to Earth for the 99th time. He found that it was not as gray as it had seemed to him the last time. There was much that was lovable and beautiful to be found: butterflies, nightingales, cedars, sunrises and sunsets, a silver moon, a singing waterfall. The wild animals and especially the humans pleased him less. But he recalled the great words that had once been spoken: "To those who are good to me, I am good, and to those who are not good to me, I am also good." Buddha founded an academy, "The Voice of the Forests," and taught young Indians as he had been taught: gently, quietly, and kindly. To teach them, he wrote various small and large poems in the tradition of his people. These spoke of butterflies, nightingales, cedars, sunrises and sunsets, a silver moon, a singing waterfall. These verses were nothing special, but entirely typical of Indian poetry. A thousand Indian poets had written such and similar verses. But then the wind carried some of his sounds, like scattered blossoms from India, to Europe, where they sounded unheard in a barren, unnatural, inhuman world. In Europe, a benefactor and philanthropist, the inventor of the murderous dynamite, had established a foundation for poets: for every few million that he sent to their death, one poet would be brought back to life — meaning to fame and glory — and this poet, when his verses were known, became Buddha, who out of modesty called himself Thakur. Thakur was greatly pleased by the deep impression his gentle, quiet teachings made on wild Europe. He put on his silk coat, stroked his white full beard, and set off for Europe to give his thoughts more emphasis through his personality. He spoke at the University of Berlin, and the gates that had never opened to a great German poet sprang open for him. He spoke of the wisdom of the forests to people who only knew the cleverness of machines. He preached: "Love your enemies!" And the rapier blades of the students clanged joyfully against one another, and from their lips rose the "Watch on the Rhine." He said: "To those who are good to me, I am good; to those who are not good to me, I am also good." And Geheimrat Roethe shook his hand. Butterweck, the chairman of the board of the Nirvana Operating Company Ltd., had him introduced and emphasized that they were united by common interests. He whispered to him aside: "In confidence, I need ten thousand Buddha statues, immediately available, 15 percent commission." – – – And Buddha, who did not understand German, was pleased with the deep impression he left everywhere. He had set out with a white full beard; but upon his arrival in Darmstadt, he was completely beardless, for the enthusiastic young girls had plucked all his hair as a memento. He also wore an elegant European coat, for his silk garment had been placed in the Berlin Cathedral next to the cuirassier helmet of Kaiser Wilhelm II as a relic. In Darmstadt, Buddha sat without his beard, in his coat, with eyes wide in amazement, on an old discarded throne. A former Grand Duke made him his *maître de plaisir* and steward, and a German philosopher with a blond full beard, whom Buddha envied, held Buddhist gatherings. He had a bass drum behind him, which he occasionally struck, shouting: "Here is the one true, only real Buddha! Not to be confused with similar enterprises! There is only one Buddha, and I am his prophet!" And he beat the drum. Buddha did not understand what all of this meant. He smiled helplessly and kindly. The blonde philosopher, who was already quite adept at beating the drum for himself, also skillfully struck it for his master. Small children came and strewed white flowers at the Buddha, just as they had once done for their Serenissimus. Yes, the Serenissimus himself scattered flowers and incense. A male choir sang the song of Andreas Hofer, probably because Andreas Hofer, like Buddha and the blond philosopher, had worn a full beard. But then, from the mouths of the people who had come from far and wide to see Buddha — arriving with wives, children, beer, and bread — came the improvised German song for the summer sky: "I don't know what it means." But Buddha still did not understand what all this was supposed to mean. He only saw the reverence shown to the god in his person. He closed his eyes and thought of butterflies, nightingales, cedars, sunrises and sunsets, the silver moon, and the singing waterfall. The singing had ended. He heard the former Grand Duke giving the tone and rhythm, and the crowd roaring in unison: "His Eminence, the Buddha — hurrah! hurrah! hurrah!" Buddha opened his eyes. The sun had set, and a night butterfly was gently swaying on his delicate hand. He stood up, wiped his forehead with his hand, and said: "I am tired. I want to sleep." He descended the steps of the throne and walked through the crowd, which made way for him reverentially. The twilight had descended. He walked through the lonely park. Here and there, a white statue glowed. In front of one, with the word Goethe written on its base, Buddha stopped. He raised his arms, then sank to the base, and tears fell from his empty, inward-turned eyes.

Fidelity to Women

My ladies, I hope you will not take offense at the little story I am about to tell you, for it is rather frivolous. But I would like to reassure you by mentioning that it took place in distant India. In Europe, as is widely known, marriage is considered a sacrament, and never has a woman in Europe broken her marriage vows. – – –

Once upon a time, there was a gentleman named Viradhara and a lady named Kamadamini. The latter was a young, delicate, and joyful creature, while her husband Viradhara had already reached that age, of which the Indian proverb says: "An old donkey does not pull anymore." Kamadamini thought that there were still enough young donkeys who would be happy to pull her little cart, if only she would harness them. Thus, Kamadamini acted and became the subject of a reputation that even reached her old husband. The husband was deeply distressed upon hearing this, but remained silent and decided to test his wife. One day he said to her: "My dear dove, forgive me if I leave you alone for a few days, for I must undertake a longer journey for business," kissed her on the forehead, and left the house, only to return by a roundabout way and sneak through the window into the room to hide under the bed. No sooner had Viradhara left the house than Kamadamini began to beautify herself, bake little cakes with the finest butter and the best flour, and sent her servant with an invitation to a young man who had often pulled her little cart. The young man appeared with great joy, they ate and drank, and then went to the room and to the bed.

Now, as Kamadamini accidentally touched the body of her husband, who was hidden to test her, with her foot, she, being as wise as women often are in all things wicked – pardon me, my ladies, in India... – immediately knew who was lying there and what was happening. When her lover tried to embrace her, she pushed him away and said: "Sir, you must not touch me." The young man replied angrily: "I beg you, beautiful lady, tell me why in the world you have had me called then?" She said: "I visited the temple of Kandika before sunrise. There, suddenly a voice sounded: 'Unfortunate one, you will be a widow within three months.' I was terribly frightened, for I love my husband more than anything in the world, even more than my life or my honor. And I begged: 'Goddess, is there a way to save my husband from this fate?' She replied: 'Yes. I will tell you this way: You must embrace a stranger – thus, the death destined for your husband will pass to him, and he will live for one hundred years.' So, know that you may now embrace me, but the death from the goddess Kandika is surely upon you..."

The young man smiled, for he began to understand the young woman, while the husband, in his hiding place, twisted and turned like a cat being petted. The young man said: "I gladly accept the death that will come to me after I have been allowed to embrace you," and so they embraced and loved each other, while the husband, moved by the sacrifice his wife made out of love for him, shed tears of emotion.

When the young man was about to leave, the husband crawled out from under the bed. With tears still in his eyelashes, he embraced him, pretending to be terribly shocked, and said: "My lifesaver! My truest friend until your inevitable death!" He kissed his wife and said: "You are the most faithful woman who ever walked on Earth. Be blessed."

Thus, my ladies, my story is at an end, and I would like to note, to avoid any unpleasant misunderstandings, that such unfaithful wives, useless young men, and silly old husbands are, of course, only to be found in India.

The Typewriter Bureau

"Winged Hand," Bureau for Typewriting Work, was written on a black-bordered porcelain sign on the door.

I rang the bell.

The door opened silently, and I found myself in the office. It was entirely wallpapered in black. The shutters were closed. On a desk, a green electric lamp burned.

An severely consumptive gentleman, who in the green light looked like someone who had long been dead, approached me, coughing hoarsely. His lungs rattled. From his mouth crawled, almost physically, like a slimy mass, the smell of decay.

"How may I help you?" whispered the consumptive.

"I wish to dictate something. Do you have employees you can recommend?"

The consumptive shook his head.

"I have no employees" –

"And the Winged Hand?" –

"– is me"...

He bowed ceremoniously.

I involuntarily looked at his hands; they were delicate and slender, like a woman's hands. They alone seemed still pulsed with blood, which reached the head only in sparse strands and channels.

It was a strange situation. Unquestionable sympathies drew me to this decaying man, yet his presence painfully oppressed me.

"I would like to dictate my life to... you," I said hesitantly.

"Radiotelegraphically. Will you be able to follow? I am still young. I am feverishly aflame. Even my calm is raging. See my eyes! They examine things a thousandfold, like the arms of an octopus. My fists shatter the stars and the doors that do not wish to open for me. I believe I am fortunate enough to count for something. My grandchildren will still be alive to me. I will come before you shortly before my death and correct the manuscript. Write! I will pay with my blood.".....

The consumptive bowed, and I left. Life grew more colorful with each passing day. The seasons swung past me like butterflies: silver, green, red, and gold. A chain of women wrapped itself around my sleep.

I piled up deeds. My will was effective. My fame resounded to the throne. Medals proved that I promoted order. Money proved that I was valued. Fame proved that I was praised. The crowd applauded enthusiastically at the gentlemen and heroes who staggered across the stage, aghast at my pen. Students were already reverently reading my moral stories, my divine poems, in their school textbooks. Lectures on my works began to be given at universities. I was visibly aging.

When I felt my last hour was near, I made my way, laboriously with a cane, out of the car and into the Bureau of the "Winged Hand."

The consumptive greeted me with a measured smile and a hoarse cough.

"The work I gave you," I said, sinking wearily into a chair.

"You didn't give me much to work with. Less than I suspected. Here is the manuscript." And he handed me a tiny piece of paper, which bore these words: "He was a man, no more, no less. He died before he died. May he live after he lived."

I screamed, crushed by the few words: "Seventy years I have lived, and written seventy books: is this the result of my reckoning? The worth of my being?"

Then the consumptive ran his bony hand over my forehead: "Please calm yourself, my dear fellow. Millions go to their graves with an empty, white sheet. If only one word of yours remains for eternity, then you live on, immortal, in the song of human suffering".....

I leaned my bald head against the chair's cushion: 'What do I owe you, please?"–

Utterly exhausted, I fell, crying like a child, inconsolably shaken into the final sleep.

I only noticed how the gaunt man cut the heart from my body, the eyes from my head, and began again to monotonously clatter away on his machine.

Part Nine:

The Last Emperor

(Published in 1923 by Fritz Heyder Verlag, Berlin-Zehlendorf.)
With illustrations by Erich Büttner

The Last Emperor

(For Countess and Count Arco)

The imperial boy awoke. He pulled back the yellow silk curtain. He listened like a hare sitting upright. The regular breathing of the sleeping servants and eunuchs reached him through the thin sandalwood wall from the antechamber. He rose; an ornate European clock — a blacksmith hammering on an anvil — began to strike seven. He rang a small golden bell that lay on a mahogany table beside the daybed. The double doors swung open, and the chief chamberlain, a mandarin of the highest rank, appeared. Nine times, his forehead touched the ground before the emperor, who stood in red leather shoes, a yellow robe embroidered with symbols, on a blue fox fur. Three servants seemed to leap from the belly of the corpulent mandarin: the first offered a cup of tea, the second a dish of preserves, the third a lacquered box with cigarettes. The emperor sipped the tea while standing. He studied the spring landscape depicted on the cup: blooming apricot trees, beneath them a pair of lovers; in the distance, a pond, a gondola; in the background, a hill with a pagoda. The emperor curled his lips as he saw the lovers, lost in innocent bliss. A crease broke his smooth, childlike brow. The servant holding the tea tray trembled, barely able to remain on his shaking knees. The emperor set the cup down with a clatter. He made a motion with his hand, and the three servants withdrew swiftly. The fat mandarin renewed the ninefold kowtow. Then, with his gaze lowered to the ground, he whispered, "The cup in which the servant Yuan Yng served tea displeased Your Celestial Majesty. I will order the servant to be flogged." The emperor ignored the whispered words. "Send for Hi."

Hi, the nursemaid, waddled in on her swollen feet. The boy's eyes lit up as he saw her: "Dress me, Hi." "Which robe does Your Majesty command? The sky-blue one embroidered with orange blossoms? The black one with stars and celestial figures? The brown one depicting agriculture and animal husbandry? The crimson one with symbols of blissful love?" The boy had turned pale. He stamped his foot on the prepared skull of the blue fox so hard that it cracked. The nursemaid looked up at him askew, her arms humbly folded over her soft belly. He turned to the wall, hastily crushing a tear unworthy of a god and emperor. "They've taken Fey-yen from me. They've wounded my heart." The nursemaid remained silent. "When I visited the chambers of the Empress, my wife, last night, accompanied by two eunuchs, a ceremonialist — a gaunt, dubious intriguer — met me with nine bows and a grin of regret: Her Majesty, the Empress, had been summoned on urgent political business late in the evening to Her Majesty, the Dowager Empress Tsze-hi, in the Summer Palace. A messenger had been sent to inform me but had not reached me in time. Now tell me, what political mission could Fey-yen, who is a child of fifteen, a year younger than I, possibly undertake with her small, unknowing hands? These hands are meant to soothe me when I am in pain. When will Tsze-hi, the wicked toad with warts, return

Fey-yen, my dragonfly, to me? She will devour her, as she devours everything that comes near her. And yet she dresses as Kwanyin, the goddess of mercy! She tortures me because I am the emperor and because she has plans for me as dark as the plots of the northern demons." Hi still remained silent, pretending not to hear the emperor's words.

The emperor approached a window. A young gardener was trimming shrubs outside. "I want no more of these imperial garments on my body," the boy said, grinding his teeth like a horse biting on its bit. "Hi, go to that gardener, give him some cash, and assure him of my imperial grace: he is to lend me his clothes." Hi tried to speak, but the emperor cut her off with a sharp gesture before she could utter a word. Hi waddled away. She returned with the filthy rags. The emperor was delighted and clapped his hands. He threw them on and examined himself in the mirror. "At last, I look like a human being — what do you think, Hi? If I step among my army in this disguise, will they recognize me as the emperor?" He flung the window open, leapt into the bushes and shrubs, and disappeared. Hi screamed, violating all etiquette. Then she crawled wailing to the chief chamberlain, who immediately sent several mandarins of the first rank after the emperor.

The emperor made his way through side paths and thickets. He came upon a crumbling tower, climbed it, and looked down. The land still lay before the first signs of spring. Trees, houses, meadows, roofs, domes, earth, sky– everything was yellow in gray and gray in yellow. These colors had dominated Peking for months. They wearied him. He longed for the blue sea, for green meadows, for red lips – specifically, the painted red lips of his young empress, whose lips were as red and delicate as those of the mysterious goddess in the Temple of Abstinence, known only to him.

He had discovered her one day in a half-buried vault that had been shattered by the artillery of foreign barbarians. She was the finest, the purest, the most beautiful goddess. He prayed to her in every painful moment of his existence. The emperor lay on the tower, where furry, gray-silver moss thrived. He then heard wailing and looked into a courtyard, where the servant who had served him tea that morning was being beaten with bamboo rods. Small, bright red streams of blood flowed over the yellow skin. The emperor felt a faint sense of satisfaction as he saw the red glimmer amidst all the gray and yellow. He descended the frail tower, disturbing a bat that fled into the daylight. He continued walking through the endless gardens. He passed through small groves of cypress trees, lotus ponds, small temples, marble structures, and landscapes he had never seen before. He climbed onto a bridge that arched like the back of a camel: nine arches spanning nine canals.

At the peak of the bridge, he stopped, leaning against the railing, and looked down. Below, gardeners were relocating old lotus plants in the pond to make space for the young ones. In the middle, they left a narrow waterway for gondolas and pleasure boats. Some of the gardeners stood in the water up to their waists. A few of them sang a monotonous song:

> Lotus blossom,
> Daughter of heaven,
> Born of pleasure, crowned with delight,
> How soon you wither, fade, and rot,
> Even you —

One of the guards happened to look up at the bridge and spotted the emperor in his gardener's uniform. He swung his bamboo stick: "Hey, you lazybones, you scoundrel, you idler, you want to watch like the emperor from the throne how others work! Get down, or I'll have you bastinadoed on the soles of your feet!" The emperor laughed and ran briskly down the bridge on the other side. He found a boat loosely chained and poled himself to the other bank. Ducks and water pigeons accompanied his silvery path. He jumped across a meadow, then into a thick fern bush. In a clearing he threw himself on the ground and immediately fell asleep.

When he woke up, a girl was sitting next to him, perhaps seventeen years old. She smiled sheepishly and scratched her scabby head. She was pretty, but dirty and neglected. "Am I disturbing your dreams? May the winds of the south be favorable to you and stroke your forehead more tenderly than the hand of a lover." "May the demons of the north always stay away from you and may Kwanyn forever give you the water of life from the Yu springs from the silver jug that she holds in her left hand. I am pleased to meet you." The emperor sat up a little straighter. Dragonflies flew overhead, yellow butterflies that looked like fluttering tangerines. "You ran away from your job, I suppose?" She looked searchingly into his face. "Show me your hands."

She took his hands. "They are delicate, as if they've never done a day's work. And here: what do these rings mean?" The emperor was frightened. During his transformation he had forgotten to take off the imperial rings: the huge sapphire set in diamonds, the ring of nine sacred pearls. He smiled embarrassed: "The stones are fake. I once bought them from a stallholder in the suburbs for a few bucks." The girl turned her hand with the stones in the sun that was beginning to break through the bushes. "But they are pretty and shine delicately. Give me a ring! If you like, I will love you for it." The emperor thought: if I give away the rings, I am no longer an emperor. They are part of the insignia of the empire.

For centuries the sons of heaven have worn the blue sapphire as a symbol of the vault of heaven, and now I am supposed to throw it to a dirty girl whose father is a rickshaw coolie and whose mother is a girl from a lowly teahouse. A girl I don't know, who I don't love and who, may the gods protect me, I won't let love me either. Who doesn't even suspect the immeasurable value of the ring and will give it away to the first Manchu soldier or cake baker who comes along. -

The thought of the senselessness of this gift and the profound self-abasement and humiliation delighted him so much that he slipped the ring with the sapphire from his finger, hesitated for a second and then put it on her hand. She whistled with joy like a dormouse and put both his hands on her young breasts. "Who are you?" he asked. "I serve as a kitchen maid in the Yu Schau summer palace of Her Exalted Majesty the Empress Dowager Tsze-hi." The Emperor jumped to his feet. "I gave you a ring, and even if it is not worth much, you still owe me a small service in return. I am currently unemployed, the gardening profession no longer suits me, take me to your head chef. He should employ me as a kitchen boy. With my knowledge of vegetables and mushrooms and fruit and salads, I can certainly be of service to him." The girl clapped her hands. "Come." A few steps behind the fern hedge was the wall of the palace garden. There was a tiny opening in the wall through which they both squeezed. A few more steps through a hedge of wild roses and they were on the street by the large wall. The street was alive with shouting, rushing rickshaws, traders, jugglers, donkeys, mangy dogs, tripping women, howling children, and street musicians. Tents and stalls had been set up. Here someone, wearing a pointed, impossibly matted hat, was selling dog's heart fried on sticks. Here they had donkey meat, frog legs in white egg sauce. Here was a bakery that made rice cakes and sugar cakes. It smelled of bad oil and rancid fat. Of musk, of garlic. Of onions, which every third person was chewing in their mouths. A cripple, missing both legs, who moved forward in a small wooden cart with two sticks, offered the women smelling pillows. A criminal, with a wooden ruff around his neck, was driven past by soldiers. He grinned cheekily and mocked the passers-by with rude phrases, of which "daughter of a turtle" was the least rude. Fortune tellers and magicians had their stalls. One predicted fortunes from grains of rice, another from lines on the hand, a third from the signs of the heavens.

Depending on the amount of cash, one was given predictions of good or bad fortune. The rich could expect good fortune and happiness. Guitar music could be heard from teahouses. A theater troupe was performing a historical tragedy in the open air, "The Last Emperor of the Ming Dynasty." The emperor arrived just in time to see the last of the Ming Dynasty tie the rope around his neck. He shuddered slightly. Had the man of letters who taught him history kept the terrible end of the Mings from him? Or was the actor merely fantasizing, a garishly made-up boy with the airs of a sex toy? The emperor bought a paper kite from a kite seller. He let it fly above the stalls, the sacred yellow dragon. It danced wild and unruly in the wind. Then the thin string broke. The dragon flew headfirst to the ground and disappeared. The emperor was frightened again. What kind of bad omens were all these? The last emperor of the Ming dynasty, the holy dragon, which first rose steeply to the top only to suddenly sink. Was the thread on which China's fate hung so thin and easily torn? The emperor approached a fortune teller: "Tell me the truth!" The fortune teller weighed the few cash in his hand. He was a magician who lived in the ruins of the Yuang Ming Yuan, the old summer palace. He stroked his beard and said: "If you disturb the wind and water gods, you can expect storms and wild floods. You should not elevate yourself to the status of the gods if you are only a human being. Build temples small so that they cling to the earth: the more easily the spirit of heaven will find them. You cannot expect a peaceful disposition from people who are forced to live with rats and bedbugs. Make people happier and they will become better. The great sacrifice himself for the sake of a small thing, the small for the sake of a great thing. Sacrifice is the meaning of life and the meaning of death. Grace drips from the gods like resin from a tree trunk."

The Emperor departed thoughtfully. Behind him the kitchen maid tripped along, vainly turning the blue sapphire in the sun. She led him to a side gate of the new palace, where a Manchu soldier, with whom she seemed to have some connection, was standing guard. He was chewing tobacco and spitting lazily. The Emperor approached him and bowed: "May my elder brother forgive him if his younger brother disturbs him in his meditations. I have met a wild goose and followed its flight. I would be delighted to welcome you as my friend, for I intend to accept the position of kitchen official in this illustrious house." "Come in," said the soldier, a little harshly, but not unkindly; he liked the handsome boy: "You have come at a strange hour. If you had asked for entry at one of the main gates, you would not have been allowed in." "What is the meaning of your speech, Tu-Wei?" said the girl, "you are making me very afraid." "The arrows that hit the proud heron are already sharpened. The colorful dress of the imperial peacock will soon fade. There is revolution in the city." "Revolution?" asked the emperor, having to make the word clear to himself. "Why revolution and against whom?" "Against whom else but the emperor," said the soldier, "have you never been involved in politics?" The emperor shook his head. "Politics is what the old, evil empress dowager Tsze-hi does. It cannot be good." The soldier frowned. "Don't be so cheeky. And above all, speak of Her Majesty the empress dowager in a different tone. Perhaps you yourself are a revolutionary?" The emperor smiled from his pale face. The soldier continued without waiting for an answer: "Some literary figures of dubious status, lawyers and legal twisters from abroad, have returned from America. They have cut off their pigtails and wear top hats and frock coats like the white barbarians. Now they want us all to cut off our pigtails and wear top hats and frock coats: that is why there is revolution. Do you understand that?" The emperor nodded. "So they are in league with the white barbarians. They are traitors to our people. How horrible." The soldier nodded. He spat the brown juice in an arc at the wall. "They have founded secret societies and agitated among the people against the emperor and the dowager empress in the name of human rights: freedom, democracy, the right of peoples to self-determination." The emperor spelled out to himself: "Human rights... what does that mean? China has been an empire for thousands of years. The emperor is the son of heaven, the mediator between mankind and Shang-ti, the spirit of heaven. How will they deal with the gods if they no longer have an emperor?" "Dear boy," said the soldier tenderly, "everyone wants to be an emperor and to personally communicate with the spirit of heaven." Then the soldier laughed and made a gesture with his right hand of counting money and pocketing it. "By the holy dolphin, you are slow on the uptake: they want to earn - what the mandarins have earned as the emperor's representatives, they want to earn themselves. Tael! Tael! Cash! Cash! Kwai zau for the little scoundrels, after the big ones have stepped down."

The emperor was astonished by the soldier's tirade as he stormed toward him. He didn't fully understand it. Since when did tael or cash matter in a person's life? These were completely irrelevant, ridiculous metallic terms with which one could buy a dog's heart on the grill, a paper kite, or perhaps even a woman.

But the Spirit of Heaven — what did he have to do with taels? The girl urged: "Just come in. The gate will soon be closed, and you must know where you stand." The emperor bowed to the soldier, asked him to recommend him to his noble family, and followed the girl. The girl led him to the Head Chef Wang, who was stirring a tureen with a face as red as a lobster. "I am bringing Your Highness a servant eager to serve." The emperor presented his request with decorum. "Very well," said the good-natured Wang, who could never say no, not even to women; he suspected that by accepting the kitchen boy, at least something would jump out or in for him with Noa. "Very well, we'll give it a try with you. Can you serve too? You have a pretty, slick face, as if your mother, the cat, licks you three times a day. You could be presented to the court." The emperor had been able to study the manners of the servants from his own. He believed that he could appear at court in style. "Very well. We will see. Noa will take you to the master of the wardrobe."

Just as the emperor was being dressed in the servants' elegant white attire, a commotion arose in the palace, which spread from the gates to the center of the dowager empress's chambers and from there into all the side wings. The emperor had disappeared from the old palace and could not be found despite the most diligent searches. They had wanted to bring him to safety in the new palace: he had certainly fallen into the hands of the rebels, the accursed republicans and insane followers of the western barbarian ideology. The dowager empress was beside herself. She shuffled up and down in her secret chamber, which smelled of perfume, with asthmatic excitement. Yng, the chief eunuch and her confidant, always following her like a chicken following a hen. "Yng, what should I do?" She took a drag from an opium pipe that was lying in a corner. "He has run away. That's it. He is a rebel himself, the son of heaven, Yng. He is a wayward boy whom we have always overlooked too much. What will he do? He will manage to join the rebels and conspire against me: as an imperial republican, as a republican emperor. Chang-tü-tsf, whom they want to make their president, is an old fool and a child molester. He will fall in love with the emperor, and we will have a mess." She panted heavily and looked like a large brown frog breathing heavily on land. "Yng, what is the young empress doing?" "She cried herself to sleep, Your Majesty." "Have the guards been reinforced? Is everything in order in case of an escape through the secret underground passage?" "Everything is in order, Your Majesty!" The old woman fell on a pillow, whining, and reached for some candied nuts that were in a bowl on a small table. "Yng, what would have become of the Manchus if I hadn't been here?" She shook her head like a marabou. "We must have the emperor back, one way or another. Fortunately, the young empress is pregnant. I will make sure that she gives birth to a son..." –

The young empress had dinner served to her in her bedroom while she was lying on the kang. By chance, her gaze fell on one of the servants. She lowered her eyelashes and ordered the eunuchs and two servants to leave the room. The third remained. "Kwang-sü!" she cried passionately and pressed him to her breast, barely having time to put the pie aside. "The winds of the south have blown you to me. How I longed for you! Me and your child!"

She led his hand under the blanket, where he felt the first stirrings of his child under her silk shirt. A tear tried to well up in his eye again. He controlled himself. "I am being persecuted and I do not know by whom. I have been kidnapped and I do not know why. Her Majesty, the Empress Dowager, sent word to me that everything is being done for my personal safety and that of the dynasty. There is an uprising raging in the city." "Down with the Emperor," they shouted. "Is that true, Kwang-sü? What have you done to them? You cannot harm anyone, can you?" The Emperor shrugged his shoulders. "But perhaps I am evil, perhaps I am the evil principle for the rebels, and that is what they want to destroy. I was raised to believe that I am the son of heaven, God's representative on earth: by the grace of the spirit. Did I earn this grace, fight for it? Where did I make a sacrifice? Fey-yen: I am a miserable human being, nothing more. I have never done anything: neither good nor bad, now I must do something: but what?" He fell into thought. Fey-yen stroked his forehead: "You fled from the old palace in the garb of a servant?" The Emperor smiled: "Oh no. What should I have fled from? I knew nothing of the rebellion when I left home in the garb of a gardener's boy. Fate ran ahead of me. When I arrived here, it was already here and told me what had happened in the form of a soldier from the gate guard." The Empress stroked his hand, her sense of touch missed a golden bump, she pulled her hand up in alarm: "Kwang-sü, where is the heavenly sapphire? The symbol of your imperial power?" – The Emperor struggled: "Fey-yen – will you understand me? I gave the stone away, do not turn pale, Fey-yen, quite simply, yes, actually, gave it away senselessly and pointlessly. The person who received the stone has no idea what it means. And I gave it away because, yes, because I no longer believe in the tradition of the centuries, but only in myself. Perhaps I do not believe in myself either, perhaps I only doubt myself: but faith and doubt are children of one father. Either the empire exists without the ring in me - or it does not exist at all. Perhaps we have already lost it. And besides," he smiled politely, "I still have the ring with the nine sacred pearls." The empress lay there, her eyes closed, tears between her eyelashes. He left her on tiptoe, walked through the line of eunuchs in the anteroom, who avoided him without knowing why. He left the palace with his friend, the soldier of the third guard, entered the park of the old palace through the hole in the wall and crept along side paths to the castle. The window to his bedroom was open. He swung himself in. He heard the servants and eunuchs whispering excitedly in the anteroom. He threw a yellow robe over himself and rang the bell. The door opened, servants appeared with candlesticks. The emperor stood in the middle of the room: "Hi, summon the nurse!" Like wildfire, the news spread that the Emperor had returned. Wang nearly shattered his forehead in his bow out of joy. He would have lost his head had the Emperor not come back. Hi waddled over, still drowsy, poorly combed, and not fully awake. Her face bore a few more wrinkles than it had during the day. "Hi, anoint my hair, oil my body, and dress me in the black robe embroidered with stars and celestial figures. I have a sacred task to perform." "Your Majesty, the black robe is the attire for the imperial sacrifice at the winter solstice on the marble altar." "Do as I say."

Once again, the Emperor invoked divine judgment. He chose the bamboo oracle, nine bamboo sticks of varying lengths. Closing his eyes, he drew one stick. It was the shortest. God had spoken. Anointed, oiled, adorned, a pearl diadem on his head and a golden scimitar at his side, the Emperor stepped out of the palace and ascended the sacred tripartite road toward the temple. A crow crossed his path. The first light of dawn glimmered on the horizon. In the early breeze, the bells and chimes of countless pagodas rang out. He walked the central path — the path reserved for spirits, a path no human foot had ever tread.

He passed through the Hall of Austerity. In a hidden niche stood the Kwanyin of Yadq, her lips painted red like Fey-yen's, her left breast slightly exposed. The Emperor kissed the breast arched above her heart. He continued ascending the nine-times-nine marble steps to the sacrificial mound. When he reached the top, he paused to catch his breath. No ministers or attendants, no dancers or choirs, no musical ensembles accompanied him as they usually did during the Emperor's nocturnal sacrifice at the time of the winter solstice. Wrapped in the mantle of stars like the one who sat enthroned above him, whose likeness and messenger he was, he stood alone and solitary before his god and, proudly yet humbly at the same time, offered him the sacrifice of his body and life. Three times, he knelt before him. Nine times, he bowed his forehead in the kowtow. Shangdi, the Spirit of Heaven, rode over the horizon in the chariot of dawn. Then the Emperor opened the vein in his neck with the golden sword and let his blood flow into the marble basin. The blood of the Son of Heaven mixed with the bloody tears that the Spirit of Heaven wept down from the morning glow. The sixteen gates of Beijing emerged from the dust of the night. There, in the heart of the palace, stood the innermost gate, the Gate of Heavenly Purity, which he had not been allowed to enter. The western hills rose out of the twilight. At the train station, the Siberian Express arrived. At that hour, the rebels stormed the palace. They found the Emperor, his head bowed over the marble basin, clutching it with both hands. The Empress Dowager and the young Empress had fled the Summer Palace through a secret underground passage, surrounded by imperial troops, escaping beyond Beijing. Noa gave the ring with the blue sapphire to the soldier of the third gate watch. He was the same man who, as General Tu-Wei, would later hold China's destiny in his hands for several years.

Part Ten:

The Poet and the Emperor

Published in *Young Germany*, vol. 1, 1918.

The Poet and the Emperor

(A Chinese Fairy Tale)

In ancient China, during the time of the Tang Dynasty — which was embroiled in great and dangerous wars with its neighbors — there lived a young poet named Hen-Tsch-Ke. One day, he dared to cut off his braided pigtail and walk through the streets of Peking like that. The boldness of this act so astonished the yellow-robed policemen that they took him for a madman and let him pass unchallenged.

He wandered through Peking — across the countryside — always without his pigtail, and eventually crossed the border into the province of Tsch-Wei-Tz, which had declared neutrality in the Tang wars. From there, he wrote a letter on fine silk paper, gracefully and vividly stylized, addressed to Emperor Tang, in which he dared, with youthful freedom, to say what everyone thought but no one dared to speak: namely, that the emperor himself should be the first to cut off his outdated queue, thus setting a noble example for the children of his land (not: subjects — for one is subject to the gods or to Buddha) and offering a shining symbol to the new age. It was unworthy of a great and supremely powerful empire to be so strong on the outside and so weak within.

One summer evening, the young poet — intoxicated by rice wine and noble sentiment — read this letter aloud to his friends in the neutral province of Tsch-Wei-Tz, after which he sent it by a mounted messenger to Peking.

The emperor's advisors were thrown into great consternation. They withheld the poet's letter from the Son of Heaven and forbade, on pain of death, the dissemination of the ideas it contained. The young poet loved his homeland deeply. It was this love that had placed the brush for the letter in his hand, and the little box of black ink. But his truly innocent act was misinterpreted from all sides. Informers seized upon him while he was away from home and accused him before the emperor's authorities of treason, *lèse-majesté*, desertion — yes, they even went so far as to claim he had written the letter on behalf of the enemy and was in the service of the Mongolian Entente. He was said to be an Entente spy. Others cast suspicion on his Chinese blood and called him a hook-nosed Korean.

The poet dared a secret journey back to his homeland and learned, to his horror, what was being said and believed about him. He, who had devoted himself only to flowery verses and delicate tragedies while abroad, was now accused of having sent revolutionary pamphlets across the border to the emperor's soldiers, urging them to surrender the empire to the enemy. The young poet was shaken and brought to tears. Like a snail, he withdrew entirely into himself, lost trust even in his few remaining friends, and slipped away, as secretly as he had come, back to the province of Tsch-Wei-Tz.

He gave thanks to the mercy of the gods that he made it across the border, for the pursuers were on his trail. A military patrol was chasing him. A sudden downpour halted their advance. Ordered to bring the poet to the northern Chinese fortress of Küs-Trin, they reached the blue-and-white border posts half an hour too late. The emperor never learned of the poet or his letter and continued to rule with the sword, not with love. The poet lived thereafter in solitude by a melancholy lake in the province of Tsch-Wei-Tz.

With his head resting on his chin, he gazed upon the green palms and the violet mountains. Gulls shrieked and wheeled above him. Many nights, his heart sought the heart of the emperor. And the emperor too, seated on his golden throne, sometimes felt a strange yearning — though he knew not for what. He would rest his head in his hand and ponder deeply... But the hearts of the poet and the emperor never found each other. A mountain range rose steeply and stonily, treeless and without paths, between them — and if they have not died, then they are still alive today...

(from: *Young Germany*, vol. 1, 1918)

Part Eleven:

Thu-fu Recalls the Great Chinese Poet Li-tai-pe From Exile

Date of publication unknown.

Thu-fu Recalls the Great Chinese Poet Li-tai-pe From Exile

Thu-fu, a man of letters of low rank and a minor official at the imperial Chinese court, sends his reverent greetings via an express courier to the great and illustrious poet Li-tai-pe, the brother of the sun and companion of the moon. Not a single day of the past year has passed without him thinking of you in tears — while you could only guess at the peach blossoms of spring through the bars of your prison, and were only permitted to write verses about walking through the golden summer. Night after night, you appeared in my dreams, burdened with chains; you know — the welts of abuse and the clanking of the chains still echoed horribly into the break of day. Your eyes stared at me, rigid and unrelenting; they did not merely search my thoughts, they pleaded, they demanded: Do not only think of my freedom — grant it to me!

How can I describe to you the multitude of events — the overwhelming rush of incidents that have accumulated in recent weeks like the thronging crowd before the imperial palace — within the narrow space of this paper scroll? What years could not achieve, a single day has done: Emperor Ming-hoang-ti suffered a decisive defeat in the Gobi Desert, which immediately caused the Tartar prince Lu-lan to break off the alliance. In one stroke, the extreme program of conquest that the emperor's generals had imposed on him for four years — underestimating both the will for freedom of our own people and the resistance of the enemy — was shattered.

People remembered, with painful reflection, the advice you gave last year to Emperor Ming-hoang-ti, for which you had to tread the stony path into exile: to begin the long-announced internal reforms before it was too late. For only a people free within, a people who possess not only duties but also rights, a people who know no masters and slaves, but only brothers of one nation — only such a people can endure the mighty assault of its enemies in the long term and bring the war to a good end.

Some cities have already reported rebellion and uprising. The emperor has thus resolved, to bring peace to the people and clear the way for new men and new principles of state, to abdicate in favor of his son. Su-tsung ascended the throne yesterday. In a solemn proclamation, he has declared the rights of man, granted amnesty to all political exiles, and graciously appointed me as censor of the new realm. He has asked me to immediately recall you, Li-tai-pe, to court.

He seeks your counsel regarding the new measures to be taken to restore both the inner and outer peace of the empire. He awaits your swift arrival and promises you atonement and compensation for the injustice you suffered in the service of justice.

Hasten, therefore, do not delay! All of China will rejoice to see the champion of the people's rights — whom it also honors as its greatest poet — freed from prison. And do not forget, upon your return, to visit your ever-willing servant and most devoted friend, Thu-fu, who considers it his highest duty to pave for you the path that leads, over the Milky Way, to the eternal stars.

Part Twelve:

He - A Story

Date of publication unknown.

He – A Story

"Quand partirez-vous, monsieur, quand... quand... quand?" He smiled. She looked up at him from below, scrub brush in hand, the rag slapping across the stone tiles of the kitchen floor.

He reached for her waist, and she leaned into him.

"Soon, soon, Faustine... You must hurry —"

"Quand?"

"Monday."

So there were still six days.

Her fevered eyes sparkled. She listened into the corridor.

"Personne n'est là. Il faut profiter..."

"So?"

But she was still afraid.

"J'ai peur." If monsieur came — or madame...

"They're out walking in Ouchy. That'll take at least two hours, Faustine. Il faut profiter de la solitude."

"But Elise? What if she suddenly comes back? I'd be mortified!"

"Elise promène le chien."

Yes, but only as far as the Sallaz. For the milk. To cancel Monday's order. Monsieur Georges (Georg) Leiserloh drank a liter of cow's milk every day. Doctor's orders. Because of his weakened lungs. Faustine didn't know about his tuberculosis. She thought he just drank it... for strength. He looked remarkably healthy: a fresh brown complexion, white healthy teeth, large blue eyes, messy brown hair — the typical handsome young man. He had just come from Gardone, where he'd taken the cure in February and March, after passing his law exams. Faustine called him le plus joli garçon de Lausanne. But not only she — Elise thought so too. She was in love with him, but didn't show it. She was from the Pays Vaudois, and women from Vaud would rather bite their tongue off than show love to a man who didn't return it.

"Monsieur... I'll come one night... at five in the morning... to your room... no one will hear me... and the gentleman next door has moved out..."

"Good, Faustine, I won't lock the door the last few nights... You can come whenever you like. But remember: I leave Monday!"

He pulled her close, kissed her neck, and went to his room. If she came, fine — but if she was too cowardly, afraid of monsieur chasing her off... or simply ashamed of being caught in a man's room at night — if she didn't come: also fine. One fling more or less didn't matter to him.

Faustine suffered terribly those last nights before he left. She was afraid... and her longing was so deep, so animal, so senseless. But every time she sat up in bed at 4 a.m., Elise would sigh in her sleep beside her, or Mademoiselle, sleeping in the next room, would cough — and Faustine wouldn't dare.

So the day of his departure came — and she had never visited him. He hardly thought of her anymore, and when he handed her a tip, he looked at her like a stranger — like any other maid.

"Take care, Faustine. Adieu. Voilà, c'est pour vous!"

She had to accept the tip — otherwise Elise would have wondered. But it burned in her hand, and that evening, when she was off-duty, she threw the six francs into the pond.

By chance, during dinner, she overheard talk while serving: Georg Leiserloh was engaged and had gone home to prepare for the wedding. The roast dish wobbled in her hand. That evening she cried — and cried so hard that Mademoiselle from next door came to give her compresses, thinking Faustine was hysterical and claiming cold compresses cured hysteria.

The next day, Faustine made a decision. She read in the newspaper that in a week the first entrance exam for the midwife program would take place in Geneva. "Applications now open." She applied immediately. Then she approached Madame.

"Madame, I'd like to ask for a day off next week — to go to Geneva."

"What's the matter, Faustine?"

She fidgeted with her white apron.

"Madame... I'm over thirty... and I'd like to have a stable job..." (she turned scarlet — she wasn't used to lying), "...and I thought I'd take an exam... I want to become a midwife. My cousin is one, and she has a good position."

Madame laughed so hard that tears ran down the folds of her kind, plump face.

"My God, Faustine — who put that idea in your head! Well, I won't talk you out of it. I'm only sorry to lose you. When do you want to quit?"

"The first of October, I think, Madame."

Thank God — the resignation was out. It hurt her deeply, for Madame had always treated her well.

Faustine went to Geneva, spent all her savings — 300 francs — paying the city treasury for exam fees and a one-year course to become a certified midwife starting October 1st. Faustine passed the preliminary exams with flying colors. They tested arithmetic, French, composition, and oral skills—just the essentials, to make sure basic schooling was present. The topic of the French essay: Morality. The examiners were lenient. Afterward, they served tea. Only 4 of 36 failed. Faustine was overjoyed. She scored a 9. (10 was the highest, but rarely awarded.)

"Vous êtes toquée," Elise said with a laugh when saying goodbye. Faustine said nothing. With a quiet strength no one would've expected from her, she threw herself into her new calling — as if it were sacred, her life's purpose. She was one of those who never forget where they once loved. After a year, she passed the state midwife exam as well.

She knew that Georg Leiserloh lived in Zurich. She had subscribed to the *New Zurich Newspaper* just for that reason — devouring it nightly before bed. With obsessive energy, she also began learning German. She wanted to work in Zurich. And one day, six months before her exam, she saw the announcement she'd been waiting for:

"Georg Leiserloh, Licentiate of Law, and Miss Lilly Bosshardt announce their recent marriage."

This time she did not cry. She folded the newspaper carefully and placed it in a small, inherited mahogany chest — alongside a lock of her mother's hair, her late father's tobacco pouch, and some dried flowers from her childhood garden high in the Jura hills.

After passing her final exam, she packed her few belongings and traveled to Zurich. She rented a small room in the dark Kruggasse — not far from the apartment of Licentiate Georg Leiserloh, who lived in a stuccoed modern building by the quay. He was now, in a sense, part of her domain.

And she waited.

Three months later, around one a.m., on a stormy night, with the moon flashing in and out of clouds above the lake, the doorbell rang — twice, sharply, in panic. She knew instantly who it was. Trembling, she dressed and rushed downstairs.

Georg Leiserloh stood at the bell.

"For God's sake — come quickly to my wife."

He didn't recognize her. He grabbed her blouse, desperate, the cries of his suffering wife still ringing in his ears. He rushed ahead, she breathless behind. In minutes, they stood before his home. The lights burned on the second floor. The doctor, summoned by the maid, arrived at the door alongside them.

When Faustine stood before the woman who had brought her beloved happiness, such a wave of love overcame her that she kissed Lilly's hand.

"It won't be long, madame. It's not so bad. And it'll be a boy," she whispered.

Lilly Leiserloh smiled, "Yes, a little boy..."

With gentle skill and care, Faustine went to work, and by two a.m., after a relatively short labor, young Leiserloh entered the world — a boy, as foretold — carried into it by Faustine's soft hands, his first cries echoing with life.

"His son," Faustine smiled, "I brought him into the world."

She stayed for 14 days, caring for the ailing mother and the healthy newborn. On the thirteenth day, when Georg returned from his law office and saw her in the kitchen, he finally recognized her.

"Ah — Faustine... I didn't recognize you at first."

He wasn't surprised she was now a midwife. Didn't think of their past. He had long since forgotten her.

"What a pale complexion the master has," Faustine said to the cook.

"Yes," the cook whispered, "I heard the doctor say — he has tuberculosis. Consumption. He won't last long. Such a pretty wife..."

Faustine went to bathe little Leiserloh — christened Athos, after one of Dumas's Three Musketeers (a fancy of Lilly's imaginative mind).

Tuberculosis! If he truly had it — and he certainly did — he wouldn't live long. Faustine had learned enough from her medical training to know: consumption heightened romantic illusions even as it destroyed the body. A young marriage — with a beloved wife — only hastened the grave.

Could she save him? Her heart beat in her throat. Then she looked at little Athos Leiserloh, whom she held above the steaming bathwater: he, he would live.

Faustine was so kind and capable with little Athos, so indispensable, that Lilly Leiserloh asked her to stay on as a nanny. It was also a great advantage, she said, that Faustine spoke French—Athos could learn both languages from her. And she convinced her husband.

So Faustine changed professions again — fcr the second time.

Two weeks later, Georg Leiserloh was sent urgently to the Riviera. He never returned. Six weeks later, he died.

In dreamy sorrow, Faustine pushed little Athos in his yellow pram along the quay. The sun sank into the lake, dazzling the air that shimmered like silver netting over the Rütli massif.

"He is dead," and her grief was too deep for tears.

"But in you," she whispered, leaning over to fix Athos's cushions, "in you — I have saved him for myself..."

Part Thirteen:

Letters to Walter Heinrich

Letters to Walter Heinrich

Walter Heinrich was a bank clerk in Crossen on the Oder, a writer in his spare time, and a long-time literary mentor of Klabund.

Berlin, Oranienburgerstr. 53 – December 1, 1910
Dear Herr Heinrich,

With sincere thanks, I am sending the Planck speech back to you. You will be surprised to receive a rather lengthy epistle at the same time. Please allow me to get straight to the point. First: I consider myself a poet. You will say others do too. Second: perhaps I am one. You will think: in case you don't even know that yourself! To which I will pull out a phrase as cheap as it is defenseless: Doubt is the beloved child of faith.

To impress you a little, here are a few numbers and titles. I have written 597 poems, 29 novellas, 13 one-act plays, 1 novel, 1 collection of aphorisms, along with fragments and material collections for dramas and novels of the greatest style (Don Juan, Nausikaa, Adam and Eve, etc.), essays, and so on. To mention a few titles: (I place great importance on titles and headings and have written stories that consist only of titles – I don't know if this is an original idea of mine?) *Pierrot on the Organ, The Macaw, Mademoiselle Potiphar, The Cavalier, Violinist Lehmann,* and *Honorable Men,* and so on, and so on. That will suffice. They may not sound particularly charming.

I can sometimes only express things that seem truly tender to me through crudeness. Like the farm boy, when he has something very beautiful to share with his sweetheart, but which is incredibly difficult to express, tenderly nudges her in the side. And the girl understands him and nudges him back accordingly.

I ask for your advice because I really have no one else to ask, and I don't want to keep everything bottled up inside forever. I further ask that you do not take this request as impertinence. It is both less and more. Perhaps you can render me — and thus the world—a great service through a few well-aimed rib jabs. I would hardly recover from them. Please forgive me for this — this little push. Yours sincerely, Alfred Henschke.

N 24, November 17, 1911
Dear Herr Heinrich,

The documents are coming rather quickly and almost intrusively. But that is not their intention. I just packed them together because I didn't know what to do with the short time before lunch. — I've included the two little fairy tales again because "they seem significant enough to me for the recognition of his poetic individuality" (why can't I still become a feuilleton editor or theater critic?). As for the *Kakadu,* it is in no way to be taken seriously, not even in its style. It can safely be used in some places as a model for *Wanda, the Master Detective of*

Brandenburg (or whatever it's called). "Quod erat demonstrandum." The *Pierrot Songs* are uneven, the Faust parody (which is not one) you need not read for God's sake, just perhaps glance through it. *Peter* is (I expressed myself inaccurately yesterday) not the man with 12 women (12 women turn a man into 12 monkeys), but *Semper idem*, i.e., always the same monkey. I consider the comedy to be stage worthy, the simple, erratic character of the schoolgirl quite understandable. — One more thing I wanted to ask: don't you think one could try to place one or the other of the little character sketches in *Part*? Since he counts Heinrich Mann and Wedekind among his favorites, he's at least "free" — perhaps he's also free to take something from me. Or Light and Shadow? I would, of course, revise the pieces again.

I once wrote to Fleischel (who brings the most hair-raising stories about Auernheimer). He was very cold and reserved... overwhelmed with work... he said he had more than enough new things to feature, etc. Couldn't one somehow make friends with *The Island*, they also publish trash occasionally? I remember bumping into an accountant from *The Island* in Schreiberhau. Couldn't one — marry her??

With warmest regards — please also convey my best regards to your mother.

Yours sincerely, Alfred Henschke

Berlin, February 20, 1911

Dear Herr Heinrich,

Many thanks for your kind card. I hope it suits you if I visit you tomorrow evening, Tuesday. (The rest of the week, except for Saturday, I am occupied. And Saturday is probably quite unsuitable).

Yesterday, Sunday, I had a ghastly-lovely celebration of the ghastliest-loveliest drunkenness. *Redoute en miniature*, a separate room, champagne (which I, however, did not pay for). I believe you can tell from my handwriting.

With best regards, yours sincerely, Alfred Henschke

Crossen (O.), March 17, 1911

Dear Herr Heinrich,

I still don't feel well at all, despite the good air and good "nutrition." It's always the case that after this kind of "recovery" in the small town, one has to recover even more once back in Berlin. If I were a schoolgirl, I'd say: completely miserable. But it will all settle in: once I'm back at my work ("work!" God forbid you mention this to my mother, who has declared my relationship with the lady to be thoroughly indecent and illegal, and she can't get enough of making annoying and persistent allusions) — I will feel better again. I've already done something: gone through a few novellas (in the process, I've heavily cut some older ones: my imagination has learned in a year to "think" more concisely). I might combine the *Kakadu* and the letter from the small town (along with other small-town things). — In terms of sexuality, I also feel miserable. Going to war here requires the cunning and instincts of a Sioux chief. — Now at the end, I still have something nice for you, which falls into your favorite area: the fine arts: In a local art shop, pardon me, a rubber goods store, the *Apollo of Belvedere* is on display in the window in a strange, but attractive, transformation: he is clothed with — a jockstrap, a suspensory bandage, and knee braces!! That's how to make art useful to life.

With the warmest regards, yours sincerely, Alfred Henschke

Crossen (Oder), Easter Saturday 1911
(or as they say here: Sunday-baking-cakes.)
Dear Herr Heinrich,

I have now finished revising most of the novellas that were at hand here. I haven't changed the situation in any way. It still seems very daring to try to improve the initial fresh pictorial impression with later retouching. Nothing good comes out of such intellectual experimentation; on the contrary, the effect (in the proper sense) goes to the devil. I have directed all my attention — as far as I have any attention at all — to improving the style and concentrating the plot, and I have severely shortened many pieces, especially the older ones (e.g., *Little blonde Liselotte*, which will probably be even smaller [but all the blonder] in a year). — I am sending you a few novellas as a replacement for *Don Juan*, which you will hardly get to see. After two rounds of corrections, it has become so unbearable to me that I get fits just from seeing it from afar. — I am looking forward to Berlin; I hope to arrive on Friday. Your cards both came to me like greetings from a "better world." One is so overfed with intellectual people here. The headmaster Calvary is the only one with whom it is socially acceptable to associate. — He is also the one who once introduced me to ancient sculptures. I have reveled in their images. Do you know anything more venerable than the breasts of the Nike of Samothrace? (You know, my fondness for breasts runs deep — deeper than anyone might think.)

With the warmest Easter greetings, your grateful and devoted Alfred Henschke.

The Comet is an apparently new satirical weekly, published by Fuhrmann and Frank Wedekind. Issue No. 4 published a poem of mine. One of the upcoming issues will probably feature my *Conversation between Girls*.

Crossen (Oder), Schädestraße 123, April 1911
Dear Herr Heinrich,

My esteemed representative, *Don Juan*, will visit you in the next few days (in typewritten form). I hope his visit will not be inconvenient for you. This time I fear your judgment. What will you say? I am very undecided myself: sometimes I find him abominably silly, sometimes he seems quite nice to me. — So far, in Crossen, I've managed to do some work by correcting novellas and *Don Juan*, but haven't really created anything. For this, I've used my father's postage fund and sent manuscripts to several magazines. The results remain to be seen. Probably negative. So far, one minus (*Velhligen*), one plus (*Comet*). I'm surprised that

Reading Munich hasn't replied yet; it's already been four weeks since I sent the novellas to them. The one-act chat sent to *Youth* has vanished without a trace. It's certainly lost. — In contrast to Berlin, I've read quite a bit here: by Potonie, Bölsche, Fontane, Eckermann, Unus. The *Student Diary* was primarily intended as a piece of propaganda, wasn't it? Recently, I dug out a Reclam book I hadn't read since my high school days (my friend Th. Blum can still recite half of it by heart from school): *The Ballad of Reading Gaol* and was quite astonished when I saw the title page: Walther Unus. — Did you only translate from English? By the way, as a warning: your relatives here are bragging about you. Even in the only bookshop in town, they knew you. I innocently asked about *Student Diary*, and the bookseller said: "Isn't that the relative of the Doerings? Of course!"

I kindly ask you to give my best regards to your mother, and best greetings from your grateful Alfred Henschke. Goethe once said in Eckermann (February 25, 1824), "Had I waited to depict the world until I knew it, my depiction would have become a parody."

Berlin, Auguststr. 3a – May 2, 1911

Dear Herr Heinrich,

I really enjoyed finishing and writing *Peter.* But now it's done! Fifteen stories and possibly an epilogue and obituary as a preface (perhaps Pastor Stiehel's speech at Peter's grave?) are enough. I've only hinted to the typist. I won't write about Peter and the boys, as you advised me. I'll also leave Erika, the millionaire widow, as she is. There's no need to have her get pregnant by a jockey and go to England. Peter is too passive a character for him to not be overwhelmed by that one cold ray — the letters. Internally, it's still smoldering, but he no longer has the courage for new attacks. I hope you can read the last stories well. They were written quickly and under the auspices of an annoying old fool. I would like to discuss Sebellina [one word illegible] with you further. I took her as the climax of the entire story, and accordingly raised Peter in this his best moment (in the inserted fantasy piece). With "Peter and the Little One," I don't know what else to do in context, except to put it as No. 1 or 2. — What do you think if I go through the whole *Peter* again, have it typed up, and perhaps send it to Fleischel? It would be a trial. I will visit you next week (perhaps Friday, May 12th). Until then, with best regards, your grateful Alfred Henschke. I've received a philosophical paper! On the concept of "motive" in literary history! Phew! Apologies for the handwriting!

N 24, Auguststr. 3a – May 26, 1911

Dear Herr Heinrich,

Please take a look at *Dr. J.* and see if you like it? Just look, nothing more — God forbid: perhaps Act III, Scene 1, or Act IV, Scene 2 — that's where you'll find the whole mess.

At the university, I'm already feeling unwell again: as usual around mid-semester.

the other day I slept so soundly during Dessoir's lecture that they started shuffling their feet. If only I could take something for it! By the way, I sent something to *The Beauty* after I had flipped through a few issues at the Royal Library. I must confess: the lack of temperament and the sluggishness that is fabricated in this sensuality is astonishing. On top of that, the absolutely deceitful and vulgar poetry of those like Stangen, Ulrich, Madeleine, which thrives here in abundance. Occasionally, a hint of the little wit-sheet blows over (in the exchange of thoughts — as it is called). Still, each issue comforts one with a respectable name: the unknowing might wonder how they got there and why these beauty asthmatics aren't left to themselves? But why shouldn't a decent person play an assistant waiter (understood as in their own establishment!) — if it's well paid (which I hope, that is not from me, for I am too modest (meaning: unknown), I know this from my other literary experiences). If you don't respond, I'll visit you on Saturday, June 3ʳᵈ. Hopefully, I'll feel more reasonable by then (more reasonable than last Friday). It's partly due to a small illness. Please give my regards to your esteemed mother — your very devoted Alfred Henschke.

N 24, Auguststr. 3a – June 25, 1911
Dear Herr Heinrich,

Thursday, June 29ᵗʰ? — And then I would have two requests. The first, harmless one: could you please, if you happen to meet the gentleman from "Beauty," ask him to return my manuscripts to me? A reminder from my side has not been effective. Secondly: I hope this request does not seem too intrusive: you are going to Munich, aren't you? Could you, since you surely have connections, ask at "Simpl" if he might publish one or the other novella of mine? Of course, only if it doesn't go against your principles and you find my novellas decent enough. — *Simpl* is almost the only way for me to get into literature. Perhaps you will disapprove of or misinterpret this "haste" of mine to get into literature. Let it ripen first! Why the rush — or this ambition to see oneself in print! It's not such a common ambition (I don't care about my name, for all I care, anything else can be put under it) — I just want to have a guarantee, a backup for myself, when I stand in front of others — as I do not foresee where my ship will sail in the next few years. The thing with the headmaster or doctor: when I talk about it with my father or with you, then it is perfectly clear to me; you have to do something, you're not a fool, don't be so sluggish. And in front of myself, alone, (I am 99% of the time completely alone, that contributes to something too!) I can't come to terms with it: you are, after all, a fool — for that, I tell myself often enough (is this just plain laziness?) — That's why I want to finish *Peter* by winter (if it's nothing then, it will never be anything). I have never asked you before; today I would like to: please, do you believe that I am or will become a decent literary character? Your grateful and devoted Alfred Henschke.

Undated

Dear Herr Heinrich,

Yesterday evening brought me two more stories from "Peter." (It seems you are kind of a second muse for me!! (left hand).) Perhaps you might still be interested in them. Since I have to go to Charlottenburg anyway — to pick up a lady — I will bring both of them along, or the whole "Peter." Wouldn't your friend like to see it?

With heartfelt regards, your very devoted Alfred Henschke.

Berlin N 24, Auguststr. 3a – June 27, 1911

Dear Herr Heinrich,

Many thanks for your card. But you'll really have to explain to me in person what you meant by calling "Siml" a reactionary publication. I've started to take more and more interest in philosophy — I'm even reading philosophy and being "enlightened" by a philosophically educated man I recently picked up. I haven't done any real work, neither in one direction nor the other — a few poems excepted. I plan to make up for that once I'm back home. There's a short trip planned (or rather, my father has planned it) to Dresden. I have a request for you, since you surely know Dresden very well: would you briefly tell me what one ought to see there — especially the things off the usual tourist track? I'm sending this card to your Berlin address, since I don't know whether you're still living in Hallstadt or have moved on. What's the story with the Hungarian language? Or are you only going to Hungary later? I hope you're getting a good rest — maybe you've even produced something — if so, please let me read it. As for your last question, I can't answer it to my satisfaction: I'm still not well. But it seems to be getting better (and it's about time — the week of reckoning is approaching). With warmest regards, yours gratefully and sincerely, Alh.

Brückenberg, Riesengebirge German Emperor August 16, 1911

Dear Herr Heinrich,

Unfortunately, I was not sent here for pleasure: I brought a nasty cough with me from Berlin, and the doctor thought immediate fresh air and mountain air were necessary. My parents and the doctor took the matter very seriously — I take a lighter view of it. Work is forbidden, idleness has been made a principle. So far, it is still bearable. I would have liked very much to finish "Peter," as I had already started rewriting it from the beginning. Naturally, Dresden is out of the question now as well. My father, who brought me here, has gone back home to play mayor.

The mountain air — 890 meters above sea level, after all — must have a thoroughly cleansing effect on the mind. I feel incredibly hollow, and not a single idea comes to me. But one of these days, I will ambush you with pieces that grew in Berlin during my fertile period — although you do find my poems atrocious.

I breathe deeply, eat eggs, drink milk, freeze, and take pleasure in the purple silk stockings and patent leather shoes of the postcard lady at the Schlingelbaude, though she has no other charms to offer. All the women here look dreadful: they wear loden skirts, saggy white blouses, and little Tyrolean hats. Their back ends are tightly laced with tape.

I am tired and do not wish to weary either you or myself further. I would be very pleased if you wrote to me once — from "Berlin," which I will likely not see this winter. That truly saddens me. With best regards, gratefully yours,Alfred Henschke

Brückenberg, August 31, 1911 German Emperor
Dear Herr Heinrich,

I had actually intended to write to you philosophically — but I have fallen unhappily in love, unhappily through my own fault, and now all philosophy has scattered like chaff before the wind. However, I will concede one thing to you: the possibility that I may have been mistaken in my appreciation of Simmel. As an admirer of language, I am always impressed by beautifully and elegantly crafted words — purely for their own sake. Besides, I am too untrained in philosophy to always correctly separate or properly connect concept and word. But surely part of the blame for us laymen misunderstanding or misinterpreting philosophy lies with philosophy itself. The pure philosopher — it is like in tennis — hits a ball, the other returns it, but then the ball falls to the ground. The first one calmly picks up another ball and serves again. The second one actually wanted the first ball back, but now he gets a ball that looks almost the same as the first, yet isn't quite the same. That's how philosophical concepts seem to me. They are not exchanged in the same currency. Like lightning, the penny transforms into a groschen, the groschen into a centime — and then one is supposed to deduce the "concept" of the penny from the centime. Those who have learned the different philosophical currencies can of course distinguish them. But beyond that, the business seems rather dubious, as Mauthner demonstrated in his *Critique of Language*. What one person calls *a*, another calls *b*, a third *c* — and in the end, they all mean *x*, the same thing, but none of them can admit it.

Health-wise, I have no complaints. How much longer I will stay here, I don't know: 14 days — 5 weeks. I have no social interactions here. If you have no objection, I will send you a one-act play, *Laura at the Piano*, or some verses when the occasion arises.

With heartfelt greetings, always your very devoted, Alfred Henschke. What has pleased me greatly: Wilhelm Schäfer has acquired four of my poems for *Rheinland* (German Monthly Journal). I have also once again turned to my much-courted friend, *Simpl*.

Crossen (O.), September 15, 1911
Dear Herr Heinrich,

Quidquid id est — my inclination toward studying certainly did not grow in

Brückenberg. That sky-blue, sweet "idleness" that shone before me there would not be an unsympathetic program for a life that isn't too long (which I probably don't have to fear — rather the opposite). I was alone almost the entire time, except for two days — and never felt bored (how proud that sounds!). I read hardly anything, wrote a short story, and otherwise only drifted lyrically.

A dozen poems that I actually quite like. — Whether I'm a bad or good "poet," in any case, the organs for a different way of life have atrophied. The dilemma I find myself in is becoming quite painfully clear to me — and more so with time. On one hand, I feel the burden of still living off my father for an indefinite period, but on the other, I lack the energy for studying. Simply because I detest it. It's not that I don't want to work. So where to spend the winter? I'd like to go back to Berlin (or Munich), though even in Marburg, my philosophical zeal wouldn't last long. Or Geneva? There's hope that I'd learn French there. Or does one not actually learn it there? Besides, the air there is probably better than in Berlin. If I were to return to Berlin, I'd live in Zehlendorf or somewhere on the outskirts. I'd have to — for my lungs' sake. Good advice is as expensive here as this year's potatoes. (I inherited my indecisiveness from my mother. Incidentally, she is very ill.) At the beginning of October, I'll be visiting an acquaintance in Wismar for two or three days. He's lucky — he already has his own fortune. I fear I might end up a journalist. "In the apartment of the worker Mappler on... Street, a gruesome family tragedy occurred today at around 2 a.m. Not only did he attack her with an ax, but the brute also shattered his recently emptied liquor bottle over the delicate skull of his three-year-old son. Neighbors who..." One just has to pay attention. With warm regards, yours sincerely, Alfred Henschke

Crossen (O.), Thursday ?/11

Dear Herr Heinrich,

Voilà, a manuscript that has hopefully changed for the better: *Peter*, the Werther of our time, the thwarted debauchee, in the form in which I wish to leave him. I will submit him to a publisher — though I don't yet know which one. Please, how do you like him now? He is certainly not too small for a book; one would just have to print him in the style of the good, late Hartleben — that is, with an enormous margin. Then it would amount to about 150 pages. And perhaps it could even be a commercial success, for he isn't boring, is he? But maybe these are just the utopian dreams of a beginner, and you will smile at them. I have been toiling over *Peter* for more than three weeks and have worn my fingers raw with fair copy writing. He has given me at least as many headaches as my teeth, which have also been troubling me — since I just had another seven fillings put in. Equilibrium? Oh, I am not in equilibrium — anymore. I was in Brückenberg. Now the doubts about my own worthiness return. One does not lay the foundations of one's "education" firmly enough; one builds and sets down one stone while the other is not even securely in place, and so on. One is sluggish, complacent, and so forth — the usual reproaches... It will probably pass.

I have been disenrolled from Berlin. So where to? My father suggests Geneva

— at least I would learn French there. Munich is also worthwhile. I must decide within fourteen days.

I would have liked to include a typewritten copy for you — but of course, the lady has not yet finished.

With warm regards — and may you find something good in the new *Peter*. Yours sincerely, Alfred Henschke

Today, I read a notice: American Theater, 8:30 PM: "Abysses"—Sensational Drama in Two Acts. That's what you recommended to me, isn't it? Now it has already reached Crossen. I will go see it.

Crossen (Oder), October 12, 1911
Dear Herr Heinrich,

Thankfully, the visit did not take place. I had time in abundance and dedicated it entirely to *Peter*. As you will see, I have changed a great deal in the details (and have taken to heart your admonition — which Flaubert should have already instilled in me: no empty phrases, but rather movements, gestures, "nature"). Since I plan to come to Berlin in the middle of next week, and *Peter* will certainly not be fully copied by then, I am sending the fellow to you once more. You wanted to see him again before he is dressed up in typewritten form, didn't you? My thought was this: if you consider him improved and matured, and if you would be so kind as to speak with Mr. Reiß, then perhaps, while I am in Berlin, I could read the manuscript to Mr. Reiß myself. He might have half an hour for it, which would surely be more convenient for him than having to read the (currently not very presentable) manuscript himself. For me, this would also save the costs of making another copy, which would amount to at least 40 marks if the manuscript is not accepted. If he does accept it, then it wouldn't matter. Please, would you write me a brief note with your opinion? I will inform you of my arrival as soon as I know it myself.

Many thanks for all your — may I say — friendship? Yours sincerely, Alfred Henschke

Regarding individual points that might still be up for debate: The prologue, *The Retarding Moments* (which I would be reluctant to part with) would be better discussed in person. The only sections that could be considered for removal would be: the prologue, the café scene, the scene before the night café, and the depiction of Sidonie's room.

Munich, Heßstraße 25 – October 25, 1911
Dear Herr Heinrich,

I can finally breathe again — away from Berlin, truly. There, the air is oppressive, far too much *sub specie veneris vulgivagae*. Here, I feel free once more, similar to how I did in Brückenberg. I think I could write poetry — if I hadn't devoted myself to Old High German grammar and its i, o, u and consonantal declensions. I am working. And as a pastime in my leisure hours, I am reading

Wilhelm Meister's *Theatrical Mission*. The details are marvelous, but the whole (as far as I can see) feels like a draft, barely or not at all revised. Wilhelm Meister's youth story bears a striking resemblance to the psychological "development novels" that were in fashion not long ago.

So: Goethe of Theatrical Mission — a man of the 19th century. Goethe of the Apprenticeship Years — a man of the 20th century. And I prefer the latter.

You speak so harshly about Munich — but you mean the beer-drinking crowd. What about the rest? The streets, the English Garden, the people — aren't they more charming than in Berlin? Best regards, Alfred Henschke

Munich, Heßstr. 25 – October 31, 1911

Dear Herr Heinrich,

Enclosed is *The Affair with Ellie*. (I could possibly still write *Peter* in a Nuremberg brothel (on his way to Munich), but that would be too much. Better to leave it as is.) I would be very happy if Mr. Reiß were to take it, as the matter with Hanns Sachs Verlag and my verses has fallen through. He thought they had too little "form." What nonsense.

Unfortunately, I have written verses again, in the following styles:

> Whoosh across three octaves
> Glissando our delight.
> Let me sleep once more
> Upon your breast.
>
> The morning creeps in softly,
> No rooster, no mutt is barking.
> You don't need to be at work
> Until eight o'clock.
>
> Let the mattress creak.
> The landlord in back is asleep.
> How your eyes stare.
> Your breath is whirring.
>
> Around your brow, the morning
> Weaves a pale wreath.
> You rest within it, protected,
> Like a saint and a pure virgin.

Or:

> Take off the rubber shoes
> And the corset.

Why all the drama — good grief!

Or:

Her mere presence
Fills the air with stench and soot.
Better to stretch out dead
Than lift a hand in greeting.

A fine "anthology!" Hopefully, *Peter* will have luck. Best regards, your grateful and devoted Alfred Henschke. Please extend my regards to your mother.

Munich, November 9, 1911

Dear Herr Heinrich,

I feel dreadful today — I'm having my quarterly misery. It's very good that you haven't read P. yet, as I wanted to ask you to strike the following passages while reading: The café scene at the beginning, at Ruth's stair railing, the part from: "a lover!" to "On Thursday, Müller visited me." Also, the speech of the morality apostle — entirely. I'll have to rewrite that at some point. In general, of course, I would also go through the whole thing again myself. On Sunday, I was in Tölz. Do you know it? What do you think of a dissertation on Büchner? Warmest regards, your devoted, Alfred Henschke

Munich, Heßstraße 25 – November 17, 1911

Dear Herr Heinrich,

Forgive the pencil — I'm writing in the library (which should show you that my good intentions are still intact). I come with a question that is really a request: Is it within your power and willingness to introduce me to Heinrich Mann (or Karl Henckell)? Certainly not for literary exploitation — but don't you think it would be beneficial for me to meet Heinrich Mann, with whom, without otherwise comparing myself to him, I share a certain similarity of purpose?

Karl Henckell, as a creator, is much more distant from me — but he is said to be such an outstanding and fine person — and I don't really know any examples of that kind here. You might say: For God's sake, then you'll end up in the literary gossip I wanted to keep you away from! — I'm already halfway in.

Yesterday, I heard Max Halbe privately read aloud his newest drama (still unpublished), *The Juggler's Ring*, listened to his (appalling) views on art, and even exchanged a handshake with him. The day before yesterday, Wedekind read his newest mystery play, *Franziska*. A marvelous first act, then it dwindles; I don't understand the fourth act at all. I attended the premiere of *The Dragon Grauli* by Dauthendey — one of the most unbelievable plays I have ever seen: insincere emotion, slovenly language, unintended comedy, all dipped into a sauce that's half Nick Carter, half Maeterlinck.

"One hand washes the other." That is the guiding principle of today's literary cliques. Leaving aside my personal involvement with this or that person, I would call myself a fool if I missed the opportunity — now that I stand on firmer ground than before — to familiarize myself with the literary circles here. I am open to your — perhaps contrary — opinion. Please don't feel the need to rush your response. There is time. With warm regards, your grateful and devoted Alfred Henschke

Munich, November 26, 1911
Dear Herr Heinrich,

I have written a parody of Wedekind: *Brigitte*, a modern mystery play, along with some sketches and a great many verses. I feel completely split, lying around like a chopped log. Should I gather myself? These pieces of wood? What is truly genuine about me, and what is merely intentional? I can't separate the two. Do you know Büchner's novella *Lenz*? Something like that. The nonsense I spout in such a state (to myself and others) is indescribable. The peacefulness with which I left Berlin is gone. But don't think Munich is to blame — it would have happened anywhere. I have an utterly undisciplined temperament. Sometimes, I manage to bottle it up, like the changeable spirit in a fairy tale, but I can't hold it for long. The cork pops, and a giant swells up. Today, I plan to visit Muncker — I haven't been there yet. Hopefully, he won't throw me out.

Munich, Heßstraße 25 – November 30, 1911
Dear Herr Heinrich,

Thank you very much for your letter. I had expected a serious reprimand (which I surely deserved), and now — my condition is always the same: loud, quiet, self-assured, contrite, enthusiastic, disgusted — and all at the same time, bathed in the mild sauce of a physical exhaustion that sometimes seems to settle in my brain. I feel like the former Simplizius Simplizissimus when he was to be made a fool — except that I am performing the procedure on myself, and perhaps will truly become a fool.

I recently compiled a small book of lyrical poems: *The Fountain*. Furthermore, I have here some adventures — about 20 anecdotes — and just as many novellas, a pamphlet of ironic poems, and several one-act comedies (in Crossen). But what of it is actually finished? Please let me know if I should send you the lyrical poems. It is probably unnecessary, and I'm sure R. would least of all warm to them. But perhaps as a "proof of talent." A few of the novellas and anecdotes are somewhat finished. (The latter are literary in their form and sexual psychology alone.) The comedies are probably just as unnecessary. Please don't send me *Peter* yet — it would only disturb me. I will of course go over it once more, but please, not now. If you would introduce me to Henckell, I would be very pleased and would thank you very much. I have little news from home. At times it feels so distant that I recently held a letter from my father in my hands, read it, and thought: who is this, actually? Where do I know him from?

In contrast to before, I am now possessed by a desire for socializing. I can rarely be alone in the evenings: a sign of the slowly beginning dulling of my mind. I haven't even been to the Pinakothek yet. With the warmest regards, your grateful and devoted Alfred Henschke.

Munich, Heßstraße 25 – December 12, 1911
Dear Herr Heinrich,

I have just come from Burger. He received me very hastily and flustered. He had wanted to write to Wolff every day, but he was so busy... that he hadn't confirmed the receipt of the painting (with a distinguished rubbing of his hands). My God, it was just a small formal mistake... he was, as mentioned, very busy... he had already written to Wolff months ago that he couldn't place the painting... Wolff was probably a bit upset... he was very sorry... but if he perhaps wanted to send him a few smaller good paintings, like the ones he had seen at the Essen or Barmen exhibition... he would then certainly try... of course, he couldn't demand exorbitant prices... The painting was, in any case, with the house manager at the university (I understood) and available to us... he would have it brought down today... Something like that. Burger is tall, elegant, in a slim frock coat, with a pointed beard and sharp eyes. I am very skeptical of him. I believe he fights for art in this case more with his mouth than with any real effort. I don't think it would be advisable to suggest to Wolff that he send Burger the aforementioned smaller paintings. It would probably be the same dance.

What now? I am very willing to be of further service to you and Wolff in this matter. Is Wolff in such dire financial straits? I think Burger mentioned that in passing. I couldn't defend him as I would have liked, as the backstory of these paintings is a bit unclear and only to be guessed at. Should I perhaps have the painting picked up and temporarily store it with me?

As for books from your library, I have nothing. I will take the Hungarian grammar with me when I come to Berlin. I am planning to go home for Christmas, and if I can see you, I'll make a stop in Berlin. Maybe next Tuesday or Wednesday. Do you have time in the evening? With warm regards, please also send Wolff my greetings. Your very devoted Alfred Henschke. Written at Café Stefanie, where I unfortunately spend a large part of my Munich life.

Crossen (Oder), January 1, 1912
Dear Herr Heinrich,

A happy and healthy New Year! I hope the "Officers" have reached you safely by now. I quite like them, though now and then (perhaps in the book form) they are a bit unclear, and the main character (his name is probably Ernst) is too typical, lacking individuality, too stuffed with moral values. He seems to me the least successful. I will be in Berlin next Sunday. Do you have time in the afternoon? Please let me know briefly. I also need to make stops in Halle, Marburg (with relatives), and Nuremberg. I am undecided about Leipzig... If you show H. Reiß the one-act play, please show him "Peter" as well. If he feels some sympathy for it (which doesn't commit him to anything), I will rework it in Munich during Carnival time (the right time for it). I also would like to send you the verses from Munich. The situation is this: my father is possibly planning to travel to Northern Italy with me in the spring, and I want to slowly prepare him for this idea. I think this will be quite easy if I can offer him some "reality" for the future (for example, a book). I hope I am not mistaken in this.

I have recently written some novellas and am currently working on a three-act comedy, of which one and a half acts are finished. Unfortunately, I am too lazy to finish it. The actors are students, and a young lady named Eva (no, not Lulu!). Have you heard anything from Burger? The photographs? Warm regards, your very devoted Alfred Henschke.

Munich, Heßstr. 25 – January 16, 1912

Dear Herr Heinrich,

I was very sorry to have missed you. I left the manuscripts with you, as at the moment I wasn't quite sure what to do with them. I hope they're not in your way. The verses are currently with Dr. Kutscher (whom I believe I've already told you about). Once I get them back, I'll gladly send them to you. Henckell has also read the verses and wrote me a letter in response, which I'm enclosing. By the way, it's not entirely clear to me whether he sees himself, at least halfway, as a candidate for "pure lyric poetry." I myself, of course, don't believe in the dogma of pure lyricism. I don't see why lyric poetry should be more egocentric than drama. There, one strikes a note on a single string; here, several tones are struck — but it's still the same string. I expect a great deal from that objectivity in lyric poetry which is expressed, for example, in Goethe's Calm Sea. I traveled here by way of Halle (where I visited a friend who ekes out a living there as an editor on 75 marks — a wonderful guy, by the way), then through Kassel — the Dutch are seldom so well represented as they are here: Dyck, Rubens, Hals, Rembrandt. Rubens, whom I couldn't stand in Berlin, revealed himself to me anew here. The Italians, however, are miserable — then on to Marburg, Frankfurt am Main (Goethe's house).

Carnival season has now arrived here, and people mostly live either in bed or at masquerade balls. I feel quite well, am reading Nietzsche's *The Gay Science* from time to time, occupying myself with Feuerbach and — spurred on by the Reichstag elections — political ideas. That's more or less all. With warmest greetings, yours most sincerely, Alfred Henschke

Munich, January 19, 1912

Dear Herr Heinrich,

Enclosed is the "Fountain." Dr. Kutscher is returning it to me. He said (literally): he hasn't found anyone in a long time to whom he could so firmly assure how strongly he believes in it... an immense liveliness... of course, a few weak poems... he is very pleased, as I said... What I know, I know in any case. He certainly has no reason to give me compliments. The pencil marks are from Henckell, who, although he didn't see everything, did read most of the poems. I am most curious to know your opinion. I consider the poems at least to be the most complete of my productions in their particular way. Henckell read *The Song of Life* yesterday. Three very beautiful poems. The others filled with a lot of pathos and morality about the song. For my taste, too much directness in the ideas, too weak in the bodies. This is a pity. Warm regards, and please write to me soon. Your very devoted Alfred Henschke.

Munich, Heßstraße 25 – 11. 15. 12.
Dear Herr Heinrich,

Please excuse the elegant stationery. Your package arrived just as I had (once again) gotten up from my sickbed. But it's not so bad.

I completely agree with your judgment of my verses. The real lyrical power, for me too, lies in the (according to Henckell) non-lyrical poems. But even (according to Henckell) the purely lyrical poems are not all bad; they characterize the development in lyric poetry (surprised?) as follows: (I start from the beginning:) Heine – C. F. Meyer – Goethe – Mörike – Wedekind – Verhaeren (a lecture!) – Henschke. I don't know if Verhaeren's influence is still noticeable? Of course, I never worked based on models.

I will try (though I have little hope) to get the "Fountain" published here. "Publishing a book" is, however, only impressive to amateurs. But aren't the people I'm materially dependent on also "amateurs"? Won't their respect for me swell immeasurably, and will they not reach into their wallets? But I myself swell, and I start to feel, if not impressive, then at least a little bit useful — compared to the others, can reproach me with uselessness, laziness, apparent baseness as they please. There's a beautiful saying about being enough for oneself and vomiting down from the pedestal onto whatever remains. But who can really bear that? One still wants to have an effect — to see impact and (indeed) counter-effect: to see love. One doesn't want to dissolve inwardly. (Of course, vanity plays a role too — the tendency of our comedies: all is vanity. The tendency of our comedy: therefore we are the vainest of all.)

I have rarely been to the theater. Of importance, I have only seen Eulenberg's *All about Money*. Hopefully, the Russian ballet will come here as well? You spoke enthusiastically about it a year ago. In literature, I have not made any new acquaintances. I almost met Friedrich Huch recently, but I was feeling unwell and couldn't go. I've spent my time in bed reading Heinrich Mann's *Goddesses*. I don't know why, despite all the magnificence and restraint in the details, it doesn't result in a happy overall effect. There's too much splendor, too much stucco on the house and in the house.

Georg Heym is a very heavy loss. One for whom "pure, unapplied poetry" can do absolutely nothing. Who is the person he drowned with? Ernst Blass? Incidentally, I wrote a few (hasty) lines about him in the Munich-Neuhausen. I hope you haven't happened to read them.

Light and Shadow has politely rejected me — probably for the same reason: impure lyric poetry, too little feeling. *The Theater* also sometimes publishes poems. Couldn't something be sent there (Helena: that is, theater)? How is Jacobsohn?

Please, you don't need to respond soon; I wrote just because I wanted to talk. Please, spend your time on yourself. I don't have much to lose. Warm regards, your very devoted Alfred Henschke.

Munich, Heßstraße 25 – March 12, 1912
Dear Herr Heinrich,

A warm greeting from Gardone. We traveled here via Bozen and Torbole. Thank God, it's warm — almost hot. One spends the whole day outside in the sun, without worrying about anything in the world. The food is good, the drinks are good, but unfortunately, my health still isn't quite what it should be. Additionally, there is a casino here, which I find very appealing. I've won a modest 10 francs.

Your very devoted A. H.

Hotel Germania 3. 23. 12 – Gardone Riviera Georg Ertl
Dear Herr Heinrich,

Italy! But through the open balcony door, it sounds pleasant: a toast, a toast to coziness. –

Gardone is supposed to mark the beginning of a new stage in my "destiny." Closed tuberculosis is the technical term, if I understood correctly. I didn't manage to visit all the beautiful cities and museums. My longing for them wasn't overly strong either. I've become so tired of new impressions. I'm glad when I can find my peace in contemplating the familiar or "accustomed" nature. I must leave Munich — on medical advice. I regret this for my literary career. Otherwise, I'm a fatalist when it comes to my outward life. I feel comfortable everywhere once I've been there for 14 days. My future residence will probably be called "free citizen." The Black Forest nearby, a medium-sized town, and half the mountain air.

The program I'm supposed to follow every day isn't very exciting. Lying down all day until late at night, walking little, eating well, and sleeping well. Work isn't part of the plan. Sometimes I have an urge for it — while lying down. But once you're really up, that urge disappears. I read a little. In the former Hartleben library, which was bought by the local lending library. There are some unusual literary curiosities there, such as *The Barrisons* (by Pierre d'Aubecque (Lindner)) and *Adam Mensch* by Conradi. But they bore me. *Adam Mensch* does offer some very interesting psychology of transitional people here and there — but too much: rambling, always the same self-reflection in Adam's monologues, he circles around himself like a cat around hot porridge. And even manages to be a bit disgusting. But I'm only about halfway through. Perhaps I'll change my mind.

— I've gradually become tired. I'll walk a few steps to pick up my father (who leaves in a few days) from the casino. There, the cinema shows the *Tripolitanian War*. In the gambling den, I won 200 lire. At least something. But now they won't let me in anymore — because I'm too young. This only pastime in Gardone on rainy days is sadly over. Please tell me how you're doing, (hopefully very well) with warm regards. Your very devoted Alfred Henschke.

By the way, did you happen to read the poem (No. 49) of mine in *Simpl.*? It was, of the five submitted — of course — the worst. I wrote to Rowohlt about my verses, but have not received an answer yet.

Incidentally: I don't know what my father is telling at home. You know: the small town, please don't mention my tuberculosis to Doering.

Difficult illnesses easily acquire the appearance of a moral defect there and can stain the entire family, potentially... In the past, at school, in the fourth grade, it was considered dishonorable to be nearsighted and to sit in the short-sighted row. The unfortunately non-mocking ones. They feared the compact majority too much. – I'll stay here over Easter and won't even go home.

Locarno, Villa Berta IV. 19. 1912

Dear Herr Heinrich,

I am happy to send you my picture and kindly ask you to send my regards to Mr. Wille. You showed me reproductions of his work once, last January, when I was in Berlin, didn't you? Reiß intends to publish him, doesn't he? — Do you believe that Beiß would be interested in publishing a strong (but not extensive) poetry collection of a deceased author? The author died at the age of twenty-four as a Prussian infantry lieutenant. He himself had already called the collection *Poems of a Dead Man* during his lifetime and wished for it to be published anonymously. In fact, he was already a dead man in body while still alive. I know his brother. Should I advise him to send the poems to Reiß? By the way, they are certainly not war poems. Best regards, your Klabund.

Lausanne, V. 24. 12

Dear Herr Heinrich,

Have you arrived back in Germany by now? How are you? Please do let me hear from you. By the way, I am going to emigrate to America. Here in the boarding house, there is a young American journalist who tells amazing stories about the writer's fees in American weekly magazines. And all you need is routine. This young man couldn't write at all before. And now he gets 2000 marks for an article. I think I will start writing for American journals, for example, "The Measure". The Americans' enjoyment of such things (when others accomplish them) still has something Indian about it.

Best regards, your very devoted Alfred Henschke.

Lausanne – Mont Charmant Av. de la Sallaz – VI. 9. 12

Dear Herr Heinrich,

Your postcard was forwarded to me with great delay. At least now I can see that you have returned from Italy. As for myself, I am quite satisfied with my health, aside from a few minor issues and annoyances. At least the lungs have settled down. Full recovery is probably out of the question. The rest cure in Gardone has made me lazier than I already was, and I am experiencing firsthand how much such an illness can be "demoralizing." My work here consists mainly of learning French. How I would love to write something again (since Berlin, I have written very little, almost only poems), the novel of that often quoted woman of mine. But when? This disgusting uncertainty about future goals (not set by me) often robs me of my peace.

Here in Lausanne, I am beginning to feel how much the big city is my true homeland and how incredibly boring a place like Lausanne is, so sour and so far removed from the "great world." (You may think: Aha! The big-city "eroticism" still has a hold on him.) (Unfortunately) you would add in square brackets. — But it's not just that: the desire to see something, to feel something, to do something, that's missing here. In general, Swiss culture. Does it even exist? Is it perhaps just a "word" born from the need for self-preservation and self-respect? I'd like to know what the German-Swiss would be without Germany, the French-Swiss without Paris. That's so obvious. But here, no one sees it. The former curses the Germans, the latter curses the French, as if they were their worst enemies. "Stop the thief."

Do you know the latest lyrical bloom of Germany, the proud "Condor," the "Poets' Secession?" (I am not an anti-Semite — but 11 Jews, 3 (perhaps) Germans: that is the new (critical) lyricism.) Oh! And the French Gothic novels by Gaston Leroux! Best regards, your very devoted Alfred Henschke.

Lausanne, VII. 6. 12

Dear Herr Heinrich,

I may be in Berlin the week after next and will try to stop by your place. Of course, I cannot set a specific day yet. I will be making stops in Interlaken, Munich, and Leipzig on my way home. As for my writing, I can report that after a six-month break, it seems to be starting up again (it looks like it may become chronic). The last magazines that published my poems (without "protection") are *Pan* and *New Review*. That gives me some encouragement. My other works are all with Rowohlt – Leipzig. For now, there is no news. I've managed to rid myself of both hope and fear in this regard. Best regards, your Alfred Henschke.

Crossen (Oder), 7. 31. 12

Dear Herr Heinrich,

For financial reasons, it was unfortunately impossible for me to stop in Berlin. Berlin, by the way, seems to me, when I remember it now, to be magically strange. I hardly remember ever being there; it feels like a distant landscape: the reports I get about it (such as my Novellen) sound like strange jungle fables or tales from the North Pole. How familiar Munich appears to me now, which you hate the most! (Probably because I've become lazier, and I'm only partially receptive to new, unexpected impressions.) By the way, in parenthesis, the erotic element plays a big role, to which I'm still heavily indebted. Mostly, I'm pleased by it, but sometimes I sigh.

A good topic for a psychological study just occurred to me: it's strange how the typewriter tries to shape the style of the person writing on it: like all machines, it has its own soul, and this soul imprints itself on the writer, forcing him to think in "typing language," so to speak. I, for instance, develop a perverse preference for commas and long, complicated words when typing. It's an aesthetic pleasure to write poems on the typewriter (oh! just saying that word!). Especially those exotic ones where words like Conifer, Main Tax Office, and Apricot Jam appear. I plan to enter the market with a new kind of poetry: "type poetry," which is only meant to be typed (certainly not to be read!) — and all "emotional values" will be conveyed solely through typing. I congratulate you warmly on the acceptance of your piece by Reinhardt. Please, wouldn't you send it to me to read? Mr. Henckell asked me to send you his best regards. (By the way, is it true that the Lese Publishing House has gone bankrupt? I didn't dare ask Henckell.) With best wishes to your esteemed mother, yours sincerely, Alfred Henschke.

Crossen (O), 9. 24. 12

Dear Herr Heinrich,

Yes, please send the sheet, I give you 999/1000 certainty that my father will buy it for 50 marks. Please include a few other sheets as well (good ones! We were always very much in agreement about the value) — I would at least like to show them. They will likely be too bare for him to buy, but you never know. (Perhaps you could note the prices somewhere.)

How much does the huge painting "Girl Walking in the Forest" cost? Maybe I can promote it somewhere. Best regards and many thanks for procuring this. Yours, Alfred Henschke. What kind of frame would you suggest?

Crossen (0), IX. 29. 1912

Dear Herr Heinrich,

My father has lost his courage — I have lost even more. I am (what I never thought) thoroughly deceived. He does not want to buy the head; for "unfinished, sketchy" things, he will not spend money, yes, if it were an oil painting. Besides, he does not understand the man. My mother understands him even less. My aunt understands him even less than that. They do not hold it against me. I cannot help it. There have been family scenes — following the fight against the iconoclasts — over very general matters, over "principles." The unmade doctor raised his hydra head. I should not "fragment" myself with foolish pursuits (poetry, any kind of writing). He does not like the sample style either. He considers it (literally) "literary banditry." I asked him to be consistent, and I asked him what his advertisement about homemade mineral water and soda was about?

Tomorrow we will have visitors. A pretty 20-year-old cousin of mine, whom I passionately loved when I was in the upper secondary school on the beach chairs in Borkum. Hopefully, it won't be as dangerous this time. Best regards, your Alfred Henschke.

Crossen, X. 16. 12
Dear Herr Heinrich,

I am sending you the poems; S. Fischer has returned them with vague, polite phrases. Since I more and more believe that they are probably the best I have done, and that at least 40 of them should make a good poetry collection, I want to send them to another publisher — but to whom? Inselverlag? They would be a decent, though perhaps unwise introduction. For I have long since abandoned any hope for the blessing of "Peter." And the Crossen stories are really just a joke. I hope you will be available to speak on Sunday (or Saturday)? Best regards, your Alfred Henschke.

Munich, X. 21. 12
Dear Herr Heinrich,

I was sorry that you weren't there on Sunday — but by chance, the evening still ended gracefully: I met a girl at Potsdamer Platz, someone I had liked a little more than the others two years ago. We went for a walk. However, my fate has now been fulfilled, without me being able to seek your advice: I am joining a local art dealership on November 1st. Goltz, the well-known aesthetic bookseller on Briennerstraße, has just opened it, and it's full of former super-Inta Impressionists. The location is Odeonsplatz. After a trial month, I plan to sign a one-and-a-half-year contract. I'm still enrolled as a student on the side. One can never know (with regard to the doctorate). I've taken this step to reassure my parents, etc. (to silence them for a while). Secondly, I want a counterbalance to my fantastic powers.

The layover in the art and book trade seems to be the given. And how tempting: the prospect of my position! Student, "artist," merchant (how healthy this will be for the "soul," assuming the body stays intact). Poet, critic: and floating above it all like a serious adventurer. (It occurs to me: maybe I can do something for Wolff now!?) Please write soon. Yours sincerely, Alfred Henschke.

Munich, Kaulbachstraße 56 part. – XI. 18. 12
Dear Herr Heinrich,

I have never felt quite like this before: nice girls love you in full bloom, you're eager to work, you have your freedom again (because, if you haven't guessed it yet: I'm no longer with Goltz. I just couldn't stand it; I was bored to death – for the first time in my life) – if only the cough weren't already barking faintly through the gray Munich fog.

Another inconvenience, which at first seemed unpleasant to me, I now view from above with calmness. Someone in Geneva claims to be having a child of mine and bombards me with letters in a foreign language. She wants to have it aborted and asks me for a few hundred francs for that purpose. I persistently refuse with silence. If I were to kill a child (which I would think very carefully about) — it must be mine. The aforementioned child is (for reasons I won't go into) by no means mine. I can swear to that. And, of course, I have no desire to get involved in any discussion about children of other fathers. (Although I don't know to what extent the law supports me, as determining the exact identity of the real father from a distance would be beyond my abilities.) One must wait and see.

As for dramatic works, I have now completed the one-act plays "Father and Stranger" as well as the three scenes "Alcestis" and the 3-act comedy "The Betrothed." "Alcestis" is in verse and very stylized. I will reconsider it (I think it's very suitable for chamber plays) and then send it directly to Reiß. May I ask you to inform him, occasionally, of the arrival of the piece? (Nothing more. He is primarily a theater publisher, right?)

Through Mr. Henckell's kind mediation, I frequent the "Halbesche" bowling alley and the "Young Crocodile." I'll save my opinion about that for a later letter. With warm regards, your very devoted, Alfred Henschke.

Munich, Kaulbachstr. 56 – XII. 30. 12

Dear Herr Heinrich,

Happy New Year! I have stayed in Munich and didn't go home this time. To avoid getting involved in difficult conversations and also because I wanted to work. I've just completed a three-act comedy (it is completely free of prostitutes), and since I'm still considering the "Alkestis," I would actually like to send the comedy and a previously written three-act student comedy to Mr. Reiß to see if he could take them on for his theater distribution. I will write to you later about how I've decided, and then please do me the favor of drawing Mr. Reiß's attention to it. I wouldn't want to trouble you with reading the pieces, although I think the comedy is good. Since I saw in an ad that Reiß also publishes poetry (by Braun), I will attach the newly assembled poetry book to the comedies, as I truly believe I can compete with Braun. Did you read my "Helena" in the December issue of the *New Review*? (It is already old.) — I now socialize in the "first literary circles." I spent Christmas evening with Mühsam at Halbe's. Halbe is a delightful person — and he can tell stories better than he writes — but his daughter is even more delightful. He treated me to a goose liver pâté and a bottle of Danziger Gold, which I found refreshingly unliterary, as I already saw the heavy work of Dietrich Stobäus looming over my head. — I'm earning a fortune with my verses! I made 70 marks just in November! But I still can't make ends meet. And no one wants a novella. I find that very strange. — My father wrote to me that I've already once made myself unpopular in Crossen again. There's a little story that appeared in the *Frankfurt Oder Newspaper*, which is read a lot in

Crossen. And in that story, various people from Crossen felt depicted: foremost a high school professor and a letter carrier's daughter. Yes: thanks from the House of Habsburg. — I'm doing quite well, if only the cough weren't there. I want to go to the Riviera. I always think the comedy should be taken, and then I'll leave on advance payment. Warm regards, your devoted Alfred Henschke.

Bad Reichenhall, Bergweg 7 – II. 11. 1913
Dear Herr Heinrich,

Enclosed, I am finally sending you a selection of poems by my friend Klabund and kindly ask you to give them to Mr. Reiß after reading, to see if he might consider publishing a small booklet of "this vagabond's charmingly bold lyrical power" — as Kerr aptly puts it. On poor gray paper, 30 pages, paperback, price one mark or so — with a preface by Kerr!! (I think it could become a business, especially if the poems are published in time for the trial!!) In parentheses: there are more Klabund songs than the ones enclosed, but they are of a different kind. — However, Mr. Reiß must not know who Klabund is yet (i.e., before the trial for possible testimony). Please only hand him the material with a nice greeting from Klabund. — If he writes to Kerr and refers to Klabund (because of the preface), Kerr will surely do it. Especially because he will have to comment on this phenomenon at some point, whether he wants to or not — due to the fierce attacks he has faced because of it, not only from the police but also from the art- and state-preserving press like "Imperial Messenger," "Art Custodiam," and so on. I am diligently undergoing my treatment here (if only the girls weren't around! They ruin the whole diet): inhalations, air, and saltwater baths, massages, drinking and lying therapy from seven in the morning (it's horrifically early) until nine in the evening. And the weather... a better deluge. Please write soon — mail is, with the rainy weather and apart from more or less boring novels, the only distraction. Warmly, your devoted Alfred Henschke.

Reichenhall, Bergweg 7 – VII. 1. 13
Dear Herr Heinrich,

Many thanks! However, the other Klabund poems are even more unsuitable! I will send some of them and then simply include some unknown poems of my own. I still need to think it over because I have just received an offer for Klabund from the publishing house Kurt Wolff (formerly Rowohlt) in Leipzig — a fairly secure one, at that. However, he only wants to include about a dozen poems, presented in a more refined manner, in his collection *The Judgment Day* (for one mark, I believe), which already features people like the ever-popular Werfel and the cabaret poet Emmy Hennings.

A few days ago, I received a summons to Munich. I didn't go. Now they will probably track me down here. Always your most devoted, Alfred Henschke.

Reichenhall, Bergweg 7 July 5, 1913

Dear Herr Heinrich,

Enclosed are another 50 poems by Klabund, most of which he had to borrow; his remaining legitimate poems are unusable (both literarily and otherwise). But please don't tell Reiß who made the offer — just speak in general terms! Hopefully, Kerr won't catch sight of the enclosed selection in any way, as there are certainly verses among them that may have appeared before under a different signature. If he remembers, which I doubt. I have chosen the enclosed poems so that they at least all have a touch of the Klabundian style.

Many thanks for your great effort! Hopefully, it will succeed. On Tuesday, I will be questioned here — as a witness.

(By the way: I assume Reiß is interested in Klabund's poetry? He doesn't intend to publish an erotic special edition, does he? In that case, I would have sent the other Klabundian stanzas, which, as mentioned, are otherwise unusable.) Yours gratefully, Alfred Henschke.

Munich, Herzogstr. 42 – VII. 31. 13

Dear Herr Heinrich,

I have signed the contract with Reiß. Many heartfelt thanks once again for drawing his attention to me. I would very much like to go to Berlin — to Zehlendorf, where there is pine-scented air and the dry Mark Brandenburg sun. At the moment, I hate Munich. I'm having another attack, coughing and spitting all day long. I want to get away again for a few weeks (the urge to wander has seized me once more), but I simply need money, a lot of money — far more than I could possibly receive, even in the best case, if I were to ask my parents for it again. And I must go south this winter. I still want to live — a while longer, at least. What do you think about me applying for the *Kleist Prize* on the basis of my poetry book? But Reiß would have to send the book to the Kleist Foundation — if I do it myself, it would look foolish. I don't know who sits on the commission, but people like Kerr, Wedekind, Halbe, and Dehmel would surely be in my favor. Then I could already head south in December. I haven't felt any real warmth at all this year — in Reichenhall, it rained constantly.

Please, what do you think about this?

And you're not doing well either? It seems that almost nothing else can be talked about anymore except one's failing health. It seems to me that even illness can become a profession — one in which one might advance very quickly and overtake all those ahead.

With heartfelt greetings, always your most devoted Alfred Henschke.

VIII. 9. 1913

Dear Herr Heinrich,

Many heartfelt thanks for all your efforts. I must have misunderstood your card, which is why I sent the telegram. From now on, I will write to R. directly as Kl., that is also your opinion, isn't it? I will also send him the poems that were objected to. It would be very nice if he were to take on Kl. — it could become a good poetry book if the selection is done properly. Moreover, this could also establish a connection for a future novel, a book of stories, and other adventurous plans. I will press R. for a decision and a quick selection.

I don't like at all that you are unwell. But the weather has been dreadful here for three weeks too — rainy and cold (down to 5 degrees! Yesterday, it even snowed on the surrounding hills). That I haven't caught a cold is a miracle and proves that the cold-water cure has actually done some good and strengthened me.

Tomorrow, I am returning to Munich. Address: Herzogstr. 42. How long I will stay in Munich, I don't know. Perhaps I will move on. If only Berlin didn't have such filthy air and such dreadful women, then one might consider going there again. It's a pity you're not in Munich. I have often missed you. I am becoming more and more one-sided in my development and don't know where it will lead. And I find so few people with whom one can talk and live without preconditions, without detours through the great generalities.

I wish you a swift recovery, a good journey, and a few wonderful days in Paris (Paris is also one of my many longings). If you happen to meet a painter named Utrillo there, have him show you his paintings — they were still available for 50 francs not long ago. He is a marvelous painter. Yours ever gratefully, Alfred Henschke.

Munich, 8. 11. 1913
Dear Herr Heinrich,

You don't know the latest news yet. The day after tomorrow, I'm leaving for Davos. I have wrung an advance out of *Youth* and *Simplicissimus* (and also Reiß). How things will go with the trial, I don't know. Of course, I would have loved to come to Berlin — my personal presence would have been beneficial for publicity alone. But I have no desire to tie myself down for the sake of such a ridiculous trifle as this court case. I really need to leave Munich right now (not that I want to, but unfortunately, I have to). The doctor considers it absolutely necessary. Reichenhall didn't help at all. So that's that. But then, in spring, I hope to be in Berlin. For a longer time. After all, it was my first love. With warm regards, always yours very devotedly, Alfred Henschke.

Arosa (Graubünden), VIII. 18. 13
Dear Herr Heinrich,

As the doctor says, I will probably have to stay up here for the winter — then there is a chance for lasting recovery. I am allowed to work, but not too much (?). Walking is not allowed. Any movement is forbidden. Lie down, lie down, and lie down again. I have just sent Mr. Reiß a book of humorous sketches. I want to work diligently on my novel. (But there is no girl here.) Sincerely, always your devoted Alfred Henschke.

Arosa, VIII. 24. 13
Dear Herr Heinrich,

No, not as you think: on the contrary, it will be a really great book — hopefully, Reiß will print it. (I will send you some chapters on occasion: compared to them, *Peter* appears gentle and meek as a lamb.) –

The *Kleist Prize* (Office at E. Fleischel) is for young talents, regardless of genre. — Yes, I would also prefer to see "Klabund" standing alone on the title page. But what about publicity? Promoting two names is very expensive. And in magazines, I am quite well known as Henschke. Perhaps I should switch entirely to signing as Klabund. What do you think? After the novel, I am already considering another unusual plan: the correspondence of two lovers. With warm regards, always your most devoted Alfred Henschke.

Arosa, Beau-Rivage, 9. 20. 1913
Dear Herr Heinrich,

On the 23rd, the trial will take place. I feel some anxiety — not about the outcome, which is indifferent to me — but because I do not know how my defense attorney will handle the case. I haven't been able to give him any directives; everything happened too quickly. There wasn't enough time to procure more detailed expert opinions and bring in Berlin literati as expert witnesses, as originally intended. Still, Wedekind's judgment on the two incriminated poems is remarkable. I laughed so hard while reading it that tears ran down my face (though it was not condescending laughter, but laughter born from the matter itself; I am certainly very akin to Wedekind. He is, incidentally, one of the few people I love). Of one poem, "How beautiful, after a night of love, to be alone in bed", he describes the mood as "Shakespearean" and the form as "". In the other poem, "My peace is at an end. Is it syphilis...?", he compares Klabund to Goethe and Wilhelm Busch (in the same breath!). I hope the book is a success so that there is a solid fund for the novel I am currently writing, which is three-quarters finished in its original draft. I plan to call it *The Ruby* and would very much like to dedicate it to you, if you permit. If you have time, please write me a few lines about Klabund's book and what you think of this parody — which is not one. The selection was mostly done by Reiß. I disagreed with about seven poems, but he praised them so highly that I left them in. I haven't even seen the cover. Hopefully, it is nice.

The snow falling on the mountains here has almost reached Arosa. One only notices the cold indoors. Outside, it is beautiful. Warm regards, your devoted, Alfred Henschke.

09.28.1913

The Embryo

A young man and patriot
Entered service as an embryo.
This is a delightful profession,
Which he created from his own inspiration.

Since birth rates, according to statistics,
Are steadily declining:
To halt this downward-going trend,
He hired himself out as an embryo.

Like many a woman, otherwise childless,
She pushed him from her womb in delight!
As Fritz, as Klaus, as Franz, as Hans,
He's recorded in the registry office.

The impact of this youthful feat
Was truly wondrous and unique.
The statistics clearly show
Him as savior of the fatherland.

Klabund.

Arosa, 10. 14. 1913

Dear Herr Heinrich,

You will receive my latest comedy in the next few days (if you like?). A romantic Berlin comedy – Berlin N 24, my first poetic love still occasionally wells up inside me. I think it's good (unfortunately not quite long enough for a full evening's performance; a one-act play should be added). I would have it included in the "Little Theater" (Altmann, about whom I have heard many good things). It would be an experiment — but Altmann is supposed to be willing to try all sorts of experiments. It seems to me a big step from my first Berlin comedy (still very personal and awkward, it was called "Abysses," do you remember?) to this "objective" romance of a pimp who sacrifices himself for his child.

I hope you can read it. There's a typewriting institute here, but the owner is English and simply cannot write in Berlin dialect. Please pass it on to Reiß afterward (unless you have major objections). I am including the three one-act plays that have been printed. What should one do with them? Only the middle one, "The Servant in Red," is interesting.

By chance, I recently read your essay on Johannsen in Westermann and remembered some drawings you once showed me of him. You had such an affection for the character "Peter." What do you think of us writing a comedy "Peter" together? The character of Peter still feels quite present to me, but I am unable to come up with a plot to surround him. Can't you do that? (If necessary, claim "Peter" from Reiß.) What do you think? I am sorry that Reiß didn't read Gorsleben's play back then. It would have been a great complement to Unruh, and he is both a wonderful person and a fantastic artist. Now Wolff has it. His play has already been accepted by Berlin, Vienna, Cologne, and Munich. With warm regards, always your Henschke.

Arosa, 10. 20. 13

Dear Herr Heinrich,

You will receive by registered mail the comedy *The Child* (I like it very much), the play *Alcestis*, and three one-act plays, where probably only the middle one would be usable. Reiß also has a three-act comedy: "Wedding Journey" there, which I think is quite effective. The plot is entirely farcical, but turns into a tragedy (in the last act). So: 1st act farce, 2nd act comedy, 3rd act tragicomedy.

Work on the novel has not been left undone. Unfortunately, I am now at the point where I would have to dictate it to the typewriter. It is impossible for me to rewrite (the novel, which has been sketched out in its entirety) by hand again.

At the moment, I feel relatively well. It is possible that one day I will leave the local tavern in a rush, but I won't do it until I am finished with the novel! With warm regards, always your devoted Alfred Henschke.

Arosa, 11.9.1913

Dear Herr Heinrich,

This is what Arosa looks like now! – As for *The Child*, could Reiß at least print it? (Some expressions are softened.) I will also present it to him soon when I send a new (Japanese) lyrical manuscript. If he doesn't want it, I will give it to another publisher, for example, Wolff-Leipzig, who once agreed to publish my works. — The way Arosa's healthy, clear air stimulates the working energy is incredible. Never have I felt so eager to work. Warm regards, your Henschke.

11.12.1913

Dear Herr Heinrich,

Aren't these two touching parental letters? (Of course, I mean it without any irony.) Please send them back. If you see anything about Klabund in the newspapers, I would be very grateful if you could send it to me. (You must have read the pamphlet in the "Daily Review" about Klabund-Henschke-Jucundus Fröhlich?) Warm regards, your Alfred Henschke.

Arosa, 11. 27. 1913

Dear Herr Heinrich,

You are probably right about my restlessness, but it is too essential a part of me for me to ever lose it. With *The Child*, I don't agree with you: I certainly wouldn't be able to revise it after years, as you say. By then, I'll be God knows where. And have other children. Also, it is too much of the storm and stress of youth for it to be published then. Now is the only time to do so. I've been madly in love for ten days (you can probably tell by the handwriting!). And since then, I haven't had a single sensible thought. No talk of working on the novel. — It's a girl from Uruguay, but she's been in Germany for a long time. Quite brown. — Today is the trial! Warm regards, always your most devoted Alfred Henschke.

A German in Italy

Fields are chirping. People, minds intertwined,
Have sung away their deeds,
And the golden moon has never waned.
It always stood above our cities,
When the winds blew from Italy,
Misted with tatters of blue sky.

Some have been driven over the mountain,
To love the southernmost infinitude,
And Venice shattered the spell.
In green, sickly-sweet alleys,
It let its stranger grasp the strangest things,
So that he could never forget that woman.

But sometimes, it surges overpoweringly,
And the Adriatic sparkles at night,
And the steel of the gaze flashes murder,
And intoxication rises to prayer:
My homeland! My gray cities!
O you coldness! Clarity! North! O North!

Alfred Henschke, 11.27.1913

XII.I.1913

Dear Herr Heinrich,

I am having an exceptionally bad day today: especially during the night, I thought I was on my last legs again. Thank you for your letter. You are certainly right — but when will I finish the novel? Since I lack the absolutely necessary comfort of being able to dictate it while lying down. — And then: don't you think it's best to adopt the name Klabund for all my respectable work? Who knows Alfred Henschke? Can't Beiß give *The Child* to *The New Art*? Maybe they'll take it on.

Oh no, I shouldn't ask for news. I was just pleased that Richard Dehmel spoke so strongly on my behalf. His speech is said to have been brilliant. Warm regards, always your Alfred Henschke.

Arosa, 12. 3. 13
Dear Herr Heinrich,

Today I received a letter from Herr Reiß, which certainly does not make me feel like continuing to work on my novel, although I am certainly not angry with him about it.

By the way, did you know that I have not been acquitted — despite the newspaper reports? And that a special trial will take place against me! An absurdity of the highest order... and only grounded in the legal technicalities of German law. — What do you think of the Zaberner scandals? — I am feeling absolutely unwell. And then this senorita. Perhaps I will leave. Warm regards, your Henschke.

Arosa, 12. 9. 13
Dear Herr Heinrich,

I'm fine again! I feel well once more. Today, I wrote a very beautiful chapter of the novel. I believe the novel will turn out well after all! Only five more chapters, the course of which is already set, then the first draft will be finished! Can you have it typewritten in Berlin? (But please don't read it yet!) And with carbon copies! It's not psychological, it's a lyrically grotesque style!

Yesterday, some Italians were here in red tailcoats with violins and guitars. We danced. Warmly devoted, your Alfred Henschke.

Arosa, 12. 15. 13
Dear Herr Heinrich,

I am surprised that I have not received any response from R. to my recent postcards and letters. He hasn't taken offense, has he? I asked and requested him to return the *Humoresque*, *The Child*, and *Geisha Songs*. I want to publish the *Humoresque* in magazines (I don't even dream of a book edition for now), *The Child* should go to Kerr, who is interested in it — *Pan* will be published again soon, with the lively participation of Klabund, of course. Regarding the *Geisha Songs*, as I wrote to R., I reserve the right to handle them freely if R. does not want them. He can't take offense at that. — Health-wise, I am a little worse off (according to the doctor). I don't feel much of it. I will probably have to stay for another four months. Is there a Klabund evening at Reuß and Pollack? Who is organizing (reading) it? Warm regards, most devotedly, Alfred Henschke.

Arosa, 12. 19. 13

Dear Herr Heinrich,

Apologies for bothering you again with a request: could you please send me the essay by Poppenberg? (It won't upset me: I have other, pleasant things to think about and do.) Merry Christmas wishes! It's terribly cold today. — 15 degrees. It's almost impossible to write. Warm regards, Alfred Henschke.

Arosa, 12. 27. 13

Dear Herr Heinrich,

Many thanks for the *Voß*. But I am pleasantly disappointed. The review is much more positive than I thought, and above all, the main thing: that the *Voß* has published it. It advertises better than lukewarm praise. It is banal, but not brutal — and Klabund will rise and surprise them in a very strange way. I know my Poppenberger. Always yours, Henschke.

Arosa, 1. 1. 1914

Dear Herr Heinrich,

Once again, all the best for the New Year! — As for myself, I have no complaints about the old one: I was happy and, for my part, content with it. The illness is a special chapter. In my life, I keep double books. On one side, illness does take up considerable space; but it is only "noted"... acknowledged. The devil may fricassee me if it ever gains influence over the other side — my real life. Moods won't change that. —

Yesterday, Mr. Sarx from Berlin visited me and brought greetings from you. He seems to be a very likeable person and official. — In my love (it is no longer just infatuation), I am now very happy and (appropriately to the circumstances) calm. I have already dictated several chapters of the novel to her. I am writing this letter in her room. She is lying in bed and is looking at me right now.

A funny story: an old white-bearded gentleman from Braunschweig declared his love to her. And in quite an ingenious way: he gave her a letter from his son to him, in which the son, in an enthusiastic contemplation, makes the old man and the young, beautiful being (in a grandiose style) appear in ridiculous relations, and he presented it to her with a gracious bow, out in the corridor, asking her to translate the letter... into Spanish. (The lovable fool lives in our boarding house!)

Today, I received another business letter from a very respected Berlin publisher, proving to me that Klabund has made quite an impact in the past three months. Since this is already the second publishing offer from prominent publishers, I don't see why I should maintain my modesty in business matters. It would also be pleasant for me to have all my books published by Reiß, but since he doesn't want to, there's nothing I can do. — The *Geisha Songs* are absolutely no risk for him — and if he sees "no progress" in them, that would still not be an obstacle to publication. He "really appreciates them otherwise" and wants "to do everything to keep me." (As you say!) But what does "everything" mean? He still hasn't responded to my letters and postcards, sent three weeks ago! Warm regards, always yours, Alfred Henschke.

Arosa, Graubünden, Beau-Rivage 1. 12. 1914
Dear Herr Heinrich,

I ask you not to interpret this letter as an alarm message. There is no reason for that. You don't need to reply to it (it doesn't require a response). Just please keep it. — Since one never knows how a chronic illness will develop (and sometimes in quite an unexpected way), I would like to make my literary will below and appoint you to carry it out.

As things stand now, I primarily wish for the publication of the (quite advanced) novel and a second volume of poetry. My lyrical manuscripts are organized in a file folder; a list of the poems I will select for the second volume is attached. *The Geisha Songs* are not suitable for this volume but should be published separately, should a publisher be found. I would like all manuscripts to first be offered to Reiß, and then to the Hyperion Publishing Company. Regarding the larger and smaller dramas, I leave it to your discretion. Perhaps a volume of small dramas, as you once suggested, could occasionally be compiled. — The *Humoresque* will already have been published by then. — The honorarium (it surely won't be extravagantly high) I bequeath temporarily in equal parts to my brother Hans and you. I ask you not to misinterpret this provisional decision: I may find myself in a position where I will have to give it to my child. With heartfelt thanks for your friendship (I may call it that?), always your loyal Alfred Henschke.

Arosa, III. 10. 1914
Dear Herr Heinrich,

I haven't touched the pen for the novel in two months. I couldn't. Now the weather is so unfavorable here. Foehn, snow melt. Much too early in the year. I feel like writing a play, mentally and sensually in one. What do you think of Gentz and Fanny Eisler? Where could one get material for it? Can you suggest sources? I also thought of Simson: but Wedekind? What I've written so far: I sometimes feel like throwing up. I wish I could get away from here! Adventure! Adventure! Adventure! I need it! Always yours, Alfred Henschke.

Arosa, III. 25. 1914
Dear Herr Heinrich,

Please advocate for "Blonde Hair" so that the title search can finally come to an end. From now on, I will always write the titles first! — One question: do you know a reliable Berlin film studio? A director or someone like that personally? Maybe Reiss? I want to get some eerie films made, but I don't know where. If you don't know the people, they steal your ideas. I've written a shepherd's play in Alexandrines. That, together with "Alcestis," "The Child," and "The Servant in Red" would make a nice book later on (after the novel) called "Small Dramas" (Four styles: Classicism, Rococo, Romanticism, Realism). Each one more different than the other. (I wrote an article in the *Crossen Newpaper* about a possible Crossen art gallery, for which I — suggested myself as director. Fine!) Yours faithfully, Henschke.

Arosa, IV. 2. 1914
Dear Herr Heinrich,

I am sending a selection of 25 titles to Reiss at the same time, but I can also send more. *Torches in the Wind, Tightrope Walkers, Smoldering Torches* are the best, I think. —

I'm feeling a bit down. I just got back from the doctor. My condition has worsened somewhat since the last visit. But he allows me — with careful living — to spend the summer in Berlin and Munich. In winter, I'll have to go back up. — It's awful to be sick and not have much money. Yours sincerely, Alfred Henschke. The novel is (provisionally) finished!

Munich, 5. 5. 14
Dear Herr Heinrich,

Mrs. Resi Langer is sending me the reviews of the Klabund evening (she seems to be a charming woman). What is written in the *Stock Exchange Courier* is directly fine. S.Z. and *Local Gazette* are also okay, but the *B.T.* (it seems it sent its editorial fool) and the *Vossian Newspaper*! "New and amusing stage talent..." Unfortunately, Reiss is nourishing this mindset when he calls the new book *Klabund's Carousel* (the *Vossian Newspaper* is right about that!). I had specifically asked in the last telegram to omit the adjective. Well, now the misfortune has happened. The critics are quick to strike. — A lot of reviews are now being handed to me. Reiss probably knows them all. Does he know the one in the *Hamburg Correspondent*, the one in the *Merker*, and the essay about me in the *Rhineland-Westphalian*: "Modern Cynicism?" — Well, one thing Klabund has certainly managed: he has brought life to the place, it's stirring up. And excitement is the main thing. Tepid praise falls under the table and rots. Warmest regards from your devoted Alfred Henschke.

Munich, V. 28. 1914
Dear Herr Heinrich,

You will receive my novel *The Ruby* by registered mail with the next post, which I dedicate to you. As thanks for your intellectual and active friendship!

This novel is not about psychological tricks – something actually happens: Twice: above and below, outside and inside. It is an expressionist novel, please, do not approach it (and Reiß) with false expectations. No analysis. No tragedy. (The hero dies – but he simply dies.) Objective daydreams. The people around

Josua are variations of his fine self, motivations of his self. Probability is not good. But the truth of the sound.

Once you have read the novel, please pass it on to Reiß.

I received a letter from Reiß today, which I do not understand. He calls me in breach of contract if I publish an anthology (with someone else) – meaning not even anything I wrote myself! – with Müller. With someone else. I am only obliged to him with my own works, not as an editor. Have you spoken to him recently? Health-wise, I feel very unwell. Warm regards, always yours, Alfred Henschke.

Munich, 6. 8. 1914
Dear Herr Heinrich,

On Tuesday, I wanted to bless Berlin — and once again something (and someone) gets in the way. So I must prolong my stay here. You'll definitely get the novel tomorrow. Did you receive the letter in which I expressed myself a bit on principle about it?

As for my serious work, I've gotten back into lyrical waters. Otherwise, I'm busy with the anthology and a little comedy that I'm writing alongside with someone else.

You can tell me your concerns about "Klabund" verbally. I understand you well, but I intend to (pleasantly) disappoint you. Hopefully.

As for my health? Up and down. One week like this, the next week like that. Please send my regards to Reiß; with the anthology, everything will probably fall into place. I've had enough excitement (on top of everything else) because of it. Warm regards, always yours, Alfred Henschke.

Charlottenburg, 7. 1. 1914
Dear Herr Heinrich,

Farewell. See you again in the fall! Last night, I had an encounter with a man, of whom I later learned that he was Mr. Rudolf Johannes Schmied and also an author for the Erich Reiß Verlag. I almost slapped him, because even when he tried to apologize, he did so in such a cheeky and drunk manner that I left him standing. Of course, he didn't know who I was. In any case, I ended up getting annoyed. When are you going on vacation? My next address: Crossen/Oder, Adler Apothecary. Warm regards, always yours, Alfred Henschke.

Munich 8. 3. 1914
Dear Herr Heinrich,

I am enlisting as a voluntary soldier with the Bavarian Light Cavalry. Hopefully, they will accept me. I believe that lying inactive behind the front causes one to rot and wears more on you than even the most exhausting service. At the very least, they will give me a weapon to hold. I can't even get any Berlin newspapers anymore (very delayed). Austria is completely silent. Here, they are working: yesterday, seven Russians were shot for subversive activities. Warm regards, H.

Munich VIII. 24. 1914
Dear Herr Heinrich,

I will probably have to give up hope of getting to the front in any way. I will have to retreat to my military designation: Landsturm without a weapon, and into the mountains — so at least I won't have to see those damned extra editions. In the meantime, I have been quite annoyed with Reiß, to whom I had offered a lyrical pamphlet of mine, *War Songs* (one sheet, a pretty, colorful title design, 50 pfennigs). He rejected it — lightheartedly! I am all the more annoyed because he does not seem inclined to apply to himself the moral demands he made of me in our correspondence regarding Georg Müller (you remember). If I now publish the pamphlet with another publisher, it is completely lost as propaganda for my works that have appeared with Reiß. And yet, what propaganda it could generate if, for example, it sold 10,000 copies — which is not at all impossible. But now exactly what Reiß so strongly accused me of back then is happening: that I am scattering my work to the winds. Who guarantees me that Reiß will print my next poetry book? That he won't just pick out the raisins — the novellas and novels — from the cake? Who is supposed to guarantee me that, if not his moral sense of responsibility? Could you perhaps speak with Reiß about this sometime? Many warm greetings, always your devoted Alfred Henschke.

Munich 9. 6. 1914
Dear Herr Heinrich,

I am going to be examined once more for the Landsturm. Probably: fit for clerical duties. If only they could at least use me in Brussels. I will write to Goltz. It is terrible to just sit around in Munich and in cafés, waiting for the dispatches. I should really absorb myself in something and go to the mountains, to Murnau (which I actually need again — I should: last night and this morning, my head wobbled as if on a stick, my limbs felt torn apart and seemed to exist separately from one another, and exhaling was excruciatingly painful. That lasted until this morning at seven. Now it's one o'clock, and everything has vanished like it was blown away). But of course, one cannot just leave. Obeying necessity, I wrote a small dramatic scene: *Russia Marches*. Characters: A policeman, a Jew, an innkeeper, a soldier, a girl, a Baltic German, two Russians. Setting: Petersburg, August 1914. The play will likely be performed in a private production at the Intimate Theater here (for the benefit of those suffering in East Prussia) the week after next. I have sent it to Reiß. Now I am completely satisfied that he did not take the pamphlet. It will be published by the Gelber Verlag (a publishing house that, given its current editorial direction, can promote it in the best possible way). Still, I don't understand Reiß. Whoever says A must also say B. He will have to grant me dispensation for a second pamphlet as well. I hear that only Erich Reiß is in

Berlin. According to his correspondence with me, Walther Reiß would never have gone along with it: "...I will not lend a hand in allowing even the smallest thing to be published by another publisher..." What have you been up to otherwise? Berlin newspapers are reporting that I have enlisted and been deployed with the Bavarian cavalry. Oh, if only. If only. I suppose I now feel almost obliged to at least learn how to ride. Warmest greetings, Yours, Alfred Henschke.

Munich 10. 25. 1914
Dear Herr Heinrich,

I want nothing more to do with one-act plays. They can go to the devil. Bloody nonsense. I have better things to do now. (What, I won't reveal in its early stages.) I just got back from Haag, Upper Bavaria. A small market town. I visited a girl and stayed with her parents — old, shriveled farmers. Very friendly and natural people. (And probably worth more than their daughter.) When I left, they picked the last roses and dahlias — or whatever they're called — from their garden for me and stuffed my handbag full of pears and apples. There are no people like that in northern Germany. It was raining, the girl was crying, but once I was past Thann-Motzbach, the sun shone into my compartment. I had the entire compartment to myself and, for the first time in weeks, had peace to read. And what I read really gripped me (partly, no doubt, due to my long abstinence from reading): *Out of the Land of Damnation* by E. Reichsfreiherr von Binder-Krieglstein (Vita). It describes prisons and adventures in Russian Manchuria (especially life in Harbin). For the first time, I grasped the Chinese national character, which I had never understood before. The Russian character, of course, is familiar to me. I think this is exactly the right book to read in wartime, and I'm amazed that it is still in its first edition. This fact brings me to the wretchedness of humanity in general: they never know what is good. My observations over the past six months (since I returned from Arosa) will soon turn me into a complete melancholic — if I wasn't one already. The times reek. Will they no longer stink after the war? I don't know. My brother Hans is deploying tomorrow or the day after. He wrote me a postcard saying: "We will only see each other again as free Germans." But, unfortunately, I received a letter from my father at the same time, which significantly dampened the patriotic tone of the postcard. Apart from his undoubtedly generous allowance, he has racked up debts like a major and, since he isn't particularly fond of alcohol, the only way he could have spent the money was in the company of certain friendly ladies. What kind of friendly ladies those are can be guessed by anyone who has set eyes on Cottbus. There are an endless number of soldier's taverns with red lights in Cottbus. The idea that patriotism, too, ultimately finds no other outlet than eroticism is a hypothesis that was never believed, even though I tried to prove it statistically (singing, gymnastics, and veterans' association festivals). But with the war volunteers, we now have irrefutable proof. I remember when Austria declared war on Serbia — I was in Leipzig. Thousands of us marched (myself included) under the leadership of a drunken journeyman baker to the Austrian consulate. Respectable people, all of them. (The journeyman baker eventually had to be driven in a requisitioned carriage because he refused to let go of his flag.) When we dispersed, no one knew where to go. The tension hadn't broken, the energy hadn't been spent. No one said anything, but everyone ended up ... in the brothels. I had never seen anything like it before — there wasn't a single free girl in any of the houses. But in Leipzig, I saw it. The alleys echoed with the footsteps of marching columns. Every man was a warrior, parading out the gates, admired by the whores and adorned with flowers.

Excuse my handwriting — I don't have my pen. I'm racking my brain trying to figure out how I can still get to the war. If I learned to shoot, to fly... I already know how to ride. I ride almost daily and do everything I'm not supposed to — smoke cigarettes — and my doctor has to admit that I am livelier than ever before. (Knock on wood, three times under the table!) Best regards, please give my regards to Reiß, yours always, Alfred Henschke.

Munich, Monday (in Sept/Oct. 1914)

Dear Herr Heinrich,

"Russia Marches," "The Cowardly Capon," and "Tommy Atkins" are, of course, merely means of getting through this time. And, in my opinion, quite decent means. The entire trilogy is set to be performed at the Munich Intimate Theater and the Theater Society in Berlin. Do you have any suggestion for a good overarching title? All three are comedies — the second takes place in Bordeaux, the third in a recruitment office in London. The second is a collection of absurd foreign press reports. (I read the *Echo of Paris* in the original.) It's a play, but I was unhappy until I had written it. The first weeks of the war were torture. Please impress upon Reiß that he should print all three together in a nice little volume with a drawing by Szafranski as soon as the bread is still warm. I hope he won't let me down now (and hand over all my war pieces to other publishers). That would pain me after such a good start with Reiß. You will believe me when I say I'm not boasting, but I have more than enough offers from other publishers. I don't want that. And I hope Reiß doesn't want to see my works with other publishers either, and that he won't overturn the agreements his brother made. (His brother has accepted the novel. It's possible that I might need the royalties one day.) Excuse me for always talking about Reiß, but it's on my mind since I've heard nothing from him. And lately, I've been working furiously, like a horse — sometimes from ten in the morning until three at night. I'm a bit overstimulated, even though I spent the last two days in the mountains, which did wonders to calm me. Do you know Mittenwald? The most architecturally beautiful town in Bavaria. A peasant's song, with the Karwendel mountains as a sheet of music. Did you know that I have a collection of soldier's songs? Probably the best one out there right now? Hundreds? Real soldier's songs! I want to publish them now. Beiß probably won't want them. He has his *When the Soldiers...*, which is very nice, but it makes no claim to completeness (Bavaria and Austria are completely missing).

Could you discuss it with him over the phone? I don't dare to write since I don't get any response anyway.

Best regards. At the moment, I'm just a terribly agitated bundle of nerves. Yours, Alfred Henschke.

Munich, X. 31. 1914

Dear Herr Heinrich,

Great things are happening on the moon, things even the calf isn't used to, or so they say somewhere. The events (including "within us," if one may say so) overtake and surprise each other. Maybe I'll somehow make it to the front. A faint hope! I ride — you know that. I am learning to shoot. I will travel around the world and ride across Mexico. What won't I do! (Reiß needs to change my contract — to a monthly pension. Will he do it? 200–300 marks.) I have found the painter Seewald. War is on! You will soon hear from the two of us. Will (or can) Reiß do something with the two of us? Most sincerely, Alfred Henschke.

Crossen, 12. 23. 14

Dear Herr Heinrich,

All the best for Christmas and for 1915! Here, one feels more of the war in two hours than in Munich in half a year. That's because of the many captured Russians one sees. Six thousand of them. Most are excellently equipped with light brown, sturdy coats and large shoes. Some, however, are pitiful: wrapped only in dirty cloths. Some are small, elderly fellows. Mongols. Bearded Jews. Balts with fringes. I have a lot of proofreading to do for the thick book I'm publishing with the "Yellow Verlag." I'll be passing through Berlin on my way back to Munich. Have you read the novella *Marietta*? I spoke with Mr. Döring. Mrs. Döring spoke favorably about your poems, which she bought. Sincerely, Alfred Henschke.

Berlin, 1. 29. 1915

Dear Herr Heinrich,

Too bad I missed you today. Didn't you get my card? I'm planning to leave tomorrow (Sunday) evening and would have liked to speak with you one last time about Reiß. I really don't know what to do. I'll probably go to see him tomorrow morning. At the very least, I need money to get back to Munich. (Things didn't work out with D.T., unfortunately.)

Yesterday, I spoke with S.S. She was more beautiful than ever. A heavenly vision. Afterward, I ran into the young lady from Eberswalde. And also a girl from Halensee who called herself an "artist" and paints floral still lifes. I'm completely exhausted today and can only think about S.S. (I'll elevate these words to magical tokens!) Best regards, Alfred Henschke.

Munich, III. 15. 15

Dear Herr Heinrich,

I am reveling — how long has it been? in the greatest poetic union of my life. You shall soon be informed about it. Reiß must have it printed for Christmas despite the war. Always yours, Klabund.

Munich, 5. 9. 15

Dear Herr Heinrich,

It seems that Reiß no longer wants to take anything from me at all. Yet right now, there is a real demand for good literature that has nothing to do with the ___ war. Whether "Insel" will take it, I don't know. I'm inquiring. With God's help, I am now with five publishers: Reiß, Insel, Georg Müller, Goltz, and Yellow Verlag... But there are still more. (Walther Reiß will surely be pleased, I imagine, when he returns to the publishing house crowned with glory. Why is he so completely lacking in initiative?) The Italian vegetable vendors here at the Viktualienmarkt were (allegedly) beaten up. But people are colder than I expected. One is starting to almost aesthetically savor the vileness of this alliance. What a vile and filthy bunch! My God, how sweet! Always yours, Klabund.

Munich, 5. 17. 15

Dear Herr Heinrich,

As soon as the novel is published by another publisher, R. ... will no longer be my publisher. That's not gonna work. "Dull Drum and Drunken Gong," Chinese war poems (they turned out better than "Litaipe," they are translated even more freely and often retain only the Chinese motif) will be published by Insel Verlag. I am not yet settled on "Litaipe." Perhaps I will make a large edition (100 unknown poems, directly translated from Chinese with a local Chinese expert). Perhaps. I have now collected my war poems, as far as they have purely artistic, timeless value. Forty. You don't know them. I offer them to Reiß. Perhaps you could occasionally ask him to show them to you.

Schienther offers me book reviews in the D.T. I want to do it because you get beautiful books for free. Otherwise, I am so lazy.

Do you like the book by H. E. Jacob about his (alleged) journey through the Belgian war? Warmest regards, always yours, Klabund.

First of June 1915

Dear Herr Heinrich,

Thank you very much for your letter. Please don't trouble yourself with Reiß. I will manage with him on my own. Either way.

Here, too, the mood is very optimistic. It has been strengthened and lifted, especially with Italy's entry. Now all that's needed is for the King of Greece to die. And America (as well) to "strike" – then we will have witnessed the fiasco of German "diplomacy" as pathetic as any diplomacy could be, for which quotation marks are still too generous. How ridiculous of this press to try to convince the German people that their complete isolation is merely a consequence of their diligence and virtue. Biblical argument: The righteous must suffer greatly... But why are all of us enemies? Even the most neutral of neutrals: Holland, Denmark, Norway. In Sweden and Spain, we enjoy some sympathy. South and North America are against us. Switzerland is highly doubtful. Not even Turkey is culturally ours. It belongs spiritually more to France. And Austria?

We have simply ("under the prevailing regime") failed to imbue the splendid organization of our army, our civil service, with a spirit of recruitment. We have been able to provide an idealism only for private use, as a "thing in itself," detached from the earth, like the French. Like (above all) the English, who (namely) are also idealists. How could England's world domination be conceivable without "idealism," but exactly that English idealism of action? One cannot seriously believe that England governs India with brutality, with raw military force? Or Egypt? With its thousands of colonial soldiers? Where does England's power over Russia come from? Over France? Over Italy? (Which marched into the war a few days after the Allies' heaviest defeats in Galicia and the Dardanelles). Reprisals? Coal? (It could have gotten that from us, too.) That is the "other side," which must eventually be considered as well. There will be heavy internal struggles with us. (England seems invincible to me. Just like Germany. Germany for military reasons, England for geopolitical reasons.) We must experience this coming time. We want to be part of it.

"The days rise before us like islands,
Which lay undiscovered in dark seas..."

That is a beautiful poem. I enjoy reading your poems. Not actually because of the poems. Because of you. Always yours, Klabund.

Munich, 7. 6. 15
Dear Herr Heinrich,
You are right with your view on the infection of the mind by the thought of the "eternal war." By the way, I must go to Berlin again, for a longer time; here, one cannot write a single novella because the air is so soft. The whole "carousel" is ultimately a "Berlin trademark." And the same thing in pale blue, but better, should be written again. Now and then, I think of "Peter," get quite moved, and feel homesick for Berlin. N. Reiß was here but did not think it necessary to call me. In the fall, he now wants to publish a book of mine. I want to go to Mittenwald every day (you should come too! Very beautiful and relatively cheap! 5.50 daily!). Warmly, Klabund.

Munich, IX. 15. 1915

Dear Herr Heinrich,

I haven't heard from you in such a long time. (You probably haven't heard from me either...) Every few weeks, I get a longing for Berlin, today for example. For the scent of Berlin. (Munich smells so indifferent, so nothing, like flat highlands.) I was in Mittenwald. It did me good. The day before yesterday, I was examined again. For 6 months (again) back. Do you see Reiß sometimes, the gentleman who deals with printing books? Warmly, Klabund.

Munich, X. 3. 1915

Dear Herr Heinrich,

The lines to my brother are in the sketch "Mittenwald!" In the meantime, I've sent three more things: *Hölderlin — Does your watch glow at night? — The Hedgehog* — to Reiß. I believe it will be a quite decent book. Only again the worry about the title! "War Diary" alone sounds so pretentious, since I wasn't actually in the war. What do you think of "Defensive," a title that very well characterizes the defensive nature of the book (defensive against the war) and at the same time strongly points to the war itself? "Klabund's Carousel in the War" unfortunately doesn't work. What's your opinion on the title? Warm regards, Klabund.

Munich, X. 11. 1915

Dear Herr Heinrich,

I wrote to Reiß that I want to keep the clock, the general, and Hölderlin (as an excellent epilogue: a mild, more resigned conclusion to the war book) in it. Title: that's causing more headaches. "Klabund's War Book" alone — doesn't work. But maybe: "Klabund's War Book in Prose?" Reiß definitely has to follow up with the "Ladder to Heaven" in the spring. With my second novel, which I am working on daily (or rather nightly), I hope to be finished by then. It will be very curious — should I tell you about my extraliterary life? Various women and children. I now love 16-year-olds. I have, after all, a fetishist for breasts, and they are the only ones who still have beautiful breasts. I myself am getting younger and younger. Ever younger. That's actually suspicious. It smells like dissolution heading to the other side. I look so young now, as if I were my brother. And my brother looks so old, as if he were me. — The apartment I have is — finally — very nice. And central heating. I feel comfortable in it. The dry air of the central heating seems to be good for my lungs. Otherwise, I have been under medical treatment for a month already... My brother is doing better. He has been discharged from the hospital. He has leave and will then go to Jüterbog for officer training. Would you like to meet him? You know I think highly of him. Unfortunately, I haven't seen him since he returned from the front. Warmest regards, Klabund.

Munich, 10. 24. 15

Dear Herr Heinrich,

I am in a terribly irritable mood due to a thousand different complications. I wrote to Reiß, telegraphed: The title "War Book" alone is impossible for me. — I have written more war books, also with other publishers. I absolutely do not understand why the title I propose is not chosen: "The Golden Death. A War Book by Klabund." After all, this cannot go on endlessly with Klabund in the title: Klabund's first novel, Klabund's second novel, Klabund's further poems, etc. That just doesn't work.

I am also convinced that "War Book" in the title has a bad effect: commercially. People do not buy direct war books. (And that is not even what it is.) I find "The Golden Death" very memorable and effective. If Reiß wants to determine everything on his own, without my consent, writing, paper, title, format, etc., then he can write my books himself in the future. Best regards, Klabund.

Munich, 10. 28. 15

Dear Herr Heinrich,

I feel what your little nephew meant to you: probably what my brother means to me. The worst thing is death. The destruction of a young heart destroys more than the construction of a Strasbourg cathedral could ever rebuild. I, too, have repeatedly been plunged into resignation and tears by the organization of death that war produces. I am weary of so much death. Recently, when a machine gun company was restocked, I cried like a dog. — I have been in bed for a few days. A mixture of stomach, intestinal, lung, and kidney ailments, hopefully I won't need surgery. I have hot water bottles on my stomach like a pregnant woman (and cold ones further down). There are no reasonable people left in Europe. We are all "crazy." Warmest regards, your Alfred Henschke.

Munich, 11. 18. 15

Dear Herr Heinrich,

My new novel *Moreau* is already with Reiß. If you should happen to read it, I would be grateful for your opinion. It is written in a completely different style, feverish, once again full of objective romance. Un-erotic! I hesitated for a long time whether I should treat certain scenes (the capture of the fleet by cavalry), the ending (the battle at Dresden) in more detail: which is definitely a matter of stylistic insight, not at all of ability. (On the contrary: the scene mentioned above could be tempting to develop in the most detailed way due to its grotesque nature.) I have left the scene short, sparse, and feverish. (By the way, I was ill when I wrote the book!) —

The Commissary Wagon — isn't that a delightful title? Isn't it a thousand times better than all the Klabund's *War Book, War Stories,* which were so colorless?

Warmest regards, your Klabund.

Crossen/Oder, 12. 26. 15
Dear Herr Heinrich,

Thank you for your letter. I also share your opinion about *Moreau* (which, by the way, made a strong impression during my lecture in Munich: reviews have appeared in some Berlin newspapers: the evening was a small sensation for Munich — something I hardly expected myself). Reiß must, of course, bring it out in March: I will pass through Berlin on my return journey and have various things to discuss with him. I think he is far too mild in his propaganda for me. He needs to make much more of a spectacle. Like Wolff with his people. —

Did I send you *Dragoons and Hussars* and the small Insel book of more distant war poetry *Muffled Drum*? I am not quite sure. That Reiß let the two small (in my opinion, quite respectable) books slip by was — between us — a foolishness on his part. (Also commercially: the fifth thousand of *Dragoons and Hussars* is being printed.) —

Why I didn't come recently? It was a sudden whim of mine to get off in Halle. A sudden aversion to Berlin. My instinct guided me correctly: I spent two hours in Halle that I will never forget. — I will be very happy to see you again on the 4th of January. I, of course, already have many new, more or less fantastic plans. All the best for the new war year! Yours, Klabund.

Munich, 1. 25. 16
Dear Herr Heinrich,

In a hurry, just a few lines. I'm not feeling well. But after all, this condition has become so latent for me that it's no longer worth discussing. It's getting boring. I've been officially released from the military. The only one at the last medical examination. (After the 9th one.) I want, or rather, I am supposed to go to Davos. In that case, I would have to ask Reiß, though it pains me, for 200 marks a month (instead of 150 marks).—

In the winter, after *Moreau*, I want to publish a large poetry book: a selection from *Ladder to Heaven* and *Red Nightingale*, which unfortunately are with Reiß. Perhaps you'll have a look at them occasionally and make suggestions. — There's, of course, no talk of work. —

The affair with my brother has been resolved once again, but very painfully. He was indeed very morally crushed. I'm actually always feverish and very depressed. But it will pass. Warmest regards, your Klabund.

Davos, 2. 12. 16
Dear Herr Heinrich,

Here we are now, and we feel very comfortable for the time being: it seems I have made a very good choice with the pension. South-facing room with its own lounging hall. The whole pension (5 meals! Lunch and dinner, grand affairs) for only 8.50 a day. And the food is excellent. I'm not yet willing to comment on the people. Otherwise, there's significant activity here. Much of the "world." English, Greeks, French, Italians, Germans, Americans, Russians, all mixed together and overlapping. Plus, meat every day. Sunday whipped cream. In short: the only kind of "peace" available at the moment. Write soon to your Klabund.

Davos-Dorf, III. 12. 1916
Dear Herr Heinrich,

Thank you for your letter. The problem of the golden casserole continues to occupy me, but I am by no means clear about the change yet. Consider this: the scene goes back to Napoleon's appearance with Moreau. I would have to recombine about 10 pages. Now, the solution would be: to have Moreau dream the scene. This would only require a few opening sentences. But: isn't the little novel, despite all its intense romance, very direct? And wouldn't that perhaps create a rift, a cutting of the style?... I have already read the first corrections.

I've written a story here: "The Disease," about three-quarters as long as the "Moreau," and it might also be published as a small, standalone book. The style is diametrically opposed to that of "Moreau." The hero is a young man named Sylvester, who also plays a role in a projected novel called *Sylvester* and [one word illegible]. The carnival is over. We celebrated it here: I danced madly. Oh, one saw red, yellow, and purple pierrots and held them in one's arms. There were again amusingly serious carnival adventures with tears and laughter. Just now the Sunday bells are ringing. I must think about the fact that Franz Marc has fallen. He, more than anyone, loved the colorful animals. (And don't the pierrots also belong to the colorful animals?) I still see his red deer, his blue horse. He was a Bavarian: but much closer to the mountains than Franz Stuck! I know nothing about him, except that I sat with him for three days before he went off at the Munich Café "Stefanie," and grew fond of him as a person. He wrote to me once more. Then I heard nothing from him. Your Klabund.

Davos, III. 22. 1916
Dear Herr Heinrich,

As a bank clerk, do you know if there is there any way to get cheap Swiss money? Can't one pledge German war bonds, say 1000 marks, with a value of 800 francs, which could be paid back at a somewhat normal exchange rate? Please write to me soon about this. I am feeling a little miserable again. Every few days, I crawl back into bed. But the ___ women are also to blame for that. If this continues, I will leave and go to Locarno. Best regards, your Klabund.

Zürich, IV. 3. 1916
Dear Herr Heinrich,

You see, I'm no longer in Davos. I haven't been for six days now. I left in a great rush after some very painful experiences. I may be a good judge of character, but

I'm a poor psychologist. I spent five happily-unhappy days here in Zurich with a friend from Davos. Now, since the day before yesterday, I've been alone, sitting here in the hotel without direction and not knowing where to go. Or why. And so on. If only one had a homeland! People like us don't. Even Munich is slipping away. —

As for *Moreau*, I was neither willing nor able to make any major changes. I barely managed to read through the necessary corrections. I added only one tiny sentence to the casserole scene: "Then Moreau awoke." Period. One more thing: I'd like, if it's still possible, to change the narrative present tense (which I initially liked so much) throughout *Moreau* into the past tense. Who could do that? You? But perhaps it's already too late because of the printing. I'm much more tired and miserable than I was back when I came to Davos from Munich. If only I could return to Davos. But I can't. Warm greetings, yours Klabund

Oberstdorf, 5. 11. 16
Dear Herr Heinrich,
I am back in Germany. Who knows for how long! In a few days, I will go to Munich. Do you know anything about "Moreau?" Best regards, your Klabund.

Oberstdorf, 5. 11. 16
Dear Herr Heinrich,
It is a pity that the beautifully printed book is so full of typographical errors. For example, there are five in the *Song of Christophe* alone!

Contrary to my first impression, I have gotten used to Munich and Germany again. At first, I was quite down; it's no small matter to return from peace to war, and to see all those painful and most painful associations resurface that one thought had sunk away. To get to something more real (though not entirely real): in Berlin, it is said that the food supply for the population is in a dire state? Has been for months? Here, we don't notice much yet. In any case, there's still plenty of meat available on meat days. One can always eat excellent roast pork with salad for 1.20 M, and a full menu (soup, two courses, dessert) for 1.30–1.70. There are many Berliners here who bring their complaints from Berlin and stuff themselves (at least for now: until the export ban from Bavaria, which seems to be in place, is lifted). The less food there is, the more materialistic people become. This simple calculation still seems to have escaped the super patriots.

How are you personally? At times, one has the distinct feeling of barely keeping one's head above water. I find it dreadful that all those involved are already preparing for a future war, as they seem not to get fully compensated in this one. A monstrous breed, these people. Write soon, heartfelt greetings, your Klabund
. I am now putting together the poetry book for the fall. It will be as thick as the Bible.

Munich VI. 27. 16

Dear Herr Heinrich,

Come to Upper Bavaria in July! I will be in Mittenwald or Garmisch then (probably with my father). For a Berliner, Bayern should be a breath of fresh air this year, especially when it comes to the stomach.

Dear Herr Heinrich: I no longer have any hope for a "better world." I read Andreas Gryphius' sonnets and find... our time. If one did not have within oneself the compulsion and the will to formally control an utterly disgusting chaos, one would either go mad or hang oneself. – The poems I sent to Reiß have all been checked for form; the second part, however, is at times poorly readable. The sections I have already chosen are each 25–50 poems long. I don't want to cut much this time.

I've made a contract with a local publisher to release a series of plays. (Reiß doesn't know about this yet.) I will receive a monthly stipend of about 200 M for it. (The same as with Reiß.) I will also send him the Geisha songs and a free translation of Omar. Think about it: I lost a comedy manuscript! That doesn't cheer me up either. Best regards, your Klabund.

Davos-Dorf, September 18, 1916

Dear Herr Heinrich,

I've now been back in this adventurous wilderness for five weeks, and I feel infinitely well. The pressure of the "war" has been lifted from me, and I breathe a peaceful air. In these five weeks, I've written a new little novel called "Francis" — in the style of "Moreau," but calmer and more composed. I deeply regret, in the sense of the publisher, that I can't write long novels, but my entire state predisposes me to the "small novel" — which, in Germany, doesn't really exist yet, and in which I may truly accomplish something lasting. ("Gunther" may become a thick book, but how far off is it still!) I will send Reiß "Francis" in the coming days and would very much appreciate your opinion. – How are you? I still mourn our last misstep. – If only there were peace: perhaps we could be together here sometime! Today is a wonderful day: blue, cool, with transparent thin clouds on the slopes. Autumn. I am becoming ever more "ethical." "Francis" proves it. A short trip to Nuremberg made me quite thoughtful. We are indeed changing. And I hope, to quote "Francis," "for a decisive turn toward the good." Always yours, Klabund. Now, I'm interested in an idea from 1848.

Davos-Dorf, XI. 5. 1916

Dear Herr Heinrich,

Thank you for your card. "Francis" has meanwhile been received by R., maybe you can ask him to check it out. The couplets don't give me any notable pleasure, but money, and I need that so badly. I suffer directly from "money complexes." As for the success of the Wegener evening, I am — unlike Reiß — not at all delighted. From private letters and some of the reviews I read, it seems Wegener has read me into the ground: poorly, carelessly, and quietly. The letters I've received from otherwise completely harmless people are downright outraged by the way W. treated me. From the third row onward, no one understood him anymore. So it was an experiment, the repetition of which I would not recommend to R.; I'd rather read myself. — Do write again soon. I am so alone here. The warmest greetings, your loyal Klabund.

Davos-Dorf, XI. 17. 1916

Dear Herr Heinrich,

Thank you for your letter. (Apologies for the pencil, I'm writing while lying down.) — No: it's impossible to print "Francis" together with other works. It must appear just like "Moreau:" as the second part of the tetralogy or trilogy I am planning: Hero, Saint, Poet, Whore. I often hint at "Gunther." I have also written many new verses and am planning a longer epic hymn. — That Reiß intended the best with the Wegener evening: I have no doubt about that. If the evening still didn't have the success I had hoped for (Reiß may be satisfied with it), it is due to two reasons: firstly, because Wegener, as I suspect, only read for money reasons, and I am as indifferent to him as God knows who: he probably didn't find any inner connection with me. And secondly, due to the gesture of Reiß, with which he apparently staged the evening. I think it is fundamentally wrong to present me as the poet, who until now has only been known to a small number of literary friends and is meant to be introduced to a larger audience. One suggests ideas to the audience and the critics that are completely based on false assumptions. My books are now (all together) distributed in over 30,000 copies. That means at least 150,000 readers. Are they still "just a few literary friends?"

— The money question — yes, that is truly annoying. One spends so much energy on it. Warmest greetings, your Klabund.

Davos, 1. 1. 1917

Dear Herr Heinrich,

Thank you very much for your letter. No, my parents are very wrong: Arosa would not suit me anymore. The people there are too empty, and the air is too light. I feel very comfortable here, living an Apollonian life with a beautiful blonde friend, working and thinking a lot. And my only (only faintly perceptible on the surface) pain is that I can't manage my money, which is partly due to the poor exchange rate. Getting 490 francs for 600 marks is not fun.

I have worked on various things, and I would like to hear your opinion on them. If you have time, I ask you to get the two manuscripts "Francis" (The Novel of a Dog) and "Irene or the Mindset" from Reiß. The latter is a song, a call, a hymn in 40 rhythmic sections. Both clearly reveal the shift I have undergone since "Moreau:" they decisively move from the carefree, playful to the intellectually purposeful. Precisely because you loved the "carefree" in me (in my art), I am very curious about your attitude towards the new writings. "Irene" is supposed to be published in the spring. Please tell me everything you think: I consider both to be a progression from "Moreau" and "Ladder to Heaven." But I only have "visions," I am not a "seer." All the best in the new year! Always yours, Klabund.

Davos-Dorf, II. 7. 17
Dear Herr Heinrich,

You must have received my last letter. I don't know if you've had the time and, above all, the inclination to read "Francis" and "Irene" in the meantime.

The break with America (and the other neutrals, for there is no longer any talk of benevolent neutrality) has certainly shaken Berlin as well. It is certainly not a small matter, and when considering the world situation, one cannot be glad like the Farmers' Union. I understand the necessity of such a step after the arrogant and irrational rejection of the German peace offer. Let us just hope that the U-boat war will succeed.

Here in Davos, there was, of course, an agitated atmosphere on the day of the break with America. Many people babbled about a break between Switzerland and Germany and packed their bags. That is, of course, out of the question. Bern has (unofficially, so far) waved off Wilson.

In these days, I have put together a new book of grotesques: it has now become 30 pieces. The whole is much more unified, more compact, and more shaped than the "Carousel." I almost feel like decorating it with colorful pictures of mine: grotesque things — what do you think about that? A friend just wrote to me about "Francis:" he finds the introduction unnecessary (even "unclean") and would like to begin the story on page 8: "I stood at the bow..." What do you think? I answered him that from the "unclean" comes the longing for "solitude," and it is from that which the fable is resolved and redeemed. And — the human being. It is the story of a redemption. I haven't heard anything from Reiß, although I would like to hear from him urgently, especially regarding "Hannibal." In three weeks, I will be going to Ticino. The warmest greetings, your Klabund.

Davos-Dorf, II. 15. 17
Dear Herr Heinrich,

It pains me that you and Reiß have so little regard for *Irene*. But at the very least, you are such a convinced realist (even if with a romantic streak) that I'm not particularly surprised — and I only deeply regret that you turn so brusquely away from an abstract creature like Irene. I want to see all sides of my being expressed, and it is by no means enough for me to write only "good" books. The divergence of possibilities (of my experience) demands it. I want, at a certain point in my life, to be in harmony with my "idea." And yet be wild and tender, gentle and swift. Irene can certainly be improved: I've already made some heavy revisions again, but I will by no means abandon her — since she stands before the highest court, my conscience. Will Reiß publish it? He writes unclearly about it; but I would advise him, nonetheless, to publish it despite his animosity toward it. Otherwise, he would once again miss out on a work of mine that I believe is important — one that Insel or Wolff would gladly accept with a kiss on the hand! You don't really like *Francis* either? What a pity! Then what will you say to my grotesques? I'm thinking about the introduction to *Francis*, but I promise nothing. Warmest regards,your Klabund.

Lugano, 4. 15. 17

Dear Herr Heinrich,

I have just received your letter. I am in Lugano for two days. A "spring" this year! Only imaginable as something Dantean — hellish beyond imagining. Erratic boulders falling like hail. Mountain ranges of meteors. — I'd be glad to follow up on your suggestion. Only: "Mohammed" was, in fact (and actually according to my plan as well), not an epileptic. Just a — let's say — rationalist visionary! It would be nice if I didn't constantly have no money! I feel like I've been transported back to my first semester. Warmest regards, your Klabund.

Locarno, 5. 7. 17

Dear Herr Heinrich,

I cannot fulfill your wish for a "deepening" of "Mohammed:" I see him as more "two-dimensional" and not so much as a founder of religion, but more as a colorful man and a radiant person. Hopefully, you will also accept him — without a hooked nose. Warmest regards, your Klabund.

Passau, 9. 16. 17

Dear Herr Heinrich,

You will be surprised to see me in Germany again! I kindly ask for discretion for various reasons! (Only Reiß may know.) I would of course be very happy to see you again — who knows when and if the opportunity will arise again later! I hope to come to Berlin half-incognito and would telegraph you in that case. What times we are living in! The Renaissance was like a puppet show compared to this! Warmest regards (that's my only name here), your Alfred Henschke.

candidata philosophiae

Locarno, 10. 29. 17.

Dear Herr Heinrich,

I haven't heard from you in such a long time! How are you? How sorry I was that I couldn't come to Berlin. But I did the right thing. Reiß must have shown you the letter in which I wrote about all the unpleasantness that was attached to me. I don't want to describe it again. — The mail from Germany takes quite a long time now. For weeks. And since the trains on the Gotthard have also been severely restricted, one feels as if they've been transported back to the days of the stagecoaches. The German successes in Italy have made a vivid impression here. In the Cafe Swizzero, the Tessinians are huddled together in thick clumps, shouting and gesticulating. I hope they don't smash our windows as the operation progresses. Warm greetings from your Klabund.

Basel, 12.17.17
Dear Herr Heinrich,

I am currently living in Basel. My extremely old-fashioned furnished little room overlooks the Rhine. The cannons from Alsace thunder all day and night. Sometimes the windows rattle, and you feel as though you're standing at the front lines. I am freezing all day long. This is due to the damn shortage of coal. Nevertheless, I have done a lot recently, both in Locarno — after Christmas I will return to Ticino — and here in Basel. I've sketched out Platonic dialogues on politics and poetry. (I am by no means in favor of their "identity," as the latest fashion wants to suggest.) I've drawn a lyrical portrait of François Villon. I've started a "Nero" (in prose). Many dramatic sketches and experiments, including: "Silvius or the Moonstruck," a play (in 16 scenes). Almost finished: "The Rebel," a Chinese comedy. "Tacitus and Suetonius," a biography of the Roman emperors, has occupied me a great deal. It has only strengthened my pessimistic view of the outcome of this war. If, on the foundation of the free Roman Republic, such a grotesque and horrific structure as the Roman Empire was possible — this darkest and most unclear episode in human history — dark despite the richest sources — then everything is indeed possible in this world. All progress appears, in such a context, as empty rhetoric. The thesis: "Man is good," almost becomes blasphemy.

The Entente, as far as I can see, is doomed. Quite logically: due to a fundamental error. Wilson's speech before Congress in the winter (January) of 1917 was the high point of Entente politics. From then on, it's been downhill, not immediately visible, but downward nonetheless. The near-completed betrayal of the Russian Revolution for military reasons (Kornilov!), Stockholm, Clemenceau's incitement against Caillaux — about which I could tell you more if I were in Germany — Lord George's speech, Asquith's, the foehn mood in the Italian Chamber: all of these show that the Entente is on the verge of collapse, not for any other reason than that it has failed to turn its ideas into facts. The ironic thing now is that the Central Powers seem to be defending the original ideas of the Entente — against the Entente. (By the way, you know my opinion on the dynastic issue: the gray cloud before the German sun.) Warm greetings from your Klabund.

Basel, 1.22.1918
Dear Herr Heinrich,

I am always happy when you write: thank you for your lines. The past month has been filled with the most terrible turmoil, and you can imagine (or not imagine) what kind of mood I've sometimes been in. It would take a book to tell you about my experiences, for example, during the war in Switzerland. If I ever get around to writing my memoirs, it will surely be my most interesting work — as interesting for the reader as it will be stirring for the author, since he "lived" them. I have sown the wind and reaped the storm, but it shall not blow me away. I stand firmly on my two feet — Davos, Zurich, Locarno, Lugano, Basel — have gotten to know me (though not necessarily recognized me). A cloud of hatred always hangs over my head. I would not take my private life half as seriously — were it not for the pressure from the outside world. In Davos, it has come to the point where it was almost necessary to convene a protest meeting against my very existence. There are, after all, many guesthouses in Davos that will no longer take me in. If you remember me, you will hardly picture me as a devilish figure with horns, which is how I am seen by others. Ruined families, betrayed friends, extinguished girls, burned-down houses — these define my path (as they say). Curiously, I occasionally glance in the mirror, but I discover none of this, just a suffering child's face.

"Villon," "The Sleepwalkers," "Eulenspiegel" are now with Reiß. I would love to hear your opinion on the latter. A technical question: you consider it entirely proper for me to use legends and anecdotes from the people in such a folk book as I have done, don't you? I have esteemed advocates: Goethe (letter to Kestner about Clavigo) and Shakespeare (Caesar, etc.) — who thought no differently, not to mention Boccaccio. What do you think? "Eulenspiegel" is my book, despite these borrowings. (I have also made three borrowings from my Crossen stories.) By the way, I am also, for example, the most hated man in literary circles, like those in Zurich. I won't repeat what the [one word illegible] apostles of ideology, this rabble, spread about me.

The bow is finished. And the letter may end with all my warmest wishes to you. Always yours, Klabund.

Locarno-Monti, Villa Neugeboren VI. 30. 1918
Dear Herr Heinrich,

I haven't heard from you in a long time! How are you? I am still living in the Tessin, above Locarno, in a wildlife and garden idyll. Snakes (one day I caught eleven — by hand), giant lizards, and tropical butterflies are my companions. (A chapter of my next poetry book will be called "The Zodiac.") I have gotten married: to a woman who is completely animal, completely child, completely butterfly, like those beings around us. She was seriously ill with lung disease. And with a throat condition. But she is recovering. — What flies in from the outside world is dissonant and harsh. The practical reason — where has it gone? The delusion of power and the madness of a full wallet and an empty heart are speeding forward more methodically. The realization of the inexperience of our situation in 1914 comes bitterly to us. Each new year punishes us more. When will we be able to return to Germany? Always yours, Klabund.

10.15.1918
Dear Herr Heinrich,

We are not as well as you seem to assume. My wife is seriously ill. She is in the hospital and will likely have to stay there for weeks before she can undergo the serious surgery she needs, if she wants to avoid endangering her life. (It is absolutely impossible for her to survive a normal birth in her current condition.) My work — I had started writing the novel of the proletarian revolution, set in centuries past — is, of course, stalled. The "Eulenspiegel" has been printed in the meantime. (Perhaps you've already received a copy?) — I am happy about the turn of events in Germany (what a turn through God's guidance! — you know the old Hohenzollern saying?), although I still only see words. But only actions will legitimize the new government: amnesty, constitutional change, new elections to the Reichstag. The moral standing of Germany has lost all credit in the world since Brest. Do you remember my open letter from June 3rd of last year? I was right time and again — and I still am. But back then, victory was always claimed, and no one anticipated the catastrophe. My theses were suspected, mocked, and ridiculed.

Reiß seems to take pleasure in further "lifting" my mood. He doesn't respond to urgent letters at all, never sends the money by the agreed date, so I always have to wire him (and how much I need to!) and he never sends it in German currency, as I've asked him a thousand times, because then I can exchange it whenever I want. (For example, I've lost 100 francs in a month due to his negligence!)

I will collect my political essays into a small book! I hope we will see each other in the spring in Germany. Best regards, your Klabund.

Telegramm – Locarno – 10/30 4:40 AM
Dear Herr Heinrich,

Dear friend, my beloved wife passed away peacefully last night. Please inform Reiß. Your most unfortunate, Klabund.

Locarno, XI. 9. 1918
Dear Herr Heinrich,

You may have been a little surprised by the telegram: but I was so distraught and so desperate that I had to cry it out to the few people I believe think of me from time to time.

Irene was to me what her name suggests: the peace of my soul. That is now gone. With an incredibly pure heart, I had truly fled from an indescribably filthy world. We lived in Monti as if in a hermitage, surrounded only by stars, clouds, and animals. The harmony of her being was perfect. She was one with the earth and the heavens. Kind, beautiful, gentle, faithful, brave — what virtues did she not possess, all without struggle, as a divine gift?

That she would stand beside me in the light forever, I had hardly dared to hope. She was too angelic, too ethereal for that. But, as I had imagined, we might have been blissful together for some years. Instead, it became only a few months. And I bitterly regret not having let her take the child away from her in the first month, as I had initially wanted to. But she had such heavenly joy over the child that I couldn't bring myself to do it. And when she had been operated on and they placed the living child in her arms, she smiled heavenly. The child is now in the nursery. It will be named Irene, just like her.

I envy her for her death. We, the survivors, are to be mourned. Does this time not seem to you increasingly horrendous and futile? I shudder with disgust when I have to read the newspapers from both sides, which are all just one side of lies. About three weeks ago, I addressed an "Appeal to Wilson" in the "New Zurich Newspaper." I don't know if you have read it. We are so powerless. But it is probably better that way. Just as the spirit becomes infected by power, so too is it doomed. I am increasingly embracing the wisdom of Lao Tzu.

Like the man in the fairy tale who set out to unearth a golden treasure, won it, until a wicked sorcerer took everything from him, I return to Germany, tired and miserable, a true wanderer, not knowing where to go, with empty hands and an overflowing heart.

(I have also been lying in the clinic for the eighteenth day today (I was not allowed to see Irene in the last days before her death), and on Monday, I plan to return to my apartment in Monti-Locarno, Villa Newborn. Newborn... a bitter word...) With heartfelt greetings, your Klabund.

Villa Newborn, Locarno-Monti, 11. 17. 18

Dear Herr Heinrich,

I am sending you (doesn't the postal situation in Germany allow the sending of valuable manuscripts?) the last two parts of my lyrical main work, the "Trilogy" (the first was "Irene or the Mindset"): "Silvia or the Promise" and "Coelia or the Fulfillment." I am sending them to you so that you can read them; please then pass them on to Reiß. I want to tell you a few things about it; I just wrote this to Irene's parents, so I'll copy it here, because I'm too tired to say it all over again:

You, who know me a little (how few really know me, and except for Irene, no one really knew me well), know that even the seemingly most typical, the most stylized things with me are based on personal experience. Thus, the "Trilogy" is nothing other than my life with Irene: from the beginning, when she came to me, until that bitter end, when she left me. "Coelia or the Fulfillment:" that is the dirge I wrote after her death. Coelia means The Heavenly One (just as Silvia means the Forest Woman: Silvia symbolizes our idyll in Monti, our summer) — but how differently I had imagined fulfillment! I had thought to call the heavens down to earth, now the heavens have taken the earth away from me. In the child, we wanted to be fulfilled, and I wanted, carried by our own, to sing its future. Now the child has cast us out of paradise, and what I sing are the lamentations of Jeremiah, the torments of Prometheus, whose chest is torn apart by an eagle, the cries of Job.

Who of my many opponents, who were so eager to paint me as a heartless charlatan and even a villain, would believe that in me there was a Leander, a Romeo's fate? The revolution in Germany seems to me like a torch lit for its own funeral. Your Klabund.

Monti-Locarno, XI. 29. 18
Dear Herr Heinrich,

Reason proves this. But the heart cannot be guided by it when the wise man has become an orphan. This is what the Tao says (not exactly, but in a similar sense). Were I not a disciple of the Tao (the only philosophy that has something to say to man in this ___ time: for it is a living philosophy, a philosophy that must be lived and by which one must die), I would have long since despaired. Were I not to know that the soul is both star and sun, not that it is merely an object of the eyes, were I not to know that the individual soul is just as immortal as the collective soul (the "Urtao"), I would have long ago shot myself in the head. For every day I must fight for it anew. And only this is my consolation: that my awakening means it, that I breathe it, and think on it.

In the meantime, I have sent the "Dirge" first to Reiß: for practical reasons. I needed the money for the machine. But please: ask him for the verses and flip through them. In me. Yours, Klabund.

You consider — from Berlin! — the political situation as justifying the best of hopes? I believe that in the coming years, no mother in the whole world will be gladly expecting. I see everything in black.

Locarno-Monti, 1.7. 1919
Dear Herr Heinrich,

Thank you for your good wishes! If only wishes could help... I have not yet gotten over Irene's death. And I will only have overcome it when I have overcome myself, that is, my own death. What a living person I was! With such passion for life! Now I feel as if I have been broken in half, neither here nor there. Neither dead nor alive. If someone had told me a year ago, or even half a year ago, that the content of my life would one day be death, I would have laughed in disbelief. What am I thinking about? What am I hoping for? To whom does my passion belong? My friendship? To death, which, in the form of my beloved wife, appears ever more seductive to me. Our love had flared up to such a fervor in the summer that I experienced, in my own body, in my own soul, what it means to be a Romeo, a Leander. I had been through a hundred women, and because I had known a hundred women, this miracle of a woman seemed all the more unique, and I will never, never meet anyone like her again. I embraced perfection. But: whoever has gazed upon beauty with eyes is already at the mercy of death... (Platen). She combined the purity of "Beatrice," the beauty of "Laura," with the kindness of the holy "Catherine" and the childlike innocence of Novalis's bride: "Sophie."

She was regarded as a saint in the small Bavarian town from which she came: the whole town wept at her death. Now, they hate me. Certainly rightly so. For I killed her along with the child. My greatest happiness became my deepest guilt. In what labyrinth do we poor humans wander! How helpless our Earth, the black fly, flails in the great golden spider's web! I want to collect all the verses I wrote for her in one volume titled *The Cherubim*: the elegy, the sonnets, the odes, the distichs, and the small songs. And as an appendix: the short play *The Gravedigger* along with a small book of ballads. Warmest regards, your Klabund.

1.17. 1919
Dear Herr Heinrich,
Irene has called her child to her today.
Your Klabund.

About the Translator

Jim Doss is a founding editor of the bi-annual journal *Loch Raven Review*. He was born and raised in the foothills of the Blue Ridge Mountains, and is a graduate of the University of Virginia. His work has appeared in numerous publications, both on the Internet and in print. Doss has published three books of poetry: *Learning to Talk Again* (2011), *What Remains* (2017), and *The Last Goodbye* (2024). He has also translated Georg Trakl's complete poems, *The Last Gold of Expired Stars*, Ernst Toller's autobiography. *A Youth in Germany*, and *Letters from Prison* in addition to a number of Ernst Toller's plays, and a poetry anthology entitled *Nine Holocaust Poets* (2024). He recently published two books of novels by Klabund: *Bracke and Six Other Novels* (2025) and *Borgia and Four Other Novels* (2025). He is a retired software engineer.